GRISLY DISCOVERY

An excited voice. "Inspector!"

The torch beam picked out broken ground . . . raw earth mixed with decayed leaves where the top surface had been turned over. A patch about eighteen inches square. The others clustered around to study the discovery.

"Hardly big enough for a grave," ventured the moustached constable.

"It may be small," said Frost, "but it's all we've got."

The man who found it carefully shovelled out loose earth, the torch, like a stage spotlight, following his every movement.

Frost lost interest. "Just our luck it's some camper's rubbish. If so, you can have my share." The cold had found its way under the folds of the scarf and was chewing and worrying at his scar. The wind started to keen softly at the back of its throat and branches rustled.

"I've hit something!" called the digger. Then, "Sir!"

Frost spun round. The cigarette fell from his mouth.

The beam of the torch held it fast—yellow, dirt-encrusted, but unmistakable. Poking obscenely through the earth was the skeleton of a human hand.

Also by R. D. Wingfield

A TOUCH OF FROST
NIGHT FROST
HARD FROST

and coming soon
AUTUMN FROST

FROST AT CHRISTMAS

R. D. Wingfield

BANTAM BOOKS
NEW YORK · TORONTO · LONDON · SYDNEY · AUCKLAND

This edition contains the complete text
of the original hardcover edition.
NOT ONE WORD HAS BEEN OMITTED

FROST AT CHRISTMAS

A Bantam Crime Line Book / published by arrangement with the author

PUBLISHING HISTORY

Originally published in Great Britain by Sphere Books Ltd.
Bantam edition / December 1995

ISBN 0-553-57168-0

Published simultaneously in the United States and Canada

Bantam Books are published by Bantam Books, a division of Bantam
Doubleday Dell Publishing Group, Inc. Its trademark, consisting of
the words "Bantam Books" and the portrayal of a rooster, is Regis-
tered in U.S. Patent and Trademark Office and in other countries.
Marca Registrada. Bantam Books, 1540 Broadway, New York, New
York 10036.

PRINTED IN THE UNITED STATES OF AMERICA

OPM   0 9 8 7 6

FROST AT

CHRISTMAS

The 999 call came through just before midnight. An elderly man, voice trembling, barely audible. He sounded terrified.

"Police? My name is Powell, Mead Cottage, Exley Road. For God's sake, get someone here quickly. There's an intruder in my house. I . . ." A gasp. The voice broke off then rose to a scream. "No . . . please . . . no . . ." Confused sounds. The line went dead.

Despite the heavy snow an area car was at the scene within three minutes and was still slithering to a halt as the two constables, Evans and Howe, raced out. Lights were on at the cottage and a single line of footprints crept through the snow to an open downstairs window at the back. There were no returning footprints. The intruder was still inside.

The two men split up, Evans to pound at the front door while Howe took up position at the rear of the cottage, ready to pounce if they flushed their man out.

As Howe approached the open window he saw movement inside. He tensed, ready to spring, as the dark shape of a man leaned out. But it was his colleague, white-faced and shaken. "An ambulance. Get a bloody ambulance."

Inside the tiny room, with snow blowing through the open window, Powell, the householder, an elderly man in a dressing gown, sat slumped on the settee, a walking stick resting against his knees. He seemed unaware of what was happening, mumbling tonelessly to himself, over and over, "I had to do it. He would have killed me. I had to do it."

The room was in violent disarray, with chairs upturned, papers scattered, the phone ripped from the wall. And on the floor, barely alive, the crumpled figure of a man with a terrible head wound and Evans on his knees trying to stem the flow of blood. Evans looked up as Howe entered. "The bastard shot him," he said.

Powell was still holding the Luger and didn't resist as Howe *took it from him and carefully reset the safety catch. "It was him or me," he droned.*

"What the hell do you mean?" snarled Evans. "He's a police officer. You've shot a police officer!"

A police officer? Howe bent down to look at the face. At first he didn't recognize him. The face was old, tired, grey and dying. Then Howe saw the scarf . . . the familiar, tatty, maroon-coloured scarf, now discoloured and sodden with blood. It was hardly believable, but the man on the floor—the intruder—was Frost . . . Detective Inspector Jack Frost.

"He broke in," said Powell. "He tried to kill me." He pushed himself up and, with the aid of the walking stick, painfully hobbled over to the window and pointed. "Look!"

The wood round the catch was splintered where it had been forced open with a knife. The knife was on the floor. Frost's knife. Outside, the snow was filling in all traces of the footprints. Frost's footprints. And Frost's skeleton keys dangled from the bureau lock.

The two policemen looked at each other. It just didn't make sense. Detective Inspector Frost had done some pretty stupid things in his time, but this . . . ? How the hell did it happen?

It was a long story. It had all started four days earlier when Joan Uphill, a prostitute, failed to meet her eight-year-old daughter from Sunday school.

SUNDAY

SUNDAY (1)

Ten days to Christmas on a bitter December afternoon, a few minutes past four o'clock. Outside the house, day had prematurely aged into night and a grim, snow-heralding wind prowled the streets, but inside, behind heavy, drawn burgundy curtains, the bedroom was stifling. The three bars of an electric fire glared at the bed where two naked figures lay side by side.

"Was it good?" she asked mechanically.

"Very good," he answered, staring at the ceiling. He didn't look at her. He never looked at her afterwards.

Each week the man seemed more violent in his lovemaking, pummelling, pounding, clawing. He hurt her. But he appeared indifferent enough now as he swung his legs to the floor and reached for his clothes, his back modestly towards her as he dressed.

Usually so punctual, today he had arrived an hour late. By now she should be outside the Sunday school waiting for Tracey. She willed him to hurry, watching with silent impatience as his clumsy fingers fumbled at his buttons. Was he being deliberately slow? He knew that she had to meet Tracey and that it wasn't safe for the child to come home alone in the dark. The Sunday school was only at the end of the street, but there had been that scare with the man trying to lure children into his car last summer.

At last, trousered and respectable, he knotted his tie and turned to face her. She lit a cigarette, knowing what he was going to say. Always the same words.

"I'm not sure about next week." He slid the knot up

under his thin beard. "I expect it will be all right, but I'm not sure."

She nodded automatically and forced a smile. Every Sunday the doubts about next week, but he'd be here, she knew it and he knew it, he'd be here on the dot, squashing the bell-push with his thumb and furtively scanning the street like an escaped convict.

And she didn't even know his name. After weeks of the closest intimacy she knew every inch of his body but had no idea who he was, what he did, where he came from. She could make some guesses, of course. Age about thirty-four, thirty-five. An office worker, perhaps living with his mother. A good son, devoted to Mother, deserting her only once a week on Sunday afternoons . . . "Just popping out for a while, Mother. Won't be long." "All right, son. Take care of yourself. Be good."

Every Sunday he was here, at precisely the same time—today being the exception; they'd messed about with his trains. Every Sunday. The well-rehearsed routine never varied. Polite conversation over a cup of tea, excessive good manners—he would not sit until she was sitting, always sprang forward to open the door for her. But in the bedroom, an animal, a savage animal . . . And afterward the coy, shy business of dressing and the face-saving "Don't know about next week" ritual.

The man opened his wallet and took out three £10 notes which he held aloft briefly for her to see and check before folding them lengthwise and dropping them into the black and white Wedgwood vase on the mantelpiece. She receipted the payment with a nod of thanks.

He always saw himself out, hurrying from the house in his anxiety to hide his shame in the darkness outside. She sighed, expelling a stream of smoke in her relief at his departure. There was something about him that made her feel vaguely uneasy . . . made her feel frightened. But he'd gone. The dark shadow had passed from her day.

Stretching lazily, she rose from the bed, pausing to examine her beautiful naked body in the full-length wardrobe mirror, her face creasing into a frown at the bruise on her shoulder and the red marks where he'd bitten. In one place the skin was broken. Thirty pounds wasn't enough. She would tell him so next week.

But look at the time! She was never going to do it. 4:25. The kids came out of the Sunday school at 4:30. She'd never do it. There was nothing else for it. Tracey would have to come home on her own. It was just this once and it wasn't as if she had to come far—just from the end of the road.

A quick tidy-up and hasty smoothing of the bedclothes, then she dressed hurriedly and switched off the electric fire which made strange clanking and clicking noises in its death-throes. A final look round the room. No visible signs of guilt, but the acrid smell of male sweat lingered accusingly. She opened the window and the warm room choked down gulps of cold, black December air. The house across the road had a Christmas tree on display in its upstairs window, a tall fir decorated with glass globes and flaming jewels of coloured lights. She would have to see about a tree for Tracey.

A full-throated treble roar echoed from the end of the street. The Sunday school had released its prisoners. The children were coming out. She craned her neck and strained her eyes into the darkness. She should see Tracey soon.

The first wave of children washed past. Tracey wasn't among them, but she always did drag behind.

A pause before the next burst, the children chattering excitedly, "oohing" and "aahing" as they spotted the lights of the Christmas tree.

Then the stragglers. That one at the end must be Tracey. But no . . . much older. Then the street was empty. No more children. Silence.

She suddenly realized she was shivering. She closed the window and rubbed the raised goose-pimples on her bare arms. But it was not just the cold that was making her body shake and her teeth chatter. There was also the soft, sibilant, wet-lipped voice of fear whispering in her ear. Telling her that Tracey wasn't going to come. Not tonight. Or ever.

SUNDAY (2)

Sunday at Denton Police Station was the same as any other day. People got drunk and smashed pub windows. Husbands and wives fought and broke up the happy home, and neighbours phoned to complain of the noise drowning out their televisions. Foolproof burglar alarms went off by accident and truculent motorists swaggered in flourishing certificates of insurance which they'd been ordered to produce after that little accident last night. Houses were robbed, old ladies mugged . . . the same as any other day.

Station Sergeant Johnnie Johnson was cold. The gap under the swing doors invited the wind to roar across the lobby and the damn radiator, which wasn't much good at the best of times, had developed an air lock that no amount of kicking could shift. The phone on the enquiry desk rang. It was Superintendent Mullett, the Denton Divisional Commander, flapping as usual.

"Yes, sir," soothed Johnson, "it's all laid on. I'm sending a car to meet him . . . No, sir, it's very quiet, as it happens. Must be the cold weather."

The cold weather! Say what you like about the cold—he stamped his feet to move the blood around his toes—but it certainly kept the crime figures down. Criminals were no respecters of the Sabbath, but even the most hardened villain preferred the comforts of his own fireside on nights like this.

He decided to let the lobby run itself for a couple of minutes and thudded across to Control.

"We got anyone picking up that new chap? The old man's just phoned."

The controller consulted his duty sheet. "Able Baker four's doing it, Sarge . . . But how come we're giving the red carpet treatment to a lousy detective-bloody-constable?"

"Because," explained the sergeant, "the new detective-bloody-constable just happens to be the nephew of the Chief-bloody-Constable . . . and our Divisional Commander knows on which side his bread is buttered."

He lingered. It was warmer in Control than out in that windswept lobby. "Anything happening?"

"No, Sarge . . . it's quiet . . . bloody quiet . . . must be the weather."

The phone in the lobby rang, but there was no need for Johnson to race out to answer it. PC Lambert was back from his tea break. The call was from a woman whose daughter hadn't returned home from Sunday school.

The 3:45 train down from London slackened speed as it took the final bend before the run in to Denton Station. The carriage lurched and a crumpled Sunday paper fell from Clive Barnard's lap. He scrubbed at the condensation and tried to peer through the window, but met the murky gaze of his own reflection, a young man of twenty-three, fair-haired, with a nose that looked as if it had been broken and badly set.

A fellow passenger tapped him on the knee. "Just coming in to Denton."

Clive nodded his thanks and dragged his suitcase down from the rack, the case he'd packed at the last minute that very morning in glorious London, over seventy miles away. Wasn't it just his lousy rotten luck to be posted to this fleabag of a town, and so near to Christmas?

He'd seen the place once before, but once was enough. Denton itself was a pleasant little market town with Georgian houses and cobbles, but the iron hand of progress had sorted it out for special treatment. Denton was designated as a proposed "New Town" and was being enlarged, modernized, redeveloped, and ruined. Already acres of its surrounding farm land and woods had been cleared, and half of the new development completed. New, clean, and efficient houses had been built, and hard-faced money-grubbing newlyweds imported to fill them, then factories had been erected to enable the hard-faced newlyweds to slave away at monotonous jobs to pay the rent, the hire purchase on the deep-freeze and colour telly, and the cost of running the car to take them to the factory . . .

So far the improving hand of progress hadn't transformed the old market town, but it was not a reprieve, just a stay of execution. The planners were leaving that tasty titbit on their plates until the last.

Denton Police Station was in the old town and it was to the police station that Detective Constable Clive Barnard, his brand-new warrant card nestling in his wallet, was to report for duty at nine o'clock sharp Monday morning.

No-one else got out at Denton Station, and the carriage door had no sooner closed behind him than the train, eager to get away, rumbled off to more exciting venues. Clive watched its lights disappear and felt bitter, deep-seated resentment towards it for abandoning him to this miserable place on a chill and friendless Sunday evening.

A yawning ticket collector held out a hand for Clive's ticket, not bothering to lift his eyes from the pages of the *Sunday Mirror*. Clive humped his case to the booking hall, dimly lit and empty. They'd promised someone would meet him, but what could you expect in a dump like this? Then, with a screech of brakes, Able Baker four pulled into the curb, its flashing blue light reproaching him for his unworthy doubts. The driver, PC Jordan, a tall, thin twenty-six-year-old with a black moustache, opened the rear door and with a jerk of the thumb motioned Clive to get in. He briefly introduced himself and his observer, PC Simms, the moonfaced man at his side. That ceremony over, the car jerked away, heading for the lodgings assigned to Clive. An icy reception, he thought to himself. He hoped his new digs wouldn't be equally cold.

"What's up with your nose?" asked Simms after a couple of minutes of silence.

It had been broken on Clive's first day out on foot patrol. He'd tried to act the peacemaker between two brawling drunks and had been set upon by both of them for his trouble.

Simms grunted at the explanation. "I always let them fight

it out to the bitter end, then I arrest the winner. It means hiding round the corner until they've finished, but at least it keeps your nose in one piece." A few more moments of prickly silence, then Simms slipped in his leading question. "How's your uncle?"

Clive sighed. So it was out in the open, the cause of the hostility. He might have known he'd have trouble with the rustics. In London it had been treated as a big joke. The odd bit of leg-pulling, but they'd known he'd worked his way up to the dizzy heights of detective constable from scratch, expecting and getting no favours. But out here in turnip country he was the brash, spoiled kid from the big city, the one with the influential relative.

"Are you referring to the Chief Constable?" he asked innocently.

Simms feigned surprise. "Oh, is *he* your uncle? That would account for the similarity of the names, of course . . ."

"And for the fact that we're acting as your bloody chauffeur," added Jordan, sounding his horn at a dog that was taking its time crossing the road. "We couldn't expect the Chief Constable's nephew to take the common bus, of course . . ."

"Let's get this straight," snapped Clive hotly. "I never asked to be met, and if you think he gives me any favours, then I can assure you I'd have asked to be posted to anywhere but this one-eyed stinking dump."

A pause, during which tension crackled. The two uniformed men exchanged glances. "One-eyed stinking dump?" said Simms. "You must have been here before." He offered around his cigarettes and the atmosphere thawed slightly. "You're quite right, Clive," he continued, and Clive noted with pleasure the use of his first name, "this place is a dump . . . in fact it's a dump and a half. It was a little dump before they started to develop it, now it's a big dump."

"It's not so bad," said Jordan, as they waited for the traffic lights to change, although there was no other vehicle in sight.

The road was deserted. It was not only criminals who preferred to stay indoors in this weather.

"I understand I'll be working under Detective Inspector Allen," remarked Clive, trying to balance some ash on the overflowing ashtray. "What's he like?"

"In a word, he's a sod," muttered Simms.

Jordan was more generous. "He's not so bad—a stickler for the book, but do it his way and you won't go far wrong. Mind you, he's got a bit of a sharp tongue, which he has been known to use on the lazy and slovenly, as my friend and colleague here has discovered to his cost."

"What about Mr. Mullett, the Divisional Commander?"

"Superintendent Mullett is a stuck-up, pompous know-nothing sod," answered Simms.

Again Jordan differed. "He's got his faults, but he's fair. How long were you in uniform?"

"Twenty-four months."

Jordan grinned. No-one could be considered for CID until they had spent a minimum of two years in uniform. Clive had spent the bare minimum. "Couldn't you wait to get out of it?"

"I joined the Force with one idea and one idea only—to go into CID. No disrespect, but to my mind CID is what police work is all about."

A left turn at a roundabout. "You'll never get me to change," said Jordan. "For my money you can't beat the uniformed branch. Mind you, it was different years ago. Then they reckoned the chap on the beat was thick, clumsy, and slow—like my mate here—employed by the CID elite to stand outside the door and bar unauthorized entry during their investigations. He might be allowed to fetch the tea and bring back the right change and work all the hours that God sent without complaining, but that was all . . ."

"It's exactly the same now," muttered Simms, "except we do complain."

Jordan snorted. "You know it isn't. We're a self-motivated team in this car, expected to work on our own initiative. I bet we do more basic detection work in a day than your average

CID man does in a month. And unlike the CID we work regular hours."

"Sounds like a good job," smiled Simms, "I think I'll join." He turned to Clive. "I don't know what you've been used to in town, but I'm afraid your digs are a bit tatty. They're hard to come by these days—and us uniformed lads get the cream, as you would expect."

Clive was about to answer when Simms stiffened, flicked his hand for silence, and touched the knob of the radio to bring up the volume.

Denton Control was calling Able Baker four.

Simms answered and reported their location. They were requested to go immediately to No. 29—repeat 29—Vicarage Terrace and interview a Mrs. Joan Uphill who had reported that her eight-year-old daughter, Tracey Uphill, had not returned home from Sunday school since 4:30.

Even before Simms had acknowledged, Jordan had spun the car around and was heading back in the direction of Vicarage Terrace.

She'd tried all the likely places—phoned them, visited them. Then she'd tramped the streets, calling Tracey's name, hair streaming, her unbuttoned fur coat flapping in the wind. She hadn't meant to go far but in the distance, very faint, barely audible, came the shrill burble of children's voices, leading her on like a will-o'-the-wisp. Just one more corner, and the next. But when tiredness forced her to stop, and the clatter of her footsteps died in the empty street, no matter how hard she listened, the children's voices transmuted themselves into the vague murmurings of the wind.

She was too far from the house. What if Tracey went back and she wasn't there? Fear made her hurry. Her legs ached from calf to thigh, but she forced them to go faster. Outside the house, no sign of Tracey. She called and only the wind answered. She let herself in and, without taking off her coat, slumped by the phone and dialled Tracey's friends again. The other mothers, their own children safe, tried to reassure her. "I wouldn't worry, Mrs. Uphill, she'll turn up, you'll see.

Now if you'll excuse me . . . the tea . . ." The last call made and nothing more to do. The house, emptier than ever, seemed different somehow, as if adjusting itself to the fact that the child would never come back. She felt drained, lost, helpless. There was no-one she could turn to: no friends, no relatives, no-one. She leaned forward and cooled her forehead on the telephone. In the centre of the dial it said "Police—ring 999."

She dialled. The operator put her through to Denton Police Station. It was 7:06.

"Denton Police. Can we help you?"

Her call was answered by PC Ronald Lambert, twenty-three years old, bearded, and unmarried. It was the thirty-eighth call he'd taken since coming on duty at two o'clock that afternoon. He hated front office work. It was freezing in the lobby after the steamy warmth of the canteen. Waiting for the caller to answer, he logged the time of the call. 1906 hours. The caller was a distraught woman. At first he couldn't make out what she was saying. Something about a girl and a Sunday school. With the patience born of practice, he asked her to repeat it slowly.

"My little girl hasn't come home . . . looked everywhere . . . everywhere . . ."

He calmed her down and methodically extracted the vital details. "Since 4:30 you say? You should have phoned us earlier, mother. But hold on . . ."

Behind him a sliding wall panel connected the lobby to the control room. He slid it back. PC Philip Ridley, who was talking to the station sergeant, looked up expectantly.

"I've got a Mrs. Uphill on the phone. No. 29 Vicarage Terrace. Her daughter, Tracey Uphill, eight years old, left St. Basil's Sunday School at 4:30 and hasn't returned home. The mother's very worried."

Vicarage Terrace. Ridley didn't need to refer to the wall map to know it was in C Beat, one of two beats covered by police car Tango Charlie one. But Tango Charlie one was already out on a call, a husband and wife punch-up, known as a "domestic." So what else had we? Ah—the area car, Able

Baker four. It wasn't doing anything vital, only taking the Chief Constable's precious nephew to his digs. Well, he could wait. It wouldn't do the pampered swine any harm to see a spot of real police work for a change.

He flicked the switch on his transmitter and called Able Baker four. The monitor speaker crackled and Simms's voice answered.

"Hello Control . . . Vicarage Terrace? We can be there in four minutes."

On the other side of the panel, PC Lambert uncupped his hand from the mouthpiece. "Mrs. Uphill? Sorry for the delay. Stay put, Mrs. Uphill, a car's on its way round to you now. Don't worry, we'll sort it out."

He dropped the receiver back on its rest and shut the sliding panel, then he and the controller, each in his separate room, logged the incident and settled down to wait for the next call. A pretty boring Sunday up to now. The station sergeant thought he'd take advantage of the lull and have his tea break.

"Sorry about this," shouted Jordan, swinging the area car through mazes of side streets choked with parked vehicles. "It could take some time. Would you like us to drop you off somewhere?"

Clive shook his head. He was in no hurry to get to his digs. He'd be spending the rest of the dreary evening there anyway, and it was barely past seven now. If they didn't mind he'd like to follow the call through with them.

"You can point out where we go wrong," said Simms, scribbling the details on his log-sheet.

The car curb-crawled Vicarage Terrace looking for number 29 among the darkened porches. This probably wouldn't take more than a few minutes. Usually the lost kid and the police turned up at the same time, the kid to be walloped and hugged, the police to be apologized to: "Now say you're sorry to the policeman." To which the police usually replied, "That's what we're here for, madam. Glad it's turned out this way."

Usually . . . not always.

"That should be it," cried Simms, pointing, and in confirmation a street door opened and a teenaged girl waved frantically.

The two uniformed men got out, putting on their peaked caps, which were not worn in the car. Simms took a clipboard and a pen from the glove compartment and made sure he had his personal radio. Clive followed at a respectful distance. He couldn't take his eyes from the girl in the doorway with her ash-blonde hair and the simple lavender-blue woollen dress hugging the soft curves of her young virginal body. The missing girl's sister, he reasoned, but she was simply fantastic—the flawless naive innocent of his dream-world erotic fantasies.

But Jordan addressed her as Mrs. Uphill! How could this child have a daughter of eight? But she wasn't a child. She was a woman. Twenty-four years old and worried to desperation.

"Yes, I'm Mrs. Uphill. Have you found her?" The voice was on the verge of hysterical.

Jordan smiled sympathetically and shook his head.

"Not yet, Mrs. Uphill. Give us a chance, we've only just received your message. Do you think we could come in?"

She led them through to the lounge, an expensively furnished room with rosewood panelling, an off-white deep-pile wall-to-wall carpet screaming money, an enormous projection colour TV, and a corner bar with a genuine reproduction pub counter and beer engine.

They settled down in cream-coloured armchairs smelling richly of leather, Simms, with his clipboard poised on his knee, asking most of the questions.

"The boring bit first, Mrs. Uphill. The details. When did you last see her? Outside the Sunday school? I see. You took her there yourself? Good. And what time would that be?"

As Simms extracted the necessary information, Clive let his eyes wander around the room. There was money in the house, even a newly appointed detective constable could see that. It shouted its opulence. But where was the husband?

There had been no mention of him. Perhaps she was a widow, or divorced. Whatever it was, Mr. Uphill had left her well provided for. Those shelves behind the bar were crammed with any drink you cared to name; the cigarette boxes were brim-filled—name your brand—filter-tipped or plain, we have it; and there was a drum of large red-and-gold-banded cigars on the bar counter. Plenty of provisions for a man, but no mention of him. His eyes moved to the girl's face. She was listening intently to Simms, her moist lips parted, her skin flawless without make-up. He felt sexual stirrings within himself and immediately suppressed them, chiding himself for being a dirty-minded slob. At a time like this . . . that poor helpless creature. If only he could offer her some comfort, some protection.

Jordan and Simms continued methodically with their questions. At this stage there was no real need for panic. Three hours wasn't all that long for a kid to be astray; she'd probably wandered a bit further afield than she had intended and couldn't find her way back. Put all patrols on the alert and they should have her back within the hour. And then his eye was drawn by the window, where the curtains had been pulled back. Outside, a tree by the lamppost twitched and shuddered in a wind of growing strength. What if they didn't find her quickly? The real danger was the weather. At night the temperature plummeted to below zero. If she was out in the open and wasn't properly dressed . . .

He cut across the uniformed men's questions.

"How was Tracey dressed when she went out, Mrs. Uphill?"

Hostile glares from the other two as she jerked her head towards him, brushing a wisp of ash-blonde hair from her eyes.

"A thick blue coat and a scarf . . ."

"If I could butt in," snapped Jordan icily. He glowered at Clive. "We've already got that information. We haven't the time to hear it twice."

Clang, thought Clive, that's me in my place. But he was

relieved the kid was well wrapped up. It could make the difference between life and death.

"Do you have a photograph of Tracey?" asked Simms. "We want to make certain we bring the right one back."

She forced a smile at the joke and rummaged in a drawer, haste making her clumsy. Inwardly she was ready to scream. Why all these questions? Why didn't they just go out and look? And why three of them? Why couldn't two go out and search while the other one asked the questions? She found the snapshot. Clive peered at it over Simms's shoulder. A full-face colour photograph of a lovely wide-eyed child, beautiful like her mother, the same ash-blonde hair, brushed and gleaming.

Simms wrote something on the back of the photograph, replaced the cap on his pen, and looked significantly at Jordan, who nodded and stood. "Just one last thing, Mrs. Uphill. We'd like to search the house."

They searched the house, starting at the top and working down. They found nothing, but it had to be done. The number of times the missing kid had been found hiding in a cupboard or a shed while armies of policemen scoured the streets . . . All a big joke to the kid, of course, but there was that terrible lesson of a few years back when, weeks after an intensive search involving hundreds of men, rivers dragged, frogmen in the reservoir, a police officer returned to the child's home and noticed a small box that could have contained books or toys. Far too small, but he looked anyway . . . and there was the body. The boy had squeezed himself in, pulled down the lid, the catch had caught and trapped him and there was hardly any air. Weeks of searching and he had been in the house all the time. But Tracey wasn't in the house.

Back to the lounge where the woman sat huddled in a chair, systematically shredding a Kleenex tissue. She didn't look up as Jordan spoke.

"Nothing there, Mrs. Uphill, but stay by your phone. As soon as we have any news . . ."

She nodded.

"And, of course, if she should come back here, you'll let us know at once, won't you?"

Again a nod.

Jordan shrugged, then signalled for the others to follow him out. At the door Clive turned. She looked so pathetic, so defencelessly alone. "Isn't there anyone who could stay with you, Mrs. Uphill—a relative, a woman friend?"

Beautiful but vacant eyes fastened on his. "I have no women friends—or any relations . . ." A bitter smile. "But thank you."

Jordan tapped Clive on the shoulder and jerked his thumb to the front door. Mrs. Uphill pulled another Kleenex from the box.

Back in the car Simms radioed the details to Denton Control for circulation to all patrols. Control instructed them to drop Clive off at his digs and then return to the station with the photograph.

The car retraced its way through the side streets and was soon back on the main road.

"Let's have the benefit of your vast London experience. What do you reckon?" asked Simms.

Clive shrugged, "It's too early. The kid could turn up at any time." Then he remembered the question he'd been burning to ask. "Where's the kid's father—the husband?"

He caught Jordan's smile in the rearview mirror. "She's not married, Clive. The 'Mrs.' is just a courtesy title."

Clive frowned. "Then where does her money come from? The chair I was sitting on must have set her back four hundred quid at least."

Simms turned in his seat. "I'll give you a clue. She's self-employed and fee-earning. The money in her lounge was earned in her bedroom." He saw Clive was still uncomprehending. "How thick can you get? She's a tart, a whore, a harlot, a pro. She's on the bash."

Clive's jaw thudded. Not her! Not that virginal child. How simple did they think he was?

"I hope I haven't shocked you," said Simms, "I don't suppose you have such wicked women in London. It's a bit naughty, I know, but then, this is a decadent town. It'll be different when the bingo halls are built." He looked to Jordan for a smile of appreciation, but the driver was lost in his thoughts.

"Sorry," said Jordan, "I've just remembered something— the Sunday school."

"St. Basil's?"

"Yes. You remember the trouble we had there this summer."

"Blimey," said Simms. "The man trying to lure kids into his car with sweets? We never caught him, did we?"

"No," said Jordan, "we never caught him." He spun the wheel and the car deserted the main road for a narrow street of terraced houses. "Here we are."

This was Sun Street. Clive's digs were at No. 26, a house that looked no different from any of the others. As he took his suitcases from the car and said his goodbyes, the downstairs curtain behind him twitched and a shaft of light wriggled across the pavement. He watched the area car continue on its way until the darkness swallowed up its rear lights. Then he felt friendless and alone, the way that woman must be feeling now. He turned and, putting his suitcases down on the pavement, knocked at the door.

MONDAY

MONDAY (1)

Superintendent Mullett, Commander, Denton Division, gave a warning toot on his horn and gently coasted his new blue Jaguar into the crowded police car park. At a few minutes past eight on a cold and dark Monday morning the parking area should have been an expanse of emptiness, dotted with the odd car belonging to members of the morning shift, but today it was tightly crammed with a congestion of assorted vehicles: army trucks, a hired coach, the mobile canteen from county headquarters, and two small vans which, at first, Mullett did not recognize until the petulant whinings and yappings from within told him they were the dog handlers' transport.

The search party had assembled.

Mullett permitted himself a brief smile of satisfaction. To arrive at this early hour and see proof of the efficient way his phoned orders of late last night had been carried out was indeed a tribute to the efficiency of the division and its commander. His smile froze and changed to a frown of intense irritation when he saw that one of the wretched army trucks had commandeered his parking space. Couldn't the fools read? Good Lord, it was clearly marked in bold white paint "Reserved for Divisional Commander" and was regarded as a sacrosanct place by his own men. Raging inwardly at the stupidity of army drivers, he rammed his car into the first vacant space he found, jammed between the hired coach that had brought in men from a neighbouring division and a wall. Too late, he realized it would require some tricky reversing if he were not to mar the gleaming blue paint of his day-old car.

In foul temper he snatched up the black leather briefcase from the rear seat, remembering in time to open the door carefully so it wouldn't crash into the wall, and picked his way through the maze of vehicles to the side street from which he could reach the main entrance of the police station. A rear entrance led directly from the car park, but kings and princes didn't sneak in through back doors and neither did divisional commanders.

The uniformed man on duty in the lobby sprang to attention and snapped him a smart salute. Mullett acknowledged it curtly and moved briskly on, noting that the man was already on the phone to warn the station sergeant of his arrival.

Outside his office his triumphant entry was temporarily halted by one of the cleaning women who was sloshing buckets of disinfectant-tainted water over the stone flags of the corridor. He coughed pointedly and had to wait while she cleared a damp path for him with her mop, pushing back the water as the Red Sea was parted for Moses on another historic occasion.

Mullett's office provided the only touch of splendour in the entire Victorian workhouse of a building. Its walls were panelled in veneered wood like a boardroom, the floor spread with a thick, pale blue Wilton carpet on which sat a splendid "senior-executive-model" desk in satin mahogany and black. He couldn't understand his counterparts in other divisions who boasted of the meanness of their own offices, thereby degrading their positions. Senior men in industry had the trappings to go with the job, so why not the police?

He opened the clothes cupboard cleverly concealed behind the panelling and hung up his London-tailored overcoat. His reflection in the full-length mirror restored his good humour. The image before him was indeed something to be regarded with unrestrained approval: a tall, straight-backed figure, glossy black hair with a chiselled parting, commanding eyes, a neatly clipped military moustache, and a complexion glowing with health and good living. And to set it off, the immaculate fit of the police uniform, its buttons winking and gleaming, the creases lethal, and the shoes, black mirrors. At forty-two years old he looked more like a successful stockbroker than a superintendent of police controlling an area of some thirty-eight square miles and 100,000 inhabitants.

The cupboard door closed and became once again part of the wall panelling. Something caught his eye. On his desk, tucked into the corner of the blotting pad, an envelope. The typing, in red capitals, said "Strictly Private and Confidential." He slit it open with his stainless-steel paper knife, slipped on his horn-rimmed glasses, and read it. His eyes hardened. He dropped down into his chair and read it again.

It was trouble. A complaint against one of his officers, Detective Inspector Frost.

He thudded the satin mahogany with a clenched fist. Damn the man; nothing but trouble from the start. He'd have him out of the division tomorrow if he could. He looked at his watch. Nearly time for the briefing meeting; Frost would have to wait. The letter was refolded along its original creases, replaced in the envelope, and locked in the top right-hand drawer of his desk.

He rang for Miss Smith, his secretary, but of course she wasn't in yet. Mullett's usual hours were from 10:00 a.m. until 6:30 p.m. Today was different, with the briefing meeting at 8:15 and the Chief Constable's nephew reporting for duty at 9:00. The Chief Constable's nephew . . . Mullett permitted himself a smug smile of satisfaction. With his future promotion in the balance it would do him no harm to have the division under the old man's careful eye. His musings were interrupted by a polite tap at the door. Bill Wells, station sergeant for the morning shift, entered.

"Ah, Sergeant Wells. Come in. Sit down."

Wells perched himself on the edge of a chair. He found Mullett's wood-lined office overpowering. A sad-faced, balding man of thirty-eight, he'd been in the Force for seventeen years and had been a sergeant for the past six. He despaired of ever making inspector.

Mullett leaned forward. "Nothing on the girl, I suppose?" The sergeant's sad face went even sadder. "No, sir."

"It's been sixteen hours, Sergeant. Too long, far too long."

"Sixteen hours of darkness, sir; we need the daylight."

Mullett nodded grudgingly and consulted his window. It was just about light enough now, and by four o'clock it would be too dark again. But with luck they would find the kid long before then. He dealt with one or two minor problems raised by the sergeant, then reached for his briefcase to go to the meeting. He remembered the letter of complaint festering in his drawer.

"Is Detective Inspector Frost in the briefing room, Sergeant?"

"No, sir," said Wells, putting his chair back against the wall. "He hasn't arrived yet."

Typical, thought Mullett. Everyone else gets here on time, but Frost . . . Masking his anger with a tight smile, he sighed audibly. "Ah well, we'll just have to start without him, won't we?" As he moved to the door, Wells cleared his throat.

"You won't be needing me at the meeting then, sir?" It was a rhetorical question. He'd already been told he wasn't wanted. Woundingly hurtful, but it didn't surprise him. He had no doubt at all that it was Mullett who'd been blocking his promotions from going through, and excluding him from the meeting was clearly the commander's way of keeping him in his place.

Sensing the man's resentment, Mullett was lavish with reassurances. "I wish I could spare you, Sergeant, but I can't. I must have someone I can trust to keep the station running. Which reminds me, I've got an important job for you."

Sergeant Wells looked up expectantly.

"You might pass the word to our army friends that they are not to use my parking space. One of their damn lorries is parked there and they couldn't have missed the sign."

A reassuring smile and he was gone, leaving Wells nothing to do but swear silently at the vacated "senior-executive" desk.

·   ·   ·

The briefing room was packed. Extra chairs had been brought in, but even so, one or two latecomers had to stand at the back.

A thick haze of cigarette smoke rolled around the room like a Baker Street fog. The low murmur of nervous conversation stopped and all assembled jumped to their feet as the Divisional Commander breezed into the room.

"Good morning, ladies and gentlemen. Good to see such a full turnout. Please sit down."

Those with chairs sat. Mullett looked around the room as he extracted some papers from his briefcase. Most people there he recognized, the majority being from his own division, including those called back from their rest day. No sign of Detective Inspector Frost, he noted grimly. A friendly nod to the army officers whose men, including the usurper of his parking space, would be stoking up on tea and sandwiches in the upstairs canteen. Those two chaps in the corner would be the dog handlers from the police kennels at Rushfield, but who was that red-faced man smiling at him? Oh yes, a detective sergeant from one of the neighbouring divisions whose commander had spared so many of his hard-pressed personnel to join the search for Tracey Uphill.

"I won't keep you long. We're not short of help, for which I thank you, but we will be short of daylight. She's been missing now for over sixteen hours. If you heard the weather forecast this morning you'll know we're due for some very severe weather. So we've got to find her quickly. It won't be an easy search. We've got woodlands, lakes, a canal, gravel pits, derelict houses, builders' sites—a thousand and one places where a child could be concealed. We will have to be methodical, not haphazard. For that reason, I have put Detective Inspector Allen in charge of the operation. And as he is in charge, I will now shut up and let him take over."

Some forced laughter at this mild joke and a shifting of positions on the hard wooden seats. Mullett moved democratically to the chair left for him in the corner of the front row and sat with his chin on his knuckles and his brow furrowed to show he was giving his full attention to everything Detective Inspector Allen was saying.

Allen was lean, wiry, and inflexibly tough, with sparse hair above a thin-lipped gaunt face. His flights of humour never soared higher than biting sarcasm. Coldly efficient, he was universally hated as a man but grudgingly admired as a first-rate detective. He jabbed a bony finger at a wall map of the district.

"I've divided the area into sections. We'll start at the most likely places near the child's home and work out from there. As the Divisional Commander has pointed out, it's a tricky area to search, so we're going to have to be bloody methodical. You will be allocated an area to search. When you have finished you will report in to me at Search Control. You will not move on to a fresh area until instructed by me to do so." He glanced at his watch. "Time's against us, so I'll be brief. I'll just let you know the forces we'll have at our disposal. Apart from yourselves, we've been promised another hundred men from the army camp. We've already got a few civilian volunteers and we'll be appealing for more if necessary. The local fire brigade has pledged us a dozen or so men and at nine o'clock there'll be a party of sixth-formers from the local comprehensive school. Enough people to get in everybody's way and sod the whole thing up, which is why you must pander to my megalomania and do exactly what I tell you to do."

As he paused for breath the phone rang. All heads turned to stare accusingly at it. It rang again, a loud, insistent, grating ring.

Mullett frowned. "I told them to hold all calls," he said peevishly.

It rang again.

"Well, answer it, someone, for Christ's sake," roared Allen. "That's the only way to stop it."

A detective sergeant picked it up. His eyes widened.

"It's the Chief Constable, sir." He hastily got rid of the phone to Mullett who took it reverently. The meeting studiously pretended not to be listening.

"Good morning, sir. No . . . not yet, but we'll find her. Yes, sir, the fullest possible co-operation. I don't think we'll be needing any more help at this stage." An enquiring glance to Inspector Allen who shook his head emphatically. His searchers would be falling over each other as it was.

"What's that, sir? I say, that's splendid. Thank you very much, sir . . . yes, that's really marvellous." The phone was replaced on the side table.

"That," said Mullett, as if announcing the Second Coming, "was the Chief Constable." A pause to let the import sink in. "And we're getting a helicopter."

A babble of excitement. Inspector Allen's eyes glittered. If they couldn't find the kid with a helicopter . . . But back to the meeting.

"All right, ladies and gentlemen, it's a help, but not the great solution to our problems. It can't poke about in sewage pipes and dung heaps. You need highly trained policemen for that. As you leave you'll be given your initial areas of search. Any questions at this stage?"

A hand shot up—one of Rushfield's men.

"I understand the mother's a prostitute, sir?"

"Yes," replied Allen, straight-faced. "She hasn't mentioned a reward, but I imagine whoever finds the kid will be on to a good thing . . ."

A ripple of laughter. The Rushfield man waited for it to subside. "I was wondering if any of our local child molesters might have got the wrong idea—like mother like daughter, that sort of thing . . ."

Allen sniffed. "A good point, but it's been covered. I've got men out already checking every known sex offender in the division. Any more questions? Right. Off you go . . . and good luck."

MONDAY (2)

———

Detective Constable Clive Barnard's orders were to report for duty to Superintendent Mullett, Denton Police Station, nine o'clock sharp. The superintendent, he was told, was a stickler for punctuality, so he allowed himself plenty of time. He set the alarm for 7:15 and went to bed early. But sleep eluded him. At four o'clock he was still awake; the bed was lumpy, there weren't enough blankets to keep out the cold, his mind was a whirl of ash-blondes and missing children, and some damn sadistic church clock punctuated his sleeplessness with clanking chimes every quarter-hour.

The exhausted sleep into which he eventually plunged was so deep that the alarm clock rang itself hoarse and he didn't hear it. He overslept. If his landlady hadn't banged on his door at 8:20 he'd be sleeping still.

So, no time for breakfast, just one mad rush to avoid the shameful crime of reporting late on his first day. A perfunctory buzz with the electric razor. Not perfect, but with his fair beard he'd get away with it. On with the brand-new grey suit with the red stripe, the one he'd bought especially for CID work from that little shop near Carnaby Street. He'd been told that clothes were important. Wear a tatty suit and you got the tatty assignments; good clothes earned the superior ones. So he'd bought this suit. It had cost him £107, a lot more than he usually paid, but it was an investment, and why not let the Denton yokels see a bit of London quality for a change?

He opened his suitcase for the light blue shirt, moving his law books to reach it. He was studying for a law degree in his spare time. He was determined to make it to the top by the quickest route and had realized that many of the younger senior men had law degrees. And he'd have plenty of time in this dead-and-alive hole to study his law books during the long winter evenings when he was without a female companion to run her gentle fingers down the ridged slope of his sexy broken nose.

By 8:45, his empty stomach complaining, he was thudding down Bath Hill, pushed by a cold wind. He wondered if they'd found Tracey Uphill. There certainly seemed to be an unusual amount of police activity for such an early hour. Three police cars had roared past him already.

Bath Hill led into Market Square where there was another policeman examining the door of a bank, but Clive gave him no more than a fleeting glance. Most of the shops had not yet opened and the tall Christmas tree outside the public lavatories was swaying in a wind that rattled its coloured electric lights. He clattered over the cobbled road to reach Eagle Lane and the police station.

And there it was, red-bricked and solid, the welcoming blue lamp over swing doors leading into the lobby where the wall clock in its wooden case showed 8:54. He'd made it. The familiar police station smell of disinfectant, polish, and cooking from the canteen met his nose as, panting with relief, he advanced to the enquiry desk where a sad-faced, balding sergeant was on the phone.

Bill Wells, station sergeant for the 6:00 a.m. to 2:00 p.m. shift was in temporary charge of the front office. He'd sent the duty constable, young PC Stringer, upstairs to the canteen for his breakfast and was keeping an eye on things until his return. The damn phone would have to ring: a woman with some rambling story about teenagers smashing her window two weeks ago and she'd only just decided to report it and what were the police going to do about it? A blast of air sent his papers flying as the lobby doors opened, but he trapped them with a practised elbow and looked up at the visitor. A young chap with a crooked nose and smart overcoat. He looked supercilious enough to be someone important, so Wells cupped his hand over the mouthpiece of the phone and said, "Be with you in a moment, sir."

Clive nodded curtly. As he had managed to arrive in good time he hoped the sergeant wouldn't take too long on the phone and make him late for his appointment with the Divisional Commander. He roamed the lobby, studying the posters on the wall. Missing Persons, Foot and Mouth Disease Movement Restriction Orders, and, everybody's favourite, the Colorado Beetle poster.

His heavy overcoat felt cumbersome, so he slipped it off and carried it over his arm. Then he caught sight of his reflection in the murky glass of the swing door. It brought him to an abrupt halt.

The new suit! It shrieked!

In the dim lighting of the shop it had seemed tastefully conservative with, perhaps, a barely audible refined whisper of trendiness, but in the sombre surroundings of the station the trendy whisper was a raucous shout. It was a disaster, and no time to race back and change. He huddled himself into a dark corner.

PC Stringer, the duty desk man, returned to his post replete with bacon, beans, tea and two slices. With his honest, open, freshly scrubbed schoolboy's face surmounted with dark curly hair, he looked more like a sixth-former than a policeman. He smiled at Clive with an air of helpful enquiry.

"I'm attending to the gentleman," hissed the sergeant from one corner of his mouth while carrying on his phone conversation with the other. The young constable shrugged good-naturedly and settled down to peck out a report on an ancient black Underwood.

At last the sergeant slammed down the phone and rubbed a sore ear. He turned to Clive with almost obsequious politeness.

"Can I help you, sir?"

It occurred to Clive that the sergeant was mistaking him for someone important. It also occurred to him that the sergeant wouldn't take too kindly to the knowledge that he had been abasing himself before the lowest of the low, a raw detective constable whose forehead still bore a ridge from a helmet. A quick explanation was vital.

"Actually, Sergeant, I'm Detective Constable—"

On the first syllable of "constable" the sergeant's smile

froze solid: it shrivelled to a tight glitter on the second and vanished chillingly on the last. The expression "his face went ugly" could have been invented for this moment. Clive ploughed bravely on . . .

"—Detective Constable Barnard. I have to report to Superintendent Mullett at nine o'clock, sir."

So this was Barnard. This is the young bastard who's going to make it because of his uncle while people with seventeen years bloody service but without influential relatives . . . Wells twisted his neck to the wall clock. A minute before nine. Pity. It would have been a pleasure to bawl him out for unpunctuality.

Another blast of wind ruffled the papers on the desk as a figure in military uniform hurtled through.

"Meeting?" he barked.

"Third door on the left, sir." The man was already on his way. Wells returned his attention to his victim.

"Oh, yes. Barnard . . . I remember. The Chief Constable's nephew, isn't it? I should have recognized the broken nose."

Clive tightened his lips, said nothing, and stared at a spot just above the sergeant's balding head. Wells moved his gaze downward . . . and then he saw it—

"Good God! Where on earth did you get that suit?"

Clive flushed. "In London, Sergeant."

"London? The last time I saw a suit like that Max Miller was wearing it. How much did you pay for it?"

A deep breath. "£107, Sergeant."

The sergeant's jaw thudded. "£107! For that? Take my tip, Barnard, don't wear it in the daylight. There's some very nervous people about." Shoulders shaking at his own witticism and his good humour restored, Wells jerked a thumb towards a polished wooden bench and bade Clive sit.

"The Divisional Commander's tied up at the moment. I'll tell you when he's free."

Clive sat. The bench was hard. You were not meant to be comfortable sitting in a police station. Above his head was the Colorado Beetle Identikit, on the opposite wall a black-

board in a wood frame. It was headed: DENTON DIVISION—
ROAD ACCIDENTS. The board contained columns in which were
chalked the monthly running totals of accidents and fatalities
in the division as compared with the previous year.

Clive sat and waited. The bench got harder, his suit
louder. Then an icy blast as the swing doors crashed back on
their hinges and a scruffy individual in a dirty mac, un-
pressed trousers, and a long trailing maroon scarf burst in.
He was in his late forties, with a pink weather-beaten
farmer's face flecked with freckles, warm blue eyes, and a
freckled balding head, the pate surrounded by fluffy light
brown hair. He went straight over to the board, picked up
the chalk, and increased by one the number of accidents.

"What happened?" asked Sergeant Wells, watching this
with concern.

"Hit the back of a bloody car as I drove in," said the
scruffy man. "Some silly sod had poked it in my parking
space. Who owns a blue Jaguar?"

Wells went white. "Not a blue Jaguar, Jack? You didn't hit
a blue Jaguar? That's Mr. Mullett's car. Brand new . . . delivered Saturday."

The scruffy man was unimpressed. "Mullett's? At this
hour of the morning? Come off it, he's at home polishing his
buttons." He sniffed. "Hello . . . either meat pudding for
dinner or Mabel's boiling her drawers."

"This is serious, Jack," insisted the sergeant. "That *is* Mullett's car. He's here for the briefing meeting on the search for
the missing kid. You were phoned about it last night. He's
been asking for you."

The man paused, then smote his brow in horrified realiza-
tion.

"The meeting! Blimey! I forgot all about it."

The station sergeant, who appeared to find happiness in
others' misfortunes, tried to reassure him. "Never mind, Jack,
after smashing up his car, missing his meeting will seem trivial. Did you do much damage?"

He thought about it. "Not much . . . a slight knock on
the rear wing. Hardly noticeable. His rear lamp's a bit

smashed and there's the odd scratch and a couple of dents . . . Pity it was so new, actually." He hitched up his scarf. "Look, Bill, you haven't seen me; I haven't been in yet. I'm going to hide my car round the corner." He scuttled down a side passage.

"Who was that?" asked Clive.

"That, Detective Constable Barnard," replied the station sergeant stiffly, "was Detective Inspector Jack Frost."

A detective inspector? That slovenly mess? Clive began to feel much happier about his future prospects. After all, if they made tramps like that up to inspectors . . .

The phone rang. Stringer stopped his typing and answered it. He listened then muffled the mouthpiece against his tunic.

"Sergeant. It's the Divisional Commander. He wants to know if Inspector Frost is in yet."

"Tell him no," said the sergeant. "And tell him there's a gentleman in a £107 suit waiting to see him."

"Send him in," snapped Mullett and banged down the phone. He stuck the "Private and Confidential" envelope back in his drawer. He had hoped to get the unpleasant interview with Frost over before he saw the new man. He shook his head in despair. How could you run an efficient station with men like Frost? And now, because of Inspector Allen's involvement with the search, Mullett was going to be forced to put the Chief Constable's nephew—the Chief Constable's actual nephew—under the dubious care of Inspector Jack Frost. It could spoil everything. True, the Chief Constable had a soft spot for Frost, but then he didn't have to work with him, to tolerate his appalling lapses, the unforgivable untidiness of his office, the tattered clothes he wore, his hatred of paperwork and the system, his forgetfulness . . . But why go on? He was only working himself up. So long as the Chief Constable had faith, albeit misplaced, in Frost, then Mullett would conceal the man's true nature from him.

Mullett, like Clive, was a career man, determined to rise to the top of his chosen profession. He'd joined the Force as a constable and, according to his charted plan, had steadily and diligently worked his way up the ranks, passing with ease all the necessary exams. In his spare time he, too, had taken a law course and was now a qualified solicitor.

Because of his flair for leadership and organization, which he had taken pains to bring to the right people's notice, he'd been promoted three years ago to superintendent and given command of Denton Division. But this was but a stepping stone. In a few years' time the station would be demolished to make way for the enlargement of the new town and the Force would move to a modern building currently under construction and would cover a much enlarged division. Whoever was in charge of the new division would be promoted to chief superintendent and would be in line for an even more glittering position when the Assistant Chief Constable retired.

Mullett had planned that he would be the next Assistant Chief Constable. He was only too aware how easy it was to slip from grace when so near the summit, but this was not going to happen to him. The decisions and actions he took were made solely in the light of what was best for his career. Sometimes this was not the best thing for the division. But the division would survive: one wrong move and he wouldn't. For this reason, having the Chief Constable's nephew here was a bonus to be cherished. The chief was definite that he wanted the lad to be shown no favours, but Mullett knew how to interpret that. He would see that Barnard was recommended for early promotion entirely on his own merits. It might upset some of his own men with stronger claims, but it was a tough world and there was always another time.

In the meantime he could congratulate himself on running a good division with some fine men under him; morale and discipline were excellent and crime figures were dropping. If only the division didn't include Detective Inspector Frost.

A knock at the door interrupted his meditations.

"Detective Constable Barnard. Welcome to Denton. Sit down, sit down."

Clive blinked in astonishment at his first sight of the Divisional Commander's panelled office. Its opulence contrasted with the rest of the building like a silken patch on a manure sack. It was easy to see how the limited maintenance budget had been spent.

Career-man Barnard shook hands with career-man Mullett, each liking what he saw. The Divisional Commander pressed a button, a bell tinkled faintly in the adjoining office, and his efficient secretary, Miss Smith, scurried in with a tray on which rattled a coffee pot and the bone-china cups that were reserved for important visitors.

Mullett poured for both of them and was just raising his cup appreciatively to his lips when he caught sight of Clive's suit. He blinked, slipped on his reading glasses from his pocket, and peered again.

"Ahem. Er . . ." Must play it carefully, it might be his uncle's choice. "I suppose the rest of your luggage is on its way with your—er—proper suit?"

"Yes, sir," lied Clive.

The superintendent beamed and sipped happily from his cup. "I've been looking through your file . . . most impressive. And I see you're studying law. Couldn't do better. If I can help you in any way, lend you books—Archbold's *Criminal Pleading and Practice,* Green's *Criminal Costs,* plenty of others . . ."

"Thank you very much, sir." Clive's stomach wished there were some biscuits to go with the coffee. "I'm looking forward to working under Mr. Allen."

Mullett's face changed. He replaced his cup on its saucer and spooned in some more sugar. "Ah . . . There's been a slight change of plan I'm afraid. Inspector Allen is in charge of our missing-girl enquiry. We've a big search on. You wouldn't know about it, of course."

Clive knew how to name-drop. "Young Tracey Uphill, sir? I was at the mother's last night with the chaps from Able Baker four."

"Were you indeed? And before you'd officially joined us! That's what I like to see—keenness. But, as you'll appreciate,

Inspector Allen won't be able to spare you any time at the moment, so I've arranged for you to work with our other Detective Inspector—Detective Inspector Frost."

Oh no! Not that old tramp in the filthy mac!

"He's a very experienced man." He stared past Clive and considered the grim vista of Eagle Lane framed in his picture window. "He . . . had a personal tragedy last year . . . his wife. Devoted couple . . . very sad. He took it badly." Mullett's face saddened and his voice dropped to a conspiratorial whisper. "Cancer. Nothing they could do, absolutely nothing. Shocking business."

Clive nodded glumly and made appropriate noises of sympathy.

"As I said, he took it badly. Naturally. You can't expect a tragedy like that not to leave its scars. I make allowances of course . . ." He picked up his stainless-steel paperknife and tapped the blade on his palm, racking his brains for something to say in his inspector's favour.

"I'm sure he can teach me a lot," said Clive, without conviction.

Mullett brightened up. "Yes. Sometimes just knowing the wrong way to do things helps. It shows the pitfalls to avoid. Not that Inspector Frost's ways are necessarily wrong, of course . . ." Realizing that the water was getting dangerously deep he struck out on a more promising tack. "Do you see much of your uncle?"

Clive's answer was drowned in a roaring vibration of sound that made the building throb in sympathy. The two men ran to the window and craned their heads up to the sky.

There it was, disappearing over the roofs of the three-storeyed houses opposite. The promised helicopter.

Detective Inspector Frost swung his head to follow the flight of the helicopter as it thundered over the Market Square. He was making his way over to the doorway of Bennington's Bank where the beat constable and a stout little CID sergeant were examining signs of an attempted break-in. Crouched, with their backs towards him, they did not notice his approach. Frost paused. The tightly trousered posterior of the fat CID man was an irresistible target. He thrust forward a carefully aimed, stubby finger.

"How's that for centre?"

The reaction was hair-trigger. The CID man shot up and spun around, his face glaring and crimson. Then he saw Jack Frost and all annoyance evaporated.

"Oh. It's you, Jack!" He turned to the smiling beat constable with mock indignation. "Did you see what this dirty devil did?"

Frost looked at his hand. "I wish you hadn't jumped up so suddenly, Arthur. You nearly bit the end of my finger off. Now move your pregnant stomach out of the way and let me have a look."

The heavy wooden door to the bank showed raw gouges near the lock, as if something had been forced between the door and the jamb.

Frost straightened up and scratched his head. "Something wrong here, Arthur. You don't try to break into a bank by jemmying the front door. Even a burk like me knows that."

"It looks as though someone's had a go, though," insisted the fat sergeant, Arthur Hanlon, a jolly little Pickwick of a man without an enemy in the world.

"No, Arthur," replied Frost, firmly. "Crooks aren't that stupid, and if they were it wouldn't be our luck to have them: they'd all be over at Bridgely Division signing confessions like there was no tomorrow." Bridgely Division, the blue-eyed boy of County Headquarters, had the lowest crime rate and the highest detection rate in the county.

"Kids," suggested the constable, who didn't waste words.

Frost considered this. "What time was the damage spotted?"

The constable studied the report left by his colleague from the previous shift. "4:00 a.m., sir."

"And when did he last notice it was all right?"

Another consultation. "1:56 a.m., sir."

Frost dug his hands deep into his pockets and sniffed. "There you are, then. It happened between two and four this morning. You won't get kids mucking about with banks at that time—too busy reading Noddy under the bedclothes or having gang-bangs. Did you have gang-bangs when you were a kid, Arthur?"

Arthur giggled and shook his head.

"Me neither. I used to count myself lucky if I had sex more than six times a night. Any prints?"

"Millions of them, right back to the bloke who made the door."

"You're never satisfied. Which reminds me, how's the wife and kids—looking forward to Christmas?"

"Yes thanks, Jack," beamed Hanlon. "But what do you reckon we should do about this lark?" He indicated the door.

"Forget it, Arthur. I'll ask the station sergeant to get his beat boys to keep their eyes open. They'll just have to sleep off-duty. Look out . . . the fuzz!"

A police car hurtled across the road from Eagle Lane and squealed to a shivering halt outside the bank. The uniformed driver ran over to them.

"It's this fat man, Constable," said Frost, grabbing Hanlon's arm. "He was trying to break into the bank. You can see the marks."

The driver grinned dutifully. "Lot of panic at the station, sir. I think the Divisional Commander wants to see you."

A blur of maroon scarf dashed across the road.

Sergeant Wells let out a sigh of relief as the panting figure staggered in, wheezing and gasping for breath.

"I forgot all about the old sod, Bill."

Wells licked a stub of pencil and pretended to make an entry in his notebook. "When cautioned, the prisoner replied 'I forgot all about the old sod.'"

Another blast of cold air whooshed in as again the swing doors opened, this time to admit a ragged shrivelled figure wearing an ex-army greatcoat many sizes too big and stiff with dirt. He shuffled over to the desk as if on crippled feet and brought with him a thick, disgusting smell.

Frost's and the station sergeant's noses shuddered and wrinkled in unison.

The object of their nasal displeasure thumped angrily on the counter with a hand dark with ingrained dirt, complaining shrilly, "Where's my bleedin' quid? Fine thing when the effing cops rob you, isn't it?"

The station sergeant backed away until the wall stopped him, then spoke in the careful tones of an expert telling his pupil how to defuse a live bomb.

"Now step back, Sam. Don't sit down. Don't touch anything. Just stand there . . . and whatever you do, don't move! Good. Now we've only got to disinfect that one little spot." He fanned his face vigorously with his notebook.

The old tramp glowered with red-rimmed, watery eyes set deep in a grey-stubbled, leathery face.

"Never mind the bleedin' insults. Where's my quid?"

Wells held up a hand and explained patiently. "Now listen, Sam. You had six pence on you when we picked you up. Six pence is not a quid. A quid is one of these pieces of paper with the Queen's head on it, and you didn't have one. You came in with six pence and you were given six pence when we turned you out. We didn't charge a penny for our hospitality, nor for the fact that you were sick all over our nice clean floor. You had that on the taxpayers." He explained to Frost, "Sleeping rough, drinking meths, and urinating on the gravestones in the churchyard."

The old man had built up a fresh head of indignation. "I wasn't as bloody drunk as all that. I had a pound note and six pence. Your copper put it in an envelope, and when he give it back to me the quid had gone."

Wells tried again. "The quid was never there, Sam. Besides, we count the money out and you sign for it as being correct. We hold your evil-smelling mark on a receipt in full discharge of your six pennies."

Cracked lips curled back to show broken brown stumps. "I never signed no receipt."

"The cross might have been forged, Sam, but the smell

was unmistakable. You were too full of meths . . . you wouldn't have known what you were doing."

"I know how much I had. I want my quid."

"Where did you get the pound from, Sam?" asked Frost. "Not been selling your body, I hope."

Sam spun round and Frost jumped back as the aroma nudged its way towards him.

"I . . . I found it." It was said with defiance, but he wouldn't meet Frost's eye.

"So, now you've lost it," murmured the sergeant. "Easy come, easy go."

A smoulder of hate. "That young copper pinched it."

The station sergeant brought a large thick ledger from beneath the desk and banged it down on the counter.

"Right, Sam. You've made a very serious accusation. I take it you're going to prefer charges."

The face screwed up, the red dots of eyes burned as he swung his head from one to the other of them like a rat cornered between two terriers. "And a fat lot of bleedin' good that would do me. You'd all lie your effing heads off."

He hobbled out into the fresh air. It took a good thirty minutes with doors and windows open to persuade the smell he'd brought in with him to do likewise.

"You've got to know how to handle these sods," said Wells, poking the ledger back. "Who does he think is going to touch his money after he's wiped his grimy fingers over it?"

The internal phone buzzed. Wells answered it.

"Oh. Yes, sir. He's on his way."

The maroon scarf streaked past his eyes and off down the corridor to Mullett's office.

"These are the cells," said PC Keith Stringer, who had been detailed to show the new man around.

Clive grunted.

"You know," explained Stringer. "Where we keep the prisoners until we can get them to court." He pushed open an iron door. "This is the drunk cell with the drain, so we can hose the sick down . . ."

Clive's impatience burst. "Look, I have been in a police station before, you know. How long have you been on the Force?"

"Three months," replied the younger man, proudly.

"And I've been in it for two years—in one of the toughest areas of London. I've forgotten more than you'll ever know, so just show me where things are, don't explain them to me."

Stringer's face reddened. "Sorry. I was only trying to help." His expression cheered up as the door to the cell section opened and another uniformed man stepped in.

"Oh, Harry . . . this is the new chap, Clive Barnard from London. Clive—Harry Dobson."

The two men shook hands. Dobson was about Clive's age, a good-looking, curly-haired man with an innocent expression.

"Young Keith showing you the ropes, is he?"

"Nothing I can show him," said Keith. "He knows it all."

"I wish I could work in London," said Dobson. "Do me a favour, Keith. Come with me to fetch the prisoners' breakfasts. They should send them down, but you know how short-handed we are with this search."

"Sure," replied Keith. "Are the prisoners all right to be left?"

Dobson scratched his chin. "Well . . . as far as I know. The bloke in the end cell's been acting a bit queer, screaming and sobbing. Off his chump if you ask me, but he's quiet now. Keep an eye on them until we get back, Clive. Shouldn't be long."

Without waiting for his agreement, they were off.

Clive watched them go. Just trotting off and leaving the prisoners—what a way to run a station! In a properly organized station, like London, the man in charge of the cell section stayed put and the food was brought to him.

Better take a look at his charges. His feet rang on the stone flags and the familiar damp uriney carbolic smell tweaked his nose. The first two doors were ajar, the cells unoccupied, but the next was locked. Peering through the peep-hole he saw the occupant, a pimply faced youth with long, dank hair lying on the wall bed and staring blankly at the ceiling. Somehow aware he was being watched the youth jerked two fingers towards the spy-hole.

Another unoccupied cell, then the drunk cell with its floor sloping down to a grated drain. And that seemed to be it. Then he remembered the other prisoner Dobson had mentioned, the queer fellow in the end cell.

The end cell was locked. It was silent within—ominously silent. Clive put his eye to the spy-hole. His heart lurched and stopped. Level with his eye, a pair of legs hung downward, swaying and twisting grotesquely.

The occupant of the cell had hanged himself.

Clive hurled himself at the door, but of course it was locked. The fools. The bloody fools! They'd left him in charge but had taken the keys. He yelled. His voice echoed back at him but no-one came. The chap in the other cell started banging on his door, shouting to know what was going on.

Feeling sick, Clive raced up the stone corridor and out of the cell block. He saw the station sergeant going through a door marked Charge Room. But he had no breath. He croaked incoherently, tugging at the sergeant's uniform to get him to do something, anything. When Wells realized what Barnard was trying to tell him his face drained of colour. He snatched the spare bunch of keys from the charge room and tore to the end cell. As he poked the key in the lock, the door swung open.

Clive followed the sergeant into the cell. Sitting on the wall bed, tears of laughter streaming down their faces, were PCs Stringer and Dobson. Hanging from the ceiling on the end of a piece of rope was the pair of men's trousers they had stuffed with straw.

The station sergeant smiled. "It's one of the oldest tricks in the game, son. I thought you'd been in a police station before."

MONDAY (3)

Superintendent Mullett was taking sadistic pleasure in making Frost wait. The man had eventually slouched into his office in his usual insolent manner wearing that disgrace of a mac with the frayed sleeves and that ridiculous scarf.

"You wanted to see me, sir?" No apology, nothing.

Without raising his eyes from his correspondence, Mullett flicked a curt wrist towards a chair and deliberately took his time signing his letters, reading them through with studied slowness, and blotting them carefully afterwards.

He heard Frost fidget in his chair. Good. The display of his superior's displeasure and the humiliation of being ignored were having the desired effect. His pen crawled at a snail's pace to intensify the torture.

More fidgeting sounds from Frost.

Mullett's pen crawled on.

The sound of a match being struck.

A match? Mullett's nose twitched. A smoke-ring gently nudged his pen and drifted across his desk. He followed it with incredulous eyes.

This was intolerable. Frost was smoking. Without even asking permission—which would have been icily refused—he was smoking, leaning at ease in the chair, swinging an unpolished shoe from side to side. He gave Mullett a reassuring smile.

"When you're ready, Super . . ."

Mullett winced. He hated being addressed as "Super." Everyone knew it but Frost.

"Put out that cigarette," he snapped with such ferocity that the cigarette immediately dropped from Frost's startled lips and landed on the carpet. There was a smell of burning wool from the blue Wilton. Frost ground at the pile with his dirty shoes and managed to distribute a mess of broken cigarette and charred wool over a wide area. He moved his chair to cover up the burn and smiled enquiringly at Mullett.

"You wanted to see me, sir?"

As soon as Frost had gone, Mullett would go down on his hands and knees and inspect the damage. In the meantime he contented himself with a long hard stare.

"I wanted to see you more than half an hour ago. You've kept me waiting, Inspector."

"I had to have a look at Bennington's Bank. Someone jemmied their door."

"I would have thought your Divisional Commander's summons took priority. And you weren't at the briefing meeting!"

A theatrical smiting of palm to freckled forehead. "The meeting? Clean forgot all about it, sir."

Mullett took the envelope from his drawer. "I've had a complaint about you, Inspector." He unfolded the memo. "From Superintendent Gibbons of the Police Training Centre . . ."

Frost's blank expression masked his relief. This was a comparatively trivial matter. He'd been asked over to the training centre to speak, as an experienced officer, to new recruits and to give them practical hints that would assist them in their chosen career.

"So, you told them how to fiddle their car expenses," accused Mullett.

"I only mentioned it in passing, sir."

"In passing, or not, that was what you were talking to them about when Superintendent Gibbons entered the lecture room. I was ashamed to get his memo. Fortunately he wrote to me confidentially, as a friend, and didn't copy it to HQ. I'm most concerned about you, Frost. I had occasion to look in your office today. Frankly, I was appalled. The mess, the untidiness . . . *and* I found that statistical return that County has been screaming for still uncompleted."

"Ah, yes. I must get around to that. Anything else, sir?"

Yes, there was. Mullett gathered himself for his main attack.

"Were those the clothes you wore at the training centre?"

Frost looked down at his apparel with surprise. "Why, yes."

The superintendent smoothed his moustache carefully as if it was insecurely fixed with spirit gum. "Superintendent Gibbons thought you had turned up in your gardening clothes . . ."

Frost shot up. "Of all the bloody cheek!"

"It's not a bloody cheek, Inspector! I've been meaning to talk to you about your dress for some time. That mac's a disgrace. And those trousers—when were they last pressed? And as for your shoes . . ."

Frost tucked his shoes under the chair to hide them from view. "With respect, sir, I'm supposed to be solving bloody crimes, not tarting myself up like a tailor's dummy."

Mullett sighed and slumped back in his chair. How could you get through to people like this? Very carefully, and explaining all the ramifications and dangers, he told Frost about the Chief Constable's nephew.

Sergeant Wells flung open the door to Inspector Frost's office. "You'll be working in here, Barnard."

It was a mess. A tiny dingy office; two desks, buried in paper, a filing cabinet that wouldn't close properly, and a hatrack. The room was overheated by an enormous cast-iron radiator running beneath a window that overlooked the car park. The wall calendar still showed the previous month and untidy heaps of paper and opened files carpeted the brown linoed floor.

Wells stepped on to an oasis of virgin lino. "You'll have to get the place tidied up a bit, Barnard. Paperwork was never the inspector's strongest suit."

Clive was speechless. This wouldn't have been tolerated for a single day in London.

The door crashed against the wall and Frost entered, eyes blazing. He kicked a heap of papers and hurled himself into a chair.

"That bloody four-eyed bastard!"

The station sergeant smiled knowingly and gave Clive a broad wink. "Just come from the Divisional Commander, Jack?"

"I'd like to pull his bleeding moustache out, hair by hair." He spotted a fresh memo on his desk, gave it a brief glance, snorted, and screwed it up. It missed the wastepaper basket by a good six inches and joined the other debris on the floor. "Do you know the latest? I've got to wet-nurse the snotty-nosed illegitimate son of our Chief-bloody-Constable."

Wells grinned and jerked a thumb towards Clive. "Not his son, Jack—his snotty-nosed nephew. And this is him."

Frost overflowed with apologies, handshakes, and offers of cigarettes. "Don't take any notice of me, son. I'm not usually like this—only when I've been rubbed up the wrong way by some horn-rimmed, hair-lipped, stuck-up cow's son of a Divisional Commander who shall be nameless."

The station sergeant coughed pointedly. There was a newcomer in their midst.

Frost took the hint. "Yes, you're right, Bill, I'm supposed to imbue our young hopefuls with respect for rank even though I haven't any myself. Flaming arseholes—!"

He had just noticed Clive's suit.

"One hundred and seven quid," announced Sergeant Wells gravely.

Frost's eyebrow shot up. He tested the material between nicotine-stained fingers and shook his head. "For that money you could have got a proper one, son. And for work the criterion is never wear a suit you wouldn't be happy letting a drunk be sick all over."

Behind an impassive face, Clive's resentment flared. Have your fun, you bucolic sods, he thought. We'll see who has the last laugh.

Frost, who had a cornucopia of tasteless anecdotes to suit every occasion, was telling a story about his early days in CID.

"I'd bought myself this suit from the Fifty Shilling Tailors and the very first day I wore it this little fat drunk lurches up and deposits his lunch all over me. Naturally, I admonished him with a sharp knee to the groin, but that suit never looked the same again."

"It doesn't, Jack," agreed Wells, straight-faced, "and it's about time you had it cleaned."

Frost grinned. "Funny you should mention my clothes, Bill. Our beloved Divisional Commander has just informed me I'm doing the ragman out of a living. I suppose my mac compares unfavourably with that £107 creation."

"He didn't care for this either," admitted Clive.

"If he said that, son, then I'm going to have to force myself to like it." As he spoke, he worried something on his right cheek with his fingertips.

Clive eyed Frost more closely. The right cheek! He hadn't noticed before. It was scarred. A knot of white puckered scar tissue under the right eye. He found himself staring and pulled his eyes away.

Frost's internal phone buzzed. It was buried beneath the papers on his desk, but he dragged the receiver out by its flex. A terse message from Inspector Allen—would Frost report to his office right away. Click. No "please," just the bare message. Frost reburied the phone. "Another bastard I hate. You might as well come with me, son. Give you a chance to see what a real detective looks like."

A real detective looked thin, wiry, and sour, but on top of the job, his chilly office reeking of floor polish and uncluttered efficiency, with the desk clinically clear, the "In" tray empty, the "Out" brimful of memos and instructions in Allen's neat hand.

Allen frowned when he saw Frost had brought someone in with him, but forced out a wintry smile when he realized it was the Chief Constable's nephew. As soon as he'd restored Tracey Uphill to her mother he'd take the new DC under his wing. Another career man, Allen knew his promotion to chief inspector would be announced shortly and he was aiming to be detective superintendent within a year. He'd overtake Mullett yet. The commandership of the new, enlarged division wasn't the one-horse race his superintendent blithely imagined.

Shaking hands briskly with Clive he nodded his visitors to chairs.

"You weren't at the meeting this morning, Frost?" It was barked out as a question.

"No, Allen," beamed Frost, lighting a cigarette and dropping the match on the polished lino, "I forgot."

Allen rose from his chair, picked up the discarded match, and deposited it carefully into his empty wastepaper basket.

"Thanks," said Frost cheerfully.

Allen took a couple of deep breaths and returned to his seat.

"The missing girl. I want you to question the mother. Something's wrong. If this was a straightforward missing-from-home we should have found the kid by now."

"There's always the possibility she's done the kid in," suggested Frost.

Clive smiled tolerantly at this outrageous suggestion. You'd only got to look at the woman . . . But Inspector Allen seemed to agree with Frost.

"Precisely. That's what I want you to check. Have a nose around. It wasn't searched properly last night."

"Right," said Frost, stretching out his legs and drawing on the cigarette.

Allen's eyes narrowed. "I mean now!" he barked.

That's the way to treat lazy buggers like Frost, thought Clive as the inspector shot to his feet.

"Congratulations," said Frost.

"On what?" asked Allen in surprise.

"On your promotion to chief inspector coming through."

"But it hasn't," said Allen.

"Oh," said Frost, "I thought it had," and he sat down again and finished his cigarette.

Frost took Clive with him to the control room to pick up a personal radio, but the constable in charge was loath to part with any more.

"You've already got two and you haven't returned them,

sir," he said, pointing to the signed receipts in his issues book.

"Important job for Inspector Allen," said Frost, breezily signing for a third. "You'll have them all back this afternoon, without fail." He snatched a radio from the shelf and hustled Clive out before the constable could protest further.

His car, a grey, mud-splattered Morris 1100, was hidden in a side street. It was a cold day and as soon as Frost had cleared the passenger seat of a pair of dirt-caked gumboots and some yellowing *Daily Mirrors,* he slid in and rammed the heater switch to "High." Then he chucked the keys across to Clive and allowed himself to be chauffeured.

Inspector Frost was the sort of navigator who screamed "Turn right!" just as the car was passing the appropriate turning. He didn't bother with advance warnings; Clive was forever slamming on the brakes and executing tight U-turns and the gumboots on the back seat kept falling to the floor.

They had left the town and were winding their way eastward down a rutted road running alongside forlorn miserable fields, unfarmed and overgrown, sites compulsorily purchased for the future expansion of Denton New Town.

To the right was one of the search parties, a thin straggle, moving slowly and methodically, poking the undergrowth with sticks, a cumulus cloud of smoky breath hovering over their heads in the cold air. Frost leaned over and honked the horn. One of the searchers turned and waved, then resumed the slow, patient prodding. Even at that distance the mud-splattered Morris was plainly identifiable.

Frost settled back in his seat, then drew Clive's attention to a large clearing where a smoke-belching bulldozer was rooting up the stumps of trees.

"Used to be woods there when I was young, son. Thick woods—with birds, squirrels, the lot. Many's the time in the hot fiery days of my youth when I've taken the shy trembling lady of my choice for an advanced anatomy lesson under the green bough." He sighed deeply. "That was weeks ago, of course. Oh, we should have turned left back there, son. All right, back a bit. More . . . more . . . you've bags of room."

She was waiting for them on the doorstep, skin scrubbed clean of make-up, ash-blonde hair pulled off her face and tied with a black boot-lace ribbon. She could have been a child, until you got close and saw the lines of worry, the eyes puffy from crying and lack of sleep. When she heard the car pull up outside she was sure they were bringing Tracey back, but when she opened the door she could see there were only two men. Please, please, she thought, don't let it be bad news.

The untidy man with the scarf gave her a reassuring smile. "No news, I'm afraid, Mrs. Uphill. Couple of questions you might help us on though."

She led them through to the lounge, buttocks wriggling in tight slacks, even in grief arousing strong sexual responses from the two men.

Frost settled down in an armchair and worried away at his scar for a minute before starting his questions. He was going to have to upset her and he hated upsetting anyone. The question he should ask was, "Have you killed your daughter, Mrs. Uphill, and hidden her body somewhere? If so, you might tell us so we can call in those poor sods searching in the cold." Instead he said, "Any further thoughts as to where Tracey might have gone, Mrs. Uphill? We've covered all the obvious places."

She brushed back a straying wisp of hair. "If I had I'd have phoned the police."

"You had no quarrel with the child? Any reason why she might have left home?"

"No. We went through all this last night!"

Frost pushed himself up from the chair. "We'd like to search the house, if you don't mind."

She looked startled. "It was searched last night."

"Children can be devils, Mrs. Uphill. She could have sneaked back in and hidden somewhere."

"She's not in the house." The woman hugged herself as though for warmth. The room was hot, but the cold was inside her. Her teeshirt had ridden up, showing naked cream beneath. She looked like a frightened, lonely child and Clive wanted to put his arms around her—and not just because he wanted to reassure her.

"We haven't got all sodding day, son," snapped Frost. "We'll start at the top and work our way down."

The upper floor contained two bedrooms and a bathroom. They looked in the main bedroom first. Thick drawn curtains shut out the daylight. Clive found the switch and a tinted bulb slashed the bed with rose-coloured light. The large double bed was unmade, a crumpled, flimsy lemon nightdress lying on a pillow. A pyramid of half-smoked cigarettes in the ashtray testified to a sleepless night.

They searched the room thoroughly, moving the bed and the large dressing table. Then Clive slid open the door of the built-in wardrobe and his startled gasp of horror sent Frost running over. But it was a doll; an expensive, life-sized, blonde-haired doll, the hidden-away Christmas present Tracey had asked Father Christmas for. Clive braced himself for some biting comment, but Frost mildly remarked, "Blimey, son, it looks bloody real, doesn't it?"

It was a large wardrobe, but apart from the doll, it held only clothes swaying on hangers; lots and lots of expensive clothes.

Frost pulled back the curtains and looked out on Vicarage Terrace. You could just see the vicarage and the Sunday school at the end of the street. What had happened to the child after she left that Sunday school? He shifted his gaze back to the room and the ceiling . . .

"Blimey!"

Clive followed his gaze. A mirror was fixed to the ceiling, positioned to reflect the occupants of the bed. The detective constable's mouth went dry as he pictured a naked, writhing Joan Uphill, her body splashed with red light, her hair spread over the pillow . . .

"Must be a sod to clean that," said the down-to-earth Jack Frost, adding, as an afterthought, "Perhaps the man has a feather duster stuck up his arse."

The other bedroom was the child's, the walls papered in a Tom and Jerry pattern, with nursery characters decorating the lampshade and the door of the white-painted cupboard. A row of dolls sat solemnly on a windowseat staring at the small bed which was neatly made. A small radiator heated the room, but it seemed cold . . . and empty.

Frost casually opened the cupboard door and an avalanche of toys cascaded to the floor at his feet. He found a yo-yo and demonstrated some tricky variations to his detective constable who tried not to show his contempt for Frost's childish behaviour.

Frost unhooked the string from his finger and dropped the yo-yo back on the heap. "Tell you what, son, you do one of your thorough London searches in the bathroom while I poke this lot back in the cupboard."

The large bathroom, with its panelled tangerine bath, toilet, and washbasin, didn't take much searching, but Clive wasn't going to let the inspector show him what he'd missed. It was really too small, but he checked the bathroom cabinet. Just the usual toiletries, body cologne, talcum powder, bath foam, and an electric razor. He unscrewed the cap of the talc and sniffed the loin-stirring Joan Uphill perfume. He put the talc back and closed the cabinet. The only real possibility was the airing cupboard. He opened it up and looked inside. Most of its space was taken up by the hot-water tank and the wooden racks each side holding ironed linen. But they'd taught him to be thorough in London. Sliding out a couple of the wooden racks, he slid his hand around the back of the tank until it was wedged between hot, bare metal and the rough surface of the wall. Nothing hidden there. He could guarantee that. The space above the cylinder? More racks and more clothes. Brushing his new suit free of brickdust and cobwebs, he called across to the inspector that he'd finished.

Frost sauntered over, his mac unbuttoned and flapping. He surveyed the bathroom. "No bidet? She must chuck her fag-ends down the loo." He dropped his own cigarette end to a sizzling death, lowered the toilet seat, plonked himself down on it, and lit up a fresh one, his eyes flitting about the room.

"That was quick, son. Congratulations."

There was something in the way he said it that put Clive on his guard. Had he missed anything? Of course he hadn't, how could he? But he still felt uneasy.

Frost pumped out a mouthful of smoke.

"Did you have much trouble getting the bath panel off?"

Clive groaned inwardly. He could have kicked himself. The bath was boxed-in with plastic panels screwed to internal battens. A screamingly obvious hiding place, so obvious he'd missed it. But the scruffy old fool had spotted it.

Frost gave an understanding smile and handed Clive a screwdriver produced from the depths of the mac pocket.

After a token display of reluctance, the screws turned easily and he dropped them, one by one, into Frost's palm for safe-keeping, then off came the panel to be rested up against the other wall. The space revealed was large enough for two or three bodies but contained only dust, a heap of wood shavings, and a wet patch where the waste-pipe had been leaking.

"Nothing, sir."

Frost beamed. "I found the loot from six break-ins once, hidden behind bath panels. We knew it was in the bathroom. One brave lad even stuck his hand down the S-bend of the lav. I won't tell you what he found, but it wasn't the loot. Then I had one of my rare bright thoughts. We took out the bath panels and there it was, £12,000 worth. A good hiding place. I wish a few more crooks were clever enough to use it. It's the first place I look now and I haven't found a bloody thing since."

A light tread on the stair and a rattle of cups.

"In here, Mrs. Uphill," called Clive.

She stopped dead when she saw the removed panel and Clive on his knees by the bath.

She knew.

She knew they weren't looking for a live child. They were looking for a body.

Her hands shook. The cup rattled.

Frost gently took the tray from her and passed it to Clive. "You think she's dead?" she whispered. Frost didn't answer. "And am I supposed to have killed her—my own daughter?"

Frost levelled up the ends of his scarf. His voice was soft. "We see lots of rotten things in the Force, Mrs. Uphill. You'd be surprised what people do. They kill their kids. Nice people. Loving parents with beautiful children, and they kill them. We had a mother, saw her husband off to work, kissed him goodbye, then drowned her three kids in the bath. Mentally ill, of course. Afterwards she went out shopping and bought them all sweets. Couldn't understand where they were when she got back. I doubt if that's what's happened in your case, but we have to check even at the risk of hurting your feelings."

There was silence. Even Clive was moved. Then she turned and clattered downstairs. She was sobbing.

"I wonder if she's hidden the body in the airing cupboard," said Frost.

You callous bastard, thought Clive. Aloud he said, "I've looked, sir."

Frost accepted this and sipped his tea reflectively. "Hmm. Not bad. If she makes you a cup of tea like this afterwards it's well worth the thirty quid she charges for her services. Grab a chair and come with me, son. I've found something else you must be dying to investigate."

Something else Clive had missed. A trapdoor in the ceiling just outside the bathroom. It led to the loft. Clive's torch beam crawled over the rafters. A suitcase. Big enough, but too light. He dragged it down. Inside were some infant clothes and a ball of white angora baby wool. They had been there a long time. Nearly nine years.

"We always wanted kids," said Frost, "the wife and me. She couldn't have them." He held the chair steady as Clive clambered down then diffidently dragged something from his inside pocket and offered it to the detective constable.

"I found this tucked inside Tracey's *Beano Annual*."

Clive looked at it in wide-eyed disbelief. Frost's words didn't seem to make sense. "In her *Beano Annual*, sir?"

Frost nodded gravely.

It was an unretouched black and white photograph of a nude girl sitting on a draped box, leaning back, supporting herself on her hands. The model could not be identified since the top of the photograph had been torn off, although traces of dark hair could be seen resting on the shoulders. Somehow the effect seemed vaguely distasteful, not erotic, but pornographic, although there was nothing pornographic about the pose apart from the model's nudity.

Frost took the photograph back and raised it to his nose. "Smell that, son—acid fixer. Amateurs never wash their prints as thoroughly as professionals. You can always smell traces of hypo." He studied it again. "That mark on the top of the left arm, son. What do you make of it?"

Clive moved to the open door of the bathroom for more light. "It's not too clear, sir. Could be a birthmark."

"Yes, that's what I reckon." He pulled the cigarette from his mouth, flipped it into the toilet basin, and flushed it down. "I wonder who she is . . . and how Tracey got hold of it."

"It wouldn't be . . . ?" Clive didn't like to say it. He pointed downstairs.

"Good Lord, no, son!" The photograph went back into his inside pocket. "I'll show it to her anyway. She's in the trade, she might recognize the model from the salient features. But first we'd better see how many bodies she's got buried in her back garden. I don't suppose you looked last night."

Clive assured him that they had.

Frost snorted. "A quick flash round with your torch in the dark—and you were looking for a living child above the surface, not for signs of recent digging."

The garden was mainly concrete patio and lawn. There were a couple of rose-beds, but the soil was rock-hard and had not been disturbed. Frost probed the lawn to see if it was composed of turfs which could be reassembled to conceal a grave, but it had been sown from seed. The patio was un-blemished. It contained a dustbin which they checked. Running along the side of the house there was a concrete path leading to the front. In it a black metal inspection cover to the sewage system was set. A heavy cover. It took the two of them to lift it. But desperate people with a body to hide can find hidden strength.

Frost rubbed his chin. "You'll hate me for this, son, but you're going to have to give your new suit the shock of its young life. Have a poke around down there, would you?"

My day will come, you bastard, thought Clive behind a set grin, determined not to give Frost the satisfaction of seeing his annoyance. He crouched over the hole and let his torch beam cut through to the gurgling horrors below.

Apart from the obvious, nothing. He ignored Frost's heavy-humoured request to see if his cigarette end had emerged yet.

They manhandled the cover back then poked about in the garage and Mrs. Uphill's red Mini. Frost seemed to be losing interest in the proceedings, hustling Clive on before he had finished. They gave the ground floor of the house a very perfunctory going-over. The inspector wouldn't let Clive clear out the meter cupboard under the stairs.

"She's not here, son," he snapped impatiently. "Leave it."

You're the boss, thought Clive, and followed the inspector into the lounge where the young mother sat, staring blankly into the plastic logs of the electric fire.

"She's not here, Mrs. Uphill," said Frost. "Do you think her father might have taken her?"

She didn't raise her head. "I'm not married."

"I know, Mrs. Uphill, but the child has a father."

A bitter grin made her face look ugly. "Yes, she has a father. I haven't seen him since before Tracey was born—since the day I broke the news to him that I was pregnant. That's when he decided he didn't want to see me any more. Coincidence, wasn't it?"

"Does he support his child?" asked Clive.

She stood and took a cigarette from a box on the mantelpiece. "I was paid off in a lump sum by his parents. They were willing to pay anything reasonable I might ask to make sure their poor misguided son wasn't lumbered with a promiscuous bitch like me and her bastard. And he was the first you know, there was no-one else."

A silence broken by the rasping of Frost's finger against his troublesome right cheek. "And he's never been in touch with you?"

She shook her head. "If he thinks of me at all, he probably hopes I'm dead. He never even bothered to find out if he had a son or a daughter—or if I died in childbirth."

Clive felt he would like to strangle the man with his bare hands. Eight years ago. She couldn't have been more than a schoolgirl, fifteen or sixteen at the most, and a virgin. His hatred mingled with jealousy and envy.

Frost wanted the man's name and address. She found the address in an old diary. Clive made an entry in his notebook. The man's name was Ronald Conley with an address in Bristol. He'd given her the diary as a present eight years before. The flyleaf bore the neatly written inscription "To my darling Joan from Ron" followed by a string of kisses. The two-faced seducing bastard, thought Clive.

"I'm puzzled, Mrs. Uphill," said Frost.

She looked at him.

"Why didn't you meet her from Sunday school?"

She busied herself lighting a cigarette. It seemed to require her full attention.

"It's a simple question, Mrs. Uphill. One of our chaps has had a word with the Sunday school superintendent. He says you always met her, winter or summer, rain or sunshine. Yesterday was the only day you missed. Why?"

She pulled the cigarette from her mouth and spat out the answer. "Don't you think I've reproached myself? I thought she'd be all right. Just this once, I didn't meet her . . ." And then her anger crumbled and her body shook with dry spasms of tearless grief. Clive raised himself from his chair, ready to bound across and comfort her, but a warning glance from Frost pushed him back.

Frost's hand shot out and grabbed the woman's shoulder. "Listen. There was a man lurking outside that Sunday school last summer trying to molest the kids. You knew about him. Ever since then you've met her. When the sun was streaming down you met her. But yesterday, when it was pitch dark, you thought she'd be all right. Why?"

She shook off his grip and screamed at him, "Leave me alone, you bastard!" And then she sobbed into her hands, tears squeezing between her fingers. Frost brutally pulled her hands away and shoved his face close to her. "I don't care a sod about your feelings, Mrs. Uphill. All I care about is getting your daughter back and I expect you to help, not go into bloody hysterics. Why didn't you meet her?"

She recoiled as if he'd slapped her face. "I . . . I had a man here."

Frost beamed and settled down in a chair, his tone friendly and cheerful. "A regular?"

She nodded.

"Was he late?"

She dabbed her eyes with one of the few Kleenex tissues remaining in the box and compressed it in her hand.

"Yes. Usually he was away by 3:30. That gave me plenty of time to meet Tracey. But yesterday he said his train was late, or cancelled, or something. It was nearly 3:30 when he arrived."

"What time did he usually come?" Frost, who had a memory like a sieve when it came to detail, glanced across the room to make sure Barnard was jotting down the times in his notebook.

"2:30."

"You'd better let us have his name and address."

She shook her head.

Frost insisted. "I'm afraid you must, Mrs. Uphill. I know you ladies have this Hippocratic oath to protect your clients' identities . . ."

"It's not that," she cut in. "I don't know his address, or his name. He said it was Bob, but they don't usually tell you their right names."

"What time did he leave you yesterday?"

"About 4:25. But what has this got to do with Tracey?"

"Probably nothing, but he left as she was coming out of Sunday school. He could have seen her. Describe him."

"Well, he had a beard . . ."

Frost's mind raced. A beard! The man trying to entice the kids into his car . . . He had a beard.

The description she gave was detailed—very detailed—right down to the appendix scar. Age thirty-four or thirty-five, light-brown hair and beard, brown eyes. From some of the other things she'd observed, Frost decided she must have seen him from some pretty unusual angles.

While Clive's pen was racing to get it all down, Frost produced the photograph. "Anyone you know, Mrs. Uphill?"

She stared at it. "No!"

"We found it in Tracey's room, hidden in a book."

Her face froze in disbelief. "Tracey's room . . . ? You couldn't have . . ."

"Would it be one of yours, perhaps? I understand you ladies keep a supply of stimulating snapshots to help some of your clients get ready to perform."

"I haven't found that necessary!" she snapped.

"Perhaps she found it somewhere," said Frost, blandly, pushing it back in his pocket. "It means nothing to kids. Well, thanks for all your help. As soon as there's any news . . ."

She saw them out and watched them walk to the car. Curtains twitched at windows on each side of the street.

"Bloody nosey neighbours," snorted Clive, "and none of them bothered to go in and comfort her. In London you wouldn't have been able to move for women making pots of tea."

But Frost was looking through the car window at the figure in the doorway. "If I had thirty quid to spare, son, I'd ask you to keep the engine running for five minutes." He shivered. "Hurry up, it's cold. Bung on the heater."

Clive started the engine. "Back to the station, sir?"

No reply. Frost was deep in thought. Suddenly he snapped

out of his trance. "Tell me, son, why the hell should anyone want to jemmy the front doors of a bank at three o'clock in the morning?"

"Eh?" said Clive, wondering what the hell this had to do with Tracey Uphill.

"Someone tried to jemmy the front door of Bennington's Bank in the Market Square in the wee small hours of this morning. I'm wondering why."

"To force an entry, sir?" suggested Clive, in the tones of one explaining the obvious to an idiot.

Frost snorted. "Through the front door of a bank? The big main doors?"

Clive tried again. "Perhaps someone just wanted to damage the door, someone with a grudge against the bank."

The inspector wasn't having this either. "You could do more damage peeing through the letterbox. Ah well, life has its little mysteries. Well, come on, son, what are we waiting for? Reverse and back out the way we came."

Barnard reversed. "Where are we going, sir?"

"To find this lucky sod with the beard, the appendix scar, and the weekly season ticket."

"And how are we going to do that?" persisted Clive.

Frost smiled and rearranged his scarf. "If he came by train, we start with the railway station. I'll tell you the way."

They passed a dark, gloomy building. Frost jerked a thumb. "That's the vicarage and Sunday school. The church is farther back."

"Looks a bit of a dump, sir."

"Yes. My wife's buried in the churchyard."

An uneasy silence as the journey proceeded, then: "Doing anything for Christmas, son?"

"I don't know yet, sir."

"I'm on duty Christmas Day. You can come on with me if you like."

Christ, thought Barnard, I'd rather have all my teeth out. Aloud he said, "I might have to go to my uncle's."

"Well, don't say I didn't offer," replied Frost. "Oh, we should have turned right at that crossing."

MONDAY (4)

A taxi was parked on the railway station forecourt; there was no sign of the driver. Clive pulled up alongside and the two men got out. The sky was darkening and the wind had gathered strength since the morning.

The booking office was empty, the platforms deserted, no signs of porters or ticket collectors.

"The mystery of the *Mary Celeste*," murmured Frost, leading Clive past the ticket barrier to a door painted olive-green and marked "Staff Only." Voices bubbled gently from inside. The inspector quietly turned the handle and crashed the door open.

"All right—nobody move!"

A tiny room reeking of shag tobacco, over-stewed tea, and sweat. Four startled heads jerked to the door. A small bald man clutching an enormous brown-enamelled teapot was the first to recognize the intruder.

"It's the bloody fuzz! They can't catch crooks, but they can smell a teapot a mile off." Then he smiled. "Come on in, Jack."

They squeezed in. The room now held six people and very little air. Apart from the detectives there were the three absent railwaymen—the bald teapot holder who was the booking office clerk, a fat ticket collector sucking at a spittle-soaked, homemade cigarette, and a gangling young apprentice porter in jeans and a railway cap wedged on top of lank, ragged hair. The fourth man wore horn-rimmed glasses, and a beaming smile. He was the missing taxi-driver, in for a warm and a cup of tea.

Two battered enamel mugs were produced for the guests, blown free of dust, and filled with strong, viscous tea.

Frost introduced Clive as his smart young assistant from London.

"Just taking him around Denton to show him where all the toilets are," he explained. "Nothing worse for a rising young cop than to be taken short and caught peeing in the gutter." He pointed in the direction of the grimy window. "If you're ever in really dire straits, son, there's one at the end of the platform. You can find it easily in the summer because of the flies buzzing over it. These lazy sods, paid a king's ransom by British Rail, spend all their time guzzling tea instead of cleaning it out."

"We daren't go in for a week after you've used it," accused the bald booking clerk. "Anyway, what are you here for?"

Frost swallowed a mouthful of tea. "Were you lot on yesterday afternoon?" They nodded. "I'm trying to trace a man aged about thirty-five, bearded, travels here every Sunday, arriving around two o'clock. Travels back about four."

The fat ticket collector had a bout of coughing and splattered ash from his homemade cigarette over his waistcoat. "Vaguely remember him," he said.

"Light brown hair?" said a voice. "Dark coat and a scarf?" Frost wheeled round. It was the taxi-driver.

"I pick him up every Sunday, 2:15, regular as clockwork —apart from yesterday. He was an hour late. Said they'd cancelled his usual train."

Frost rubbed his hands in delight. "Where did you take him?"

"Same place as always—top of Church Lane."

The inspector could have hugged himself. Church Lane was but a short distance from Vicarage Terrace and the rosy, mirrored ceiling of No. 29.

"That's the bloke." He turned to the railwaymen. "What station did he come from?"

"I don't know what station," said the lanky porter, "but the only train cancelled yesterday was the 1:47 from Cranford, stopping at all stations."

"That's right," said the booking clerk. "The driver didn't turn up. The next train was the 2:47."

"I've got him!" said the ticket collector. "Bearded fellow . . . I've placed him now." He dived under the table and produced a large tin that once had held Huntley and Palmer's biscuits but was now filled with small packets containing the daily hauls of collected tickets. He rummaged and found a torn half of green pasteboard, which he handed to Frost. "That's his ticket!"

The outward half of a cheap day return from Lefington, a small village some twelve miles down the line.

A bang shook the door and it was crashed open by a bowler-hatted gentleman with a military moustache and a brick-red angry face. He glared at the tea party. "Isn't anyone on duty in the ticket office? I've been waiting more than five minutes."

"Just coming," said the bald man and bolted out after him.

"Bloody passengers," observed Frost. "They seem to think the railway's run for their benefit. Well, we're getting somewhere. We know he came from Lefington. Do you remember him going back?"

The fat porter scratched his head. "He usually caught the 4:33, but I swear he wasn't on it yesterday."

"He was an hour late," said Frost. "What time was the next one?"

"The 5:33—but he wasn't on that either. We only had one passenger for that—a woman."

"Hardly worth keeping the bloody station open," snorted Frost. "What train did he catch, then?"

The porter shrugged. "We went off duty at six," he said, slamming the door on any further progress in that direction.

But Frost had enough to go on. Lefington was a small village and the booking clerk there should recognize the man from the detailed description. But what had he done after he'd left Mrs. Uphill? Seemingly he was in no hurry to use the return half of his ticket. But find him first. As soon as they got back to the office he'd teleprint Lefington sub-division and get them to follow it up.

A train rattled through the station and sped on its way. The railwaymen consulted pocketwatches and nodded. The train was on time.

Then Frost realized he hadn't reported back to Inspector Allen after interviewing the mother. Blimey, that'll bring the pains on, he thought.

"Come on, son—work to do."

Clive, who was being told by the young porter that his suit was fab, drank the remains of his tea and buttoned his coat.

Frost protected his neck with a couple of tight turns of the scarf and opened the door. Outside it was cold. Very cold.

By four o'clock it was too dark to continue and reluctantly, but sensibly, Detective Inspector Allen issued instructions for the search to be called off for the day. He sat alone at a corner table in the canteen with its green and gold Christmas decorations hanging from the ceiling and watched the tired, cold men returning to join the shuffling queue for hot, strong tea. The hissing of the urn and the clangour of cups and cutlery almost drowned the low-key dispirited conversations.

Allen was as tired and drained as the searchers. Something was wrong. They should have found her today. Tomorrow he'd have to draw in more men and extend the area of the search, which meant more organizing, more painstakingly detailed work before he could call it a day. He'd been on the go since seven that morning and would be lucky to see his bed before midnight. And he felt ill. He hadn't eaten all day and the thought of food sickened him. The canteen was overbearingly hot. Where the devil was that incompetent fool, Frost. Nothing from him since he was detailed to interview the mother before lunch. And the man an inspector, the same rank as Allen, who was bearing all the worry and responsibility of the search and who would have to accept all the blame if it went sour.

A burst of raucous laughter from the queue by the counter, and there was Frost in his dirty mac, sharing some coarse joke with the woman at the tea urn. No worries, no thought of reporting back to Allen, just straight into the queue for tea.

It was too much. Allen stormed over and jerked his head to the door, waiting in the corridor outside for Frost to follow. Out he came, his scarf bulging out of his pocket, the new chap, Barnard, behind him.

"Bit of luck spotting you," beamed Frost, completely unabashed. "I'll give you a verbal report—save all the bother of sticking it on paper."

Allen exploded. Was he expected to receive important reports casually in the corridor?

"You'll write the bloody thing out properly and bring it to my office. And where the hell have you been?"

"Sorry," said Frost, surprised at the outburst and wondering why the man was so touchy—although he didn't look well. "She gave us a lead and we followed it through."

Allen's eyes blazed. "You weren't told to follow it through. You were told to report back, you bloody fool. Why don't you do what you're told!"

"Why don't you get stuffed," asked Frost, turning to go. "You'll get the report when I've had some tea."

Something snapped. Allen reached out, grabbed Frost's shoulder, and spun him round. Frost's eyes flashed and knuckles whitened over clenched fists.

God, thought Clive, there's going to be a fight. He prayed that a senior officer would come on the scene before it got out of hand. What was the etiquette for such things? Should he try to break it up or look the other way and pretend it just wasn't happening?

But it didn't happen. Allen gasped and doubled up, his face sickly white and contorted with the pain that tore his stomach.

Frost was immediately full of concern. "Are you all right?"

Allen straightened up, his brow clammy with sweat. "Something I've eaten. It'll pass." He was unsteady on his feet and clutched the wall for support.

"I'll give you a hand to your office."

"No—I can manage." He composed himself. Then: "What happened with Mrs. Uphill?" He listened intently as

Frost told him. He didn't think the nude photograph was relevant but was very interested in the bearded man.

"I want to know immediately there's any news from Lefington. And I want a typed report on my desk tonight." He trotted briskly down the stairs. Whatever had been wrong with him seemed to have passed.

"I won't half pay for that when his promotion comes through," Frost told Clive blandly, pushing the swing doors to re-enter the canteen, but no sooner had they joined the end of the queue when the PA system gave a metallic cough.

"Telephone call for Inspector Frost."

There was a phone in the corridor. The call was from Lefington sub-division. Good news. The railway booking clerk not only recognized the description, but was able to turn up an application the bearded man had made for a season ticket. It contained his full name and address. He was Stanley Farnham, a schoolmaster, who travelled daily by train to Cranford where he taught English at the comprehensive school.

Frost scribbled the address down on the back of a cigarette packet and was profuse with thanks, praise, and offers of reciprocation. The face he turned to Clive beamed with delicious anticipation, like a cat's on finding the door to the canary's cage open.

"No time for tea, son. We've got a beard to interview." He tugged the scarf from his mac pocket and reeled it round his neck.

"You'll be letting Inspector Allen know, sir?" asked Clive anxiously.

"But of course. He gets touchy if he thinks I'm ignoring him. I don't know why he should feel jealous—after all, we're both the same rank." He dialled Allen's office on the internal phone, but it was Detective Sergeant George Martin, Allen's assistant, who answered.

"Oh, hello, George," chirped Frost. "Is your esteemed chief there by some unfortunate chance? Gone home for a bath? Well, about time. I'm not a fussy man, but . . . Look, when he gets back, you might tell him we've traced

Mrs. Uphill's weekly customer and we're on our way to interview him. No, I don't think I should ask him first. He likes people to act on their own initiative. Have I done what? The crime statistics? God, is it time for them already? Due in last week? Clang! Well, thanks for the whisper. I'll do them when we get back."

He hung up and swore softly at the wall. Damn those bloody statistics. Mullett was such a stickler for them going out to HQ on time and they were a time-wasting nuisance. There was no problem if your office was organized like Inspector Allen's; you just went to a file and extracted the figures. But if your papers were unfiled and your office was a rubbish tip . . .

"As soon as we get back, son, we'll do the crime statistics. Be good training for you."

When they reached the car the inspector realized he'd left his other packet of cigarettes in the office and Clive, spilling over with resentment at being used as a messenger boy, was sent back for them.

The muddle and disorder of Frost's office made him shudder. Since they were last in, fresh deliveries of paperwork had arrived and had been stacked on top of earlier layers on the inspector's desk, held down under the weight of his glass ashtray. The top item under the ashtray looked interesting. A sheet of thick, deckle-edged notepaper scrawled with spidery writing in pale green ink. Clive sat at the desk to read it when young PC Keith Stringer breezed in with roneoed copies of the new duty roster for January.

"In the boss's chair already?" he grinned, adding a roneoed sheet to the rising paper mountain.

Clive decided not to admit to being engaged in the menial task of fetching cigarettes and countered with a question of his own. "I thought your shift finished at two?"

"Overtime. We're men short on the search and I need the money."

"Tell me something," said Clive. "What time do you reckon he'll be letting me go?"

"How do you mean?"

Clive checked his watch. "I've been on now for nearly eight hours. We've got to interview a man—say another couple of hours—then he's talking about coming back for a jolly session with the crime statistics. To hear him talk you'd think the day had just started."

Keith's grin widened. "Haven't you been told about Mr. Frost? He's a smashing bloke and we all like him, but he never wants to call it a day. Since his wife died there's nothing for him to go home for, I suppose, but he doesn't think anyone else has a home either. If you're home before midnight, you'll be lucky. First in and last out, that's him, so say goodbye to your sex life." He dropped a duty roster on Frost's desk and sailed out of the office.

Clive seethed. Midnight! Well, he wasn't going to put up with that; he'd see Mullett first thing tomorrow morning. Then his heart sank. He couldn't, of course. He was the Chief Constable's nephew. They'd say he was after special treatment.

So where were those bloody cigarettes? He worked his rage off on the desk drawer by jerking it out and was taken by surprise when it shot out easily, spilling its contents all over the floor.

Down on the knees of his flash trousers to pick them up. "Damn and sod the man," he cursed, chucking the useless junk back in the drawer. Bad enough to spend all day with the uncouth idiot without spending half the night as well.

One of the things that had fallen to the brown lino was curious. A blue box about the size of a packet of twenty cigarettes, with a crest embossed in gold on the front. It rattled when he shook it, so he peeped inside. A medal of some kind, in the shape of a cross and attached to a dark blue ribbon, nestled on a velvet bed. A long-service award perhaps. It was engraved "To Jack Edward Frost."

Clive tossed it in the drawer, found the cigarettes, and raced back to the car.

Stanley Farnham dumped the exercise books for marking on the hall table and picked up the letters from the mat. Two of them, one his monthly statement from Barclaycard, and the other . . . His pulse quickened. Hanging his overcoat in the hall closet he looked again at the envelope. It bulged. It must be the catalogue he'd sent off for last week. Still in the hall, he ripped it open and pulled out the contents. Yes, a large catalogue entitled *Sex Aids and Sex Toys*. He thumbed quickly through it. He would savour it at his leisure later, but just had to see . . . What's this. A price list for contraceptives, all makes, all colours, all nationalities. He pushed it aside impatiently; he couldn't work up much excitement for latex rubber-wear. A leaflet advertising books—*Sexual Positions*. This was more promising . . .

A warning bell inside him rang a fraction of a second before the doorbell screamed.

He wheeled round, nearly dropping the envelope. Two shadows through the frosted glass of the front door.

His heart banged and raced. The envelope! He stuffed it and the catalogue into the shallow drawer of the hall table.

The bell shrilled again. A loud bang at the door.

"Who is it?"

"Police."

The police! Oh God . . . surely they weren't checking his mail? When the postman had handed him that packet last week, he had been sure there had been a knowing smirk on the man's face.

He fastened the chain on the door and opened it cautiously. He wasn't taking any chances. Sometimes men, pretending to be police officers . . .

"Mr. Stanley Farnham? Sorry to trouble you, sir. We're from Denton CID. May we come in . . . ?"

This was the elder of two men, a shabby-looking character with a scarred face. The other, much younger, wore a shortie overcoat over a flashy suit and seemed to have a broken nose. A right pair of thugs! He was thankful he'd thought to put the chain on.

He asked to see their warrant cards. This seemed to present some difficulty to the scarred man who spent ages fumbling through wedges of dog-eared papers, but the young man instantly produced a wallet which he flipped open. A brand-new, clean warrant card proclaimed him to be Detective Constable Barnard. Then the other man found his and held it alongside.

"Or if you want to see a dirty one . . ." he said.

Farnham unhooked the chain and ushered them quickly past the hall table and into the lounge.

"What's this all about? I've only just got in from the school."

Detective Inspector Frost hung his scarf on the back of a chair and sat down. The other man remained standing.

"Nice little place you've got here, sir." The inspector's eyes crawled around the tasteful room, taking in the block-mounted abstract prints, the tightly packed bookshelves, the Tippett *Knot Garden* recording on top of the stereo record player. "Nice and compact. You took your time answering the door?"

The accusation slipped out so silkily, Farnham wasn't ready with an answer. "Oh. I . . . I . . . I was doing something . . ."

A hard stare from the inspector. "How many rooms have you got here, sir?"

"Rooms? Oh . . . this room, bedroom, kitchen, and bathroom."

"Just enough," nodded Frost, approvingly. "No point in having more than you need. You don't mind if my colleague from London has a look round, sir? Shouldn't take long."

Farnham felt a nerve in his face writhe and twitch. What were they looking for? What a fool he'd been sending for that stuff: it stood to reason that some of those advertisements had been bending the law . . . that last book was positively pornographic. It wasn't in the bookcase, thank God! The inspector's eyes were on him, watching that damn nerve pulsate and throb. Well, he wasn't going to make it easy for them; they'd have to drag him to the scaffold.

"Yes, I do mind. I'm not answering any questions without my solicitor."

Frost received this with benign equanimity. "Very wise, sir. Call him on the phone. We've plenty of time."

They were playing with him. Oh God, what if it was that other business? But they couldn't have found out. The room was closing in, he felt cornered; he wanted to run, to get away. Now he knew why the young detective had remained standing. He was blocking the door, preventing Farnham from getting out. They had him trapped. He was finding it difficult to breathe. The inspector was staring at him.

"Are you all right, Mr. Farnham?"

"Yes, of course I'm all right." It was hot. The heat was stifling. He loosened his tie.

"You've nothing to hide, have you, sir?"

"Hide? Of course not. What . . . what is this all about?"

"You know a woman called Joan Uphill, Mr. Farnham?"

His heart skipped a beat. Surely they didn't know about her? "Uphill?" The face screwed in concentration. "No, I can't recall . . ."

"No. 29 Vicarage Terrace, Denton, sir. Thirty pounds a time, tea included."

He managed to look mystified. "I'm sorry, I don't know her."

Frost stood up and adjusted his scarf. "You'd better phone your solicitor, sir. We'd like you to meet the lady. She reckons you were with her yesterday afternoon. In view of what you say, she must be lying, so the sooner we sort it out . . ."

Farnham tried to light a cigarette, but his lighter wouldn't work. The detective produced his and waited patiently until the cigarette stopped shaking.

"All right. Yes, I do know Mrs. Uphill. What has happened to her?"

"Why should anything have happened to her, sir?"

"These women, they do get attacked, you know. But she was all right when I left her." The cigarette stuck to his lip and tore his skin. His tongue tasted salty blood.

"It's not the mother, sir. It's the daughter."

"Tracey?"

"You know her?"

"I've seen her once or twice. What about her?"

"You must surely know what's happened. It was on the news, in all the papers."

The young man spoke. "There's your today's paper, sir." It was on the coffee table.

"Yes, but I haven't read it."

Frost reached for it and frowned. The crossword on the back page was completed. He showed it to Farnham, eyebrows raised.

"Yes, I do the crossword while I'm eating breakfast. I don't look at the front page, or the inside, until evening."

Frost turned the paper over, unfolded it, and passed it to Farnham. The headline and photograph were half-way down on the right.

POLICE SEARCH FOR MISSING GIRL.

Farnham's lips moved as he skimmed through the story.

"Good Lord! How terrible. I never knew . . ." He paused as the penny dropped. "You think she's here? You want to search because you think she's here?" The relief was overwhelming. "Go on then, search. I've got nothing to hide."

A nod from the inspector and Clive sidled out of the room. Frost settled back in his chair.

"You left Mrs. Uphill's about half-past four, sir. I suppose you didn't meet Tracey coming out of Sunday school?"

"I didn't meet her. I saw her, though."

Frost jerked forward excitedly. He'd seen her! They'd found someone who'd actually seen her! "Where was this, sir?"

"Walking away from the Sunday school."

"Towards her house?"

Farnham sucked more salt from his lip. "No. The opposite direction. She was with a woman."

Frost wriggled in his chair. They could have done with

this information hours ago. He'd radio it through to Allen the minute they were back in the car.

"Can you describe this woman?"

"Well . . . I didn't take an awful lot of notice. I was in a hurry, and it was dark. Medium height, wearing a white fur coat."

A white fur? Well, that was something.

"How old was she?"

"No idea."

"Did you see where they went?"

"No. I soon out-paced them. I didn't particularly want Tracey to see me. As I said, I was in a hurry."

"Why were you in a hurry, sir?"

The questions came bouncing back hard on his answers, but his brain was working quicker now. They'd obviously checked at the railway station and found he hadn't taken the first train out.

"I had to visit my aunt. She's an old lady of seventy-eight or so. Lives in the senior citizens' bungalows on the Southern Housing Estate. I was due there for tea."

The inspector sniffed. "Your Sundays are one long round of pleasure, sir. First Mrs. Uphill, then tea with your aunt. I'd like her address if you don't mind."

Farnham was startled. "You won't go round worrying her? She's an old lady, and her heart's not too good."

"I specialize in old ladies with weak hearts, sir—have no fear."

Frost wrote the address down on a scrap of paper he found in his pocket, then he tried to dig a hole in his cheek with a finger. Something was worrying him.

"Do you own a car, Mr. Farnham?"

"No."

"A red car?"

"No."

"Some time ago we had reports of a bearded man in a red car trying to pick up young kids outside that Sunday school." His eyes bored into Farnham. "Have you ever owned a car?"

"Yes, once. I couldn't afford to keep it."

"Yes. Red cars are expensive to run. It was red, wasn't it, sir?"

"No!" shouted Farnham.

"Then you've got nothing to worry about," said Frost unconvincingly. He stood up and stretched his arms. "I'd better go and see what that detective constable of mine is doing."

Barnard was in the bathroom, shirt-sleeves rolled up, his jacket hanging from the door. The bath panel had come off all right but was refusing to go back on again. With a couple of bangs in the right place from Frost, it was eventually coaxed into place.

"Not a very good fit, I'm afraid," said Farnham.

"Don't say that, sir," cried Frost. "It cost him one hundred and seven quid."

They went at last. Farnham watched through the curtains until their car turned the corner. He slumped back in his chair and pleaded with God not to let them check with his aunt. He'd never touch another woman again, he'd never send for another catalogue, but please, don't let them check with his aunt.

MONDAY (5)

Detective Inspector Allen rubbed his eyes and concentrated again on the sheet of paper where the list of names blurred, then slowly edged back into focus. He read that all the mothers who had been waiting for their children outside the Sunday school yesterday had been contacted and questioned, but not one of them remembered seeing this mysterious woman in the white fur coat. He dropped the paper into his "Out" tray and snorted with smug satisfaction. His earlier scepticism was justified. The woman didn't exist. She was conveniently invented by Farnham in an attempt to divert suspicion from himself and, naturally, that gullible fool Frost had swallowed it without question.

But where was Frost? He should be here by now. A pain jolted through Allen's body and his head throbbed and banged. He felt terrible. There were some aspirins in his overcoat pocket. He rose to fetch them but two paces across the room and he cried out as the fire in his stomach flared and sent flames of agony rippling through his body. The pain was more than he could stand and the room was spinning and a roaring noise got louder and louder.

Detective Sergeant Martin heard the crash and dashed into the office. Allen was out cold, sprawled across the polished lino.

Martin phoned Mullett from the hospital. They were keeping the inspector in for observation. There was some concern, but it was probably a virus of some kind. Blood samples and other tests were in hand but there would be no firm news until a specialist saw him some time tomorrow.

Mullett put down the phone and thoughtfully drummed a rallying tattoo on the satin mahogany. Why couldn't Allen have picked a more convenient time? Someone else would have to be put in charge of the search, but who? The division was sadly under strength as it was. Detective Sergeant Martin, Allen's assistant, would be able to cope, but, of course, he was only a sergeant. If Frost were capable there would be no problem, but he wasn't so the idea was unthinkable.

Mullett scratched his chin, then his eyes brightened. County Headquarters! They were crawling with superfluous staff. It really was a disgrace with so many divisions starved of men. If he could get them to send him a senior officer . . . and once they did, he'd hang on to the man, even after Allen returned to duty.

But this called for strategy. He would have to go to the top—a direct call to the Chief Constable, no less. Mullett straightened his uniform and smoothed back his hair. When he felt he was presentable, he dialled the Old Man's home number.

"Sorry to bother you at this outrageous hour, sir. If anyone's entitled to some peace and relaxation, it's you. Me, sir? Oh—I'm still in the office. No rest for us Divisional Commanders, I'm afraid." He gave a modest, good-natured laugh and explained about Allen. ". . . Which means, of course, sir, I'll have to put someone else in charge of the Tracey Uphill investigation." He let his voice trail off, leaving a gap for the Chief Constable to fill with a suggestion to which Mullett could give his whole-hearted agreement.

"Well," said the chief, after a pause, "we've got no-one to spare at County—but you knew that, of course."

"Of course," echoed Mullett sincerely.

"But I don't see your problem. You've got Frost. I'm surprised you didn't put him in charge in the first place. He's a good man."

"They come no better," croaked Mullett. "I'm glad we're of one mind, sir. I shall put Frost in charge right away." He put the phone down, then went over the conversation several times in his mind, trying to work out where he had gone wrong, then bracing himself, he dialled the number of Frost's office.

"Where's Jack Frost?"

Clive looked up wearily from the jumble of papers from which he was supposed to ferret out details for the crime statistics return.

The speaker was a uniformed sergeant, a hearty-looking man of forty with a weather-beaten face and a straggly handlebar moustache.

"He is with the Divisional Commander, Sergeant. I'm his assistant, Detective Con—"

He was cut short. "I know who you are, lad—flashy suit, wonky nose—the Chief Constable's nephew, right?"

Clive bristled. "I also happen to have a name—it's Barnard."

"And I'm Johnson—Johnnie Johnson, Station Sergeant."
There was, of course, a station sergeant for each eight-hour
shift.

Johnson propped himself up against a filing cabinet.
"How do you like working for our Jack?"

Still smarting, Clive snapped, "I'm not used to working
for idiots." He instantly regretted the tactless but honest answer and stiffened for the expected rebuke. To his surprise
the sergeant smiled tolerantly.

"Count your blessings, Barnard. He may be a fool but
they don't come any better. Half the people here are jockey-
ing for promotion, scrambling to get to the top, not caring
who they tread on in the process. But not Jack Frost. He's a
man who knows his limitations, who doesn't pretend to be
what he isn't. You'll never find him trying to snatch the
credit due to someone else—and if you worked for Inspector
Allen, you'd know what I mean."

Clive ventured another criticism. "He's callous and crude.
We're dealing with a woman whose kid is missing, probably
dead, and all he can talk about is how he'd like to get into
bed with her."

The sergeant rolled himself a cigarette. "Jack's trouble is,
what he thinks, he says. You probably think the same as him
but don't say it."

This was true, but Clive hunched his shoulders sullenly.
"He's a bloody mess, like his office," and he indicated the
litter. "By the way, what was that medal I saw in his desk? I
didn't recognize it. It must be a long-service award—obviously it can't be for good conduct."

The sergeant's tongue travelled along the gummed edge of
his cigarette paper and he gave the young man a pitying look.
"Two years in the force and you know it all, don't you,
Barnard? Well, two and a half years ago it was headline news.
The medal that he keeps tucked away in the blue box so no-
one can see it is the George Cross."

Clive's mouth opened and closed before he could croak
the words out. "The George Cross?"

"Yes—the civilian equivalent of the Victoria Cross, and it's his—that bloody mess you were talking about."

They hadn't heard Frost's footsteps clattering up the corridor. The door burst open.

"Bloody mess?" he breezed. "Somebody must be talking about me." And then he greeted the station sergeant with unconcealed delight, but noticing Clive's crimson face.

"Hairy Johnnie Johnson! Where have you been? I haven't seen you for weeks."

"Spot of leave, Jack," beamed the sergeant. "Came back on duty Sunday night."

"You get leave as well with your job? Who's been taking the bribes in your absence? I see you've met my assistant, Joseph and the Amazing Technicolor Dreamcoat. And how's your charming and erotic wife?"

"As charming and erotic as ever, thanks. She wants you to come for a meal one evening."

"I daren't, Johnnie," demurred Frost. "You know the effect she has on me. But in any case, I can't go hobnobbing with mere sergeants any more. I've just been put in complete charge of the Tracey Uphill investigation." He folded his arms triumphantly.

"You?" said Clive, trying not to sound incredulous.

"Yes, son. I've just received the accolade from our lovable horn-rimmed commander in the old log cabin. Poor old Allen's been taken to hospital—shock from having a bath, if you ask me."

The sergeant nodded approvingly. "Congratulations, Jack."

"Mind you," continued Frost, "I've been given my orders. I'm to stay away from the press and the TV boys, I'm to report to Mullett every five minutes and do nothing without his written confirmation, but apart from that I've got a free hand." He sniffed. "Blimey, Johnnie, what are you smoking —moustache clippings?"

Johnnie Johnson grinned. "Mr. Mullett wouldn't have put you in charge if he didn't think you could do it, Jack."

Frost waved this aside. "Come off it, Johnnie, he was

forced to give it to me. Who else is there?" He rammed a cigarette in his mouth and blazed the end with his lighter. "Be honest, if it wasn't for my damn George Cross he'd have had me out on my ear years ago." He remembered Clive and offered the packet. "Do you know about my medal, son?" He sucked at his cigarette and reflected. "Came in the nick of time it did. Mullett was all ready to give me the tin-tack in appreciation of a couple of my more spectacular balls-ups when I had my little moment of triumph. I must show you my medal sometime. They prefer you to get killed before they give it to you but make an exception if their stocks of them are building up."

His cigarette was burning unevenly so he dabbed some spit on one side. "I'm famous now. Every time I get a mention in the local press, like 'Local Detective Sods Up Court Case,' they add a little footnote about my medal. And that's why Mullett is forced to keep me on. The power of the press. He's afraid of seeing headlines like 'Handsome Detective Hero Gets Boot. Shabbily Treated by Horn-rimmed Bastard.' "

"He recommended you for promotion, Jack," insisted the sergeant.

Frost sniffed scornfully. "Only because he thought the medal would give the division a bit of prestige. He forgot I was attached to the end of it. I bet he regrets it now, poor sod. Put those papers away, son. Let's have a look in Search Control."

The station sergeant walked with them as far as the charge room where he again pressed Frost to come for a meal. "Peggy insists, Jack . . ."

Later, Frost confided to Clive why he daren't accept the invitation. "I respect Johnnie too much. He's a nice bloke and thinks the world of her, but she's a bloody sex maniac. Sticks her nipple in your ear as she serves the *hors d'oeuvre* and rubs thighs under the tablecloth. Makes you dribble your soup. Anyone else but Johnnie's wife and I'd love it. I happen to know a couple of the lads pop round there when he's on

duty. If he ever found out . . ." he sighed sadly and let the
sentence hang.

Search Control, housed in the old recreation room next to
Mullett's office, was a tribute to Allen's organizing ability.
Extra phone lines had been installed. There were teleprinters,
photostat and duplicating machines, loudspeakers relaying
messages from Divisional Control, large-scale wall maps
marking the exact position of all search parties, cars, mobile
and foot patrols, etc. Every incoming phone call was automatically timed and recorded on cassette. There was a direct
line through to the GPO Engineers in case any calls needed
tracing. Colour televisions, with stand-by black-and-white
sets, monitored all news broadcasts. Nothing had been left to
chance. In the event of a power failure a mobile generator
came immediately into operation.

Frost, the one contingency Allen hadn't allowed for,
walked into the room, looked helplessly at the meticulous
order and efficiency and, to everyone's relief, announced he
would be leaving Allen's assistant in charge. The assistant was
Detective Sergeant George Martin, a slow-talking, deep-
thinking individual with a gurgling pipe that always set
Frost's teeth on edge.

Throughout the day Search Control had hummed with
activity, phones continually busy with a constant stream of
calls from the public, ever anxious to help with reports of
sightings of the missing girl. Some of the sightings sounded
hopeful, the majority just impossible, but all had to be
logged, checked, and investigated. But with the dark came
calm. Phones rang only occasionally. Tired men were able to
catch up on their paperwork, grab a meal, plan for the next
long day.

Frost wandered over to George Martin. "Any luck with
the woman in the fur coat?"

Cinders erupted as Martin blew down his pipe stem.
"Nothing yet, Jack." He pulled the pipe from his mouth and
worried at it with a straightened paperclip. "You know . . ."

poke, poke, ". . . I was thinking . . . Has Mrs. Uphill got a white fur coat?"

Clive's eyes blazed. "You're surely not suggesting—" But Frost cut across him.

"Mrs. Uphill? Now there's a thought." He considered it then shook his head. "No, George. It couldn't have been her who Farnham saw. He'd just left her in bed, counting her thirty quid, and he was galloping away all eager to have tea with his aunt. Which reminds me . . ." He jabbed a finger at Clive. "We've got to check with auntie, son, don't forget." He turned to Martin. "Tell you what we must do, George. Give details about the woman in the fur to the press."

"Already done, Jack. Mr. Allen pushed it out as soon as he got your report."

That efficient sod would, thought Frost. Aloud he said, "Just testing you, George."

George smiled tolerantly and made disgusting bubbling noises in his pipe.

"I'd get a plumber on to that," said Frost.

A uniformed man at a desk in the corner finished a phone call then waved a half-eaten sandwich to attract attention. "Inspector!"

Frost ambled over to him.

"I've had my tea, thanks, Fred."

The man grinned. "Something interesting, sir. You know we've been checking on child molesters and sexual offenders who've been involved with children. We want to find out where they were yesterday afternoon around 4:30."

"I know I'm dim," moaned Frost, "but you don't have to explain everything to me. And what's in that sandwich—dead dog?"

"Bloater-paste, sir." He took a bite. "We've traced most of them and obtained statements." A wodge of handwritten foolscap was shaken free of crumbs. "Would you like to read them?"

"No, I bloody-well wouldn't," cried Frost. "If I had the time to read I'd read a dirty book. What do they say?"

"Most of them have alibis, sir, which we're checking on.

But there was one chap we couldn't get hold of. Mickey Hoskins didn't turn up for work today."

Frost's eyebrows soared. "Mickey Hoskins?" He whistled softly.

"The area car's been to his digs a few times, but no-one seems to be in. The neighbours say his landlady, Mrs. Bousey, is up in town shopping. They don't know about Mickey though. Haven't seen him since yesterday morning."

"I want that car parked on Ma Bousey's doorstep," snapped Frost.

"On its way, sir—Inspector Allen's orders."

Double-sod Inspector Allen, thought Frost.

The area car returned at 9:07. This time the hall light was on and the milk had been taken in. Mrs. Bousey was back from her shopping expedition, but there was no light from the upstairs room occupied by her lodger, Mickey Hoskins.

It was PC Mike Jordan's turn to knock. He put on his peaked cap and walked over to the house. A rat-tat at the knocker. Mrs. Bousey wheezed up the passage, flung open the door, and the stale smell of kippers escaped thankfully into the street.

"Yes?" She was a short, fat woman with scragged-back hair and tiny deep-set eyes.

"Mick in, Mrs. Bousey?"

"Ain't been in since Sunday."

"Oh?" Jordan took out his notebook. "What happened Sunday, then?"

She coughed, holding the door handle for support. "Had his dinner, went out, never came back."

"Unusual, wasn't it?"

"He's paid his rent till Friday, so why should I worry?"

"Can I take a look at his room?"

"If you like. But it won't be available until Friday."

He followed her into the stuffy kipper-scented atmosphere and up the worn linoed stairs. Mickey's room contained a bed, a wardrobe, a table, and a chair. On the table lay a paperback book with a lurid cover; a folded toffee paper acted as a bookmark. Alongside the book was an expensive all-wave transistor radio. A single suit of clothes and ladies' underwear stolen from washing-lines swayed in the wardrobe.

Jordan took out his personal transmitter and radioed Control.

"Highly mysterious," said Frost when George Martin brought him the news. "Nip down to records and get Mickey Hoskins's form-sheet, son."

Martin waved Clive back. He'd brought the form-sheet in with him. Inspector Allen would have expected it automatically.

Frost ran his eye down the long list of past convictions. Indecent Exposure, Indecent Assault, Posing as a Doctor, Obscene Phone Calls, Stealing Underwear, etc., etc. He pushed it from him distastefully. "He's a great one for exposing himself, isn't he? If mine was as small as his I'd keep it covered up." He pinched the skin of his cheek. "So not only are we looking for a woman in a white fur, we're also looking for a runaway toucher-upper. Perhaps they've eloped." He gave the form-sheet back to the sergeant. "Hang on to it, George, I've got enough paper of my own. And put out an All Patrols message for Mickey. I want him brought in."

"Already done," said Martin, hurt. Why did Frost think he had to be told everything?

Frost was trying to balance on the two back legs of his chair. "So Mick left Ma Bousey's *after* dinner? If he was in his right mind he'd have left before. I had to go there once to bring him in after he'd nicked thirty pairs of calico drawers from the convent clothesline. Ma Bousey was boiling up handkerchiefs and cooking a meat pudding in the same saucepan." He shuddered at the recollection. "I think the handkerchiefs came off worst."

As Martin made his departure, Frost's chair crashed to the ground. He scooped up the top layer of papers from his desk and passed them over to Clive. "Try and find room on your desk for these, would you, son?"

On top of the pile was a deckle-edged sheet of notepaper scrawled with green ink. Clive read it.

Old Wood Cottage, Denton
Dec. 3

To the Chief Policeman:

Dear Sir,
A lost soul in Limbo cries for Justice. The earthly Coroner may say Matthew Finch killed himself but the spirits know he was murdered. His Widow's hands are stained with GUILTY BLOOD.

Yours sincerely,
Martha Wendle

Clive read it again. He wasn't sure if it was meant to be a joke.

"There's a special file for cranks," Frost told him. "Top drawer, I think. If there's no room, bung it in 'miscellaneous.' The woman's a bloody menace, always writing in about something. She's a witch or a spiritualist or some such. According to her, no-one dies naturally. The graveyards are chockablock with murder victims and us dim sods are too thick to see it."

Clive wasn't convinced. The letter seemed so definite. "This chap Finch, sir. Could it have been murder?"

Frost pursed his lips and considered. "Impossible. That was one of Inspector Allen's cases and he never makes mistakes. Here, I was going to show you my tin medal, wasn't I?" He rummaged around in the wrong drawer. Clive was about to put him right but remembered just in time that he wasn't supposed to know. Frost stopped and looked into the opened drawer with a puzzled frown.

"You haven't borrowed any of my money, have you, son? No? Bloody odd. There was about 45p in small change. I keep it to pay for stuff I have sent down from the canteen. Fine bloody thing when your money isn't safe in a cop shop, isn't it?" He slammed the drawer shut and tried the next. "Ah, here it is." He passed the box over to Clive.

"Hooked on my swelling chest by the regal hands of Her Majesty, that was. Thrilled my wife to bits when I got that."

It was a silver cross hung on a dark blue ribbon, the words "For Gallantry" in the centre. Clive asked him how he'd won it.

Frost's fingers found the scar on his cheek. "Young tearaway he was, son. Forget his name. Held up Bennington's Bank over the road with a gun. He was a bit unstable— popped to the eyeballs on drugs. I mean, who in his right mind would pick a bank so near the cop shop? We were over there in seconds with truncheons drawn so we could knock the bullets out of the way when he started firing—one of those times when a cop wouldn't mind having a gun too, like they all do in America. Not that we'd know how to use the damn things.

"There was a woman in the bank with a kid in her arms and a baby in a pram. He grabs her as a hostage and rams the gun in the kid's ear, then looks at us cops and dares us to approach. We did all the clever things like telling him to be sensible and come and be arrested, but he just stands there, sweating and twitching and rolling his eyes. The woman was crying, the kid was screaming his head off, and the baby in the pram was gurgling. He was just itching for someone to step out of line so he could relieve the tension by pulling the trigger. Everyone saw that, except me. I thought, he's bluffing, so I march over, bold as brass and dead ignorant. The yobbo switches the gun from the kid to me. He was shaking from head to foot and the sweat was pouring off in buckets, from which I brilliantly deduced the gun wasn't loaded and all I had to do was take it from him.

"His first bullet went in my stomach and properly ruined my theory. I was too stupid to stop and just went on. The next shot tore through my cheek and the one after grazed my scalp, under my hair. By the time it dawned on me I was being fired at, I'd grabbed him, and my mates pounced and reasoned with him with their truncheons. I was lucky. The shot to my stomach hit my belt buckle so all I got was a bloody great bruise. The one in my cheek just went in and out. He got eleven years and I got a medal." He took it from Clive and dropped it back into the drawer. "There's definitely 45p missing from here."

His phone rang.

"Frost. What? The stupid sod!—and he's only just told us? You've got the right address? Right, I'm on my way with Flash Harry." He slammed the telephone back. "Come on, son. The headmaster of Tracey's school has just phoned Search Control about a girl called Audrey Harding. She's twelve, older than Tracey, but a great friend. And Audrey didn't turn up for school today."

As a schoolgirl was involved, they took a woman police constable with them and she sat huddled up on the back seat, not saying a word throughout the journey. Clive sneaked a look at her through the driving mirror, but with her peaked cap pulled down and her collar turned up against the cold, there wasn't much on show to set the pulses racing.

"We're here," announced Frost, and the car pulled into the curb, outside a group of Victorian terraced houses.

The girl who answered the door was a blood-racing blockbuster in brushed-denim jeans and a tight cotton teeshirt that adhered like cling film to the most gorgeous breasts Clive had seen for many a long day. They held his gaze like the hypnotic grip of a snake's eyes.

"Cor!" breathed Frost, adding quickly, "Sorry to trouble you, miss. We're police officers."

"Who is it?" A raucous female voice from the depths.

"The police," called the girl.

A door along the passage opened and a woman with a shop-soiled baby-doll face waddled out, wearing a dress twenty years too young for her.

"Mrs. Harding?" enquired Frost. "It's about your little girl, Audrey."

"What—her?" asked the woman, jerking her thumb to the girl.

Her? This was Audrey, a twelve-year-old schoolgirl? She looked eighteen or nineteen—a well-developed eighteen or nineteen. Clive and the inspector exchanged open-mouthed glances.

"We'll all get our deaths of cold standing here," said Mrs. Harding. "Come on in." She waddled off, leading them to a small sitting room, baking hot from the coal fire roaring up the chimney. In the centre of the room an ironing board had been set up. Frost unbuttoned his mac, unwound a few yards of scarf, and signalled for Clive to start the questioning.

Mrs. Harding said, "All right if I carry on with the ironing?"

Clive nodded. "You weren't at school today, Audrey?"

"So what?"

"She had a bad chest," offered her mother from the ironing board. Audrey coughed obligingly to corroborate the story.

"Try camphorated oil for it," suggested Frost, adding *sotto voce*, "About half a gallon . . ."

The woman police constable suppressed a giggle. Clive frowned. This was a serious enquiry. Couldn't the old fool keep his cheap jokes to himself, just for once?

"They haven't sent three cops down just because I didn't go to school, surely?" asked the girl, rubbing her hands over the chest in a way that made Clive envious and Frost uncomfortable.

"No. It's about Tracey Uphill. I believe you know her?"

"I know her," said the girl. "Her mother's a tart."

Mrs. Harding banged her iron down angrily. "Maybe she is, my girl, but you shouldn't say so. There's some things you don't talk about." In a confidential aside to Frost she added, "My uncle was an undertaker, but we never mentioned it to anyone. Some things are best left unsaid."

"Quite," said Frost, motioning for Clive to continue.

"You don't go to Sunday school, do you, Audrey?"

"Only to ballet classes and tap-dancing," chimed in the mother. "We believe in religion and that sort of thing, but we don't want it rammed down our throats, especially on a Sunday."

"Tracey's been missing from home since 4:30 yesterday afternoon, Mrs. Harding."

Her eyes saucered. "I know! Her poor mother, I mean . . . they must have feelings the same as anyone else."

"She was a friend of yours, Audrey?"

"I knew her a bit," said the girl in an off-hand voice, "but I haven't seen her outside school for a couple of weeks, now."

"Are you sure?" Clive persisted.

"My girl's not a liar," stated Mrs. Harding firmly, watching a ball of spit fry on the sole-plate of her iron.

"Can you think of anywhere she might have gone?"

Audrey shook her head and scratched her stomach. She yawned to make it clear she was getting bored.

"She was seen with a woman in a white fur coat. Any idea who that woman might be?"

"No idea." She studied her vivid orange fingernails.

Then Frost chipped in. "Do you play Bingo, Mrs. Harding?"

Flaming hell, thought Clive. What's Bingo got to do with it?

Mrs. Harding's iron delved the depths of a voluminous bra. "Yes, I do, twice a week regular down the old Grand Cinema. It's my only bit of pleasure. But how did you know?"

Frost beamed at her. "We had reports about a beautiful woman playing there. And I happened to see the Bingo cards on your mantelpiece."

Mrs. Harding simpered. "Aren't you observant? Eyes everywhere." She added the ironed bra to the finished pile.

"Been lucky?"

"I've had a couple of good wins."

"I had a feeling you had. And I've got a feeling you can make a smashing cup of tea."

"Would you like one?" she said, switching off the iron. "It won't take a minute."

When she was gone Frost leaned across to the girl. "Oi, Fanny—does your mother know you borrow her fur coat?"

The girl went white. "Shut up!" she hissed.

To the woman police constable Frost said, "Keep the mother occupied in the kitchen and shut the door.

"All right, Audrey," he continued as the door closed, "let's have it. You borrow her fur coat, don't you, without her knowing?"

"She'll murder me," whimpered the girl. "She'd belt me rotten if she knew. She bought it with her Bingo money, nearly three hundred quid, and no-one must touch the bloody thing. You won't tell her, will you?"

"You wore it yesterday, didn't you, when you met Tracey from the Sunday school?"

"I just wanted to show off the coat. I didn't want her to come with me."

"You didn't want her to—but she did?"

"That was her look-out. I said she'd have to go when he turned up."

"When who turned up?"

"My boyfriend . . . my fellow."

"What's his name?" She told them. Clive wrote it down.

"Where did you meet him?"

"Those fields along Meadow Road."

"And then Tracey went home?"

"No. The little bitch pretended to go, but she followed us. I suppose she wanted to have an eyeful. We ended up in the Old Wood."

"The Old Wood? Why did you go there?"

"To try to shake her off, but she kept following, so we ran and hid behind that big tree—the one near the lake. She went racing past, and we backtracked and belted off home."

"What time was this?"

"About 5:30."

Frost frowned. "You left a kid of eight to find her own way home in the pitch dark?"

The girl shrugged. "That was her look-out. Besides, she

knew her way back. And she wasn't going home, she was going to play in the vicarage grounds."

The vicarage grounds! Clive made a note in his book.

"Where did you go after that?" continued Frost.

"To me boy's house. His parents were out."

"And what did you do there?"

"What do you think?" The blue eyelid closed in an obscene wink.

The kitchen door opened and the tea emerged.

"You won't tell me mum?" Audrey whispered anxiously, the twelve-year-old again.

"Not unless I have to," murmured Frost. "Ah . . . tea."

So they sipped their tea and chatted and suddenly it was like a family party with everyone talking and Frost gently flirting with the girl's mother who he'd got to parade for them in the white fur coat. Clive's eyes were on the woman police constable who had slipped off the greatcoat and peaked cap and was laughing at the inspector's antics. The cap had hidden thick auburn hair which tumbled to her shoulders. She was lovely.

A sharp pain in the ribs from Frost's elbow. The inspector swivelled his eyes towards Audrey. The girl was examining the perfection of her right shoulder. To do this she had pulled back the short sleeve of her teeshirt leaving the arm bare. And there it was, on the top of her right arm, a brown birthmark—the birthmark last seen in black and white on the headless nude photograph found in Tracey's bedroom.

As soon as the mother took the empty cups into the kitchen, Frost grabbed the girl.

"Ever had your photograph taken in the nude, Audrey?"

"Of course not." But her eyes were frightened and her hand tugged down the sleeve.

"God can hear you telling these lies," purred Frost, his face moving close to her.

"Piss off, you old bugger," she snapped.

"Arseholes," murmured Frost, adding sweetly as Mrs. Harding returned, "I was just asking your little girl what Father Christmas was going to bring her this year."

• • •

Back in the car, Frost radioed to Search Control. George Martin told him the Old Wood had had a perfunctory search but was scheduled for detailed coverage the next morning. The vicarage grounds had been covered thoroughly.

"Hmm," said Frost, scratching his face thoughtfully. "Better rake up as many men as you can for an immediate search of the woods tonight. It'll be tricky in the dark, but if the kid's there, speed's vital." Outside, the wind was shrilling to gale force.

Clive didn't need further directions once he was piloted back to the main road, so the inspector was able to relax in his seat.

"Well," he said, "I don't know what was sticking out the most—your eyes or that kid's chest. Oh sorry—forgot we had a lady on board." He beamed at the woman PC in the back seat.

She smiled back. "Don't mind me."

"I'll tell you a little story," said Frost, and Clive's heart sank. Not another of his dubious reminiscences! He gritted his teeth and concentrated on his driving.

"I was sixteen," continued Frost, "and I'd been knocking about with this girl—Ivy Standish her name was—and blimey, was she hot stuff! She'd let you do anything with her —anything except swear. She couldn't stand swearing, so if your trembling hand fumbled on the last button of her cami-knicks and you inadvertently said 'Sod it,' that was your lot; you were sent packing, no matter how high your state of expectation. Anyway, to cut a long and boring story short, her birthday came along and her mum invited me to the party. It was going to be a surprise, but it turned out to be a bloody shock. You know how many candles she had on her cake? Eleven! I could have got fourteen years for that, so I had my slice of cake and left, hurriedly."

Wishful thinking, thought Clive, not believing a word.

When the car reached the Market Square the woman PC asked to be dropped off.

"Are you on stand-by duty then, Hazel?" asked Frost.

"Tell you what, I'll get off here and walk. Young Clive will drive you home."

They watched Frost, his shoulders hunched, his chin dug deeply into his scarf as he braved the wind to reach Eagle Lane. The girl gave Clive directions.

"Why, you don't live far from me," he said. "Tell you what, why don't we drop off at my place and have a cup of coffee?"

To his astonishment she agreed. He wondered if Frost was expecting him back right away. But damn it all, he'd been on duty nearly thirteen hours now and surely was entitled to half an hour's break.

It seemed colder in his room than outside. He rammed coins down the meter's hungry throat and turned the gas fire on full. She sat on the unmade bed, hands thrust deep in her pockets, and watched him.

"Soon be warm," he said, and dashed into the kitchen to make the coffee, filling the percolator with hot water for quickness and dumping it on the gas-ring.

He returned to his visitor. "Won't be long." She nodded. The gas-fire began to raise the temperature. "Warming up, isn't it?" Another nod. Not a great talker, he thought and suggested she might like to take off her greatcoat. Off it came, then her uniform jacket. Her grey and white shirt swelled out temptingly.

He kissed her. It was a long, lingering, tongue-meeting kiss, the most promising start he'd made for a long time. They parted for air. "Some music," he suggested, and leaned across her to switch on his radio. In doing so, his hand brushed her chest. She quivered. He slipped an arm around her shoulders and pulled her towards him, his mouth covered hers, his hand, with the delicate skill of a surgeon performing a tricky brain operation, gently undid the tiny buttons on her shirt. Another break for air.

A group throbbed away on the radio.

"That's number one in the top ten, isn't it?" she asked, leaning forward so he could undo the fiddling little hooks on her bra. He began to caress the soft skin of her back. His heart started to pound in tune to the pulse of the percolator. His hand dropped to her leg and began to crawl upward . . .

The door burst open and Frost entered.

Damn, damn, and sodding damn!

Frantic covering up, the girl turning aside and rebuttoning.

"Bit of luck I saw your light," said Frost, grabbing him by the arm. "They've found a scarf in the woods. It sounds like it's Tracey's. You weren't doing anything important, were you?"

MONDAY (6)

The Old Wood, about two miles north of Vicarage Terrace, straggled over some four hundred acres. Clive and the inspector crashed and floundered in the dark between rows of wind-lashed, creaking skeleton trees, as they tried to locate the two police constables who had found the scarf, and it was only by chance that Clive spotted the gleam of torches.

"Over there, sir."

The torches homed them in. "We said by the oak, sir," said one of the policemen reproachfully.

"I only know two sorts of trees," replied Frost, "big ones and little ones. Show us what you've found."

A flashlight was directed towards a bush where a flapping scarf, impaled on some thorns, resisted the efforts of the wind to pluck it off.

"How was this missed when the woods were covered before?" asked Frost, fingering the wool.

"It would take days to search this place thoroughly, sir, and they were looking for the girl, or her body. You tend to look on the ground."

"So, if she was up a tree, no-one would spot her," remarked Frost. "Still, I'm glad it was missed. I was beginning to think people who worked under Inspector Allen were infallible."

Clive was interested in the way the scarf was caught in the thorns. If he pulled it towards him, it would come off easily; tug it the other way and the thorns bit deeper.

"Assuming she was wearing the scarf when it was caught on the bush, sir, then she was moving in that direction." He demonstrated his theory to Frost who was most impressed.

"We'd already worked that out," muttered the younger of the police constables, jealous of this broken-nosed know-all.

"Then you shall have a sweet as well," said Frost, as he carefully unhooked the scarf and rammed it in his pocket. "Where does this lead?" He slithered down the path in the direction indicated by Clive's theory.

"Careful, sir!" warned the young constable.

Frost stopped abruptly. The path suddenly veered to the left, and if he'd carried straight on he'd have plunged into the murky depths of Willow Lake.

The edge of the lake was not clearly definable, with overgrown vegetation from the path sprawling into the water. They carefully traversed the circumference, looking for telltale broken undergrowth. But if the child had crashed through to the water she'd left no trace.

Clive let the beam of his torch crawl across the black, sullen surface of the lake. The light picked out the glistening ripple of thin ice. In a couple of days it would be frozen solid.

"We'll have it dragged tomorrow, first thing," muttered Frost, rubbing at his scar which the cold had frozen into a knot of dead, hard flesh. "We knew the girl was in the woods, so it's no triumph finding her scarf . . . if it is her scarf. We'll call in on old Mother Uphill on the way back, son, and see if she can identify it."

The uniformed men were stamping their feet and flapping their arms. "We'll carry on looking then, Inspector?"

Frost nodded. "Yes. I'll try and get Control to send some more men to help you. I know it's bloody near impossible finding anything in this place in the dark, but another night in the open could kill her." He looked at the lake and shivered. "If she's not already dead . . ."

An expensive-looking car stood outside No. 29 Vicarage Terrace, and Clive had to park the Morris farther down the street. In the house opposite, Christmas-tree lights flashed on and off. Mrs. Uphill's door opened and a well-dressed man came out. He waved to the slim figure at the front door, entered the expensive car, and slid away into the dark.

Frost called out so she wouldn't close the door. She waited as they walked briskly up the path.

"A client?" Frost jerked his head to the departing visitor. She gave a shrug. "I've got to live."

She showed them into the lounge, which smelt richly of cigar smoke, and lit a cigarette from the box on the mantelpiece. She daren't ask them why they had come in case the answer was what she dreaded to hear.

Frost produced the scarf from his pocket and handed it to her without a word.

The colour drained from her face and she sat down heavily. "It's Tracey's." Her finger found a hole in the wool. "I was going to mend it, but there was never time." Then she buried her face in her hands and her body shook. "I wish I could cry," she said, "I wish I could cry."

"We haven't found her yet," explained Frost. He told her about Tracey following Audrey Harding and her boyfriend into the wood. "We've got men searching there tonight and we'll be mounting a full-scale search at first light tomorrow."

Her face was expressionless. She knew the wood, she knew the lake, she knew what the weather was like. Her finger wouldn't stop worrying the hole in the scarf. The two men didn't know what to say and words of assurance would have sounded hollow anyway, so it was almost a relief when the shrill trill of the telephone shattered the brittle silence.

A flicker of apprehension as she forced herself to walk across the room to answer it. She listened without expression then carefully replaced the receiver.

"Obscene call?" asked Frost.

"The sixth today."

"There's a lot of rotten bastards about. Would you like us to have your calls intercepted?"

She shook her head. "I can put up with them. I've heard a lot worse than that."

"If it gets too bad," said Clive, gently prising the scarf from her reluctant fingers, "let us know."

The scarf was gone but her fingers were still working as if finding that hole. Frost and Barnard let themselves out, and left her huddled in the armchair, looking small, helpless, and so alone.

Clive turned on the ignition. "She shouldn't be on her own, sir. Someone should stay the night with her."

"Are you volunteering?" asked Frost. "I'll sub you the thirty quid if you are short."

The detective constable savagely slammed the car around the corner and said nothing for the rest of the journey.

"She identified the scarf, Sarge," yelled Frost as they bustled through the lobby.

Another shift had taken over and it was a bearded station sergeant Clive had not yet met who waved a hand in acknowledgement. Clive was relieved that Frost did not pause for introductions. He had met so many people that day his head was spinning with a blur of half-remembered faces and names. Tomorrow, Bill Wells and the original shift would take over again. It was like seeing a very long film around to the point where you came in, a long time ago . . .

When they reached the door of the station control room, Frost suddenly stopped dead and, finger to lips, signalled Clive to silence. Cautiously, he eased open the door. The controller, PC Philip Ridley, was bent over a microphone, relaying a message to a police car. Frost tiptoed in and crossed stealthily to the corner where returned personal radios were being recharged from the mains. A quick look to make certain he was undetected and he pulled down the issues book from a shelf. He found the entry for the personal radio issued to him a few days earlier and with consummate skill forged a signature acknowledging its return. Replacing the book he tiptoed out. The controller, still at the microphone, was completely unaware that he had had a visitor.

"Fine bloody copper he is," murmured Frost, grabbing Clive's arm and hustling him down the corridor. "A spot of forgery, son," he explained. "I had a set pinched from my car and I daren't let anyone know so I've just put the records straight."

Their next port of call was Search Control where a tired Detective Sergeant Martin had just finished working out schedules and instructions, to be presented to the various search parties at the next morning's briefing meeting. He showed them to the inspector who pretended to understand them and handed them back with vigorous noises of approval.

"What about the dragging party, George, for Willow Lake?"

Martin confirmed it was laid on for eight o'clock in the morning, adding, "We could only scrape up another three men to help search the wood. Most of our chaps have worked double shifts as it is."

"Fair enough," said Frost, tagging Tracey's scarf and locking it in a cupboard. "I'll look in on them later to see how they're getting on."

Martin paused in the act of buttoning his thick overcoat. "By the way, Jack, Mr. Mullett was in earlier screaming blue murder because someone had smashed the back of his brand-new Jaguar."

Frost's face expressed over-exaggerated concern. "Tut tut —I hope they catch the bastard who did it."

"He left a note on your desk." Martin added.

"Christ!" said Frost, and this time the concern was real.

The note, written in the Divisional Commander's firm hand, read:

County HQ advise me they have not received your
crime statistics. I have promised them they will get
them tomorrow morning, without fail. M.

Frost flopped into his chair. "Interfering sod. If he's promised them, he should do them. Did you get those figures out,
son?"

Clive reminded the inspector that he was told to leave
them.

Frost sniffed. "You may find this hard to believe, son, but
there are some rotten sods who don't do their statistical returns the proper, honest way. They cheat by doing this," and
he picked up the phone and dialled his opposite number in a
neighbouring division.

"Hello, Charlie—Jack. Of course my watch hasn't
stopped. I'm still working and bloody hard, too. You done
your crime statistics? Good, what was the trend, up or down?
Seven per cent up? Disgraceful, you should be ashamed of
yourself. Ours? About the same. Here, did I tell you the joke
about the bloke who drunk the spittoon for a bet? Oh . . .
Well, cheers. If I don't speak to you before, have a nice
Christmas."

He replaced the receiver with a triumphant flourish.

"The figures are up seven per cent, son, so we find last
month's return, we up the answers by seven per cent, and
we're home and dry. This is the wrong way to do them, of
course, and must never in any circumstances be used unless
you are sure you can get away with it."

It took them an hour. The job could have been done
quicker, but Frost, working out seven per cents on the backs
of old envelopes, kept getting a different answer from Clive
and had to do his calculations again before he could agree.
"I'm better at sums once I know the answer I'm aiming for,"
he explained, licking the gummed label that addressed the
return to County Headquarters. "How's the time, son?"

Clive screwed the sleep from his eyes and looked at his

watch. "Nearly midnight, sir." He'd been on duty for fifteen hours.

"Good," said Frost. "Just a couple more jobs to do, then we can go home."

He stuck his head round the door of Search Control where a uniformed man on night shift was keeping an eye on things.

"Just going to the woods with the new chap," he announced.

Clive winced. The new chap! He felt as if he had been trotting along behind Frost for at least twenty years.

The wind was waiting for them at the woods. It tore and bit and hammered as they wandered in the dark trying to locate the search party. Eventually the search party found them. A torch shone in their faces. The constable holding it was shivering with cold.

"Call it a night," said Frost. "We don't want you all going down with pneumonia. I can't stand funerals at Christmas. Anyway, if she's spent a day and a night in the open, she's dead, so we might as well find the body tomorrow as tonight. Let the mother hope for a while longer. Come on, son."

Back to the car. "Where to, sir?"

"The town, son."

Thank goodness, thought his detective constable, home and bed at last.

As they sped towards the town a church clock chimed . . . one o'clock on a cold and frosty morning. The streets they passed were empty, the lights out in the houses, and it seemed as though they were the only two people in the world who heard that single chime rolling across the sleeping countryside.

The Market Square at last, with its lighted shop windows and the tall Christmas tree outside the public lavatories. But what the hell was the silly old fool up to, now? The inspector motioned for Clive to turn the car down one of the dark side streets leading off the square. A couple of sharp right turns and, "Pull up here, son . . . quietly."

The car coasted the last few yards and came to a halt in

the dark shadow of the side entrance to Woolworth's. Across
the road, brightly illuminated by a tall streetlamp, the solid
shape of Bennington's Bank. Frost switched off the radio and
wound down the side window. The car sucked in cold air
and Clive shivered and silently cursed all detective inspectors.

"Little spot of observation," croaked Frost. "Shouldn't
take long."

It took an hour, a long, cold hour, marked off by two
more clanking chimes from the church clock. The inspector
was slumped in his seat, his scarf round his ears, breathing
heavily, his face child-like in repose.

Typical, seethed Clive. The stupid git has gone to sleep
and hasn't even told me what we're supposed to be watching
for.

But the eyelids were not tightly closed; they fluttered and
a hand gently squeezed Clive's arm.

In the doorway of the bank someone moved. A duffle-
coated figure, the face hidden in the depths of the hood. The
head moved from side to side, checking, then a long metallic
object was produced from inside the coat. A scraping of
metal. The shattering pistol crack of splintering wood.

Clive grabbed the door handle, ready for the plunge across
the cobbled road, but was pushed back. "Just watch, son
. . . that's all . . . watch."

Someone else had heard the noise. The running feet of the
foot-patrol police constable clip-clopped down Bath Hill. A
loud clang as the duffle-coat dropped the jemmy and ran into
the blackness of a side-turning, vanishing long before the
beat man was anywhere near. Accepting defeat, the constable
gave up the chase and returned to examine the marks on the
bank door. He picked up the jemmy, then began to speak
rapidly into his personal radio.

Frost had seen all he wanted to see. He asked Clive to
reverse quietly and at 2:15 they were straining up Bath Hill
to Clive's digs.

"Do me a favour, son, keep quiet about this for the moment. Ah—this is you, isn't it?"

Clive stepped out of the car and Frost slid into the driver's seat muttering something about an early start tomorrow.

The lights were out at No. 26. As he bent to locate the keyhole something cold and wet kissed the back of Clive's neck. He raised his head. It was snowing, idly at first, and then in clusters of thick swirling flakes. He wondered if tracker dogs were any good in snow. He couldn't remember, he was so tired . . .

TUESDAY

TUESDAY (1)

—————

". . . search for Tracey Uphill, the missing eight-year-old, hampered by heavy falls of snow. A police spokesman stated the operations would be resumed immediately the severe weather conditions eased. The Post Office reports a record Christmas . . ."

"Turn it off, son."

Clive switched off the car radio and concentrated on his driving, squinting with tired eyes through the snow-splattered windscreen at a strange, silent, soft-contoured landscape. A bright and breezy Frost had dragged him out of bed at 7:15 after barely five hours' sleep and another marathon day loomed infinitely ahead.

Strong winds drove the snow almost horizontally, and when they left the car on the outskirts of the Old Wood it was teeth-gritting hard work to push themselves along the obscured path. By the time they reached the lake they were plastered thickly with snow from head to foot.

A small canvas marquee had been erected at lakeside for the dragging party and the wind was pounding its fists on the roof and trying to pluck out the tent-pegs. They plunged inside, thankful for its scant shelter, and sat on the small upturned rowboat which someone must have manhandled through the woods in the dark. Outside, two uniformed snowmen stoically smashed the surface ice with long poles.

"Trust me to get weather like this," yelled Frost over the thunder of the flapping canvas. "Inspector Allen would have had sunshine, bluebirds singing, and little deer chasing butterflies. Who the hell's this?"

A burly figure in an anorak butted his way towards them. He ducked into the tent and shook himself like a dog, shedding layers of snow, then pulled back the hood to uncover wire-wool ginger hair flecked with grey and a beaming, florid face mottled with large freckles. Sandy Lane, Chief Reporter of the Denton *Echo*, had heard the lake was being dragged and wanted to be there when the body popped up. The story would certainly be taken by the London dailies and would merit a byline and a welcome fee that would just about make up for the chilling effort of getting up at the crack of dawn.

Frost greeted the reporter with a whoop of delight and introduced Clive, who was slumped against the tent-pole trying to keep awake, as his alert young assistant from London.

"Now I've taken the trouble to come, I hope she's in there," said Sandy.

"We'll try and oblige," said Frost, moving out of the way as a well-muffled elderly police constable, the boatman, arrived and slithered and bumped the small craft into the lake.

"We're ready to start, Inspector."

"All right, but don't fall in. I've signed for you."

A creak of oars and the boat was hidden in the swirling snow. The other two constables trudged the circumference, methodically poking the bottom of the lake with their poles to encourage a body entangled with weeds to float to the surface. The oarsman was doing the same in the centre of the lake. There were false alarms as a rotting log or a plastic bag full of rubbish pretended to be a body and bubbled up to be hooked out and tossed to one side.

Frost stared into the flickering white curtain and smoked listening to the creakings and splashings. Then the wind blew a hole in the snow and he saw the small creosoted hut on the far side. He called out to one of the pole carriers who told him the hut was used by the Denton Model Boating Club in the summer but was now empty.

"It's been searched, I hope?"

"Yes, sir. It's padlocked, but we got the key from the club secretary."

Frost thought for a while, then wound his scarf to strangulation tightness and turned up his coat collar. "I'm afraid I've got one of my rotten feelings, son."

It was no bigger than a small garden shed, the sort used for storing rakes and spades and things, about as big as a sentry box. It had no windows, just a door fastened by an impressive brass padlock on a hasp.

The hasp didn't look right.

Frost tugged at it and the screws popped out of the wood, letting the hasp and the padlock fall with a plop to the ground.

The constable was incredulous. "It wasn't like that before, sir."

Frost pulled the door open gingerly. There was something on the floor. He swore softly, then stepped back so the others could see. The wind howled and screamed and drove snow on to the face of the crumpled figure huddled on the bare wooden floor.

Sandy Lane ran over from the marquee. The boatman rowed for the shore and joined them. They crowded around, silently, looking down on the gaping ugly face of death.

But it wasn't the child.

It was a man wearing an old army greatcoat several sizes too big for him. It was old Sam, the tramp who yesterday had marched into the station demanding the return of his pound. He had frozen to death and the dribble of spittle from the blue lips was a tiny river of ice.

Frost bent and touched the face. It was iced marble, colder even than the snow-driving wind that was howling with rage because they were ignoring it.

"He must have crawled in here last night to sleep," said the boatman. "Poor old sod."

Frost wiped his hand on his coat again and again. "He's better off out of it." His foot kicked an empty wine bottle. "At least he died happy."

Sandy Lane left them and trudged back to the marquee. There was no byline story in the death of an old tramp.

Frost nudged the army greatcoat with the toe of his boot.

It crackled. "Watch out for fleas, boys. I'm told they won't stay on a dead body." He noticed the boatman. "Any luck?"

"No, sir. We'll try again to make sure but we've bashed the bottom and she'd be floating on top if she was there. There's less muck in the pond than we thought."

Frost sniffed. "Why should people come all this way with their old mattresses when there's lots of beauty spots far nearer." He took another look at the shrivelled husk on the hut floor. "I don't want to be here when you chaps find Sam's body. I'm far enough behind with my paperwork as it is and this would be the last straw. So don't find him officially until I've gone." He paused. "And some brave soul will have to go through his pockets and see if he's got a second name. Let me know who does it and I'll recommend him for the Victoria Cross."

Sandy was swigging something from a hipflask. He spun round furtively as they entered the marquee.

"Bit early for that, Sandy, isn't it?"

"Never too early for me, Jack." He stuck the flask back in his pocket. "You'd think I'd be used to dead bodies after forty-one years, wouldn't you?"

"Did I ever tell you about my first body?" asked Frost. "He was a tramp, too. Dead for weeks during a heatwave. Council dug up the street twice thinking it was the drains. Then we found him—or what the rats had left . . ." He noticed the boat party were returned. "I'll tell you the rest later."

The reporter offered his cigarettes around and murmured confidentially to Clive, "Try and avoid hearing the rest at all costs. It put me off my grub for a week when he told it to me."

A rasping noise from outside as the boat was dragged ashore. Three frozen policemen stumbled in. Tracey wasn't in the lake.

"Sorry we couldn't oblige you, Sandy," said Frost.

"That's all right," replied the reporter. He zipped up his anorak. "What about lunch today at The Crown?"

"Why not?" said Frost.

The reporter waved and was lost in the snow.

"If anyone wants us, we'll be at the vicarage," said Frost. "Give us five minutes, then nip over and discover old Sam." He studied the blizzard outside. "You can't beat a white Christmas, can you?"

The vicarage was a sprawling Victorian building, huge and cheerless enough for an army barracks, but the vicar, the Reverend James Bell, moonfaced and beaming, greeted them warmly.

"Inspector Frost! Come in, come in."

He ushered them into an uncarpeted hall with dark brown walls and a high ceiling. It was colder inside than out.

"There's a fire in my study. This way." He led them to a small room with an enormous marble mantelpiece and a fireplace large enough to roast an ox in; in it two pieces of smouldering coal fought for survival.

"It'll soon get warm," said the vicar optimistically, attacking the fire with a poker until all signs of life were extinct. "Oh dear." He knelt and began puffing and blowing into the grate in a forlorn attempt to raise the dead. At last he stood, admitting defeat. "Never mind. It's not as cold as it was."

On the marble mantelpiece were several photographs of recent church functions. One showed a group of children. The Sunday school Christmas party. Tracey Uphill was in the centre of the group. Frost picked up the photograph and studied it. "It's her we've come about, Padre," he said, pointing. "Young Tracey Uphill."

The vicar sat behind his paper-strewn desk and shook his head, sadly, "Oh yes. Terrible business. Simply terrible." He blinked in surprise as a spent match dropped into his paperclip tray. Frost had lit a cigarette.

"Sorry, Padre," boomed Frost, unabashed, "thought it was an ashtray." He retrieved the match and flicked it towards the grate. It missed by miles. "Hello, does old Martha write to you as well?" He pointed to a letter lying on the desk . . . spidery writing in green ink on stiff, deckle-edge notepaper.

"This?" The vicar held it up. "From our local clairvoyant,

you mean?" He gave a tolerant smile. "She wants to hold a public spiritualist meeting in our church hall. We can't pick and choose our lettings, I'm afraid. Our collections are not as generous as one might wish, and things are so expensive. The price of coal!" He swung round for another post-mortem examination of the fire, but stopped as he remembered the reason for their visit. "I'm sorry. You're here about that poor child. How can I help you?"

"You knew her, didn't you, Vicar?"

The vicar seemed to start. "Only through Sunday school."

Frost's eyes narrowed. Why that reaction? "I meant through Sunday school, of course, sir. Pretty kid, wasn't she?"

"Was she? I hadn't noticed." An attempt to sound offhand that didn't come off.

It suddenly occurred to Clive that both Frost and the Reverend James Bell were talking of Tracey in the past tense.

"Good looks run in her family," continued Frost. "You should see her mother. She's on the game, but I expect you know."

"Yes," replied the vicar, "I know. I've often seen the men going into her house."

Frost nodded. "She gets thirty quid a time for her Sunday afternoon service. A lot more than you get dropped in your collection plate, I bet." Frost was the only one who laughed and, to make up for the lack of appreciation, laughed loud and long. Clive looked openly disgusted, the vicar, both pained and rueful. Then Frost stopped abruptly, took a last drag on his cigarette, and hurled it in the general direction of the fireplace.

"We want to search the vicarage, Padre. The kid was sup- posed to have come here to play in the grounds, but she could well have sneaked into the vicarage without anyone knowing."

"No!" It was the shocked reaction to an improper sugges- tion.

Frost stared hard at the vicar. "Why not, sir?"

"It's not convenient, I'm afraid. We've got people coming.

Later perhaps . . ." He refused to meet the inspector's questioning eye.

Frost smiled. "We won't pinch anything, I promise you. I've got more hymnbooks than I can read back at home. We'll let you know when we've finished." He looked over the vicar's shoulder. "Hello, there's a trace of smoke coming from your fire. I'd encourage it, if I were you." A jerk of his head to Clive and they were out of the study before Bell could think of a reason to stop them.

Frost wound the scarf tighter round his neck. "Like a flaming igloo in there."

"He didn't seem too keen on our looking around," remarked Clive.

"Doesn't trust you, son. It's your suit. Not much better than yesterday's effort, I'm afraid. We'll start at the top and work down."

They trudged upwards. Staircase succeeded staircase, little sub-landings and corridors shooting off at each turn. The vicarage would be a swine to search properly. And then the stairs stopped and there were only brown cobwebby ceilings above and a gloomy passage lined with dark doors. They creaked the doors open and looked in on pokey attic cells with low sloping ceilings, flapping mildewed wallpaper, and tiny windows thick with years of grime.

"The servants would have slept up here in the old days," explained Frost, stepping back hurriedly as a floorboard disintegrated under his foot. "What a life the poor sods must have led when you think of it. Working like beavers from crack of dawn until nearly midnight, scrubbing, scouring, emptying the gentry's slop-buckets, then staggering up those flaming stairs for a few hours' kip before it started all over again the next morning."

I don't know about the slop-buckets, thought Clive, but their hours sound better than mine.

The dust and cobwebs in the attic rooms had clearly not been disturbed for years, so they descended to the floor below where the rooms were larger and the sour smell of decay slightly less pungent. On this floor the rooms were apparently used for storage, graveyards for the abandoned junk of past incumbents. They looked in cupboards and battered trunks that smelt faintly of lavender and strongly of mouldering linen and that contained stained ancient clothing and scuttling insects.

But the end room was different. The door opened easily and the smell inside was of stale tobacco smoke, like the vicar's study. Drawn, heavy curtains made it dark. Frost clunked down the old-fashioned brass lightswitch and an unshaded 60-watt bulb glimmered mournfully. He crossed to the window, dragged back the curtains, and looked down on the back gardens of Vicarage Terrace, now unified in a single plain by the heavy covering of snow. He couldn't tell which was Mrs. Uphill's garden; they all looked the same.

The room was used by the vicar as a photographic studio. The thick cord of an antiquated electric bowl fire shared a power-point with the thinner cord of a photoflood lamp and reflector on a tall metal stand. Around the walls were enlargements of photos of churches and local landmarks. Inside a corner cupboard they found more photographic equipment, including a tripod and an early model Rolleiflex twin-lens reflex camera.

But it was the sheet-draped rectangular object in the centre of the floor that claimed the men's interest.

"That's where the body is," said Frost.

Clive twitched the sheet away to reveal a battered metal coffin. A cabin trunk, well worn, its sides pasted with labels from long-defunct Edwardian shipping lines. The trunk was old, but the heavy brass padlock securing the lid was brand-new.

"Let's see if one of these will open it," murmured Frost, producing the bunch of skeleton keys he always carried with him. The third key he tried did the trick. Clive flung back the lid and they peered inside, almost fearful of what they might see.

Books. The trunk was tight-packed with books of all shapes and sizes, none of which seemed to warrant the expense of a heavy brass padlock.

They took them out. Old hymnbooks with the covers hanging by a thread. A copy of *Mr. Midshipman Easy* presented to Master James Graham Bell, Cooperley Primary School, June 1946, for good work. There were some bound volumes of *The Boys' Own Paper* dating from the turn of the century that Frost flipped through with interest. "Could be worth a few bob, son. Wonder if he'd miss them."

The next layer brought forth more ancient treasures including volumes of *The Strand Magazine* containing the Sherlock Holmes stories with Sidney Paget drawings of spade-bearded men in hansom cabs.

But in the next layer . . . Here the unexpurgated *Fanny Hill* was the tamest of the collection. Filthy books, obscene books. The sort of books kept under the counter in grubby little back-street Soho bookshops. The general theme of the collection was young girls.

Frost became engrossed in a paperback whose cover depicted a large, leather-knickered, bare-chested Amazon thrashing the posterior of a buxom, bare-buttocked blonde. The blonde wore a schoolgirl's hat. "What Katy did at school," he muttered, reading with moving lips a choice passage at random.

They emptied out the trunk. More books of the same type. "All right, son. Bung them back. Who said vicars aren't human? They're as dirty-minded as you or I, or even old Mullett." He reluctantly tossed in the paperback.

If Clive hadn't noticed the slight bulge under the brown paper lining at the bottom of the trunk, they would have missed the envelope. It contained photographs. Black and white enlargements of Mrs. Uphill in full, unretouched nudity. It also contained photographs of an undressed, nubile twelve-year-old Audrey Harding sprawling provocatively on this self-same sheet-draped cabin trunk. This time the head wasn't torn off.

Frost was looking through the photographs for the fourth time when Clive asked, "What now, sir?"

Frost sighed. "Stick them back in the trunk and say nothing, son. Don't look surprised. He hasn't committed a crime, you know."

Clive squeaked with indignation. "The girl's under age!"

Frost shrugged. "Look at the photographs. Tell me what part of her is under age. We've got more important things to do, son, than drag this poor sod to court for corrupting the morals of a twelve-year-old slut who was more corrupt than him to start with. Blimey, she could probably corrupt me, and that takes some doing!"

They carefully replaced everything exactly as they had found it, but as Frost tried to relock the lid, his skeleton key snapped off inside the padlock. He faked it shut, covered the trunk with the sheet, and hoped the vicar wouldn't notice.

Down to the next floor, but by now the inspector was becoming bored with the search. He hustled Clive along, leaning against the wall and smoking sulkily whenever the younger man tried to be thorough.

A pair of doors opened on to a large hall with a stage, benches, and the components of trestle tables stacked along the walls. This was the vicarage hall, home of the Sunday school, Boy Scouts, Girl Guides, amateur dramatic society, and similar local functions. Clive found a trapdoor on the stage and lay flat on his stomach, probing the space beneath with his torch. He was still putting the trapdoor back when Frost was impatiently pounding down the next flight, anxious to get this time-wasting job over so he could get to his over-heated little office, drink tea, and snarl at the paperwork.

At last they reached the ground floor. The smell of cooking drew them to the kitchen and the vicar's wife, a fluttering woman with a once pretty face and a nervous laugh. She constantly apologized. She apologized for the mess, for the snow, for the lack of heat. A saucepan boiled over and she apologized for that. She offered to show them around the living quarters and invited them to stay for lunch. Frost eyed what was in the saucepan and declined both offers hastily.

The Bells' living quarters were warm and comfortable, the walls adorned with more framed photographs—Scout groups, cuddly kittens with balls of wool, gnarled trees against a setting sun. "He should stick to nudes," said Frost dismissively.

All interest in the search now gone, Frost would barely let Clive poke his head round a door before bundling him off to the next room. "I'm a good starter, son, but a poor finisher. At least, that's what my lady friends keep telling me. But we're wasting our time. The kid's not here. I feel it . . ."

The only room to arouse his curiosity was the Bells' connubial bedroom. He sat on the bed, bouncing up and down on the mattress, wondering to Clive if it made the same creaking during the couple's nocturnal activities.

On the bedside table stood a silver-framed wedding photograph of a much younger version of the vicar, his beautiful girl-wife clutching his arm proudly. She looked incredibly young, almost a child. She didn't look much older than Audrey Harding.

TUESDAY (2)

Clive slammed the brakes on hard and spun the wheel to control the skid as a little red Mini shot out of a side-turning smack in the path of the inspector's Morris, then did a sharp right turn to disappear into the swirling curtain of snow ahead.

"Bloody woman driver," he croaked, gripping the wheel hard to stop his hands shaking.

Frost smirked. "And I thought she could do no wrong in your eyes. Didn't you recognize her, son? Your girlfriend, Mrs. Uphill. I wonder why she's in such a hurry? Some poor devil needs her services urgently, I suppose."

On to the Market Square where decorated shop windows appealed in vain to stay-at-home shoppers. Frost remembered he wanted to cash a cheque and asked Clive to stop at Bennington's Bank. Clive eased the car to the curb, and found he was parked alongside an empty red Mini. Frost dashed across the pavement to the bank where the fat detective sergeant from the previous morning was again examining the splintered door. He spun round rapidly at Frost's approach and guarded his rear with his hand. "I had enough of you yesterday, Jack," he protested.

"You know you like it, Arthur," replied Frost. "What's this then—another attempted break-in?"

The fat detective gave his head a puzzled scratch. "Looks like it. Two nights running now and roughly at the same time. I think I'll get the duty chap to rearrange his beat so he's waiting for him."

"Good idea, Arthur—you don't have to be thin to have brains, do you . . . ?" Frost's voice trailed off. He was looking over Hanlon's shoulder into the bank where Mrs. Uphill was having a wad of notes counted out to her by the cashier. Excusing himself, he slid inside, pressed himself into a corner, and pretended to study the astronomical figures, with infinite noughts, contained in the bank's Annual Balance Sheet, framed on the wall. The click of heels across the tiled floor was Mrs. Uphill leaving. He sped over to the cashier and flashed his warrant card. The cashier looked to left and to right, then leaned across and spoke in a low voice. Frost nodded his thanks.

Back to the car where Clive was fighting with sleep.

"The station, son."

Clive reversed and the car bounced over the cobbles.

"What do you think, son," said Frost. "Your girlfriend has just drawn out two thousand quid in fivers."

"Two thousand?" Clive whistled softly. "What do you think, sir? Blackmail?"

Frost gave him an old-fashioned look. "At the risk of soiling your lady's good name, she's more likely to be the one doing the blackmailing. No, son, I don't think so. But what about ransom money?"

·   ·   ·

The station sergeant's internal phone buzzed. He raised his eyes to the ceiling. He knew who it was. Mullett had buzzed five minutes earlier and five minutes before that.

"Wells. No, sir, I'm afraid Inspector Frost still hasn't arrived."

Mullett droned and crackled in the earpiece. The sergeant held the phone away from his ear until the sound had finished. "Yes, sir, of course, sir, the minute he arrives." He'd heard it all before. But where the hell had Frost got to?

PC Stringer, looking out of the window to the snow-covered car park, reported the prodigal's return.

"Inspector Frost's car pulling into the car park, Sarge."

Wells swivelled his chair to confirm this sighting and saw the car door open and a single figure, scarf streaming behind him, streak over to the rear entrance of the station. Then the car backed up, turned, and drove off.

"After him—don't let him escape," roared the sergeant, and Stringer darted up the corridor to head off the inspector. He returned with Frost at his heels, the pride of capture on his face.

"What's all the fuss about?" asked Frost, taking off his coat and shaking snow all over the newly swept floor.

"The briefing meeting," said the sergeant in a voice charged with significance.

Frost sagged and his eyes widened in horror. "Blimey! Oh Gawd, I forgot it again."

"You were supposed to be running it—in Inspector Allen's absence," said Wells.

"Yes, I know," sighed Frost. He got out his cigarette packet. "Mr. Mullett reminded me last night. I suppose he's upset."

"Upset," cried Wells, "he's spitting blood. It was a shambles. And to make matters worse, the Chief Constable turned up."

"Oh Gawd!" said Frost again.

The internal phone buzzed and Frost backed away as if it were a bomb. Stringer picked it up, listened, and then handed it to Sergeant Wells.

"Yes, sir, his car has just come in . . . this very minute. He's on his way, sir." He dropped the phone and smiled sweetly. "Our Divisional Commander wonders if you could spare him a few minutes of your valuable time?"

"I shall wear my medal," said Frost. "He's too much of a coward to sack a gallant hero."

He darted up the corridor to Mullett's lair and bumped into three men coming the opposite way, two in uniform. The man in the middle wore a crumpled suit and peered with frightened eyes through thick steel-rimmed spectacles.

"Hello, hello, hello . . . and what have we here? A visitor gracing our presence?"

The trio stopped. "This is our friendly neighbourhood child molester, sir. You asked us to invite him in."

It was Mickey Hoskins, missing from his digs since Sunday.

"Now what's this all about?" he squeaked, his eyes darting from side to side as if seeking a way of escape.

"We appreciate your co-operation, Mickey," said Frost, opening the door of the interview room and bowing him in. "Won't be a minute, make yourself at home." He closed the door and turned to the two constables.

"Good work, lads. Where did you find him?"

"In the public library, sir."

"The library?"

"Yes, sir. It's warm in there. I imagine he's been sleeping rough to keep out of our way. The snow's driven him out of cover."

Frost nodded. Sleeping rough . . . like that poor old tramp. He wondered if the station sergeant knew old Sam was dead.

"Have you told him what it's all about?"

"No, sir."

"That's right, let him sweat. Give him a cup of tea and leave him on his own. I've got to see the Divisional Commander to have my goolies chewed off, so I'll chat him up as soon as that treat's over." A cheery wave and he ambled off to Mullett's room.

As dogs grow to look like their masters, so his secretary emulated Mullett's varying moods. Miss Smith's face was sour, with drawn-together eyebrows and tightly pursed lips. If only that coarse Inspector Frost would show some signs of contrition for the distress he caused the commander she could soften towards him. She understood he was very well liked in the station, but all she could say was they must see an entirely different side of the man.

Frost barged in cheerfully and asked if Santa was in his grotto.

"He's waiting for you, Inspector." She spat out the words in a manner she felt would merit the full approval of her master and resumed her finger-blurring typing.

"You look beautiful when you're angry, Ida," chirped Frost, sailing into the Divisional Commander's inner sanctum.

Mullett was furious. He was shaking with the anger and the humiliation of it all. The meeting had been a complete and utter shambles. They'd started late after waiting twenty minutes for Frost, and then the Chief Constable had turned up, unannounced and unexpected. "Didn't want you to lay anything special on for me, Commander, just want to see the normal run of things." Lots of forced laughter and increased perspiration levels as the fiasco blundered on. The various progress reports and detailed instructions for the search parties couldn't be found. Eventually Detective Sergeant Martin located them buried under other papers on Inspector Frost's desk. By then, the outside volunteers had decided that the weather would preclude searching for the day, and most of them had drifted off, while the Chief Constable's snorts were becoming more and more pointedly audible.

The meeting finally died horribly. The Chief Constable had taken Mullett quietly to one side and suggested that he ought to get a little more involved in detail instead of leaving everything to others. And as a parting shot he had made that ridiculous suggestion about the spiritualist woman. A shameful, degrading morning and all because of that untidy shuffling figure before him.

He fixed Frost with an icy stare. "We started the meeting without you, Inspector—your meeting, your briefing meeting. I hope you didn't mind? We waited twenty minutes in case you decided to come, but had to go ahead. Everyone else was there on time, you'll be glad to know, including the Chief Constable." He paused to compose himself as the bitter recollection of his humiliation fuelled the flames of his fury.

Frost composed his face into what he hoped was an expression of penitent contrition and did his best to look attentive while switching off his ears. He could kick himself for missing the lousy meeting, but all the screaming and shouting in the world wouldn't put it right now. And look at Mullett, his mouth opening and shutting, his eyes popping, just like a bloody fish. Anyway, it was just as well he hadn't turned up if the Chief Constable had been there, with all the others toadying up to him, lighting his fags, fetching his tea, laughing at his jokes, and making polite conversation, while he, Frost, would have been stuck in the corner seat at the back, deeply conscious of the fact that his suit hadn't been pressed for a week.

Mullett droned on, his face getting redder and redder.

Blimey! thought Frost—the bank! He'd nipped in there for some cash, but the sight of Mrs. Uphill with her two thousand in used bills had driven it clean from his mind. All he had on him was a few pence and he was meeting Sandy Lane in the pub at lunchtime. He wondered if he could chance his arm and tap Mullett for a couple of quid until the afternoon, but felt that the moment was not opportune. Mullett was thumping his fist on his desk, reaching the climax of his tirade. Frost opened his ears slightly to let the sound slowly creep in.

". . . just not good enough. And if it happens again I shall make a personal request to the Chief Constable for you to be transferred away from this division. Do I make myself clear?"

The inspector fought back a near irresistible urge to say "Sorry, sir, what was that?—I wasn't listening," but didn't want to be the only one laughing so he nodded with as chastened and earnestly repentant a look as he could muster.

His hangdog expression was so good that even Mullett was touched, thinking, poor devil, losing his wife like that must have a lot to do with it. Time to let him off the hook.

"What were you doing this morning?"

Frost told him about dragging the lake and searching the vicarage.

Mullett pressed his moustache into place. "That's another thing, Inspector. Now you're in charge I don't expect you to be doing house searches yourself. I want you doing the paperwork, controlling the operation."

"Yes, sir. Oh—something else. Mrs. Uphill withdrew two thousand pounds in five-pound notes from her bank this morning."

"Did she?" exclaimed Mullett. "A ransom demand do you think?"

"More than likely, sir. I've sent young Barnard down to her house to chat her up about it."

"Barnard! His second day with the division and you sent him? You should have gone yourself."

"Yes, sir, but on the basis of whatever I did was wrong, I decided to send him and obey your summons to see you. By the way, we've picked up Mickey Hoskins. He's in the interview room. I thought I'd question him—if that's all right with you, of course."

"It's your case, Inspector," said Mullett, ignoring the sarcasm. "Er . . . there was one thing the Chief Constable suggested . . . might be worth following up. I said we would, as a matter of fact, even though it's a little unusual . . ." He seemed embarrassed and fiddled with his paperknife, looking anywhere but at Frost. "It seems the Chief Constable is interested in spiritualism. Did you know that?"

"I heard he was a bit cranky, sir, but I didn't know in which direction."

"Er . . . yes. His wife is a leading light in their local

spiritualist church. It's quite a thing these days, I understand. I must confess, I used to scoff in the past, but now . . ."

But now you know the Chief Constable's wife is interested, thought Frost.

"There's a woman called Martha Wendle. Do you know her?"

"I know of her, sir. A weird old cow—always writing to say she can get the spirits to solve our cases for us."

Mullett smiled tolerantly. "We shouldn't shut our eyes to things just because we can't understand them, Inspector. She's supposed to have second sight—like that Dutch chap who helps the police in Holland." The superintendent found an interesting piece of graining on his desk top and followed it with his finger. "The Chief wants . . . suggests . . . er . . . feels we should see this woman. Ask if she can help us find Tracey Uphill. It can't do any harm . . . after all, you've no positive lead at the moment."

Frost's jaw crashed. "You mean we're to ask the bloody ghosts to help us?"

Mullett showed his palms. "I know it's a bit . . . unorthodox . . . but a Chief Constable's entitled to his whims, so let's humour him! Just go along and see her . . . I . . . er . . ." He showed his teeth. "I told him you'd see her yourself and make it a number-one priority."

He rose from his chair to signify the interview was over. The great thing after tearing chaps off a strip was to end on a happy note, show them you were behind them. He gave Frost's arm a little squeeze. "Cheer up . . . er . . . Jack . . . it's not the end of the world."

He carried on with his letter-signing as Frost slouched out. From Miss Smith's office he heard a startled cry of annoyance, a guffaw from Frost who said, "How's that for centre, Ida?" He wondered what it was all about.

Mickey Hoskins lit another cigarette. He didn't want it, it tasted hot and bitter, and the ones he had already smoked had coated his mouth with thick acidy nicotine, but he had to do something. He'd been in this damned interview room for over half an hour, just waiting. It was all part of the softening-up process, of course, to get you jumpy, twitchy, wondering how much they knew. Well, he wasn't going to let it affect him.

But he wished he had something to do. Just sitting in this miserable room with its dull green walls and the tiny window too high to see out of. But, at least it was warm. These coppers sure liked their warmth. A cylinder of ash dropped from his cigarette. How many had he left? He checked. One! And he was saving that for the interview. With a cigarette in his hand he felt better. It gave him something to do, time to think when the questions got a bit too near the mark.

But how much longer had he to wait? They had no right to keep him here against his will. He hadn't been charged, he could just stand up and walk out of that door and into the street and they couldn't do anything to stop him. He'd give them five minutes and not a second more. Twelve minutes later Inspector Frost breezed in wearing the same battered suit Mickey remembered from years past.

"Sorry to keep you waiting, Mickey boy, but I've got so many ventures of great pith and moment on the boil, I completely forgot about you."

A young uniformed man slid in after him and stood by the door. Frost dragged a chair from under the table and sat opposite Mickey who blinked at him warily through those thick lenses.

"Right, Mickey. First of all I must have a fag." He lit one slowly, but didn't offer the packet, then he took a photograph from his inside pocket and laid it face down on the table. He pushed it over to the other man with his forefinger.

"Turn it over, Mick."

Mickey regarded Frost suspiciously, then looked down at the blank back of the photograph. What trick was this?

"What is it?"

"Turn it over and look."

Gingerly he flipped it over. It showed a young girl, a schoolgirl, in colour. She looked vaguely familiar. He screwed up his face. Was it one of his? He couldn't remember.

"Well, Mickey?"

"Well, what? It's a photograph of a kid." His tongue travelled along dry lips.

"Does she look anything like her photograph?"

"How should I know—I've never seen her."

"Never seen her!" Frost barked out the words as if they were of the utmost significance, then turned to the young constable who was making shorthand notes in a spiral-bound notebook. "Get that down, Constable, and underline it— he's never seen her!" Back to Hoskins. "You'd sign that, of course, wouldn't you, Mickey? I wouldn't want people to think I'd tricked you. You'd sign a statement saying you'd never seen her?"

Mickey wriggled in his chair. Frost always managed to get him confused. "I might have seen her . . . I mean, it's a small town. I could have seen her without knowing it was her. Who says I've seen her? I mean, I couldn't actually swear on a Bible . . ." The eyelids were fluttering wildly behind the lenses. "When am I supposed to have seen her?"

"How about Sunday?" suggested Frost.

"No!"

"Show me your hand, Mick. Come on, I want to see your hand."

He held out his hand. It wouldn't keep still. Frost grabbed it, squeezing the wrist in a vice-like grip. Mickey was glad the young constable was in the room. If one of them got you alone, he beat you up.

Frost was shaking the wrist. "Look at this, Constable." The young man raised his eyes from the notebook. "Have you ever seen such a soft, warm hand? Look at these long, sensitive fingers. A really beautiful hand, that is, Mick. How many knicker legs has it slipped inside, eh?" Hoskins tried to pull free, but was held firm. "How many warm young thighs has that explored, eh, Mick?"

"Stop it!" This time he managed to snatch his hand away. He massaged the white pressure marks of Frost's fingers.

"Getting you excited, is it?"

"No, of course not." Time for a cigarette. His hand shook as he lit it.

Frost rose from his chair and walked round the table to stand behind him. "Did you have a go at her on Sunday, Mick? Did she like it? Did you like her?"

Almost a scream. "Stop it! I never saw her on Sunday."

"You don't have to shout, Mick." The voice now gentle. "You can lie just as well in a quiet voice. You haven't been in your digs since Sunday."

"So? It's not a crime, is it?"

"Afraid to go back after what you did? Come on, Mick, tell us. Have the thrill of telling, then you can live it all again. What did you do to her?"

Mickey sucked at the cigarette, then blinked up at his tormentor. "I want my solicitor."

"You have but to ask, Mick," said Frost with a friendly smile. He picked up the phone, dialled for an outside line, then handed the receiver to the huddled man.

Hoskins took it, poked his finger towards the dial, then, almost in tears with frustration, slammed it back on its rest.

"You know I haven't got a solicitor," he bleated petulantly. "I've got no money. Only the rich can afford the law."

Frost nodded his agreement. "We live in an unfair society, Mick. Still, I bet the richest man in the world hasn't been up as many knicker legs as you. But back to the old police persecution. I want to know about Sunday. Come on, give us a cheap thrill."

Mickey thought for a while then asked for a cigarette. Frost gave him one. He took two deep drags, then he spoke. "I didn't think she'd mind. Some of them don't—they lap it up, they love it. She was sitting on her own, so I moved over and sat next to her."

The inspector frowned. "Where was this?"

It was Mickey's turn to look puzzled. "The pictures. The Century Cinema in Lexton. That's what you're on about, isn't it?"

Frost assured him that it was, wondering how the hell eight-year-old Tracey Uphill could have got over to Lexton and into the Century Cinema on her own. "So you sat next to her . . . ?"

"Yes. Like I said, I didn't think she'd mind. She let me get my hand right up her leg before she screamed. If she didn't want it, why didn't she complain earlier?"

"Perhaps she didn't want to miss a good bit of the film, Mick," suggested Frost. Then he saw that the young constable was trying to attract his attention. He went over to him.

"This incident," the young man whispered, "it's been reported—a man tried to molest a woman, she screamed, he hit her in the face, breaking her nose. There was a chase. They nearly got him when he couldn't get the exit doors open, but he burst through. The woman was about thirty, sir. He's not talking about Tracey."

Thirty years old? Mickey's hands usually favoured much fresher meat. At the other side of the room their suspect strained his ears, wondering what they were whispering about. Frost patted the constable on the arm and returned.

"Sorry about that, Mick—he just wanted to know how to spell 'dirty bastard.' You broke her nose, you know. Why? A bit vicious wasn't it?"

"Vicious? Vicious?" The voice rose by a major third. "She was the vicious one. Look!" He thrust out his left hand to show the blistered, inflamed area on the back of the wrist. "She did that. She clamped her legs tight to trap my hand then brought her lighted cigarette down on it. I had to hit her to get away."

Frost stroked his own scar. "Very nasty, Mick. Could have ruined you professionally for life. Come to think of it, someone did say there was a smell of roast pork. But the old dear was pushing thirty. A bit ancient for you, wasn't she?"

Mickey drew down his lips and shrugged. "Needs must when the Devil drives, Inspector. It was a restricted admission programme. They don't let kids in to see those films. In the old days you had good clean family entertainment, but this stuff today . . . it's filth . . . pure, unadulterated filth."

Frost nodded his agreement and went across to the police

constable. "Keep an eye on him, son, would you? I'll send someone in to take his statement. If he was touching up in the Century at six o'clock, I can't see him having anything to do with Tracey, but we'll keep him in mind, just in case."

Back to the table. "I'm sending someone else in to take your statement, Mickey. Can't do it myself, I get too excited when I hear about thighs and knickers and things. I can't hold the pencil steady. Oh, I'd better take this." He picked up the photograph.

"Hold on a minute." Hoskins took the photograph from him and studied it through magnified eyes. "Here . . . this is that missing kid—Tracey Uphill. You surely didn't think that I . . . ?"

"I had to ask, Mick—you'd have been offended otherwise."

"She's only eight years old." The voice quivered with indignation. "I've never touched a kid under ten in my life—well, not knowingly, anyway."

Outside the interview room Frost grabbed Bill Wells, the station sergeant, who said he'd be pleased to take Hoskins's statement. They talked about old Sam, the tramp, a character who'd been in and out of the station's cells for years and who was now stiff and cold in the morgue and cleaner than he'd ever been in his life. "It's funny," observed the sergeant. "I hated the bloke, he stank and was no bloody good, but I feel choked knowing he's dead. By the way, the new chap's waiting for you in your office."

Frost frowned. What new chap? Oh—of course, young Barnard. He'd sent him to talk to Mrs. Uphill about the two thousand pounds. There were so many things on his mind. There was the bank door business. That worried him. And the old tramp's dying. Then he had to meet Sandy Lane in the pub for a drink. And there was something else. It was important. He should keep notes, but then he'd forget to look at them. Blimey, yes! Old Mother Wendle, the witch of the woods. He had to ask her to get the spirits to tell him where the kid was. Now he'd remembered what it was, he felt happier. But first, let's see what young Barnard had got from

the juicy Mrs. Uphill, the best thirty quid's worth east of
Suez.

He trotted down the stone corridor to his office. Somewhere an outer door had been left open and a blast of cold air
roared along the passage. He glanced through a window. Still
no let-up in the snow, the sky was black, with plenty to come
down. Barely twelve o'clock, and every light in the place was
on.

Frost read the note again.

> I HAVE GOT YOUR DAUGHTER TRACEY UPHILL IF YOU WANT TO
> SEE HER ALIVE GET £2000 IN USED FIVE-POUND NOTES AND
> WAIT BY YOUR PHONE FOR INSTRUCTIONS TELL THE POLICE
> AND I KILL HER.

It had arrived at Mrs. Uphill's with the first postal delivery. The postmark on the cheap brown envelope showed it
had been collected from the main Denton post office in the
Market Square at 6:15 the night before. Inside was a sheet of
paper which could have been a page torn from a child's
exercise book. The writing was in laboriously printed block
capitals written with a smudgy ballpoint pen. At first Mrs.
Uphill had denied its existence—TELL THE POLICE AND I KILL
HER—but Clive had convinced her that she must co-operate.
"Don't worry, Mrs. Uphill. Just leave everything to us."

Frost took the page carefully by the edges and held it to
the light, looking for a watermark. He dropped the sheet on
to his desk.

"No watermark, son—not that it would mean anything to
me if there was one." He leaned back in his chair, stretching
his arms in a yawn. "Better get it over to Forensic. They'll be
able to tell us when the paper was made, the precise location
of the pulping mill, when the tree was chopped down, and
the exact chemical composition of the ball-point ink. Then
they'll put their findings in a twenty-page report which some
poor sod will have to read, but they won't be the slightest
help in telling us who wrote the bloody thing."

Clive slid the envelope and letter into a large transparent pocket and made out a requisition for a forensic report.

A brisk knock at the door and Mullett entered, his gleaming tailor-made uniform shaming Frost's office into looking even drabber.

"I hear through the grapevine there's a ransom note, Inspector."

"I was just about to bring it in to you, sir," said Frost, who had had no intention of so doing.

The glasses were pushed on the nose and Mullett read the note through the transparent cover. "Better get this over to Forensic."

"Good idea," said Frost. "Would you do that, son?"

Mullett looked for a chair to sit on, but they were both stacked with unreplaced files. Typical . . . absolutely typical. "What's your next move, Inspector?"

"I'm having her phone wired so we can listen in to her calls—so if you're one of her regulars, sir, I'd lay off for a while."

Mullett's face tightened. He didn't think that the least bit funny.

"Hmm . . . I suppose you can't make firm plans until you know the arrangements the kidnapper requires for the hand-over of the money. Now this note . . . do you think it's genuine? Do you think he's really got the girl?"

"I think it's genuine," said Clive, and Mullett beamed in his direction.

"So do I." Then, remembering Frost hadn't answered, "Inspector . . . ?"

Frost pulled a face. "I'm probably wrong—I usually am— but if she was kidnapped on Sunday, then why the hell did he wait until Monday night before posting his ransom note?"

"The kidnapper may not have had any envelopes and had to wait until Monday to buy them," suggested Clive.

"My thoughts exactly," agreed Mullett. "He may not have had any stamps, either."

"Or a ballpoint pen," added Frost.

Not sure if this was sarcasm or not, Mullett gave a wintry smile and left.

"Stupid bastard," snorted Frost as the door closed. "Send it to Forensic! What did he think we were going to do with it —wipe our arses on it? Well, nip it along to the post room, son, then get the chap in Control to send a civilian technician over to bug her phone. Tell them to send someone who hasn't got three tenners to spare. I want a quick and thorough job. And then get back here—we're meeting Sandy in the pub for lunch."

As he waited for the detective constable to return he tidied up the latest batch of papers that had landed on his desk. There was a file Inspector Allen had been working on concerning a series of thefts at a local electronics factory. He'd have to look at that some time. Then he found a note in his own hand scribbled on the back of an old envelope. It said "Check Aunt—Tea." He wasted the rest of the time until Clive's return puzzling out what the hell it meant, finally giving it up as a bad job.

"I've ordered the lunch," said Sandy. "Now what do you want to drink—whiskey?"

"You'd better make it beers," answered the inspector, "we haven't got any information for you."

The beers came with the curry. It wasn't very good curry, doubtful chunks of gristle in a violent yellow sauce, bedded down on grey rice.

"I'm paying," said Sandy.

"I should hope so," said Frost, eyeing his plate with grave suspicion.

The reporter slipped in his leading question. "I understand Mrs. Uphill drew a packet out of her bank today."

Clive fired a glance at the inspector. How the hell did Sandy know that? Frost didn't bat an eyelid; he chewed stolidly on a lump of rubbery meat.

"If this is chicken curry, I've got one of the claws," he announced gloomily.

"Come off it, Jack," persisted the reporter. "Give me a

break. I've spent my entire expense allowance on this lunch. We haven't got the resources of the big London dailies you know."

Frost pushed his plate away and rinsed the taste down with beer. "Did I tell you the joke about the bloke who drank the spittoon for a bet?"

"Yes—what delightful bloody table talk you've got. Now come on, Jack. She drew out two thousand quid—why?"

"Ask your mate in the bank," said Frost, lighting a cigarette. "I'm sorry, Sandy, as soon as there's anything I can give you, you'll have it. You don't deserve it for such a stinking lunch, but you might find something interesting in tomorrow's Magistrate's Court. Mickey Hoskins. He touched up some female in the pictures and she gave him a different sort of thrill from what he expected by stubbing her fag out on his hand."

Sandy brightened up and scribbled a note in his diary. "A crumb, but acceptable."

Frost sipped his beer. "I wish our canteen tea was as warm as this." Then he put his glass down and nudged Sandy. "The bird in the leopard-skin coat—don't look round so obviously—at the bar."

The reporter swivelled his eyes. "Cynthia Collard," he whispered and Frost nodded in confirmation. Clive eased his head round to see who they were taking so much interest in.

She had the dark olive skin of a brunette, but her hair was bleached blonde. Thick make-up couldn't conceal the dark rings under the eyes or the pinched lines around the mouth and nose. Now in her late hard-faced thirties, she must have been demurely pretty once, but now cold predatory eyes scoured the room as she sat cross-legged on the barstool, a cheap imitation leopard-skin coat cloaked over her shoulders. An overweight moustached man in the corner read the invitation in her glance and beckoned her to join him. She sauntered over with a smug smile.

"Still on the game, then?" said Frost. "I can remember Cynthia when she was free . . . and liberal. A real goer, she was. Never gave the impression she was doing you a favour, like some of the local moggies."

"That was a long time ago, Jack. She wants cash in advance, now." The reporter drained his glass and looked at his watch.

Cynthia and the man went out, arm in arm.

"I hope she's got change for a quid," said Frost.

TUESDAY (3)

Martha Wendle's cottage was in the black heart of the woods and could only be reached by a footpath. If this meant she received few callers, then she shed no tears. There was a private road riddled with potholes that gave direct access, but it was barred to the public by barbed-wire-lined gates secured by padlocks and strong chains and was only used when Martha ventured out in her battered old Morris Minor.

So Frost and Clive parked on the outskirts and trudged, heads down, along the winding footpath barely discernible through the thick snow. Wind roared in their ears and when they strayed from the path, they found themselves knee deep in cold clamminess. A long, miserable, stumbling journey, which was broken at intervals by Frost yelling "Sod the Chief Constable" into the wind.

The path forked and Frost waited for Clive, who was lagging, to catch up. "We go left," he yelled. "The other way leads to Dead Man's Hollow."

"Dead Man's what?" Clive shouted back.

"Dead Man's Hollow." He jerked his thumb in the direction of a gloomy depression overhung with diseased-looking trees crouching under the weight of the snow on their maimed branches. "I don't know what its official name is, but it's been called that ever since I was a kid. None of us would go near it. It's all puffy with fungus in the summer and the adders are supposed to be enormous."

They turned their backs on the depression and breasted the wind until the path plunged sharply and veered right and Old Wood Cottage sprang into view. Clive had expected to see something out of Walt Disney's *Snow White and the Seven Dwarfs* with latticed windows and a thatched roof, but the main building material used for Martha Wendle's home was rusty corrugated iron.

Frost hammered his fist on the front door. Creakings and pattering from within. The door was opened a suspicious chink and two black eyes surveyed them. Then a talon pulled the door open further.

"I've been expecting you. Come on in."

She had raven black hair, jet beads for eyes, a hooked nose, and a jutting chin that gave her a crescent-like profile. A couple of centuries before and she would have screamed and crackled on top of a roaring fire, together with her cat and her broomstick.

The smell hit them as soon as they stepped inside the door.

Frost sniffed delicately. "Do you keep cats, Miss Wendle?"

There were dozens of them, dirty mangy strays.

"Any cat is welcome here," she said, taking them into her living room where hostile green eyes glimmered in dark recesses.

"Please sit down."

A fat, dribbling cat was snuffling in its sleep on Frost's chair, but he knocked it to the floor with a swift cuff and was seated before the animal realized it had been deposed. Clive's chair was cat-less, but the cushion bore evidence of recent occupation. He sat very gingerly on the extreme edge.

"I expect the spirits have told you what it's about, Miss Wendle—the missing girl."

The fat cat staged a counter-attack. It leaped up to Frost's lap and, under the pretext of settling down, sank the length of its claws into his thigh. With a barely perceptible short-arm jab, he sent it flying to the floor where it spat at him.

"Your men have already been here and I've told them I haven't seen her, Inspector."

"You may not have seen her, Miss Wendle, but with the special powers you keep telling us about in your lovely and frequent letters, we thought you could find out where we should look."

Her eyes glittered. "You've mocked me in the past, why should I help you now?"

Frost stood up and rearranged his scarf. "Fair enough. My fault for sticking up for you, I suppose. Our Chief Constable reckons you're a fake and I had to fight him like mad to put you to the test, but if you can't do it . . ."

"Sit down." The dribbling cat had returned and he sat down on top of it. It squealed and flew off unaided. Martha Wendle split a coal on the fire with a crack of the poker. "What you ask is dangerous. If the spirits want to tell me, they will. To seek what they wish to withhold could be . . . unpleasant. It will be on your head, but I will try."

She lifted a heavy oak table and carried it without effort to a spot between the two men. She turned down the wick of the old-fashioned brass oil-lamp which was the room's only illumination. A coal shifted on the fire and seemed to smother the flames and the room went dark and very cold. Hard green emeralds stared and tongues rasped on fur.

Miss Wendle sat between the two men at the table and took one each of their hands in a tight crushing grip, her nails chewing into their flesh.

In the darkness the sound of wheezing, rasping breath, deep and rhythmic, and strange sobbing noises. The breathing shallowed and quickened. Outside, the wind clanged the corrugated iron and something blew over and clattered. And, suddenly, silence . . . no wind . . . no scuffling of cats . . . not even the sound of breathing. The voice didn't come from the woman whose nails were burning points of pain on their skin. It came from . . . from the air.

"It's cold . . . grave . . . snow . . . so cold . . . skull . . . bones . . . so . . . so . . . so cold."

All right, dear, thought Frost, we'll let you know—next please.

The breathing returned, deeper, more frenzied, like the climax of love-making.

"Buried . . . unmarked grave . . . snow . . . death . . . death . . ."

The voice was so unearthly, Clive felt the hairs on the back of his neck stir and rise.

"Where are you buried?" This from Frost.

"Woods . . ."

Frost stiffened. "Where in the woods?"

More breathing, slower, shallower. He repeated the question. "Where in the woods?"

"Hollow . . . in front of tree . . . Hollow . . . Dead Man's Hollow."

"Were you murdered?" A moan of pain. Frost jerked his hand from the woman's grip and shook her shoulders. "Answer me, was it murder?"

"No, sir," protested Clive urgently. "If you bring her out of a trance too soon, it can kill her."

"Then I'll apologize," snapped Frost. "Light that lamp."

A match flared and the oil-lamp glowed. The room blinked and came to life. Cats yawned and scratched and licked. In her chair, the woman was bolt upright, her body rigid, her eyes staring but sightless.

Frost shook her roughly. "Miss Wendle!" She blinked, then looked at him in puzzlement. "Who are you? Oh—the policeman."

"Who killed Tracey?" barked Frost.

"Is she dead?" She got up and stabbed the fire in the heart with the poker. It roared instantly into life.

"You told us she was buried in Dead Man's Hollow."

She squeezed out a thin vinegary smile. "No, Inspector. The spirits told you, not me. I was in a trance. They simply used my mouth to utter their words, words of which I have no knowledge."

"I see," said Frost. "Well, you can tell your bloody spirits that if I find Tracey buried where your mouth said she was, then you'll be holding your next séance in the nick on a charge of murder. Come on, son."

He spun on his heel and stamped out. A cat clawed at him as he passed. The woman didn't move, but as Clive squeezed by to get to the door he was able to see beyond the acid hate that uglied her face. Martha Wendle was frightened, terribly frightened.

Outside they sucked down lungfuls of clean air, like submariners unexpectedly saved from a suffocating death. The wind had dropped for the return journey, but hit out with a cold blast from time to time to let them know it was still lurking.

"I hope I haven't caught anything from those lousy cats," said Frost, sniffing at his coat. "Do you have intuitions, son?"

"Sometimes, sir."

"I have them all the time. That woman's a killer!"

"Where's your proof, sir?"

"You're proof-mad, son! All I want is a suspect. Forget this 'innocent until proved guilty' caper. Find your suspect and then prove he or she did it. Saves sodding about with lots of different people."

They reached the fork in the path and Frost used his torch to light the way over the slithering plunge to Dead Man's Hollow. "Well, this is it, son."

His torch beam crawled over virgin snow, through which the branches of stunted trees protruded like the hands of drowning men.

"Shall we go down there, sir?" asked Clive.

"Waste of bloody time, son. We haven't got shovels."

Clive took a deep breath. "Then why did we come, sir?"

"I wanted to get the feel of the place. Now shut up for a minute, there's a good boy."

The wind had a spasm and shook snow from branches, then went quiet. A match flared as Frost lit a cigarette.

"The kid's not here, son."

Clive looked at him amazed. "How on earth do you know that, sir?"

"I don't know—I feel it."

Clive gave a scornful snort. "More intuition?"

"Yes, son—more of my stupid intuition. We'll probably have to dig just to satisfy Mullett and Uncle Chief Constable, but she's not here."

Clive grabbed his arm. "Sir—on that bush—shine your torch to the left . . . do you see it?"

Something small and white and insignificant fluttered on the branch. The snow was thigh-deep at that point but Clive plunged over to the bush. He snatched the object and waded back to the inspector in triumph. Frost looked at the treasure, a small square of waxed paper—the wrapping from a boiled sweet.

"It could have been chucked there by the kid," said Clive eagerly, like a puppy that has brought the ball back for the first time.

Frost raised his eyes to heaven. "A sweet wrapper," he exclaimed. "The spirits are vindicated—a bloody sweet wrapper." He found a crumpled transparent envelope in his pocket and poked the wrapper inside. "If you weren't looking so pleased with yourself, son, I'd chuck it away, but I suppose I'm setting you enough bad examples as it is, so we'll let Forensic tell us what flavour the sweet was and how much a pound they are."

Back at the car the radio was going blue in the face pleading for Inspector Frost to answer. He sighed and slid into his seat. "They don't let you alone when you're lovable, do they, son?" He slowly lit a cigarette just to show the radio who was master, then announced his whereabouts into the microphone.

"Inspector Frost? We've been trying to contact you for ages, sir. Can you get back to the station at once? The kidnapper has phoned Mrs. Uphill."

TUESDAY (4)

The take-up spool on the tape recorder slowly revolved, pulling tape across the replay head. First the hissing of virgin tape, then . . .

Brr . . . brr . . . br—hardly two rings before the receiver was snatched up.

"Denton 2346." Mrs. Uphill, pathetically eager.

Pay-phone pips, then the *chunk* of money.

"Mrs. Uphill?" a man's voice, nondescript, distorted by the phone.

"Yes."

"You got my letter?"

"Yes . . . Please . . . where is she?"

"All in good time. Have you got the money?"

"Yes—exactly as you said."

"And you've told no-one?"

"No—no-one."

"Good, I'd hate to have to carry out my promise. Now listen carefully—"

But Mrs. Uphill cut across him, "I've got to know about Tracey. How is she?"

"All right—considering . . . She cries a lot, doesn't she? She's got a bit of a cold and she keeps whining for her mother, but apart from that . . ."

"Please," and her voice was a barely steady whisper, "what do you want me to do?"

"I want—"

A click, then the dial tone. Frost's head jerked up. Detective Sergeant Martin waved him to silence; there was a little more.

"Hello . . . hello . . ." Mrs. Uphill, almost hysterical as she jiggled the receiver rest. "Hello . . ." The relentless purr of dial tone going on and on. A click as the receiver was replaced, then the hiss and crackle of virgin tape.

Martin banged down the Stop key. "That's it."

Frost dragged off his scarf and draped it over the radiator to dry. "So what happened? Was he cut off?"

"I don't think so, Jack. Listen carefully to the end of the tape." Martin turned the volume control to its maximum and wound the tape back a few inches. He pressed the Start key. Tape background roared and sizzled and distorted voices boomed.

"Please, what do you want me to do?"

"I want—" *click* . . . dial tone.

"Again," snapped Frost.

Martin kept repeating the last few seconds of the recording. "I want—" *click* . . . "I want—" *click* . . . "I want—"

It was just about audible through the background mush, the faint *Pee-paw, pee-paw* of a police car on the road outside the telephone kiosk.

"One of our cars passed the kiosk while he was on the phone," said Martin, scratching his head with the stem of his pipe. "He must have thought we were on to him and bolted."

Frost buried his head in his hands. "Bloody police," he moaned. "When you want them, you can't find them; when you don't they roar past and scare your suspects away." Then he noticed a stiffening of everyone's shoulders and his eye caught the gleam of burnished silver buttons.

"Afternoon, Super," he said.

"Heard the recording?" asked Mullett.

"Yes, sir."

"What are we going to do about it?"

Frost ruffled his hair. "Blowed if I know. Did the telephone engineers manage to trace the call?"

Martin sprang forward. "I was just coming to that Jack—er—Inspector. They did. It came from a call box on the main eastern highway, by the junction with Beehive Lane. Charlie

Alpha two was in the vicinity, so Control sent him over to investigate."

"Charlie Alpha two!" snorted Frost. "It was probably those silly sods who scared him off in the first place."

"They were on patrol, Inspector," cut in Mullett, icily, ever protective of the reputation of his uniformed men, "and fully entitled to be where they were."

"With you one hundred per cent, Super—all the way— they're the salt of the earth," murmured Frost, blandly. Mullett was convinced Frost was being sarcastic, but before he could think of a suitable rebuke, bearing in mind that there were others present, Control buzzed through on the internal phone. Charlie Alpha two was reporting in.

Frost signalled for Clive to switch on the monitor speaker.

"Hello, Control. Charlie Alpha two. We're at the phone box at the junction of Beehive Lane and Eastern Highway. We've had a good look round. No-one in the vicinity."

Frost spoke over the internal phone to the controller and asked if there was any way Charlie Alpha could keep the phone box under observation without being seen. Control relayed the message and the reply came over the monitor speaker.

"Yes—there are some trees a little way up the road. We can tuck the car behind them. It's some distance from the phone box, but we'll have a clear view."

"Right, they can wait there until he comes back," ordered Frost.

"Bloody heck!" acknowledged the voice over the speaker before Control cut it off.

Frost stripped the cellophane from his second packet of twenty that day and offered them around. "We can't do much until he phones again."

Martin shook his head gloomily. "The odds are he'll use another phone box."

Frost tapped his cheek and expelled a salvo of smoke-rings. "You don't have to be so bloody pessimistic, George, just because I'm in charge. Count your blessings. We've had a lovely spate of phone-box vandalism recently—over sixteen cases in the last couple of days. He'll have a job finding another box that works, so, as long as Charlie Alpha doesn't do anything daft like leaving its blue light flashing, we might nab him yet." Then remembering, he turned to Mullett. "Sorry, Super—I'm neglecting you."

Mullett flashed perfect teeth. "That's all right, Inspector, only I'm expecting the Chief Constable to ring and I rather wanted to know how you got on with this Wendle woman."

"Oh—it was quite interesting, actually. We had a séance. According to her spiritual snouts, the kid's buried in Dead Man's Hollow."

"Dead Man's Hollow?" breathed Mullett in eye-blazing excitement. "Did you take a look?"

"Well, we looked at the four feet of snow covering it and it looked pretty much like the snow covering everywhere else."

"Organize a digging party," called Mullett over his shoulder as he made for the door. "I'll phone the Chief Constable right away."

As the door clicked shut, Frost exploded. "A bloody digging party! As if we didn't have enough to do. I'm throwing a little digging party, just a few friends—do come. Informal dress, just boots and shovels."

"Shall I put it in hand?" asked Martin.

"No, I'll see to it, George." He tugged his steaming scarf from the radiator. "Done to a turn!" Then he called across to Clive. "Important job for you, son. Nip up to the canteen and bring a couple of cups of tea to the office. I'll be along as soon as I've seen the station sergeant." He clattered out and along the corridor.

"How much longer has the stupid bugger got to go?" asked Clive.

The room went silent.

"What did you say, Constable?" the detective sergeant's eyes were cold.

"He wouldn't last five minutes in London."

"I can understand how you got your nose broken, Bar-

nard. Go and fetch his bloody tea and see if you can do that
without bitching."

The station sergeant could only spare two men to help with
the digging until he learned that Mullett and the Chief Constable were taking a great interest in the outcome, then he
managed to rake up two more and the four "volunteers" were
sent to wrap up warm and collect their shovels from the
stores.

Frost returned to his office to see if anyone had taken pity
on him and had removed some of his paperwork, but another
pile had been added, held down by a cup of tea. He took the
cup of tea and two personal letters with local postmarks and
leaned against the radiator where the hot pipes baked steam
from his sodden trouser legs. He raised the cup to his lips,
then shuddered. The tea was stone cold.

A fumbling at the door handle, then two steaming cups
poked through followed by Clive Barnard who kicked the
door shut behind him.

"Sorry I've been so long, sir. I had to wait for the digging
party to be served first."

Frost returned to his desk and accepted the hot tea gratefully. "Thought you'd already been, son." He stirred up the
thick mud of sugar at the bottom of the cup, then he suddenly realized what the cryptic note on the back of the envelope meant—"Check Aunt—Tea." Of course, Farnham,
Mrs. Uphill's regular, was supposed to have gone to his aged
aunt's for a nice spot of anti-climax after thirty quids' worth
of strenuous exercise and his story hadn't been checked. Clive
was detailed to attend to this right away.

"Take the car, son—I'll be going in the van with the
grave-diggers. When you've seen the old dear, come down to
Dead Man's Hollow and join in the fun. I reckon we'll have
to dig down to Australia before we find anything, though."
He was to remember this remark afterwards. When he was
wrong, he certainly was wrong.

Clive's hand was on the door handle when Frost had another thought. "She's probably old and nervous, so you'd

better have a woman PC along with you. Take the same one as before . . ."

Clive's face lit up. "Hazel!"

"Blimey," said Frost. "Don't tell me I've done something right for a change. Don't let anyone catch you smiling, son, they might think you're enjoying working with me."

As the door closed, Frost ripped open the two envelopes, but he knew it was just to delay what he had to do. Both Christmas cards. He dropped them on the desk, then steeled himself to pull open the top right-hand drawer of his desk. His heart sank when he saw what he expected to see.

A quick tap and the door opened before he could say "Come in."

"I've come for the empty cups, sir." It was Keith Stringer, the young PC from the front office.

Frost waved a hand to the window ledge.

"You didn't drink your tea, sir . . ." Mildly reproachful.

Frost looked up wearily. "Sorry, son, by the time I got here it was cold. Hold on a minute, would you? Put the cups down . . . shut the door."

The young man looked puzzled, but did as he was told.

Frost's thumb indicated a chair. "Sit down." He slid a packet of cigarettes across the desk.

"I don't smoke, sir."

The inspector grunted and took one himself. "Keith isn't it—Keith Stringer?"

"Yes, sir."

"Hmm." Frost rubbed his chin and patted some papers into a neat pile. Outside in the car park the sound of a car door slamming. Frost sighed and shook his head sadly.

"Tell me, son, how much money have you pinched in total—to within a couple of quid, say?"

Stringer's eyes widened. He searched the inspector's face for a hidden smile . . . it was a joke, of course. Frost met the gaze steadily. Stringer sprang to his feet, face hot, lips compressed.

Frost crashed his fist on the desk. "Sit down." The young constable jerked back in his chair, seething with resentment.

Frost stubbed out the cigarette and poked the butt back into the packet. "Look, son, you probably think me useless and decrepit, and perhaps you're right, but I'd be a real right twit if I couldn't solve a simple case of someone nicking money from my desk drawer . . . money that's always missing after you've been in with the tea . . ."

Eyes blazed. "I'm not staying here to be insulted, sir. I'm reporting this to the Police Federation Representative, so if you want to say anything further to me . . ."

The inspector knocked Stringer's hand from the door handle, grabbed him by the tunic, and slung him back in his chair. His eyes were soft and reproachful, his voice calm. "I'll call the Divisional Commander if you like, son, and tell him I want your pockets searched. You see . . . I marked the money . . ."

Stringer flinched and, as if a plug had been pulled, the colour drained from his face. Defiance shrivelled and he crumpled in the chair.

The door opened and the station sergeant's head poked round. "They're ready, Jack . . ." he began, then he felt the electric tension in the air. His head swivelled from the white-faced constable to the stiff figure of Frost behind the desk, the scar on his cheek twitching.

"Thank you, Sergeant."

The questioning raised eyebrows were ignored, so the head withdrew tactfully and the door closed.

Frost relit the cigarette butt and sat on the corner of his desk, dribbling the smoke from his nose. "It's not only my money, son. What about that tramp we found dead—the poor old sod whose quid you pinched? If he had had that quid he might have found himself lodgings for the night and still be alive. He was hunched up in a wooden hut, no bigger than a coffin, frozen to death."

The constable buried his face in his hands.

Frost's face was touched with pity. "But if it's any consolation, son, I can't see old Sam wasting a good quid on rubbish like food and lodgings . . . The odds are he'd have blown it on bottles of cheap wine and drunk himself to death a few seconds before the cold got him. So you haven't really got his death on your conscience . . . only the fact that he died *knowing* a copper had stolen his money, and when he came to us to complain, we insulted him and sent him off with a flea in his ear. I hope you feel as rotten about it as I do."

Stringer raised his head from his hands. "What are you going to do, sir?"

Frost pinched out the butt and flicked it into his wastepaper basket. "That depends on you, son. You'd better tell me about it."

The phone on his desk rang. He picked it up, said "Later," and dropped it back on the rest. The young man was staring at the floor, lips quivering, but no words came.

"I'll give you a start to help you, son. Now I'm a rotten driver. When I drive, my eyes are anywhere but on the road. I see lots of things that don't make sense at the time, but I file them away in my mind for future reference. More than once I've seen you coming out of Sammy Jacobs' Betting Shop. Not that there's anything wrong with the odd bet, of course, providing you know when to stop—and providing you visit the shop during business hours. But I've seen you coming out when the shop has been closed."

"I owe him nearly four hundred quid," said Stringer, his eyes still fixed on the floor.

Frost whistled silently. "Four hundred quid! It's going to take a hell of a time repaying that with the odd pennies from my drawer and the occasional quid from a drunken tramp."

"I'm paying him back twenty pounds a week, sir. I have to give my mother money for my keep, then there's the hire purchase on my car. I'm only left with a couple of quid in my pocket."

"I see. So any extra little pickings would be a Godsend. Pity you didn't come and tell me, son. I've got more than enough on Sammy Jacobs. But that's not all, is it?"

"No." Stringer spoke to the ground. "He says a score a week isn't enough. He wants the lot repaid, otherwise he's going to the Divisional Commander. I haven't got that sort of money."

Frost sniffed. "I suppose Sammy suggested a way out?"

"Yes, sir. He wanted some information. If I get it to him, he'd let me off the debt."

Frost felt the corner of the desk boring its way into his buttock. He stood up and rubbed himself. "What information?"

"He wanted to know when we were going to pull the beat constable off his normal foot patrol to keep watch at Bennington's Bank. As you know, he's being pulled off tonight."

"And you told him?"

"Yes, sir."

Frost clapped his hands together with delight, then dialled Detective Sergeant Hanlon on his internal phone. "Hello, Arthur—Jack Frost. Sad news. You're going to have to forgo your nightly connubials. I've had a tip-off—something big. This Bennington's Bank business, it's just a decoy to draw our chap from his usual beat so someone can pull off a job undisturbed. I've no details, so we'll have to play it clever. We pretend we don't know. The constable stays watching the bank, but you and a couple of your best men are lurking in the vicinity of where the beat copper usually is between, say, two and three in the morning . . . If I knew the exact address I'd have given it to you, Arthur—even I am not that bleeding dim. No—with the search for the kid we can't spare any more men. We keep our fingers crossed and hope for the best. I'll be in touch." He swung the phone by the cord and flicked it back into the cradle.

Stringer was now sitting up straight. He seemed to have pulled himself together. "What happens now, sir?"

Frost twitched his shoulders. "That's entirely up to you, son. I've got enough on my plate with missing kids, ransom demands, and talking spirits. I'll just say this. You've been a bloody fool and you've been found out by a dim old fool like me, so you haven't been very clever, have you? If you want to keep out of trouble never put yourself in a position where crooks like Sammy Jacobs can blackmail you. Do you want to stay in the Force?"

"Yes, sir."

"Then buzz off and behave yourself from now on. And from time to time you might repay the odd copper you've pinched from me. My top drawer's always available—all contributions gratefully received."

The phone gave an urgent ring. It was the station sergeant. "Frost. Oh—thanks. I'm coming now. What? Oh, just a private matter, nothing that concerns anyone but him and me. I'll tell him."

He dropped the phone back and looked at the young man.

"Better get back, son. The station sergeant's got a job for you."

"Right, sir . . . and thanks . . ."

But Frost had gone, his footsteps clattering up the corridor. Stringer picked up the cups with a shaking hand. He felt like bursting into tears. The open desk drawer gaped accusingly at him as he passed.

The van bumped in and out of snow-covered potholes and the two policemen in the back, with the shovels and the tarpaulins, cursed as they slithered and cannoned into each other. Frost, wedged tightly between the driver and a dark moustached young constable, was able to do little more than grunt with each jolt.

"Park by those trees," he said. "We walk from here." The moustached copper was looking queasy. "What's up, son—car sickness?"

A brisk shake of the head. "No, sir—it's just that I don't like the idea of digging up a body."

Frost snorted derisively. "It's the winter, son, not the summer. Cor, I remember my first body. All decomposing and rotten . . . half the face eaten away by rats and the weather hot and sticky. I'd have given anything for a nice fresh corpse in the winter. You don't know how lucky you are."

They waded through thigh-deep drifts at Dead Man's Hollow and Frost cursed himself for not having the foresight to grab a pair of Wellingtons like the rest of his digging party

who, properly dressed for the occasion, plodded stoically behind him.

"Right. The first thing to do is to clear the snow away."

The snow was light and fluffy, all bulk and no substance,
like candy-floss, and it was tiring, unsatisfying work, but at
last an area was cleared behind piled, shovelled snow.

"What now, sir?" asked the driver, breathing heavily and
resting on his shovel.

"Don't look all-knowing at me, son," snapped Frost. "I
reckon it's a bloody waste of time as well but I wasn't going
to call the Divisional Commander a twit to his face and risk
not getting a Christmas card. What's the ground like?"

In reply the driver struck the earth with his shovel. It rang,
frozen solid. Digging would be an illegitimate cow's son.

Frost wound his scarf to just below his eyes. "Prod
around, lads. If anyone's been digging recently there should
be traces." He poked a cigarette through a gap in the scarf
and watched them work. His feet were so cold they hurt.

An excited voice. "Inspector!"

The torch beam picked out broken ground . . . raw
earth mixed with decayed leaves where the top surface had
been turned over. A patch about eighteen inches square. The
others clustered around to study the discovery.

"Well," snapped Frost, his hands deep in his pockets for
warmth, "it won't get any bloody bigger by looking at it. Get
digging!"

"Hardly big enough for a grave," ventured the moustached constable.

"It may be small," said Frost, "but it's all we've got."

The man who found it carefully shovelled out loose earth,
the torch, like a stage spotlight, following his every movement.

Frost lost interest. "Just our luck it's some camper's rubbish. If so, you can have my share." The cold had found its
way under the folds of the scarf and was chewing and worrying at his scar. The wind started to keen softly at the back of
its throat and branches rustled.

"I've hit something!" called the digger. Then "Sir!"

Frost spun round. The cigarette fell from his mouth.

The beam of the torch held it fast—yellow, dirt-encrusted, but unmistakable. Poking obscenely through the earth was the skeleton of a human hand.

Frost broke the shocked silence and swore softly. "Just what we bloody-well need!"

The driver dropped to his knees and examined it closely. "It's human, sir."

"Of course it's bloody human. Anyone else would have been lucky enough to get a dead horse or a cow, but I have to get bloody human remains."

The earth was too hard for shovels so one of the constables was sent back to the van for some pickaxes, and also to radio Search Control to tell them that the spirits had given a false lead so far as Tracey Uphill was concerned.

In the distance the sound of a car pulling up, then approaching voices, one of them a woman's—Clive Barnard and WPC Hazel Page.

"Hello, sir—found something?" asked Clive.

"A hand," said Frost. "Why—have you lost one?"

The men moved out of the way so the newcomers could view the discovery.

"Well, if you've finished admiring it," said Frost, "what did auntie have to say?"

Clive paused for a moment to heighten the dramatic effect of his bombshell. "Farnham hasn't been to his aunt's for at least three weeks and he wasn't there Sunday."

Frost lit another cigarette. "I knew he was a liar the minute I saw him. You never can trust randy sods—present company excepted, of course."

"Shall I bring him in, sir?"

Frost considered, then shook his head. "Let him sweat until tomorrow. I'm more interested in old Mother Wendle. How did she know something was buried here?"

"She's a clairvoyant, sir."

"If the lady wasn't here, I'd say 'shit,'" snapped Frost. "I don't believe in ghosts and I don't believe in Father Christmas. She knew it was here and I want to know how she knew."

A crashing and a cursing as the policeman bringing the picks slipped and fell. He limped towards them and shared out the tools, then told the inspector that Control was sending a doctor and an ambulance.

"A doctor?" said Frost, nearly losing another cigarette. "Oh, yes, we're not supposed to presume death are we? We're so bloody thick we don't know a dead body when we see one. All right, lads, get his chest uncovered . . . the doctor might want to use his stethoscope."

It was hard going, even with the pickaxes, as they had to chip away carefully to avoid disturbing the position of the bones.

"Who do you think it was, sir?" asked Hazel.

"Probably some old tramp who crawled here to die years ago. No relatives, no-one's missed him, but we're going to have all the bother of trying to find out who he was."

Hazel tucked her head deeper into her greatcoat collar. "It'll be difficult to discover the cause of death now, sir."

Frost nodded. "You're right, love. The police surgeon likes a lot more meat on a corpse than we've got here. Which reminds me, did I ever tell you about the time we had to get the body of this fat woman out of the house? She'd died in her bath—stark naked she was and—"

Clive cut in quickly before another doubtful story was launched. The inspector was forgetting a lady was present.

"If death was natural causes, sir, who buried him?"

Something soft fluttered down and wetly kissed the inspector's cheek. It was snowing again. He asked Hazel to return to the van and radio Control to send the marquee used that morning for the dragging party. Then he remembered he hadn't answered Clive's question.

"Who buried him? No-one, I'd say, son—leaves and mould naturally built up over him. No-one comes near this part of the woods. It's got an unsavoury reputation, like the toilets in the High Street."

"But surely someone must have come across it," Clive persisted. "I mean . . . a dead body!"

"We're not nosey down here, you know—not like you lot in London. And don't forget, he'd be stinking to high heaven after a few days—enough to put anyone off who wasn't frightened of the snakes already. People would have thought he was a dead animal and kept clear."

The earth, loosened by the pickaxe, was being gently scraped away. A cry from the constable sent Frost running over again. "What do you make of this, sir?"

Frost made nothing of it. Encircling the wrist was a band of metal to which was fastened a length of steel chain. The other end of the chain buried itself deeply in the rock-hard earth and no amount of pulling would prise it free.

And then, something even more puzzling. By scraping away the earth, more and more of the arm bone was uncovered, but then, before the elbow was reached, the arm just stopped.

They didn't have a complete skeleton. Just a hand, part of an arm, and the metal wristband . . . and the chain.

Frost decided that animals must have dragged the arm away from the rest of the body and his diggers were spread out over a wider area to prospect for the remainder.

The snow was falling in great white fluffy flakes and would soon cover the excavation. A distant car door slammed and they hoped it was the promised marquee, but the approaching light bobbing along the path was carried by Dr. McKenzie, the little tubby police surgeon.

"Who's in charge here? Oh—it's you, Inspector Frost. I should have guessed. If you had to find a body in a Godforsaken hole like this, did it have to be during a snowstorm?" He wiped the snow from his glasses and peered down at the excavated arm, then shook his head solemnly. "You've called me too late, I'm afraid . . . a few minutes earlier and I could have saved him."

"I tried to give it the kiss of life," remarked Frost, dryly, "but it stuck its fingers up my nose. Well, come on, Doc— time of death?"

The doctor licked a flake of snow from his nose. "You know as well as I do, Jack . . . years . . . ten, twenty, perhaps longer. You'll need a pathologist."

Frost held the doctor by one arm and led him out of earshot of the others. "Do we really need a pathologist, Doc? Couldn't you just say he died of natural causes and let it go at that? Honestly, I've enough work to keep me going for a month, even if I applied myself—which I rarely do. I don't want to be sodding about with this ancient relic." He offered the doctor a cigarette as a bribe.

Grunts and clangs as pickaxes bit. The doctor accepted a light. "I couldn't say natural causes, Jack—for one thing, how do you explain the chain attached to the wrist? In any case to tell you anything definite I'd need a darn sight more than half an arm. It'll require all sorts of tests and soil analysis. Your forensic boys will take it in their stride. I'm only a GP. If it's not broken bones or constipation I'm out of my depth. I give a letter for a specialist, and that's what you want —a specialist." He coughed with the cigarette still in his mouth, spraying the inspector with hot ash. "I'm off home. I'll let you have my report."

"What report?" demanded Frost. "You haven't even examined it."

But the doctor was already moving off. "You want the pathologist. Besides, it's snowing and he's paid a lot more than I am."

Frost swore silently at a man who would desert him after accepting one of his cigarettes. There was a cry from the moustached PC. He'd found what looked like the rest of the skeleton. It was some eight feet away from the hand. Clive was sent running back to the radio car to ask for a pathologist. Halfway there he met the men bringing the marquee.

By the time the pathologist and the forensic team turned up, the marquee had been erected and the canvas was flapping with sounds like rifle-shots, as the wind searched it out for weaknesses.

The pathologist, tall and cadaverous in a long black overcoat, had brought his medical secretary along—a faded, puffy-eyed beauty, who recorded her master's comments in the loops and angles of Pitman's shorthand. The pathologist seemed to find the wristband and chain more interesting than the human remains.

"I'd like to know what's on the other end of that chain, Inspector."

A busy beaver from Forensic got to work and began scraping away with practised, economical movements, until enough chain was uncovered to permit a firm grip to be taken. He pulled. The earth released another three feet of chain, then held the rest fast. More patient scratching with a trowel, then some work with a pickaxe.

The end of the chain was fastened to a metal box, about 2'6" × 1'6" × 4" deep.

Frost plucked the pathologist's sleeve. He thought he knew what it was.

"Could he have been here since the war, Doc?"

The great man winced at the "Doc." "Possibly, Inspector. But I've done no tests yet so anything is a possibility until proved otherwise. Why do you ask?"

"I think I know what that thing is. It's a sort of metal attaché case. They were used during the war for confidential dispatches, chained to the courier's wrist. We had some plane crashes here during the Blitz—British and German. Could he have been thrown—or fallen—from a plane blowing up in the air, perhaps?"

The pathologist pushed his lower lip into his mouth and sucked hard. "Again—possible. There's no telling how long the remains have been here." He dropped on one knee and scraped some dirt away from a rib. "If he fell you'd expect to find broken bones, but until we can get some of this encrusted dirt off . . ." He stood, rubbing the tips of his fingers. "When it's completely uncovered and photographed I'll have it moved to the crime lab for a thorough examination. I'll be able to give you facts then instead of theories. Oh—and I'd like all the surrounding earth crated up and sent for tests."

"All of it?" asked Frost.

"Well—where the arm and the rest of the skeleton have been lying, down to a depth of about three feet."

The inspector's cigarette dropped. "That's going to take some digging, Doc."

"Yes," agreed the great man, drawing on his gloves, "but it's necessary. Oh, and you might let me have a complete list, with dates, of all the air crashes that occurred in this vicinity during the war years."

"Certainly, Doc," said Frost, wondering where the hell he could obtain useless information like that. He gave orders for the earth to be crated, then quickly tiptoed out with Clive before the pathologist could think of any more stupid jobs.

The wind hurled handfuls of snow at them as they trudged back to the car, where Hazel was waiting. There had been calls galore for the inspector, she reported. Would he report back?

"Control here, Inspector. Can you return to the station at once, please? The Divisional Commander wishes to see you urgently."

Frost groaned. Gawd, he thought, what have I done wrong now?

Mullett was boiling with rage. He couldn't wait for Frost to close the door behind him before he started.

"I found this on your desk, Inspector," and he held up the envelope containing the crime statistics. Frost looked at it with horror, then dropped wearily into a chair and swore to himself as vehemently as Mullett was shouting at him. The bloody crime statistics! In the ecstasy of getting the sodding things completed last night, he'd completely forgotten to post them off . . . nosey bastard had to find them on his desk . . .

Mullett was beside himself. He, the Divisional Commander, had made a promise to County, had instructed Frost that the statistics must go off, and now he had to bear the odious, stinging humiliation of being shown incapable of getting his own men to carry out a specific order.

Frost half closed his eyes and let the scalding tirade wash

over him. Didn't the bloody tailor's dummy have better things to do than poke his ugly nose in other people's desks? And if he was so bloody clever, how come he didn't know who had smashed the rear of his car?

A timid tap at the door halted the lashing tongue in mid-invective, and Miss Smith looked in to wish the commander goodnight. No need to look at the clock—the hands would be quivering at 6:10 exactly. Mullett snatched up the envelope and handed it to her. "As Inspector Frost is incapable of obeying the simplest order, perhaps you would kindly drop this in the County postbag on your way out." Frost blew her a kiss behind the commander's back and she scuttled out with a brick-red face.

Mullett returned to the attack. "I also happened to notice, Inspector, that the file for the electronics theft case was still on your desk. As far as I can see, you've made no progress on it."

You had a bloody good look round, thought Frost. Aloud he said, "I'll get around to it when I find time, Super."

"Make time, Inspector, it's urgent. Now what happened at Dead Man's Hollow? I promised to ring the Chief Constable." His face darkened with annoyance as he was told about the skeleton. "We could have done without this," he snapped, as if it was all Frost's fault.

"If you like I could stick it back again and we can dig it up when things get slack," said Frost, adding, "do you want me any more?" He pre-empted Mullett's reply by pushing up out of his chair.

"Anything further from the kidnapper?"

"I haven't looked in on Search Control yet. I came straight here when I got your message—at the time I thought it was urgent."

And he was gone before Mullett could think of a suitable rebuke.

All was peace, calm, and orderliness in Search Control. The odd telephone rang apologetically and a few routine messages purred from the loudspeaker. Frost wandered over to George Martin who was rearranging schedules for the following day in case the weather worsened.

"All quiet, Jack. We had a couple of teams searching the uncompleted section of the new Burghley Estate, but they found nothing."

"Then they had more luck than I had," said Frost. "What about the phone tap?"

"Dead quiet."

"Are we still watching that phone box?"

"Yes."

"Heard about my bloody skeleton?"

Martin laughed. He had heard. Then he turned his head away as if he was embarrassed about something. "Have you had a word with Johnnie Johnson?"

"No, why?"

"He—er—wanted to see you."

And Frost knew there was more trouble.

He was queuing for tea in the canteen when he spotted the handlebar moustache at a table in the far corner. He took his cup and ambled over.

"Hello, Johnnie."

"Hello, Jack—sit down." Yes, definitely trouble. The sergeant wasn't meeting his eye. Johnnie stirred his tea deliberately, then, "What was that business this afternoon with young Stringer?"

"Oh . . . a private chat, Johnnie, nothing that would interest you. Is that what you wanted to talk about?"

"No, Jack." He pushed his tea to one side. "Did the CID overtime return go off to County last night?"

Frost froze, the cup an inch from his lips. "Oh God!"

"For Heaven's sake, Jack, it's the second month running. I phoned County this evening to check. It hadn't arrived. They had to make special arrangements to get your men's overtime paid last month—had to get someone in specially to feed the figures to the computer at three o'clock in the morning. They said they'd never do it again."

Frost rubbed a weary hand over his face. His scar was hurting. "You know how good I am with paperwork, Johnnie. It was different before, I used to pass all the overtime claims through without checking—I trust everyone—but that silly sod Davidson at HQ found out and I got a rollocking. Now I'm supposed to check each and every one, but it takes time."

Johnson took out his tobacco pouch. "But you've had time, Jack."

"All right—but it's not a job I like doing," and his head whirled as he thought of all the other jobs he had left undone for the same reason. "I suppose they wouldn't like two lots next month?"

Johnnie Johnson lit his homemade cigarette. "They wouldn't, Jack, and you can't blame them. The men have already missed two months this year because you forgot to send off the forms and it's not fair they should have to suffer. They work all hours and they don't do it for charity. Besides," and he looked away, "there's been an official complaint."

Frost flinched as if he had been struck. "Who to?"

"To me, Jack. I'm the Police Federation man."

"Am I such a shit they couldn't come to me?"

Johnnie shook his head. "The opposite, Jack. They like you too much and you would have joked your way out of it and they wouldn't have got their money." His cigarette wasn't drawing well and he had to suck hard to keep it lit. "As it's been made official, I'm taking it up with Divisional Commander tomorrow morning," and he studied the scanty Christmas decorations hanging from the rafters.

Frost spoke quietly with the barest hint of pleading. "You'd be the answer to his prayers, Johnnie. He's just waiting for a legitimate excuse to bounce me."

The sergeant stood up. "I had to tell you first, Jack. I couldn't do it behind your back." He hesitated, then gripped Frost's shoulder tightly. "Sorry, Jack . . ." and was gone.

Frost buttoned his coat. It was cold in the canteen. He sighed. All he seemed to do these days was stagger from one crisis to the next. Overhead, the PA system cleared its throat and asked Inspector Frost to go to the nearest telephone.

Clive Barnard, sharing a table with Hazel, heard the message and saw the inspector leave. He pressed the key of his digs in her hand and rose to follow the inspector. "I'll probably be late, but wait for me. Promise?"

He found Frost on the phone outside the canteen and waited until he had finished. Frost grunted, scribbled some hieroglyphics on the back of the telephone directory, then hung up.

"That was Forensic, son. They've sifted through the crates of earth and found some coins from our skeleton's pockets. The latest coins were dated 1951, so we can forget about his being killed in the war. They've also cut open the steel case chained to his wrist and it contained absolutely sod all. So what was he doing with an empty steel case double-locked to his wrist?"

"Perhaps whatever was in the case had been delivered," suggested Clive.

"Possible, son, but then you'd have thought they would have unlocked the case from his wrist." He rasped his chin thoughtfully, "1951! Festival of Britain year. We really went to town here, then—the toilets stayed open an extra half-hour and the Town Hall flagpole was illuminated weekends." His mind clicked back to the present. "When's this bloody kidnapper going to phone again? I hope he realizes he's sodding us all up." He clattered off down the stairs back to his office and Clive had to hurry to keep up.

Frost chucked himself in his chair and riffled the papers on his desk. A couple more Christmas cards had arrived and there was the electronics theft folder with a note from Mullett attached: "Please treat this as urgent." He dug deeper and found the overtime return which he quickly checked and initialled, but what was the point? It was too late. The computers at County HQ were kept going on a twenty-four-hour-a-day basis doing work mainly for the county council, but a few hours each month the police were allowed to squeeze their business in, and the allotted time for wages was this morning. He slipped the return in an envelope and stuck it in his jacket pocket. He'd bung it in the postbox. Too late for this month, but at least it would be out of the office. He dreaded facing Mullett again in the morning.

"Everything I touch goes wrong," he announced to Clive, who was surprised at the self-pity from a man who gave the impression that nothing on earth could get him down. Clive accepted a cigarette and they lit up.

"I'll tell you something," continued Frost, confidentially, "something I've told no-one. This tin medal of mine—" he opened his drawer and took the medal out "—do you know why I tackled that gunman? I wanted to get myself killed, that's why. I didn't want to live. It's not a joke, son, I'm being serious for a change. They'd just told me, that day, that my wife had cancer . . . that she'd only last a few months and was going to have a bloody rotten death. That nut-case with the gun was the answer to my prayers. I thought, 'Sod it, I don't care if I live or die, so let's die a bloody hero.' So he fired, and he missed—he was as useless as I am—and I couldn't even get myself killed properly." Then suddenly, in a puff of expelled smoke, the black mood was gone. "I'm a morbid bugger, aren't I? Come on, son, let's go to Search Control and find out the latest on the kid."

Turning the corner at the top of the corridor they bumped into a police dispatch rider, crash-helmeted and water-proofed, his goggles rimmed with unmelted snow.

"Divisional Commander's Office?" he asked. "I've an urgent package to pick up for Statistical Department."

Frost directed him, then as an afterthought asked, "Are you going back to County Headquarters tonight?"

"Yes, sir."

"Do us a turn, would you?" He fumbled in his pocket for the overtime return envelope. "Drop this in Accounts. It's the overtime return . . . should have been in this morning."

The dispatch rider slid the envelope into a leather pouch. "You'll be all right, Inspector. They're all behind in Accounts —half of them down with flu. They won't be doing the police wages until tomorrow night."

Frost almost sweated as warm relief flooded his body. "I

may sod up a lot of things," he told Clive, "but I have much more luck than anyone's entitled to expect."

In Search Control, the feeling of standing down. Time to file stuff away and tidy up desks. A photograph of Tracey had been shown on the television news and people had been phoning in all day to report seeing her in London, Cornwall, Dover, on a lorry heading up the M1 motorway, in a café in Leeds with a Pakistani, outside a cinema in Bromley . . . everywhere but in Denton. All well-meaning but probably useless leads, each of which had to be followed up, fortunately mainly by other police divisions who had been sent details by teleprinter.

A phone rang. An agitated Mrs. Uphill, concerned that the alleged kidnapper hadn't been back to her. Frost calmed her down and told her it was important she keep off the phone so the man could make contact. She hung up immediately. Then it occurred to Frost that she had two thousand pounds lying around loose and if the man didn't have Tracey, his intention might be to break into the house and steal the money. He phoned back to tell her to bolt all doors and windows and not to let anyone in.

"As robbery could be the motive, shouldn't we have someone watching the house?" asked George Martin.

"I daren't frighten him off in case it's genuine, George," Frost said. "Don't forget he's threatened to kill the kid if Mrs. Uphill contacts the police."

Forensic phoned. Could Frost get over to the lab right away? Something interesting.

"You'll remember to switch your radio on, sir, so we can get in touch with you?" asked the detective sergeant.

"Of course," said Frost, in feigned surprise, "don't I always?"

In the lobby Johnnie Johnson was taking details of a driving licence and insurance certificate from a truculent youth in a brown leather jacket. Frost nipped over and whispered a few words, telling him about the overtime return.

Johnnie put down his pen and looked at Frost in joyful disbelief. "You jammy old bastard," he said.

It was a cold, slithery ten-mile drive to the county forensic laboratory. The weather had worsened and they passed two cars abandoned in drifts.

The laboratory, a modern, single-storied building, stuck in the middle of nowhere, welcomed them with the warm antiseptic breath of its hot-air system as they trampled slush over the two-tone grey carpet tiles in the reception area and walked past an unmanned mahogany counter draped with potted plants. There were two old friends on the wall, the poster identifying the Colorado Beetle and a Foot and Mouth Disease Movement restriction order which made them feel at home in alien surroundings.

They followed a dimly lit corridor to swing doors, through which they found the laboratory proper. Frigid bluish-white fluorescent lighting glared down on the pathologist and three white-coated assistants who were crouching busily over a long bench.

The pathologist beckoned them over and led them to a table draped with thick polythene sheeting on which lay the completed jigsaw puzzle of the skeleton, the gaping eye-sockets staring blindly into the white fluorescent sun.

"He's cleaned up nicely, hasn't he?" said the pathologist proudly, scraping a blob of dirt from the lower jaw. "Have a look at this," and he picked up the remains of the lower right arm. "This wasn't broken or chewed off by animals. It was deliberately hacked off—apparently with an axe."

"Hacked off?" exclaimed Frost.

"Precisely. There can be no doubt."

"Before or after death?"

The pathologist stroked the bone with loving care. "We can only guess, but I'd hazard shortly after death, before serious decomposition took place. It's only a theory, of course, but my guess is that the arm was severed in an attempt to remove the chained case."

"But it was still on the arm," Frost pointed out.

"Agreed. Whoever chopped it, chopped too high up and wouldn't have been able to slide the metal wrist band over the severed end. The victim was probably fleshy and a little fat. You try and drag your wristwatch up your arm, you'll find it gets stuck half-way."

"Why cut off the arm to remove a locked and empty case?" asked Frost.

"You're the detective, not me," replied the pathologist, scratching his chin with the severed bone before carefully replacing it in its allotted place. "But you've missed the best bit—look," and he pointed to the skull. It was so obvious that at first Frost missed it, then he and Clive saw it at the same time.

"Good God!"

The skull had a third eye smack in the middle of its forehead. The third eye was small, neat, and precision drilled.

"This is what made the hole," said the pathologist, and he dropped a small transparent envelope containing a dull mess of flattened metal into Frost's palm. "It's a revolver bullet. We found it inside the skull, mixed up with the dirt."

Frost held the envelope to the light and examined the discoloured metal from all angles. "So this is what killed him, Doc?"

But the pathologist wasn't going to be led into saying anything definite. "All I can say after all this time is that if he was alive when this bullet was fired at him, then this is what killed him. I can find no other cause of death. We're having the soil analysed, but after all these years . . ." He finished the sentence with a hopeless shrug, then led them to a side bench where a bald man was scraping away at bits of rusty metal.

"Show the inspector the other things we found, Arnold."

Arnold was only too happy to oblige. "Nothing spectacular, I'm afraid, Mr. Frost. Everything rottable had rotted, so all we're left with are metal objects. For example, these metal trouser buttons. No zips, of course—men didn't trust zips back in the 1950s."

"I don't trust them now," said Frost. "I had an unfortunate experience. That's when you reckon he died, then—1950s?"

Arnold nodded. "We're doing more tests, but everything points that way." He raked among the rest of the deceased's effects and found a flat, round pitted object. "This is what's left of his wristwatch. A cheap pallet movement, probably pre-war. Over there is the money, which you know about, and there's these . . ." He rattled a crusted keyring containing two small desk keys, a larger key, and a flat Yale key, all in surprisingly good condition. And that was all the skeleton had to show for itself.

"No car keys," Clive pointed out.

"Not an awful lot of private cars about in the fifties," said Arnold. "Petrol rationing was still on, I think."

Frost spotted a tiny heap of rusty crumbs. "What are they?"

"Remains of cobblers' tacks from his shoes. They used to nail the soles on in those days."

Frost dug his hands in his pockets and stared for a moment at the pathetic piles of scrap, then turned and regarded the bones stretched out on the polythene sheeting. "So what do we know about him? He was shot, he had a few bob in his pocket, he buttoned up his fly, and he died more than thirty years ago. Not much to go on. Any special features, Doc, that would help us identify him, like a ten-foot dick or eight fingers on each hand?"

The pathologist gritted his teeth. "I can't give you much, Inspector. He was between thirty-five and forty, he'd had extensive dental work carried out on his teeth . . ."

"That's the best place to have it carried out," observed Frost, ignoring the withering glance.

"If I may continue . . . He broke his left arm about five years before he died. If you look carefully you can see the line of the fracture. That's all I've got at the moment."

"The case," prompted Arnold.

"Ah yes . . . I was forgetting. We've paid a lot of attention to the case chained to his wrist. It was very strong and obviously specially made for the job—the sort of thing cashiers use for carting large sums of money about. We managed to read the maker's name on the lock—Smith-Curtis—they used to specialize in safes and strongboxes and things."

"Used to?" asked the inspector, warily.

"They went out of business in 1955, so no help there, I'm afraid. By the way, how is Inspector Allen? I was very sorry to learn of his illness."

"Not half so bloody sorry as I am now," replied Frost.

TUESDAY (5)

It was as if he had the power to provoke reaction. The minute Frost walked in to Search Control, the previously dumb loudspeaker monitoring Mrs. Uphill's phone gave a little click and the spool of the tape recorder began to revolve. Someone was dialling her number.

Brr . . . brr . . . Brr—She answered it on the third ring.

"Remember me?"

Everyone in the room stiffened and held his breath. It was the kidnapper. Frost hissed for Barnard to ring Control on the internal and ask if Charlie Alpha two could see anyone.

"Yes," said Mrs. Uphill, "I remember you. How is Tracey?"

"Her cold's a little worse, I'm afraid. There's no heat where she is, you see, but if you get her home tonight, I think she should live."

Charlie Alpha two had the phone box in clear view. It was empty.

"Damn," snapped Frost, "he's found another one. Let's hope the GPO can trace it in time."

"Please," said the loudspeaker, "I want her back. I'll do anything."

"You only have to do what you're told . . . but do it to the letter. I'm saying it once and once only. Put the money in a carrier bag, then go for a walk down the Bath Road towards Exham."

"I've got a car. I'll go by car."

"You will walk . . . do you understand? Walk on the left-hand side. Just past the antique shop there's a public call box. Wait there for my call. I'll give you further instructions."

A click and the death rattle of the dial tone.

The office phone rang. It was the telephone engineers. Very sorry, but they hadn't been able to trace the call. They were told to monitor the call box outside the antique shop. Frost yelled across for George Martin to get Mrs. Uphill on her phone before she left, then he spun round and ordered Clive to ask Control to send Charlie Alpha two tearing round to the other phone box to wait for Mrs. Uphill. Immediately she received the kidnapper's fresh instructions they were to radio them back to Control.

Frost leaned back in his chair, happy. This is what he could understand, this is what he could do. Action. But something was wrong. George Martin, the phone pressed to his ear, was drumming impatient fingers on his desk.

"Mrs. Uphill isn't answering, Jack."

"You sure you got the right number?"

In reply the detective sergeant leaned over and turned up the volume of the monitor speaker. The ringing tone of his call roared out. He hung up and the ringing tone was replaced by the dial tone.

"All right, turn it down. You've made your point. Couldn't the stupid cow have waited a minute?"

Barnard, his shoulder hunched to hold the internal phone to his ear, called across. "Message from Charlie Alpha two, sir. They're at the new phone box and are waiting for Mrs. Uphill to arrive."

Frost acknowledged with a nod.

George Martin thumbed some tobacco in his pipe. "We should have someone following her, sir."

"She's on foot," retorted Frost, "and she's going up Bath Road which is as straight as a bloody die. Anyone following would be spotted a mile off. If this bloke's keeping tabs on her, we'd frighten him away. Apart from that, I didn't bloody-well think of it." He yawned and offered round his cigarettes. Everyone who smoked took one to relieve the tension and the room was soon blue-hazed. No-one spoke. The clock ticked. All eyes were on Barnard who was waiting for Control to pass the message from Charlie Alpha that Mrs. Uphill had reached them.

Frost found his chair suddenly hard. He stood and stretched wearily, then looked out of the window. It was snowing again. He flicked ash into the wastepaper basket.

"What was that? Control?"

All eyes swivelled to Clive. They saw him nod, then ease the phone from his ear. "Charlie Alpha, sir—nothing to report."

"Then tell them not to be so bloody efficient. I'm not interested in nothing!"

The minute hand on the hall clock clunked round to the next division.

The warning buzzer sounded in the inspector's brain.

"Something's gone wrong. She should have reached there by now."

Martin tried to reassure him. "You can't walk very quickly in this snow, Jack—especially in heels."

"She won't give a sod about high heels," snapped Frost. "She'd run to get her kid back . . . she'd run." He paced up and down, kicking at imaginary balls. The minute hand on the wall clock clunked relentlessly on.

"She's had time to walk all the way to bloody Bath and back by now. Are you sure those two bright herberts are waiting at the right phone box?"

Barnard relayed the query to Control and then reported the reply back to Frost. Charlie Alpha two was waiting in a side road near the phone box by the antique shop. They could see some way down the Bath Road. There was no sign of Mrs. Uphill.

Frost phoned her house again. It was just possible she had returned for something. *Brr . . . brr . . .* The speaker relayed the sad, lonely sound a phone makes when it isn't going to be answered. He thumped the receiver down. "I remember phoning a girl once . . ."

But the anecdote was left untold. The hairy face of the station sergeant poked round the door.

"Excuse me butting in, Inspector, but you've got Charlie Alpha two standing by on Bath Road, haven't you?

"Yes, Johnnie—why?"

"We've just had a motorist phone in. He's found a woman unconscious at the side of the road. We've sent for an ambulance, but Charlie Alpha could be there in a couple of seconds and I'd like them to get some details."

The silence was electric. Everyone in the room was thinking . . . fearing . . . the same thing.

"Yes—tell Control it's all right, and say that Charlie Alpha has got to wait for me. Come on, son!" Clive prided himself on his fitness but had a job keeping up with the older man charging across the car park in the snow. By the time Clive had reached the car, Frost had already started up the engine, but he moved to let his detective constable take the wheel.

"Which way, sir?"

"Just follow that ambulance."

The flashing blue light led them through the darkness like a frantic Pied Piper, hurling round corners, ignoring traffic signals. And then, ahead, another flashing blue light. Charlie Alpha. They skidded to a snow-spraying halt, just avoiding running into the back of the ambulance whose brakes were better than Frost's. A police constable, bending over a shape on the ground covered by a police greatcoat, straightened up as the ambulance men ran over with their stretcher and thick red blanket. They moved so quickly, they were sliding the laden stretcher into the back of the ambulance before Frost and Barnard could reach them. The inspector yelled for them to stop and pulled the blanket from the face. It was Mrs. Uphill. Eyes closed, face chalk white, looking about fifteen years old.

"How is she?"

"She's had a nasty wallop on the head. Don't think the skull's fractured, though. Lucky that chap found her, otherwise she could have frozen to death."

The man, wearing a sheepskin motoring coat, was leaning against a yellow Escort and was being questioned by a policeman.

The rear doors of the ambulance clunked shut and its flashing blue light dwindled to a pinprick along the straight-as-a-die Bath Road.

Clive bent and picked up something from the ground. It was Mrs. Uphill's handbag. Frost opened it and flashed his torch inside. The usual female bric-a-brac, but the change purse that should have been there was missing. Clive was detailed to search the vicinity for the two thousand pounds in the carrier bag, not that Frost had any hopes it would be found.

The man in the sheepskin coat had just finished giving details to the police constable as Frost sauntered over and introduced himself.

"You didn't see anything then, sir?" Frost asked the man when the constable had filled him in.

"No. I just saw her lying there—my headlights picked her out. I thought she'd been knocked down by a hit-and-run. I phoned and waited for your chaps, but I didn't really expect I'd have to stand here and answer all these questions. I've got an urgent appointment and I'm late now."

Frost sympathized with him. "It's usually the way when you try and help, isn't it, sir? Makes us all the more grateful when, in spite of it all, the public still bothers to assist us. You've got the gentleman's particulars, Constable?"

The police driver handed him the man's driving licence. Frost flipped through it; it was all in order. Barnard returned from his search and gave the thumbs-down sign.

"You didn't spot a carrier bag, I suppose, sir?" asked Frost on the off-chance.

The man shook his head emphatically. "I'm afraid I can't help you any more." His hand moved to the door handle.

"Just before you go, sir, do you think we could take a look in the boot of the car?"

"The boot? Look—I just stopped to report an accident."

"Won't take a minute, sir. There's some money missing and my superior would take it amiss if I deviated from my usual high standards and let a car go off unsearched. If I could have the keys, sir . . ." He held out a demanding hand. The keyring was thrown into it.

Frost opened the boot and switched on his torch. "Be over in a flash, sir, I—" And then Frost paused, at a loss for words. The boot was full of small, expensive electronic calculating machines of the type reported stolen from Buskin's Electronics on the Factory Estate. The case inherited from Inspector Allen. The case that Mullett had ordered him to treat as urgent. A quick radio call to Control confirmed that the serial numbers tallied.

The inspector sighed at the thought of all the paperwork this would involve. "On any other day I'd have been overjoyed to have copped you, sir. Why did it have to be tonight?"

"What rotten stinking luck," snarled the man bitterly. "I could have driven straight past . . . left her there to die and got away with it."

"You couldn't, sir," said Frost, softly, "you're not that sort of person. You're very much like me. We do the right thing and get ourselves into trouble. You wouldn't have a cigarette on you by any chance, would you?"

Frost pressed down his stapler and impaled details of the evening's arrest in a prominent position on the front of the Electronics Theft file which he proudly dumped, with a two-fingered salute, on the Divisional Commander's barren desk. That would wipe the smile off Mullett's face when he came in the next morning.

What to do now? Barnard was still at the hospital waiting for Mrs. Uphill to regain consciousness, and no-one had time for a chat as they were all busy clearing their desks ready for the next shift to take over at 10:00 p.m.

Sounds of a commotion in the lobby promised a welcome diversion and he followed the unintelligible swearing, grunts, and calls for assistance to find young Keith Stringer struggling with a fat drunken Irishman from the local building site who'd apparently staggered out of a pub, slipped in the snow, and broken a leg, and had then dragged himself through the slush to the station where he demanded immediate medical attention and flailed his fists at anyone who tried to get near. As Frost arrived the man was sprawled on the lobby floor, his hands locked round Stringer's legs, trying to crash him down.

Frost ambled over and kicked the labourer's hands away. Small, red-rimmed pig's eyes squinted up with unveiled hatred and the slobbering mouth spewed mindless obscenities. The inspector lit a cigarette and looked down with disgust. The man's clothes were filthy and sodden and at some stage he had been sick down his coat. He stank of whisky, vomit, and blind hatred. Anaesthetized by drink, the man felt no pain from the fracture and was able to heave himself up, pulling on Stringer's trouser legs for assistance then, looking slyly apologetic, suddenly swung a meaty fist at Frost which, had it landed, would have felled him. But Frost saw it coming. His foot shot out and hooked round the man's good leg, sending him crashing to the floor with a scream of pain which hinted it hadn't done the broken leg much good.

"What's his beef?" Frost asked Stringer.

"I'll tell you," screamed the Irishman. "He's pinched my wallet."

Oh no! thought Frost, not again, and he turned to Stringer who shook a drawn face in mute denial.

"Fifteen pounds there was in it, sir. Fifteen pounds I had when I came in."

"Shut up!" snapped Frost, steeling himself. He'd have to search the man and the thought of going through the pockets of that sodden jacket churned up his stomach. He wished the Chief Constable's nephew was here so he could give the job to him.

He walked behind the man who followed him with piggy eyes screwed up to keep him in focus. What a ghastly sight, the enormous seat spread over the floor, the back seam of the trousers gaping where the thread had given up the struggle to contain the vast, flabby girth. And then Frost's eyes narrowed and he spotted a fat bulge in the back pocket.

"Is this your wallet, Paddy?"

The man squinted suspiciously at the brown leather object dangled in front of his face, then something like a smile revealed black stumps.

"Well . . . and how did that get there? I never keep it in my back pocket."

Frost opened it and flipped through the thin wad of notes. "Fifteen . . . All right, you drunken sod, count them."

"No need, sir, if you say they're all there . . ."

Frost's foot swung back threateningly. "Count them, you sod."

"Yes, sir, of course, sir, all there, sir. Thank you, thank you . . ."

The young constable expelled an audible sigh of relief.

"Right, son, now call the ambulance and see how soon they can get this stinking rat-bag out of here. If he shows his face again, think of a charge and book him. I'll support you."

Stringer suddenly caught sight of someone behind the inspector's back and his face tic-tacked a warning. It was Mullett, resplendent in a beautifully tailored topcoat, white gloves in hand.

"What's going on here?" he asked, coldly.

Seeing a possible ally, a crafty look crossed the drunk's face. "I broke my leg outside, sir, and I've had nothing but abuse since I've been here. And that man kicked me."

Frost caught Stringer's eye and jerked his head towards the phone. The young constable took the hint and slipped off to call the ambulance. The sooner they got the drunk off the premises, the better.

"Bit of a new development with that skeleton, sir," ventured Frost, hoping to change the subject, but Mullett, deeply concerned with an allegation of police brutality towards a poor injured Irishman, waved the inspector to one side and moved forward to question the man on the floor. At which instant the labourer turned a pale shade of green, gulped, and was copiously sick all over Mullett's shoes.

Frost suddenly felt a warm, friendly, loving feeling towards the drunk and wished he'd been kinder. There's good in all of us, he thought, as Mullett scuttled away to clean himself.

The diversion over, Frost returned to his office for a smoke and a bloody good laugh, when his phone summoned him to the old log cabin where Mullett, who had heard about the attack on Mrs. Uphill, proceeded to give him a roasting. How could Frost, an experienced officer, let her go out on her own with all that money? If that wasn't asking for trouble . . .

Frost countered by sniffing repeatedly, staring at Mullett's shoes, and asking if they could have the window open. The bloody man never let a wound heal without grinding half a pound of rough salt into it. Of course he should have had Mrs. Uphill followed, but he couldn't think of everything. He wasn't bloody Gideon of the Yard, he was Detective Inspector Jack Frost, GC, jumped up from being a lousy sergeant to a lousier inspector. He hadn't asked for promotion.

These silent thoughts were stopped from being put into words by the intervention of the telephone. Mullett handed it to him. It was Clive Barnard from the hospital.

Mrs. Uphill had regained consciousness.

"Right," said Frost, "I'm on my way." Then he turned to Mullett. "By the way, sir," he said, trying to sound casual, "I've put the Electronics Theft file on your desk. We caught the bloke tonight."

"Oh yes?" said Mullett, giving it a curt glance and dropping it in his "Out" tray. "One of Inspector Allen's cases, wasn't it? He had it all but tied up before he went sick."

Frost shut the door carefully behind him, then swore loudly, long, and ineffectively into the empty passage.

TUESDAY (6)

As he pushed through the hospital entrance door, it all came back to him. The smells—over-cooked food and disinfectant. The sounds—moans, muffled sobs, hushed worried voices. He'd had them, twice a day, for six months when his wife was slowly dying. The end bed with the screens, and "You can stay as long as you like, Mr. Frost."

Clive Barnard, slumped moodily on a hard wooden bench, rose at the inspector's approach and led him into a side ward where a white-faced Mrs. Uphill, head bandaged, lay propped up on plumped-up pillows. Frost dropped his eyes to the chart clipped at the foot of the bed. Temperature a trifle high, pulse slightly fast. She wasn't too badly damaged.

He gave her an encouraging smile. "They're letting you go home tomorrow, Mrs. Uphill."

Her head sank into the starched depths of the pillow. "I want to go home now. I've got to be there when he phones again."

Frost dragged a small wooden bench from under the bed and sat down. "What makes you think he's going to phone again?"

"He's got the money, now he must tell me where Tracey is. That was the bargain." She struggled up, eyes burning. "She might even be back at the house now, waiting . . ."

"Easy, love, easy . . ." He pushed her down gently, then drew Clive to one side and whispered some instructions. Mrs. Uphill had pointed out something Frost had overlooked. The possibility—the extremely remote possibility—that the alleged kidnapper really did have Tracey and would now return her. Barnard was to contact the station and get them to ensure that Mrs. Uphill's phone was still continually monitored and to arrange that the house was kept under permanent surveillance.

Frost returned to the woman. "We'll be watching your house, monitoring your phone, and taking your calls, so don't worry."

"If the police answer, you'll frighten him off."

"No. One of our women PCs will take the calls. He'll think it's you. Now, tell us what happened."

Her hand plucked at the sheets. "He phoned me. He said—"

Frost cut her short. "We know about the phone call. Go on from there."

"I put the money in a bag, as he said."

"What sort of bag?"

"One of those blue and white plastic carriers from the supermarket. I walked down Vicarage Terrace, then cut through to the Bath Road."

"Were you aware of anyone following or watching you?"

She thought, then shook her head. "No. I don't think so. I just wanted to get to the phone box as quickly as I could. I was afraid he'd ring before I reached it. Halfway down Bath Road I heard a sort of rustling noise behind me, then something hit me." Her hand touched the bandage. "The next thing my head was hurting and I was in here. I don't remember the ambulance or anything."

Frost smiled sympathetically. "Did you have your change purse with you?"

"Yes. It's in my handbag."

"Not any more. He must have helped himself to that as well. What was in it?"

"About twenty pounds in cash, my house keys, and the keys for the car."

The night nurse entered with a sleeping tablet and a glass of water. She glared at Frost, who decided it was time to leave.

Barnard was waiting outside after making his phone call. As they walked down the long corridor to the main entrance, Frost brought him up to date on the interview. "Even nicked twenty quid from her purse. We're not dealing with a kidnapper, son. This is a small-time crook out for anything he can get."

A grim-faced nurse carrying a hypodermic syringe in a kidney bowl brushed past them and pushed through swing doors into a darkened ward where someone was moaning.

Frost averted his eyes and walked much faster. "My wife was in that ward, son. After I'd visited her, I always felt I could do with a drink. There's a little pub round the corner . . ."

It was a cheerful little pub with a crackling log fire and glittering Christmas decorations. There was only one other customer, a small man in a heavy overcoat, drinking at a corner table. Frost warmed himself at the fire, letting the friendly atmosphere unwind him as it had always done after those ghastly visits to the hospital when they kindly told him he could stay as long as he liked. That meant he had no excuse for cutting the visit short. He just had to sit there, with a false smile, nothing to say, sharing her pain, watching her die.

Clive returned with the drinks and Frost's change. "Not a bad little pub this, sir," he remarked. But Frost wasn't listening. He was staring at the corner table. The little man had gone, leaving behind an almost full spirit glass. Frost walked over to the table.

"Did you see him go?"

"Who?" asked Clive.

"Little bloke, sitting here. Couldn't get out fast enough when we came in. Even left his drink." Frost picked up the glass, sniffed the contents, then drank it down in one gulp. "Scotch. And bloody good stuff. See if you can see where he went."

Clive got outside just in time to see the rear lights of a departing car. He returned and told Frost.

Frost shrugged. "Never mind, probably not important. I've got a job for you, son."

"Oh yes?" said Clive, warily.

"Nip out to our car and radio the station. I want all surveillance removed from the Uphill house."

Clive was incredulous. "Removed? But you've only just asked to have it put on."

"I know," said Frost. "I'm afraid I'm having one of my fickle moods at the moment. So hurry up and do it, then wait for me in the car."

Control was equally incredulous. "Are you sure you've got the message right?"

"Of course I'm sure," snapped Clive. "He wants all surveillance removed."

"No disrespect," said Control, "but I think I'd like to hear it from the inspector."

The car door opened. Frost took the handset. "Frost here. I want all surveillance away from the Uphill house, pronto. Up and under, over and out." He returned the handset to Clive and slammed the car door. "Finger out and foot down, son. We're going to Mrs. Uphill's house of pleasure."

As they neared Vicarage Terrace, Frost directed Clive down some back streets and they eventually emerged at a side turning from which they could see No. 29 without being too obvious. The car lights were extinguished. They waited.

"What exactly are we doing here?" asked Clive after five minutes of watching an empty house in an empty street.

"Thought you'd never ask," replied Frost. "While you were radioing through to Control, I got on the blower to the hospital. I wanted to know if anyone had phoned, or called, asking about your lady friend, Mrs. Uphill. And someone had. Guess who?"

"I give up," said Clive, wishing Frost would get to the point.

"A shifty little bloke in a heavy overcoat. He'd called at the Porter's Lodge not fifteen minutes before, asking how poor Mrs. Uphill was and when she'd be coming out."

Clive was unimpressed. "So? It could have been a neighbour."

"And it could have been a client wondering how long he'd have to have the cold showers. But it wasn't. Apart from the police, son, who the hell knew she was in hospital? No, it was our little bloke from the pub. The one who left his whisky. The porter told him she'd be kept in overnight, so off he went."

"I still don't see—" began Clive.

"Her attacker is a cheap crook, son. He's got her change purse and her house keys. He knows the house will be empty all night, so he can just walk in and help himself."

"Then why did you send away the surveillance car?"

"Because I want to catch the little sod, not frighten him off. Duck down, quick. I think this is him."

A light-coloured car cruised to the end of Vicarage Terrace, reversed, and slowly made its way back again. A couple of minutes later the car returned, drove past Mrs. Uphill's, stopping three houses away on the opposite side of the road. For a while nothing happened, then a small man got out carrying a large suitcase. He looked up and down the street, then walked briskly across to No. 29. The sound of a key in a lock, a door opening and quietly closing. He was inside.

Clive's hand reached for the door handle. "Shall we go in and get him?"

But Frost settled back in his seat. "No. He's got to come back to his car, so let's wait for him."

They waited. Frost was on his fourth cigarette. "I spy with my little eye, son," he said. The little man was leaving the house. The suitcase seemed almost too heavy for him as he staggered across the road.

They jumped on him as he was bending to unlock his car door. His yell of surprise roused the sleeping street. Dogs started barking, nervous householders dialled 999. The area car sent to investigate was ordered away by Frost. "Go and find your own crooks."

Their prisoner offered no resistance, but complained bitterly once he had caught his breath. "Frightened the flaming life out of me, Mr. Frost. What a silly thing to do. I've got a weak heart, you know."

"As long as you haven't got a weak bladder," replied Frost. He peered at the man, who apparently knew him.

"So that's who you are. Meet Dapper Dawson, son—housebreaker, petty crook, and con man. What have you got in the suitcase, Dapper?"

"Encyclopedias, Mr. Frost. I'm working my way through college."

The suitcase was packed tight with furs, jewellery, and small valuables from the Uphill house. On the back seat of Dapper's car was a blue and white carrier bag. It was full of used five-pound notes.

They took him back to the station and sat him in the interview room with a cup of tea and one of Frost's cigarettes. He needed no prompting. All they had to do was listen as Dapper's story flooded out to produce a long, four-page statement. He had read about the classic Lindbergh kidnapping where a man had obtained ransom money by pretending he had the Lindbergh baby.

"So I thought I'd try the same. After all, she's only an old bag. What's two grand to her? She can earn that on her back without even getting out of bed. What's up with the bloke with the wonky nose?"

Frost glared at Clive, who should have known better than to react when a suspect was making a statement.

"The kid?" continued Dapper. "Of course I haven't got the kid. Kidnapping's not my style, is it? Search my house if you like. If you find any kids, my old woman's been having it off with the milkman."

They didn't expect to find Tracey at Dapper's house, but an area car investigated just in case. She wasn't there. She had never been there.

Dapper signed his statement, thanked Frost for the cigarette, and was locked up in the cell next to the man in the sheepskin coat.

"We won't have enough cells if you go on like this," commented the station sergeant.

To Frost's regret, Mullett had left for home and wasn't there to witness his moment of triumph. "If it was one of my usual balls-ups, he'd be there sneering from ear to bloody ear," he reflected ruefully. He went back to his office to shuffle some papers about and found Clive waiting hopefully for permission to go home. Hazel would be at his bedsitter, her uniform folded neatly over a chair, her face scrubbed of make-up . . .

"It's 11:15, sir," he announced loudly, looking hard at his watch and yawning.

"What's this?" asked Frost, picking up a scribbled note from his desk. "Sandy Lane, Denton *Echo*, phoned. Wants you to phone him, urgent." Then underneath, in the same hand, "Phoned again, 10:30—extremely urgent—please call."

"11:15 did you say, son? We'll ring him now," and he dialled the newspaper office. A few words with Sandy, then he banged down the phone and sprang from his chair.

"Chuck us my scarf, son. It's definitely my lucky day. Sandy reckons he knows the identity of our skeleton, so come on, you can drive me to his office."

Clive trailed after the inspector to the car park, scuffing the snow peevishly. It was a cold, miserable, and never-ending night and he thought of his warm, cosy flat, the gas-fire popping, Hazel peeling off her microscopic knickers, rubbing her hands sensuously down her thighs. The mental picture forced a groan of frustration as he turned the ignition key.

"What's up?" asked Frost. "Not sickening for anything, are you?"

Sandy Lane squeezed his visitors into his tiny office, a partitioned corner of an open-plan stockade of tightly packed desks, phones, and typewriters.

Frost had to raise his voice over the hammering of typewriters. "So, who's our skeleton, Sandy?"

"You'll read all about it in tomorrow's *Echo*, Jack," said the reporter, dumping a badly smudged proof copy of the following day's paper in front of the two detectives. The black banner headline screamed out at them:

MISSING BANK CLERK FOUND AFTER 32 YEARS.

A sub-heading read: "Echo of £20,000 Bank Robbery,"

followed by another, "Spirit Medium Leads Police to Mysterious Woodland Grave." Then there was a photograph of
Frost, cupid-lipped with a bit more hair than now, captioned,
"Detective Inspector Frost, GC, who is in charge of the
case."

"That picture looks as if *I've* been dug up after thirty-two
years," said Frost.

The rest of the front page was filled with a greatly enlarged
full-face photograph of a sad-looking man with receding hair,
aged about thirty-five. The caption said, simply, "Timothy
Fawcus."

Frost frowned. "Fawcus?" he asked. The name nagged a
memory.

"It's his skeleton," explained Sandy.

"Then tell him to come and claim it, we don't want it."
He opened the page for more clues, but the inside was blank
and unprinted. Then something clicked. Timothy Fawcus!
Of course. He spun round to Clive and explained. "This was
1951, son—before you were born. I'd just joined the Force.
Eighteen I was, sturdy of back and randy as hell—and you
had to fight for it in those days, it didn't come crawling
round to your flat waiting for you." The blood rushed to
Clive's face. How the hell did Frost know?

"Fawcus was a cashier at Bennington's Bank and the case
chained to his wrist held twenty thousand pounds. When he
went missing, all leave was stopped for the search. We looked
everywhere . . . and he was buried in Dead Man's Hollow
all the time." He tapped his scar. "I wonder if they'll dig up
Tracey's skeleton in thirty-odd years' time."

Sandy leaned forward. "You reckon she's dead then,
Jack?"

Frost nodded towards the tall window where outside a
cutting wind screamed and hurled flurries of snow against the
glass. "What do you reckon?" And then he was back again in
the distant past. "Remember the chap in charge of the Fawcus case, Sandy? Inspector Bottomley, as fat as a pig with an
enormous gut; he had to have his trousers specially built."

"What happened with Fawcus?" asked Clive.

It was a simple story. On the twenty-sixth of July, 1951, Fawcus left Denton in the bank's pool car, driven by a junior clerk, Rupert Garwood—their destination, Bennington's Exley branch, some seven miles away—to deliver twenty thousand pounds, locked in a case chained to Fawcus's wrist. The car never arrived at its destination. It was found later that afternoon in a side road well away from the route it should have taken. The junior clerk, Garwood, was slumped across the wheel, unconscious from a savage head injury which left him with no memory of what had happened. Fawcus and the twenty thousand pounds were never seen again.

"I got my first byline on that case," said Sandy, proudly. "It made the London dailies."

"Poor old Fawcus," said Frost, "wrongly accused for all those years and all the time he was decently dead and buried. He had a family, didn't he?"

"A wife," answered the reporter. "Don't know what happened to her, though. Er . . . how was he killed?"

"Shot," Frost tapped his forehead, "through the brain."

Sandy's hand streaked to his internal phone and he jabbed the button marked "Printing Room." "Mac—Sandy here. Hold everything. We're going to tear down the front page. The police say Fawcus was shot." He dropped the phone and fidgeted, obviously anxious to usher them out and get cracking.

"You've given me quite a scoop, Jack."

"You know me," said Frost modestly, "one cheap curry and you've bought my soul. Come on, son."

"Hold on, Jack. The money—it was gone, I suppose?"

Frost smiled sweetly. "Dumb as we are, Sandy boy, if we'd found twenty thousand pounds in the case, we might just about have worked out who he was for ourselves." He went to grab the door handle, but the door retreated as a studious young reporter entered.

"Sorry to butt in, Mr. Lane, but the bank manager refuses to make a statement, and I can't get a reply from Garwood's house."

Frost braked sharply. "Garwood? You mean Rupert Garwood, the kid who was driving the car?"

"Yes," replied Sandy. "He's back at Denton again, didn't you know? He's Assistant Manager at Bennington's Bank."

TUESDAY (7)

Police Sergeant Tom Henderson put down his pen and yawned. He'd never get used to working nights. No matter how much sleep he had during the day, his body still insisted on feeling tired and ready for bed as midnight approached. He wriggled his shoulders in a shiver. It was so cold in the lobby and every time that rotten door opened . . .

His phone rang.

The leather-jacketed youth slumped dejectedly on a wooden bench under the Colorado Beetle poster jerked up a face tight with apprehension.

Henderson listened, said, "No, not yet," and hung up. He looked across to the leather-jacket and shook his head. The youth slouched back and resumed his mindless study of the opposite blank wall.

An icy blast roared across the lobby as Inspector Frost and the new chap with the bent nose came in.

"Hello, Jack."

"Hello, Tom. Here, you didn't shave today, did you?"

Henderson grinned and fingered his new beard, the result of many weeks of careful growing and much rude comment.

Frost caught sight of the youth. "What's up with him?"

Henderson leaned over, keeping his voice low. "He ran an old lady over. She's having an emergency operation and he's waiting for the result. Touch and go, they reckon."

"Oh!" Frost let his eyes slide over the kid. Barely eighteen and worried sick. "His fault, was it?"

The sergeant nodded gravely. "Didn't look where he was going. Staring back at his mates out of the rear window. Never saw her until he hit her, and she was using the crossing."

"Poor little sod," murmured Frost, a rare look of pity on his face.

"Poor, sir?" asked Clive, puzzled.

"Yes, son. I've nearly killed people in my car time and time again . . . it was only luck that saved me. He didn't have the luck."

"And neither did the old lady."

Frost sniffed. "You're hard, son, very hard. I'm sorry for her, but I'm sorry for him, too."

Another roar of cold air and the papers on the desk were sent flying. A big red-faced man in a fur-lined parka thundered in, ready to bellow at the first uniform he saw.

"You! Where's my son?"

"Dad!" The youth didn't turn his head. He spoke to space.

"Come on—you're going home." An angry face thrust at Sergeant Henderson. "I'm taking him. You've no right to keep him here."

"We're not keeping him here, sir," explained the sergeant patiently. "He's free to go. He's given us a statement and we've got all his details."

"Statement?" He turned angrily to the lad. "You bloody fool—a statement? Tell them nothing!" Back to the sergeant. "His statement is invalid. It was made without a solicitor being present. We repudiate it."

The youth tilted his head up to his father and spoke as if explaining to an uncomprehending idiot. "I'm eighteen, Dad. I made the statement of my own free will. I wasn't looking . . . I hit her." His face showed pain at the recollection.

The man's hand slapping his son's face was the crack of a whip.

"Keep your mouth shut, do you hear? I'll tell you what to say."

The phone on the desk rang. The youth, ready with an angry retort, froze. Henderson raised the receiver and listened.

"Henderson. Oh, I see. Yes, thanks for telling me." He replaced the phone with care, then spoke quietly.

"You might as well go home, son. She died five minutes ago."

The boy stared at the sergeant. At first it seemed that the news hadn't sunk in. There was a puzzled frown on his face, a face drained of colour except for the angry mark of the blow on the left cheek. The lip quivered, and then his face crumpled. He cried with body-wracking sobs. His father, now a different man, placed an arm around his shoulder.

"All right, son, all right. We're going home." He led the sobbing youth through the doors and out into the cold white night. The door swung shut behind them.

"As I always say," said Frost, dragging off his scarf, "there's no bloody justice. If he'd kept his mouth shut or lied and said she stepped in front of him without warning, we couldn't have touched him. He's the only witness. But he's been honest. He really cares that he's killed someone. And we'll probably throw the book at him."

Then, trailing his scarf along the ground, he was off along the corridor to his office. With a despairing look at the wall clock whose hands stood vertical at half-past midnight, Clive dashed off after him.

"They knew how to tie knots in 1951," muttered Frost, tearing his nails on the fossilized string tied round the Bennington Bank Robbery—July 1951 file that had been disinterred from the upstairs storeroom. The string broke unexpectedly and yellow-edged papers were disgorged on top of the litter already on the desk. He scooped the papers up, and in doing so uncovered an internal memo from Mullett reminding all staff of the last day for the submission of expense claims, stressing that any received late would be held over until the following month.

Frost passed the file over to Clive and began to scout through his drawers for an expense-claim form.

"Find a description of Fawcus, son, see if it matches in with the skeleton. If he only had one leg, we've got a mystery on our hands."

It was a fat file, the pages smelling stale and musty from their long entombment in the unheated storeroom. Near the front was a photograph of a young man in army uniform, the forage cap perched on top of lots of wavy hair, glistening with brilliantine. Handwritten on the back were the words "To my darling Rose with all my love—Tim," followed by a string of kisses. A typed police label read "Timothy Fawcus— early picture—much balder now." Clive turned the photograph over and looked at the smiling, unworried face. Was this the dirt-encrusted skull prised from the frozen grip of Dead Man's Hollow?

He showed it to Frost.

"I used to have hair like that, son—it drove the girls mad." He read the inscription on the back. "Balder now— me and him both. Who's Rose—his wife?"

"I haven't come to that yet, sir." Digging deeper, Clive unearthed another photograph, the original of the one they had seen earlier on the front page of the Denton *Echo*. A full description was on the back. "Timothy Fawcus, aged 38, height 5'11", weight 12 stone 4 pounds, sallow complexion, receding hairline, dark hair, thin features. Appendix scar. Tattoo on right wrist, 'Rose' in a red heart."

Frost pursed his lips. "The ubiquitous Rose. I hope she doesn't turn out to be a bloody sledge, or something, like in that Orson Welles film."

"*Citizen Kane,* sir—the sledge was called Rosebud."

The inspector chucked his expense claim over for Clive to check the totals. "That description might have been all right at the time, but when your suspect has been rotting in the ground for more than thirty years it doesn't do much for your tattoos and receding hairline. Still, we'll get it over to Forensic, and they can see if it fits."

"What about checking on the broken arm, sir? And there's

the dental chart, of course. If we had that we could compare it with the skull's teeth."

"You're blinding me with science, son. But that'll be your job for tomorrow. Try and trace Fawcus's doctor and dentist. Now what have you found?"

It was a photograph of a young, wide-eyed girl with a Judy Garland hairstyle—Rose Fawcus, the missing man's wife. Her address was shown as No. 172 Longley Road, Denton.

"She won't be there any more," said Frost. "It's being pulled down for the new public library."

The next photograph was of a bright-eyed lad in his teens. The label on the back said, "Rupert Garwood. Junior Clerk, Bennington's Bank." The hospital doctor's report was attached. The skull had been fractured but would mend. Garwood was now back as Assistant Manager, Frost remembered. They'd see him first thing in the morning.

And then he realized they were messing about with this ancient, long-forgotten case which had nothing to do with Tracey Uphill, missing since Sunday. He looked through the window. Outside a muffled figure was walking across the car park, treading gingerly and leaving no footprints. The snow was polished glass, frozen solid. Frost shivered. Continue the search the next morning and if they didn't find the stiff, frozen body then, perhaps they'd find it the following day.

He'd had enough. On with the scarf and overcoat. "Pack it in, son—we're going home."

Clive needed no second bidding. He slammed the file shut and rammed it in a drawer, then cannoned into Frost who had stopped dead.

"Good Lord, son. I've just realized. No wonder we've been so lucky. Do you know what today is? It's my birthday."

And it was . . . at least up to midnight it was. And no-one to remember, no-one to send him a card.

"Many happy returns," said Clive, hoping this didn't mean they couldn't go home.

But Frost was already off on his record-breaking trot along the echoing corridor, pausing to poke his head round the door of Control. "If Detective Sergeant Hanlon radios in for me, bung out a call on my personal radio. I'm off home."

In the lobby, Henderson was taking details from a man whose car had been stolen. He gave them a cheerful wave.

Outside the night was bitter with air so cold it scoured the lungs. Frost took the driving seat, spun the car into a U-turn, and crawled over gleaming ice to the main road.

"Just a short detour, then I'll drop you off, son."

Clive's heart missed a couple of beats. He knew the inspector's short detours. But they didn't go far. Down some side roads leading out of the High Street into a darkened turning without street lights, where Frost halted in front of a black row of blind-windowed terraced houses.

"Longley Road," he announced.

This was where Fawcus had lived back in 1951. Clive looked hard at the houses and realized they were derelict, windows covered with sheets of corrugated iron, heavy planks nailed over doors bearing cryptic messages—Gas Off, Water Off, Electricity Off.

Frost walked up the crumbling steps of No. 172 and peeped through the letterbox into pitch blackness smelling of damp plaster and sodden mattresses.

"No-one at home, son. Still, we've got a key." And he produced from his pocket the keyring found in the earth beneath the skeleton. He poked a key in the lock. A click and the lock mechanism turned, but the door, gripped by six-inch nails, held firm. Frost put the key back in the pocket.

"So it fits, sir," said Clive, trying to sound impressed.

The inspector grinned. He was pleased with himself. "Looks like it, doesn't it, son? So this is where our skeleton lived back in 1951." He looked into the barrenness of the street. "And now he's dead, and the whole bloody street's dead and whoever shot his brains out and chopped off his arm is probably dead." He shrugged and descended the steps. "There used to be a little newspaper shop on that corner where I bought my comics when I was a kid. Now I'm a bloody comic myself."

He dropped Barnard at his digs a little after 2:15 a.m.

"You can have a lie-in tomorrow, son. I won't be round for you until eight o'clock."

Clive staggered to the door, his sleep-weary brain calculating he would be getting less than five and a half hours sleep, if he was lucky. Actually he was going to be very lucky and would get far less sleep than basic mathematics suggested. Frost noticed the bedroom curtains twitch as the car door slammed and caught a brief glimpse of auburn hair and naked flesh.

He sighed. There'd be no-one waiting for him when he got back. His house would be as cold and dead as Longley Road. Gas Off, Electricity Off, Naked Women Off. He remembered he was expecting to hear from Detective Sergeant Hanlon about the bank decoy job, and radioed Control who hadn't any news. The lights went on in Barnard's window. Feeling like a Peeping Tom, Frost saw two shadows merge, then the light went out. That decided him. It is my birthday, he told himself, slamming the car into gear and roaring eastward towards Bath Road, which the Council had newly garnished with salt. He pressed his foot down and the car leaped forward and telegraph poles swished past, his speedometer needle flickering near its limit. That's right, kill yourself on your bloody birthday!

He nearly missed the turn-off. Down the bumpy lane with the car bucking and rearing as it found all the ruts and potholes. Half-way down he stopped and switched off the engine. The house was a black lump where the lane turned, but in spite of the late hour a hopeful light gleamed in a downstairs room.

A moment of indecision, then he was out of the car, head down into the stinging wind, floundering ankle deep in snow. The front gate etched a curved groove when he pushed it and deep footsteps followed him up the path. He jabbed the doorbell. A pause. A woman's voice called, "Who is it?"

"Jack Frost."

"Good God!" Bolts were drawn and the door opened. She was wearing a dressing gown, the glass in her hand half full. "What the hell do you want?"

"Just popped round to day hello," said Frost.

"What? At 2:30 in the morning? Well, you've said it. Now you can pop off home again."

"Oh!" said Frost, crestfallen.

"All right, come in. Quick, before I freeze to death."

He stepped into a hothouse. The front door slammed on the snow, on Tracey, Mullett, the skeleton, and the entire outside world.

She led him through to the lounge, dimly-lit and thickly carpeted, a hi-fi unit in the corner oozing syrupy late-night music. A soft, chocolate brown studio couch absorbed the heat of a gas fire.

"Well, now you're here you might as well take off your coat."

He shrugged off his coat, stuck his scarf in the pocket, and went to the little cloakroom just off the hall. When he returned she was sitting on the studio couch, her head on one side, watching him. "I've poured you a drink." He flopped down beside her and took the well-filled glass from the side-table.

"Here's to us, Jack." Her drink was sunk in a single gulp, but he sipped his slowly, letting his eyes run over her. She still looked good, even if the figure was now just a shade on the plump side, and she was at least forty, even by the kindest calculations.

"So what happened last Wednesday?" she asked.

"Wednesday?" He furrowed his brow, then groaned. "Hell, was I supposed to take you out?"

"Yes, you flaming were. To dinner. To make up for Monday, when you also forgot."

"Oh, Shirl, I'm sorry. I'll make it up to you, I promise."

" 'Sorry!' You're always bloody-well sorry. I waited for hours . . . hours. And now you calmly turn up at 2:30 in the morning and expect to jump in bed with me."

"It's not *quite* 2:30," said Frost.

She lay back on the studio couch and watched him drop the last of his clothes on top of her discarded dressing gown, then she moved so he could join her. His hands were reaching for her when a man's voice suddenly said, "Inspector Frost. Control to Inspector Frost."

"What the hell's that?" she asked huskily.

Frost put a finger to his lips, then stretched out an arm for his personal radio. She ran the tips of her fingers gently down his back. With as much composure as he could muster he said, "Frost here. What is it, Control?"

"Message from Detective Sergeant Hanlon, Mr. Frost. Goodtimes, the jewellers in the High Street, has had a break-in. About twenty-five thousand quid's worth of stuff taken."

Her fingertips were now tracing an intricate pattern at the base of his spine. He tried to keep his voice steady. "Have we nabbed anyone?"

"No, Inspector. We were on the scene within seconds, but they got clean away. Shall we set roadblocks up?"

"Forget roadblocks. They'll be a waste of time. Tell Mr. Hanlon I want him to put a man front and back of Sammy Jacobs' betting shop. Keep them out of sight, but they are to detain anyone who tries to leave. Right?"

"Understood, sir."

"Tell him I'll meet him outside Sammy's in about . . ." Shirley pressed herself close to him and breathed heavily ". . . in about half an hour, perhaps a bit longer. Over and out."

He clicked off the transmitter and let it drop on the expensive carpet. The fire was warm, the couch was soft, and Shirley was marvellous. In the distance, the personal radio chattered inanely on about crashed cars, drunken brawls, suspicious noises . . .

It was 3:25 in the morning, the car was purring sweetly, and Frost was humming to himself as he puffed away at the cigar Shirley had given him as an extra birthday present. He hadn't realized before what a beautiful night it was with the snow sparkling like white silver. He parked well short of the betting shop and walked stealthily the rest of the way, noticing that although the wind blew as hard as ever, his overcoat seemed to have grown in thickness. A shape loomed from a shop doorway.

"Jack!"

Tubby Arthur Hanlon in tweed coat and pork-pie hat, his nose as red as his cheeks, motioned towards the betting shop.

"No-one's been in or out, Jack."

"Good," grunted Frost. "Fill me in on the details."

Hanlon told him the story. The owner of the jewellers lived on the premises and at 2:45 had been woken up by insistent knocking. He looked from his upstairs window and saw the beat constable who informed him that the shop's burglar alarm was ringing at the station and could he come in and look around. The jeweller slipped on his dressing gown, scurried downstairs, switched off the alarm, and opened the shop door. Whereupon the "beat constable" coshed him and ransacked the shop.

"Right," said Frost, "then let's see if Sammy is still open for business."

They crossed the road to the betting shop, Sammy Jacobs, Turf Accountant, and Frost leaned on the door buzzer.

"Why here?" whispered Hanlon. "Did you have a tip-off?"

"Intuition," mumbled Frost, and gave the door a kick to reinforce the summons of the buzzer.

Then something happened. Movement from inside the shop, a door banged, then a scuffling sound. Someone was trying to get out the back way. But a uniformed man was waiting.

"Oh no you don't!"

Frost pressed his face against the glass of the door and could make out the uniformed man pushing in from the rear, frogmarching a struggling figure. The constable shoved his prize through and unlatched the front door.

"Caught him trying to sneak out the back, sir."

Hanlon's torch splashed the man's sullen face. "Sid Sexton!" he exclaimed triumphantly. "What are you doing here?"

What Sid was doing at that precise moment was uttering a

string of profanities. Hanlon had indeed caught a big fish. Sid Sexton was a break-in expert with five convictions for robbery with violence and a form-sheet several pages long.

"Where's Sammy?" asked Frost, rocking on his heels and puffing at his cigar.

In answer to his question a door opened at the head of some stairs and a shaft of light sliced the darkness, backlighting a fat, bald man in an expensive dressing gown, armed with a poker. He peered down into the shop.

"Who's there?"

"Police, Mr. Jacobs," called Frost. "Real ones."

Sammy lowered the poker and thudded downstairs.

"Mr. Frost!" he exclaimed in surprise. "What's this about?"

"Do you recognize this man, sir?" The flashlight shone on the break-in expert's face, which Sammy made a great pretence of studying, finally shaking his head reluctantly.

"Never seen him before in my life. Why?"

"We caught him running out of your premises a couple of minutes ago. He must have broken in."

Sammy frowned. "Broken in? Impossible."

"He came running out of here, straight into the constable's arms," insisted Hanlon.

Sammy dug into his dressing-gown pocket and found an enormous cigar which put Frost's to shame. He lit it carefully. "Well, nothing seems to have been taken . . ."

"We don't know that for sure, sir. We'd better take a look around."

The bookmaker caught the crook's eye and they both stiffened.

"No! There's no need for that."

But Frost was already halfway up the stairs. "Up here, is it, Mr. Jacobs—your living quarters?"

"Yes, you can look if you like." The note of relief was so strong that Frost came straight down again. He nodded to the room behind the counter. "What do you keep in your office, Sammy? He could have nicked something from there."

The fat shoulders shook with laughter. "A few pencils and some betting slips. If he took them, he's welcome."

"You're too charitable, Sammy, but we'll look, just in case. We owe it to you as a rate-payer and an upright citizen."

The safe, painted grey, was cemented into the wall. Sammy tested the handle. "It hasn't been touched. Without the key it's impossible. Look—it's late. Let him go. I won't prefer charges."

"Won't hurt just to look inside," murmured Frost.

This was inconvenient. The key was upstairs, somewhere. And it was so late. If they'd care to come back in the morning . . .

"Nip up and get it, Sammy, there's a good chap."

The bookmaker took the cigar from his mouth and studied the glowing end. "I don't have to."

"No," agreed Frost, cheerfully, "you don't *have* to. It's a citizen's privilege to sod up the police, but it means we'd have to go to all the bother and expense of getting a search warrant, which all comes out of the rates, and they're high enough already."

Sammy shrugged expansively. "So. I pay my rates. You get your search warrant."

"Please yourself, Sammy, but it means a couple of my men would have to stay here, by the safe, until we got it. And you'd be all on edge, up and down to the toilet. We're definitely going to see what's inside, so why prolong the agony?"

The cigar was hurled to the ground and trampled to death. "You lousy bastard, Jack. You *know*, don't you?"

Frost beamed affably. "I'm afraid I do, Sammy. One of my rare infallible days. I think the key's in your right-hand pocket."

It was. With shoulders slumped in defeat, Sammy moved to the safe, but Frost stopped him. "Hold it a minute, Sammy." He asked Hanlon and the constable to wait outside with the prisoner. "I want a quick word in private with Mr. Jacobs."

Hanlon gave the inspector a searching look as he closed the office door.

"So what is it?" asked the bookmaker, the key poised in front of the lock.

Frost stuck his hands in his pockets and looked up at the ceiling. "It's a bloody serious offence, bribing and corrupting young police officers, Sammy. You'd cop at least double the sentence you'd expect just for robbery. But as it's my birthday, and it's near Christmas, I'll be generous. You keep your fat mouth shut about a certain member of the Denton police force, and I'll keep mine shut about bribery and corruption charges. How does that sound?"

"You lot look after your bloody own," snarled Sammy. Then with a shrug, "But what have I got to lose. It's a deal, Jack."

"Let's have his IOU, then."

The safe door swung open and Sammy thrust his arm past the neat heaps of expensive jewellery and watches lying on top of a folded police uniform, and pulled out an envelope which he handed to Frost. The inspector checked the contents, took out his lighter, and burned it to ashes. Then he called the others in.

As he climbed back into his car the church clock chimed four times. He backed out of the side street and headed for home. He'd told Detective Sergeant Hanlon to take over the entire case. "I wasn't there, Arthur. I've already had two arrests of my own tonight, which is more than my fair share of glory and form-filling. Grab this one with both hands. You've got kids and a fat stomach to support. Just say you were acting on information received. Sammy will keep me out of it, as it's my birthday."

He jerked his head and blinked. God, he was falling asleep at the wheel. He'd never done that before. Where was he? He stared unbelievingly through the windscreen at his house. He'd been driving in a trance, turning corners, crossing traffic lights without knowing it. If anyone had been in his path . . . He shuddered and thought of that miserable eighteen-year-old kid in the lobby. He wound down the window to let the cold air jerk him back to life. That poor kid. He just didn't have the luck.

Switching off the engine, he staggered to his front door. He didn't remember getting undressed, but was asleep as soon as his head touched the pillow. He could have dreamed of death and decay, but he dreamed of Shirley.

When he went out the next morning he found he'd left the car unlocked, with the window down, and the keys swinging in the ignition. Anyone could have pinched it, but his luck had held out just a little while longer.

WEDNESDAY

WEDNESDAY (1)

————

Wednesday morning at 8:05, Station Sergeant Bill Wells leaned across the enquiry desk and studied the morning paper, a look of intense pity on his face.

"What's up?" asked Frost, pausing on the way to his office with Clive.

Sadly shaking his head, Wells jabbed a thumb at the front page. "I've seen some terrible things in my time, Jack, but this is awful. The poor devil—you'd think they could do something with plastic surgery."

Frost snatched the paper and looked at a photograph of himself taken at the time he'd received his medal at the palace.

"God, what a handsome brute," he exclaimed. "Who is it —Errol Flynn?"

The banner headline bellowed SKELETON OF SHOT BANK ROBBER FOUND IN 32-YEAR-OLD GRAVE. Tucked away at the bottom was a tiny, blurred photo of Tracey, captioned "Hopes fading for missing girl." Frost shuddered. The snow had stopped and the search parties would be out in force and he wondered if it would be today that he'd have the rotten job of taking the mother to the mortuary.

"Hear about the arrests Arthur Hanlon made last night?" asked Wells.

"Yes," snapped Frost, already on his way to the office, "he's a good chap. He doesn't waste his time reading bloody papers."

They made an early start and were well stuck into the Bennington's Bank robbery file when Frost let out a sharp groan and reminded Clive they should have been at the briefing meeting ten minutes ago. Mullett stared pointedly as they clattered their shamefaced way to their seats, mumbling apologies.

"I suppose I'll have to start again for the benefit of the latecomers. I was suggesting we should extend the area of the search."

"It's no use extending it until we get some more men," said Frost. "We haven't even got enough to cover the more likely places as thoroughly as we should."

"Agreed," purred Mullett, "but if you had been here when the meeting started, Inspector, you would have known that I intend to ask the Chief Constable for more help."

Game, set, and match to Hornrim Harry, thought Frost, and didn't say another word until the Divisional Commander left when he blew a soft raspberry at the closed door. That courtesy out of the way, he heaved himself to his feet and sidled over to Detective Sergeant Martin. "You don't need me, do you, George? I'll be over at the bank solving the case of the three-eyed skull. If anything exciting happens, give us a buzz on the radio." He stopped at the door. "Oh—one other thing. Mrs. Uphill will be waking up in a strange bed without the mirror in the ceiling this morning. Better get one of the policewomen to take her home. What's the name of that one with the mole on her stomach?"

"Hazel!" said George Martin and Clive in unison.

Hudson, the manager of Bennington's Bank, was plump, dark-haired, and blue-chinned. He shook hands with a warm pudgy palm, ushered them to moquette-covered chairs, and announced his secretary would rustle up some coffee.

"It's about the skeleton, isn't it? I read about it in the papers this morning."

"Yes, sir. Looks as if it might be a long-lost cashier of yours. Reckon you can let us have details of everyone who worked here in 1951?"

Hudson scratched a note on his memo pad with a chunky, gold-banded pen. "Our staff department at head office holds all personal files. I'll have to get the details from there." He smiled and offered a suggestion. "This was before my time, of course, but why don't you have a word with our assistant manager, Rupert Garwood? He was here then—in fact he drove the car and got coshed for his troubles, I understand."

"Good idea, sir," said Frost. "May we see him?"

A light grey phone was lifted with a flourish. "Brenda? Mr. Hudson here. Ask Mr. Garwood to come to my office, please. What?" His eyes travelled up to the wall clock. "Unusual for him, isn't it? And he hasn't phoned? Oh dear, I hope he's not sick. Ask Mr. Fox to take over his post." The brow was deeply furrowed as he replaced the phone and turned apologetically to Frost.

"Bit of a snag, I'm afraid. Mr. Garwood doesn't seem to be in today. Brenda's phoned his home, but there's no reply. Most odd—and so unlike him." He made another note on his pad.

The two detectives exchanged glances. "Let us have his address," said Frost, "and we'll call at his house on our way back. If we miss him, and he turns up here, you might ask him to give me a ring at the station. I've got a card somewhere."

Eventually a grubby dog-eared card was located from the depths of a crumb-lined pocket and passed across. Hudson took it doubtfully and was about to tuck it in the corner of his clean blotter when he decided it would look less offensive under his paperclip tray, in which, he noticed with annoyance, the inspector had stubbed out his cigarette.

No. 38 Priestly Court, where Garwood lived, was a pebbledashed residence of 1938 vintage. They followed the milkman's footprints up the snow-covered path to the porch where the morning's pint of milk shivered on the step. All the curtains were drawn. Frost pressed the bell. They could hear it ringing inside. The ringing died. Silence. Frost rang again, then rattled the letterbox, causing the morning paper to drop down on the doormat.

"Sounds ominously empty, son," said Frost. "The woman

next door's peeking at us through her curtains. She looks a right nosey cow. Let's see if she can tell us anything."

She was a homely body in curlers and a quilted mauve dressing gown, and she talked non-stop. If they wanted Mr. Garwood, he'd be at the bank. No, he wasn't married—lived on his own with Roy . . . Of course not! He wasn't that sort of a man. Roy was his golden retriever. I'm surprised you didn't hear it barking its head off when you rang the bell. It usually does.

Nodding his thanks, Frost backed away, leaving her still talking, then he sped back to the car with Clive. "I don't like it, son. Radio through to Control and get them to contact the bank. If Garwood still hasn't arrived, they'd better do a quick audit. He might have run off with the tea money." He watched Clive fumble among the litter on the ledge under the dashboard. "What's up, son?"

"I can't find your personal radio," Clive explained.

Christ! thought Frost. He remembered where he'd left it. On Shirley's studio couch the previous night.

"On second thoughts, son, scrub it. Let's go round to the back of the house. There might be a door open."

On the way they took a look at Garwood's garage. The doors were padlocked, but they forced them open enough to poke a torch inside and it lit up the radiator of a grey Hillman Avenger. Wherever Garwood had gone, he hadn't taken his car.

But the back door was securely locked and bolted and the closed venetian blinds stopped them from seeing into the kitchen. A small patio extended from the rear of the house for about ten feet or so before the lawn took over. Thick, crusty snow made it one unbroken blanketed expanse, except for an oddly shaped little mound, longish, slightly curved. Frost prodded it tentatively with his toe. A crackling sound of thin ice breaking. Curiosity aroused, he bent and scraped away the snow with a gloved hand, calling for Clive to help. A little way down the snow was tinted pink, and then there was thick, bright, ruby red ice, and something stiff, golden, and spiky. Frozen animal fur. They'd found Roy, Garwood's golden retriever, the head darkened with dried blood running into frozen rivulets, soft brown eyes staring dully and reproachfully at the inspector's unpolished shoes.

Frost turned his head away. Tracey's body would be like that, stiff, cold, and reproachful.

They were crouched at the back door, Frost trying one of his skeleton keys, when the two men jumped on them. Frost's arm was seized and jerked brutally upward in an agonizing hammerlock, while Clive's head was slammed into the woodwork of the door. Frost kicked back, savagely, and there was a scream of pain. Then he turned his head and saw the police uniforms.

"You silly sods!" The policeman holding him, gritting his teeth against the pain of the kick, abruptly froze, then slowly released his grip.

"Inspector Frost!"

"Who were you hoping for, you great tart—Jack-the-bloody-Ripper?" The constable rubbed his leg and Frost worked the shoulder muscles of his right arm to ease the pain. Clive was soaking up blood from his nose with a handkerchief. "Are you all right, son?" Clive nodded and dyed the handkerchief red.

"Sorry, sir," apologized the second policeman, "but we had this 999 call about two suspicious characters . . ."

"Lucky for you we're not burglars, otherwise I'd sue you for police brutality—look at what you've done to his nose, it's all bent." Clive's eyes glared at the inspector over his sodden handkerchief.

"We're trying to break into this house," said Frost. "What's the easiest way?"

"Through the coal-chute," said the first constable and limped around the front to show them.

During the summer, while the householders were away on holiday, there had been several break-ins in the locality, the thieves gaining admittance through the coal-chutes which were alongside the front doors. Most of the burgled houses had their doors fitted with strong, sophisticated thief-proof locks, but the coal-chute doors were secured by very simple locks—after all, who would want to steal a few pieces of coal? But with the coal-chute door forced open, all the intruder had to do was slither down into the coal cellar and out through the inner door, straight into the house.

They got the door open without any trouble. An enormous pile of anthracite hid the inner door.

The constable cleared his throat. "Be a mucky job clambering over that lot, sir."

Frost flashed a benevolent beam at Clive. "Fortunately we have in our midst the Chief Constable's nephew. A new boy's perks, I'm afraid, son. Try not to drip blood on his nice clean coal."

Impassively, Clive heaved himself up and slid down the gritty chute to land ankle deep in the anthracite, which kept shifting underfoot and sending up clouds of dry, penetrating coal dust to creep down the collar and into the eyes, and to stick to the blood from his nose. With pumping legs he tried to climb to the top of the heap, but the coal ran away from him and it was like trying to run up the down escalator, but at last, sweat trickling channels of white into his grimed face, he was there. The inner cellar door had no inside handle and a push proclaimed it to be bolted from the other side. Garwood must have heard about those burglaries.

"Give it a kick, son," called Frost.

The first kick sent him sprawling on his face, but the second crashed back the door, and there was the hall with its off-white carpeting daring him to spoil it with dirty shoes. He tiptoed to the front door, which wasn't bolted, and opened it to Frost who tipped his hat and handed him the bottle of milk.

Frost suggested the two constables wait outside—"This gentleman doesn't want you mucking up his nice clean floor with your beetle-crushers"—then he ventured inside. The first door he tried led to the lounge. He whistled softly. It was in some disarray, with drawers open and the contents trailing to the floor as if someone had been frantically searching for something. But they gave it just a cursory glance and moved on. The next door led to the kitchen, which was in darkness, with the venetian blinds closed. Frost felt round the door frame and switched on the light. A compact kitchen in stainless steel and Formica. On the floor, spread across the blue and yellow checkered tiles, was a man.

The man wore a blue paisley dressing gown over grey nylon pyjamas. He lay on his back, his mouth open as if surprised, his left eye staring in perplexity at the ceiling. Where the right eye should have been was a cavity overflowing with congealed blood. The blood had welled over down the side of the face and on to the blue and yellow tiles.

The smashed eye held Clive in a repulsive but hypnotic grip. He didn't want to look, but couldn't turn his head away. Then his stomach revolted and he staggered from the room. Frost heard his retching outside and hoped he'd managed to avoid the off-white carpet.

Sensing trouble the two uniformed men bounded in, recoiling at the sight of the mess on the floor. Frost waved them out. The kitchen was too small with the corpse taking up so much room.

"You'd better radio the station, lads," he said. "Get a full forensic team. Tell them someone has shot and killed Rupert Garwood."

WEDNESDAY (2)

And then it was organized chaos with experts stamping all over the house, measuring, examining, photographing, dusting for fingerprints. The pathologist and his secretary were closeted with the corpse in the kitchen after being assured by the inspector that it had a bit more meat on it than the last one.

Frost didn't like experts. They spoke a language he didn't understand, a language where things were exact and precise

and where hunches, intuition, and blind luck didn't enter
into it. So he sat on the stairs, smoking, keeping out of
everyone's way, flicking ash on the thick sheet of polythene
that had been laid to protect the deceased's off-white Wilton.

Clive staggered in from the garden, his face chalk white
under the coal grime. He flopped down on the bottom stair,
ready to charge outside again should the need arise.

"Feeling better now, son?"

Clive nodded. "Sorry about that, sir—it was seeing his
eye . . ."

"Don't apologize, son. It's to your credit that you've still
got some decent revulsion left in you. I bet, in a couple of
weeks, you'll be flicking your butts in it like the rest of us."

Clive sat quietly, willing his stomach to settle down. Frost
kept the conversation going to cheer the lad up.

"The pathologist and his girlfriend are in there now, admiring the spilled brains. I remember a choice corpse we had
once when I was on the beat. It seemed this bus had gone
right over his head . . ."

Clive was thankful that two ambulance men bearing a
stretcher caused a diversion as Frost directed them, with a
jerk of his cigarette, to the kitchen, but they were immediately rejected. The pathologist was not yet ready to yield up
the body.

A fingerprint man emerged with his case of equipment,
humming happily to himself.

"If you've done the kitchen, do the lounge," called Frost.
"Someone's turned it over."

"Right," beamed the fingerprint man. "Let's hope he had
the manners to take off his gloves. He kept them on in the
kitchen."

"How I hate cheerful little sods," said Frost, and then the
kitchen door opened again and the photographer squeezed
out with his equipment. Frost asked for three enlargements
of the eye, in colour, to send as Christmas cards, then went
in with Clive to see the pathologist.

He was dictating notes to his secretary as Frost's head
poked round the door. The corpse, respectably draped with a

sheet, was now just something to be stepped over. Frost stepped over it.

"His dog's outside, Doc, as dead as he is. Do you think you could take a look when you've finished in here?" He nudged the sheeted body with his foot. "What's the verdict on one-eyed Riley?"

The pathologist winced, delicately. "Well, he was shot from a distance of a few feet. The bullet has ripped through the eye and is now lodged in the skull somewhere. I'll fish it out for you when I do the autopsy. He would have fallen back with the impact and cracked his head on the tiles, but he wouldn't have felt it. He was dead before he hit the floor."

"Some people have all the luck. What time did he cop it?"

The pathologist scratched his chin. "We're now going into the realms of speculation. Pinpointing the time of death is very much a hit-and-miss affair, but from my preliminary calculations I'd say that death occurred between ten o'clock and midnight last night. I'll be more precise after the post mortem."

The ambulance men were allowed to remove the body and Frost led the pathologist out to the stiffened little mound on the patio. Squatting on his haunches the medical man gently explored the sodden fur on the animal's head. "Beautiful creatures, aren't they?" he murmured impassively, then straightened up and rubbed his hands briskly together. "A blow from our old friend, the blunt instrument. A nasty knock, but I don't think the intention was to kill. The dog was stunned and this crippling weather did the rest. It just froze to death."

Frost evened up the ends of his scarf. "Thank God we're not dealing with the sort of swine who'd kill a dog in cold blood. Parliament would bring back hanging for that. What time did Fido expire?"

The pathologist gave a hollow laugh. "You do ask the most impossible questions, Inspector. The dog's frozen solid. It's like giving me a piece of meat from the deep-freeze and wanting to know when it was slaughtered. My guess is that it died some time last night."

"That's bloody obvious, Doc," snorted Frost. "Garwood was a fastidious man. He would never have left a dead dog out on his patio all day. He'd have shoved it in the dustbin. They both must have been killed around the same time, but who went for walkies in the sky first—the bow-wow or his master?"

"If it's all that important," sniffed the pathologist, "I'll do a quick PM on the dog as well." He called out to one of the ambulance men to ask if there was a polythene bag to put the dog in.

The ambulance man looked at the golden retriever, his eyes clouding with compassion. "Poor old thing. What bastard would do that to a dog?"

"If I ever get myself murdered," announced Frost, "I'll make certain my dog is scabby, mangy, and smelly, so if any sympathy's going, I get the lot."

The black Daimler carrying the pathologist purred away, followed, after a frenzy of door-slamming, by the ambulance bearing the mortal remains of Garwood and Roy. And then the house was peaceful again.

Frost closed the front door, lit his thirtieth cigarette of the day, and ambled back to the kitchen with its traces of fingerprint powder on polished surfaces and the distorted chalked outline, like a child's drawing, on the floor. He wandered over to the Ideal Standard boiler in the corner, opened the fire door, and peered inside. It was full of light grey fluffy ash and lumps of cold unburned coal.

"Why did he let the fire go out, son? You'd expect it to be going full blast, day and night, in the winter."

"I imagine he was killed before he could make it up for the night," answered Clive, trying not to sound too patronizing.

"I'm glad you said that, son. It gives me one of my rare chances to shine. He was in his pyjamas and dressing gown, all clean from his weekly wash. A methodical bloke like Garwood would have made the dirty fire up first."

Clive thought again. "Then perhaps the boiler was due for

a clean-out. You have to let the fire go out every few weeks to rake out the ashes, otherwise it gets clogged up."

Frost smiled thankfully. "I'll buy that, son. We can eliminate the boiler from our list of things to worry about, then. Thank God for that, there's enough bloody mysteries as it is. Are you going to the Christmas Dinner and Dance?"

"Dance, sir?" frowned Clive, unable to keep up with these abrupt changes of subject.

"The Denton Division Annual Dinner. It's next Saturday. Entirely voluntary, of course, but you don't get promotion if you don't go. You can have my ticket." He opened a drawer and closed it aimlessly. "You can smell death in the house, can't you, son? A sort of empty, final feeling. You know what I mean?"

Clive didn't know what the old fool meant so gave a noncommittal shrug. It was clear the inspector was completely out of his depth, without the faintest idea of what to do next. Surely the superintendent wouldn't leave him in charge of a murder investigation?

"What's our next move, sir?"

Frost consulted his wrist. "Too early for lunch, even if his eye hadn't taken the edge off my appetite. You know, son, after my wife died, my house was like this—still, silent, achingly empty. It was frightening. And she'd been in hospital for nine weeks, hadn't even been at home, so why should her death have made the house different?"

"Perhaps the difference was in you, sir, not the house."

"More than likely, son." His mood brightened. "Do you realize I'm averaging a body a day—more if you count dogs. What you might call an embarrassment of riches. What's your theory about the murder? I think the dog shot Garwood and then committed suicide, but I'm open to alternative suggestions."

"Garwood surprised a burglar, sir, and the burglar shot him."

Frost thought for a moment, then shook his head reluctantly. "I hate to pour wee-wee on your suggestion, but have you taken a look in his bedroom? His bed hasn't been slept in, so presumably he was up, with the lights on, when he copped it. Even a burglar as stupid as me would wait for the householder to go to bed."

For once he's right, brooded Clive, then, "Sir, I've got it!" and he pounded up and down the small kitchen expounding his theory while Frost smoked and listened.

"Garwood would be holding the keys to the vaults at the bank, sir. That's what the intruder was after. Garwood must have made a false move, so the man shot him."

Frost pressed his cheek and popped out a smoke-ring. "A bank job, eh? So what does the intruder do after he's shot Garwood?"

"He looks for the keys himself, sir—that's why the lounge was turned over."

"The rest of the house hasn't been touched," mused Frost, dribbling smoke, "so he must have found the keys—unless he was disturbed. And if he found them, why didn't he rob the bank?"

"The beat bobby was watching the door, sir—remember?"

"It seems to fit," said Frost grudgingly. "It doesn't have the right feel, but I can't think of anything better . . . Arseholes!"

The expletive because someone was ringing the doorbell.

"See who it is, son. If it's the baker, no bread today; if it's the cat's-meat man, tell him he's lost a customer."

It was Mullett, immaculate in his tailored topcoat. "Trouble seems to be following you around, Inspector," he said, studying the chalked outline on the floor.

"You're only doing your job, Super," said Frost, genuinely misunderstanding him, and then all his forebodings came to the boil when Mullett asked Clive if he would mind leaving him alone with the inspector for a moment.

He's found out I smashed his bloody car, thought Frost, his mind racing through, and rejecting, other possible alternatives.

A heart-thudding pause while the superintendent seemed to be rehearsing what he was going to say, then he produced a packet of untipped Senior Service from his pocket. "Cigarette . . . er . . . Jack?"

Frost felt the ominous tell-tale prickling at the back of his neck. The cigarette was offered in the way a prison governor would behave when he had to break the news to the condemned man—"The-news-on-your-reprieve-is-not-all-that-good-I'm-afraid" sort of thing.

Frost took the cigarette and waited for the blade of the guillotine to come crashing down.

"This murder case . . . er . . . Jack. I think we should call in the Yard."

"Sod that," snapped Frost, choking with indignation. "We do the work and the Yard gets the credit—no thanks!" He puffed savagely and stared at the far wall.

"Right," said Mullett, giving in surprisingly quickly, "I shall tell the Chief Constable you are violently opposed to that course. But, can you cope—I mean, with the missing girl as well?"

"Providing I can call on extra men, if necessary."

"You have but to ask, Joe . . . er, Jack. Good, that's settled. It'll only be for a couple of days."

Frost's head jerked up. "A couple of days?" he said warily.

"Er . . . yes. Inspector Allen should be fit by then and he'll take the cases over from you."

You crafty sod! thought Frost, so that's what the "Jack" stuff and the free fag was about! Mullett didn't want the Yard in either, he wanted Denton Division to get all the glory, but had managed to slant it; should things go wrong, then Frost would get the blame for insisting the Yard be kept out. But if it all went right, Allen and Mullett would cop all the praise. At least he had the decency not to meet Frost's gaze.

Frost took Mullett's gift cigarette from this mouth, coughed, and regarded it suspiciously. "Are these cheaper than Weights, sir?" he asked innocently, but Mullett was already on his way back to his panelled snuggery.

Clive returned to the kitchen after showing the superintendent out. The man had what Frost lacked, dignity and authority.

"What now, sir?"

"Ask Control to send some men down to question the neighbours in case they heard something last night. There's a slim chance nothing good was on the telly." Then he stopped dead in his tracks and clouted his forehead with his palm. "Excreta!"

"What's up, sir?"

"Did you spot my deliberate mistake, son? The bloody body! I never had it identified. It could be any Tom, Dick, or Harry tarted up in grey pyjamas. We'd look bloody fools if it wasn't Garwood, wouldn't we? Never mind, we'll get Hudson the bank manager to do it. We'll break the sad news about his staff vacancy then slyly slip into the conversation that we want him to identify the corpse in the morgue."

At first Hudson couldn't take it in. He stared at Frost as if the inspector had said something disgusting, then he collapsed in his chair and pulled off his glasses.

"Dead? Rupert Garwood, dead?"

"I'm afraid so, sir."

Hudson blew his nose loudly, then dabbed the corners of his eyes. "Garwood was very good to me. His help, when I took over this branch, was unstinting and he must have hoped he would have got the managership himself." He blew his nose again.

Good job I didn't tell him about the dog, thought Frost, he'd have cried his bloody eyes out. He put forward Clive's theory that an intruder was after keys to the vaults, but Hudson's head shake emphatically nailed the possibility.

"Garwood didn't have the keys, Inspector. Two sets are required to open our vaults. I hold one and the other is held by senior staff on a rota basis. Mr. Garwood won't have the keys for another—" the lip quivered, "—he won't ever have them again."

"So that's your theory booted up the arse, I'm afraid, son," murmured Frost. Clive tightened his lips. Was it necessary to be so childishly crude?

Hudson pulled himself together. "Those files you wanted,

Inspector. Our head office is sending them by Red Star passenger train and we'll be picking them up from the station at 2:30."

"That's what I call real co-operation, Mr. Hudson. It's much appreciated."

A brave smile. "If there's anything more I can do to help . . . anything . . ."

Smack into the trap, thought Frost. "As a matter of fact, sir, there is . . ."

"Oh," said Hudson, his face all eagerness to assist.

"Just a formality, sir, won't take long. We'd like you to identify the body."

The colour drained from Hudson's dismayed face and he shrank visibly. "Oh . . . Is this absolutely . . . ? I mean, I've never really seen a dead body in my life."

"Be an experience for you then," beamed Frost. "There's nothing to it. A quick look under the sheet and we'd have you back in good time for your dinner."

The mortuary was in the large grounds of Denton Hospital next to a tall-chimneyed incinerator, which was belching black greasy smoke.

"A few arms and legs going up there," commented Frost breezily to the trembling figure in the back seat.

In the small lobby the steam heat was overpowering, but Frost advised Hudson not to take off his overcoat, as it would be freezing in the room where the body was—the stiff-store as he put it.

A notice on the wall read "All Undertakers to Report to Porter Before Removing Bodies." They reported to the porter, and there was a minor altercation, as the man didn't have Garwood's body booked in his custody. This meant, he explained, that if the body was here, it was still being worked on. To prove this point he stabbed a disinfectant-smelling finger at the appropriate page of his stockbook which was patently devoid of corpses named Garwood, the last entry being the old tramp found frozen to death in the woods the previous morning.

"Hold on a minute, Mr. Hudson," said Frost with the air of a man who is going to sort everything out. Hudson's glance was straying furtively to the exit doors and Clive moved slightly to block any last-minute attempt at flight.

The illuminated sign over the door read "Autopsy Room" and as the inspector barged through, there was a breath of air colder than cold, and the glimpse of something waxy and sheet-covered with bare feet.

Hudson decided he must make his position absolutely clear. He could not go on with it, he told Clive. He was sorry, but there it was. Some things were just not possible and this was one of them. Clive spoke soothingly, trying to reassure him, but was not helped by Frost's voice, clearly audible from within.

"You haven't sawed his head open yet, have you, Doc? I've brought someone along to identify him."

And then the door to that awful room opened and Frost's finger firmly beckoned. Clive took Hudson's arm in a tight grip and half steered, half dragged him through. It was like walking a condemned man to the scaffold.

Inside were white tiles, pipes, hoses, running water, and things gurgling and spitting. Annoyed at being disturbed at an interesting bit, the pathologist moved back scowling and wiping his hands on a red rubber apron.

Frost pushed Hudson forward. He first saw the table, an item of horribly specific design with a perforated and channelled stainless-steel top, with pipes at each corner running down to drains. He let himself look at the body occupying such a small space on that large table. How clean Garwood looked in death, the naked skin pale under the blaze of the dazzle-free lamps, a towel draped demurely across the middle and the toes sticking so obscenely in the air.

They waited. A hosepipe dribbled tinted water. Hudson steeled himself and let his gaze creep up to the face. He looked away quickly, being aware of some damage to the eye and of an electric bone-saw, waiting to be plugged in, on a side table.

The inspector said he had to look at the face properly. If

It's cold in here, thought Hudson, why am I sweating? A quick look, then away. A swimming, blood-filled socket screamed up at him, filling his entire field of vision, then roared away to be replaced by anxious faces looking down on him as the floor hit his back and the lights went out.

He came to in the lobby with streaming eyes and jerked his head away from the stinging fumes of the ammonia bottle.

"I'm sorry, Inspector, truly I am. It was just . . ."

"That's all right, sir," soothed Frost. "I understand. I can remember the first body I ever saw. An old tramp it was . . ."

Clive cut in with a warning cough. One of Frost's disgusting stories was the last thing the manager should hear about in his condition.

"It *was* Mr. Garwood, I suppose, sir?"

Hudson managed a nod and remembered that eye. Through the door came the bone-grinding whine of an electric saw and they just managed to catch him before he fell again.

Hudson's secretary watched wide-eyed as they brought him back to the bank, his legs rubbery, his face damp and green.

"What's up with Mr. Hudson?" she asked.

Clive explained.

She shook her head and carried on with her typing. "Shame about Mr. Garwood. He wasn't all that old."

"His dog was killed as well," called Frost, steering Hudson through the door to his office.

Her face darkened with anger and her eyes spat. "It was a golden retriever. The rotten stinking bastards . . ."

"Rustle us up some coffee," said Frost.

WEDNESDAY (3)

Detective Sergeant Hanlon's stomach rumbled and whined in querulous protest as it realized its owner was walking past the stairs to the canteen where the Wednesday lunch of meat pie and great slabs of steamed currant pudding was screaming out its siren call. Before Hanlon could eat he had to report to Inspector Frost about his visit to the schoolmaster. He rapped at the door and entered into steam heat and a thick haze of cigarette smoke, and there was Frost at his desk, pushing papers about, his face beaming at the sight of a welcome diversion.

"It's the Fat Owl of the Remove. Grab a chair."

Hanlon lowered himself gently into the rickety chair reserved for visitors and remembered to thank Frost for his Christmas card. "Any chance of us seeing you over the holidays?"

Frost shook his head. "I'll be on duty Christmas and Boxing Day, Arthur, guarding the divisional peace." Hanlon's face expressed sadness and concern, but Frost reassured him. "I volunteered, Arthur. There's nothing for me at home and it's not too bad here—just the odd drunk spewing seasonal fare all over the lobby, but that's what Christmas is all about, isn't it? And our beloved Divisional Commander usually phones in to give us all his blessing, so what more could a man want, except for a bit of the other and a mince pie?"

Hanlon chortled, his whole body enjoying the joke. "I've seen that chap Farnham, Jack."

"Who the hell's Farnham?"

"The schoolmaster."

Frost snapped his fingers. "Of course—Mrs. Uphill's bearded regular. He was supposed to have staggered from her emporium last Sunday to have tea with his aunt, but auntie hasn't seen him for weeks. What's his story now?"

Hanlon pulled a notebook from his pocket and Frost snorted with disgust.

"You're not going to read it out, are you? You only saw him five minutes ago."

But Hanlon did things his own way, and he read from the notebook. "He said he lied to you and he's sorry. He didn't go to his aunt's."

"You're reading beautifully, Arthur."

"Then don't interrupt. He said he was walking back to the railway station when he was accosted by a woman in a leopard-skin coat."

Leopard-skin coat, thought Frost, his finger sawing away at his scar. Now, where have I . . . ? "Sinful Cynthia!" he exclaimed, joyfully, then, seeing Hanlon's puzzled face, added, "Cynthia Collard—you must remember her, Arthur —got a pair like a couple of Christmas puddings."

The culinary reference gave the fat sergeant the required mental picture. "I didn't know she was back in Denton."

"Still, I expect you managed . . . But go on with your reading. When he was accosted, he said 'Sorry, but I don't do things like that on a Sunday'—right?"

Hanlon waited patiently for Frost to finish, then went on. "Farnham went with Cynthia, in her car, to her room."

"So she's got a room, now?" murmured Frost with surprise. "The doorway of the butcher's shop isn't good enough for her any more." He flicked the point of his ballpoint pen in and out, then scratched his ear with it. "So he'd had two women in one day. He must have been ashamed to tell us about the second one in case we thought he was greedy. Well, we'll have to see if Cynthia confirms this story of debauchery. Have you had your lunch, Arthur?"

Arthur's stomach woke up and growled. Meat pie and double chips. "Not yet, Jack."

"Good, then you can have it at The Crown. She plies for hire from there."

A roar of protest from his stomach—the food at The Crown was notoriously poor. "I'm not certain what she looks like, Jack."

"Then use some subtlety, Arthur. Sit there with it hanging out and she'll come to you. But you'll recognize her, Arthur —bleached hair, leopard-skin coat, and a tattoo on her stomach saying 'No money refunded in any circumstances.'"

Clive returned from the washroom where he'd spent a quarter of an hour scraping at the coal-dust with the nailbrush. His back still felt gritty and itchy and his suit was filthy. He'd be wearing the Carnaby Street monstrosity tomorrow, so that should give the yokels something to laugh about. He nodded warmly to the fat detective who'd done a magnificent job with the jewellery-shop robbery the night before. A pity Frost wasn't as efficient as that.

As the inspector filled Clive in on Farnham's further Sunday exploits, Hanlon heaved himself up to brace the cooking at The Crown. "Will you be here after lunch, Jack?"

"Doubt it," said Frost. "We'll probably be over at the bank. Did you know I found another body today—Garwood, their assistant manager?"

Hanlon was shaken rigid and he had to grab the back of the chair to steady himself. "Garwood? I knew him, Jack. He arranged the bridging loan for my house."

"Shot through the head, I'm afraid," continued Frost. "That's two bodies yesterday, one today." He shrugged. "But I'll probably go all day tomorrow without finding any."

His phone rang. It was Forensic. He listened, frowned, then whistled softly and scribbled something across a memo of complaint from Mullett. He hung up and stared at the phone in disbelief. "Ballistics. They say the bullet that killed Garwood last night was fired from the same gun that killed Fawcus thirty-two years ago. They suggest it might be significant."

Clive gaped at the inspector. "They were both killed by the same person?"

"I hope so, son," said Frost. "It means we can eliminate anyone younger than thirty-two from our enquiries. Now hurry up, Arthur, before they sell out of curried rissoles."

·   ·   ·

Mr. Hudson couldn't face lunch. He'd sipped delicately at a tiny glass of sherry, and had taken the merest nibble from a ham sandwich before the dead touch of cold meat revolted him. He'd returned early to his office and was sitting quietly, trying to blank out the memory of the awful morning and subdue a rebellious stomach. His internal phone buzzed like the sound of the bone-saw ripping through poor Garwood's skull. He lifted it to his ear and croaked his name. His secretary told him the two policemen were back for the files.

And in they came, that dreadfully scruffy one with the scarf and his assistant with the nose and grimed black fingernails. The inspector scooped up the files with a nod of thanks and asked if they could question the other members of the bank staff and also have a look through Garwood's desk.

Eager to get rid to them, Hudson agreed immediately and led them over to the olive green partition and through the frosted-glass door bearing the name R. Garwood—Asst. Manager.

Frost flopped into Garwood's swivel chair and dragged off his scarf. "Did Garwood have any relatives?"

"No," said Hudson, "none at all. All alone in the world, it seems," and he retired to his own office, managing a brave smile until the door closed behind him.

"We'll take half his desk each," said Frost, emptying out a paperclip container for use as an ashtray. He pulled open a drawer. "There's something sneaky about looking into other people's desks, isn't there, son? I feel quite guilty when I rummage through Mullett's drawers on Christmas Day."

The drawers yielded nothing significant—social club files, a duster, a towel, an envelope heavy with silver, which turned out to be the collection for the tealady's Christmas present. They buzzed Hudson on the internal phone and announced they were now ready to have the staff in for questioning, and in they came, one by one, in strict order of seniority, starting with the chief clerk.

Like all things Frost did, the interviews started well, but the inspector soon became bored. No-one could tell them anything that could help. Their colleague's death still weighed heavily upon them and they were all full of praise for a man who was apparently a living saint, barren of faults and never a bad word to say to a living soul. He hadn't spoken to anyone about the 1951 robbery and no-one knew what his social life was outside the bank.

Frost thought that such a man sounded so boring he deserved to get shot and he let his detective constable ask all the questions while he smoked cigarette after cigarette and swivelled from side to side in the chair, occasionally studying his wristwatch and sighing deeply.

Clive had worked his way down the office social scale and was now questioning a seventeen-year-old typist with a lisp and a quivering, mouth-drying, figure. Frost scribbled something on a piece of paper, folded it carefully, and passed it across to Clive who excused himself to the girl and read it. It said "She isn't wearing a bra!" and, for the rest of the interview, Clive heard little of what she was saying, his eyes firmly fixed on her vibrating sweater, which showed clear proof of his superior's powers of observation.

At last she was dismissed, leaving a hint of perfume and a beautiful memory.

Frost spun a complete circle in Garwood's chair. "So, it seems he was a saint? If we came back in a week's time, I'll bet they'd all have remembered what a bastard he was. Come on, son."

As they entered the lobby with the staff files, Johnnie Johnson called out to Frost and beckoned him over. He was holding aloft the inspector's personal radio.

"A lady brought this in for you, Inspector."

"A lady?" asked Frost, warily.

"Yes, she said you left it round her place."

"Oh—ta—thanks." He tried to sound casual.

"Nice bit of stuff she was, reminded me of a nun, or a Sunday school teacher or something." The face was deceptively innocent, but Frost wasn't fooled.

"Sergeant Hanlon back?" he snapped in his best official manner, stuffing the radio back in his pocket.

"In his office, Inspector," and the station sergeant just managed to hide the broad grin under his moustache.

I wonder what that's all about? thought Clive.

They found Hanlon in his office worrying the life out of a glass of Alka-Seltzer with a spoon. He swallowed the bubbling liquid in one long gulp and let it do battle with his digestive system.

"That's no cure for the pox, you know, Arthur," said Frost with concern.

Fat eyes regarded him indignantly. "You sent me to a fine place, Inspector Frost. The meat was off. How can meat be off in this weather?" He suppressed a belch.

"Did you find sexy Cynthia?"

"I found her. She confirms Farnham's story. He was with her until six o'clock."

"Thank you, Arthur. Now go and wash your hands in carbolic and get on with your work."

Back in the torrid seclusion of his own office, the inspector tugged at the string tying the bundle of Bennington's Bank staff files. Clive watched moodily. He was beginning to feel useless, just trotting along behind Frost like a tame dog. He wanted to get out on his own.

"Hadn't I better do my round of doctors and dentists, sir?"

"That can wait, son. I'm content we've found Fawcus's skeleton—I don't want any more proof. When we've worked out who killed him and Garwood—and let's not forget the dog—then we can waste our time sodding about with luxuries like dental charts. Help me look through this pile of old rubbish." He spread the files out on his desk. There were ten of them, ten people who were working diligently in Bennington's Denton branch way back in July 1951, at least two of whom were now dead with bullets in their skulls.

"We'll work from the top down," announced Frost, "the manager first."

In 1951 the manager was a John Aubrey Powell, then aged 45. He had retired in 1971 on his sixty-fifth birthday. An exemplary bank employee it would seem, judging from the annual assessments contained in the file. The 1952 assessment lightly referred to the unfortunate business of the missing cashier and the lost £20,000 but absolved Powell from all blame. The last item in the file was a copy of a memo from the staff pension fund administrators to the effect that, at Mr. Powell's request, part of his pension entitlement was to be paid as a lump sum, his monthly pension to be reduced accordingly.

"I wonder why he took a lump sum," said Frost, and dialled Hudson to ask him.

Apparently it wasn't unusual. Many people opted for a lump sum. They might want to start up a little business, or buy a better house—you wouldn't stand much chance of obtaining a fresh mortgage at the age of sixty-five—or . . .

Frost pulled the phone away and let the manager babble on. "I'm sorry I asked," he told Clive, "I'm getting a bloody lecture." Then the phone was jammed in his ear and he jolted to attention. "What did you say, Mr. Hudson?"

"I said I don't know the exact reason why Mr. Powell took a lump sum, but you could always ask him."

"Ask him? You mean he's still in Denton?"

"His address is in the file," said Hudson edgily. His head was aching, the inspector was shouting, and he wanted to go home.

Frost scrabbled through the pages. "I can't see it."

Clive leaned over his shoulder and tapped a finger on a section headed Present Address.

"Oh," said Frost, "it's all right, Mr. Hudson, I've found it. It was filed in the wrong place." He hung up.

Clive jotted down Powell's address and they plunged into the murk of the next file, that of the then assistant manager, now running a branch in Glasgow. Glasgow police were teleprinted to have a word with him.

And on to the next. Timothy Fawcus. A good and industrious worker, recommended for early promotion. His medical report for the pension fund made no mention of a broken arm. The file closed with the cryptic comment "Left service of bank June 1951—see separate file."

They pulled out Rupert Garwood's file. A fairly recent photograph pinned to the inner cover showed both of his eyes. At the time of the robbery in 1951 he was earning three pounds two shillings per week, five and a half days including Saturday mornings. Following the fracturing of his skull he was off work for three months, but in return for a doctor's certificate of incapacitation a money order for the full three pounds two shillings was sent to his home every Friday. A confidential memo from Head of Staff Administration asked Manager Powell if it were possible that the lad was in any way implicated in the disappearance of Fawcus and the money, but Powell disabused head office of this unthinkable possibility. Later that year Garwood was regraded and his salary increased to three pounds fifteen shillings a week, payable monthly.

Another four files, all flat, stale, and unprofitable. Frost was getting bored.

"My head's aching looking at all this rubbish, son," he complained, staring out at the white bleakness of the car park. "It's getting dark already. They'll be calling off the searches soon. Hello—this file's a different colour."

The colour was different because in the rigid social structure of the bank in the early fifties, the files of caretakers and manual workers had to be clearly distinguished from those of the elite salaried staff and this was the dossier of Albert Barrow, fifty-three, Caretaker, who had left the bank's service at the end of 1951. His going was abrupt and without notice. He just walked out one night and never returned. The bank eventually sent him his cards and tax forms, and the envelope was returned marked Gone away—present address unknown.

Frost stifled a yawn and fluffed his hair in exasperation. "This is getting too bloody complicated, son. What would help us no end is for someone to walk in and confess."

There was one file left and it looked as dull and potentially unfruitful as the others. He decided to shove it to one side while they nipped up to the canteen for a cup of hot stewed tea and was actually pushing himself up from the chair when intuition whispered in his ear. The shout of tea was louder than the whisper of intuition, but he turned the cover of the file and gave a brief, reluctant glance inside, then—

"Christ!"

He made Clive jump. "What is it, sir?"

"I knew that old cow was involved, son. You can't beat the old Frost intuition."

Clive spun the file around. The photograph on the inner cover looked vaguely familiar. An ugly girl with tight thin lips, a hooked nose. He couldn't believe it, but the name underneath was conclusive. Working for the bank in 1951 was the wild witch of the woods, Martha Wendle, the clairvoyant, the skeleton locater, the cat woman. From May to July 1951 she had operated the bank's switchboard, but on the 10th of July she was dismissed, the reasons for her dismissal stated as "Listening in to private phone calls, rudeness to bank customers, unexplained absence from switchboard, insubordination, lack of co-operation, etc., etc."

"She got them going during the three months she was with them," said Frost with grudging admiration. He wound the old maroon scarf over the tightly knotted tie. "Come on, son, get the motor out. We've got some cats to visit."

The Morris 1100 purred along a road between rolling, snow-mantled fields. Frost suddenly grabbed at Clive's arm.

"Hold it, son!"

Clive stopped the car and followed the inspector's gaze to a distant clump of slow-moving figures flashing torches.

"Our chaps, I think," said Frost, raising binoculars to his eyes and fiddling with the focus. Blurs sharpened into men with uniforms, moving forward quickly, pointing and mouthing noiselessly. There was no way to join them except by wading through the snow-blanketed fields. Frost radioed Control who sounded quite excited.

"A lead, sir. The helicopter spotted something moving in the snow and we sent a team out to investigate."

Frost's heart beat faster. If it was Tracey, and she was moving . . . And he'd written her off as dead! The binoculars again. The men had stopped and were gathered around something; they were bending, lifting . . .

"I think they've found her, son." Somehow he managed to keep his voice steady. He handed the binoculars to Clive and radioed back to Control for a further report. Control were slow in answering. Static crackled and his hand trembled with excitement.

Clive was giving a low-voiced running commentary. "Yes, sir, there is something. They're picking her up. I can't quite see . . ."

A clattering over the radio as someone in Control picked up a microphone. "Control here. Sorry, Inspector, a false lead. It's a sheep."

"It's a sheep," reported Clive. "Must have got trapped in a snowdrift."

Disappointment crushed Frost back into his seat and he signalled wearily for Clive to drive on. "Why do I get so excited?" he said moodily. "The kid's dead and I know it. There's some things you feel. You know, like when the hospital phoned to say my wife had died. I didn't have to pick up the phone. At the very first ring, I knew."

Clive eased the car into the now-familiar parking spot at the edge of the woods and they pushed out for the long slithering slog to the cottage.

"You on duty Christmas?" bellowed Frost.

"I haven't checked the roster yet, sir."

"They could be leaning over backward to show no favouritism to the Chief Constable's nephew, so if you are on, let me know, I might be able to wangle something."

No more talk until the misshapen bulk of the cottage loomed up. No lights were showing and their knocks went unanswered. Clive squinted through the letterbox. Green emeralds sparkled in blackness. He shouted. They blurred and vanished.

The lean-to that should have housed Martha Wendle's old car was empty, and tyre tracks led towards the private road.

"The old cow's done a bunk!" moaned Frost. "Why didn't I run her in when we found that lousy skeleton?"

Clive didn't answer him. He was looking over the inspector's shoulder into the back garden where something poked crookedly out of the snow. It was a cross fashioned from two pieces of wood nailed together. In front of the cross stood a vase containing a bunch of expensive hot-house chrysanthemums.

Frost galloped over and scraped snow away with his shoe. It was deep snow, but the ground beneath showed signs of recent disturbance, and the shape was unmistakable. Frost's voice was quiet. "It's a bloody grave, son. I think we've found Tracey."

He sent Clive racing back to the parked car to radio for Forensic, for some diggers and for Martha Wendle to be picked up. Frost stayed behind, keeping vigil, chain-smoking and stamping to bring sluggish circulation back to his feet. A lurking wind suddenly spotted him and pounced, tearing and biting through his clothes, clawing at his scar. He was reluctant to leave the grave, but at last sought shelter in a small garden shed. It contained a shovel and a fork. He decided he couldn't wait for the digging party and braved the wind. It wasn't a job that could be rushed and his fork probed delicately for fear of plunging into the child's body. He was still scratching the surface when bobbing lights through the trees heralded the approach of the Forensic team. He felt a twinge of doubt. If it was a grave, it seemed empty. He dropped to his knees and scraped away with gloved hands and the men from Forensic gathered around, spotlighting the site with their torches. And then he found the body . . . small, stiff, and white. But it wasn't Tracey. It was a white kitten, its head flattened in grotesque distortion by the weight of the covering earth. And that was all the grave contained.

No-one laughed, no-one said anything, but the silence was crushing and oppressive. Frost wished the ground would open up and swallow him as well as the kitten. He straightened up slowly and rubbed his palms down his coat. "You can go home if you like, lads. I've made what you might term a bit of a balls-up."

They trudged off without a word, leaving Frost and Clive to shovel the earth back and stamp it down hard. It was a big grave for such a tiny creature so the mistake was reasonable, and Clive was wishing he could think of something to say when, cutting gratingly over the wind, a woman screamed and screamed and screamed.

It came from the cottage. Martha Wendle was screaming at them. They hadn't heard her return, but she had seen men lurking in her garden so she shrieked in terror and slammed all the bolts on the doors.

They pleaded with her through the letterbox and pushed their warrant cards under the door as proof of their honest intentions before she finally let them in, still trembling. Even her cats were cowering fearfully in dark places.

"I'm sorry, Inspector," she said when she had calmed down, "but I had no idea it was you invading the privacy of my garden."

"I'd have knocked first," said Frost, his nose twitching against the unforgettable smells, "but I thought the spirits would be keeping you in the picture."

"It's easy to scoff," she snapped, brushing past him to fetch a large brown saucepan from the kitchen. She removed the lid and dumped a mess of strong-smelling fish heads on to a plate on the floor which was immediately awash with cats spitting, biting, tearing, and scrunching. Clive slipped into the room at that point. He caught Frost's eyes and shook his head: he had found nothing. Frost had asked him to search the cottage. The size of the kitten's grave worried him.

Frost pulled his scarf up so it covered his nose and hoped it would filter off some of the aromas. "That skeleton you kindly put us on to, Miss Wendle. You were working at Bennington's when he was killed, weren't you?"

She suddenly stared at him intently. "You miss your wife a lot, don't you, Inspector?"

Clive had never seen Frost so angry before. The inspector was trembling with rage. "Keep that bloody claptrap to yourself, you wicked cow." Then he swallowed hard and regained control. "Sorry—it's a painful subject. July 1951. Tell me about the robbery."

She wiped her hands on a grimy tea-towel. "I was accused

of not passing on a vital message. The message was never given to me."

"What vital message?" asked Frost.

"It's in your file," she said.

That means I'll have to read the bloody thing, thought Frost, and Clive, feeling he had been silent long enough, asked, "Is that why they sacked you, Miss Wendle—because you didn't pass this message on?"

"That was the excuse they used," she said bitterly, fastening her eyes on the younger man, "but the truth was, I knew too much about the manager and his business."

"His business?" prompted Clive.

"Yes. You can't help overhearing the odd snippet when you work on a switchboard. That son of his was always phoning the manager up."

"What about?"

"Money. He was always whining for money. I can still hear that wheedling voice." She gave a grotesque imitation. " 'You've got to help me, Dad, I must have the money to-night.' The manager falsely accused me of listening in to his calls." A self-satisfied smile crawled across her face. "But he was punished for his wickedness."

One of the more unpleasant-looking cats had discovered Frost's leg and was rubbing up against it.

"How was he punished?" asked Clive.

Her eyes went blank as she savoured the recollection. "His son committed suicide, didn't you know?" She chose that moment to look down as Frost's foot was swinging and her expression changed abruptly to acid hate. "You dare touch that animal!" She scooped the cat up and hugged it protectively to her chest. "I'm glad your wife died," she spat. "Now get out!"

Frost gave her a look of contempt. "You nasty bitch!"

"Go!" she said, and squeezed the cat until it squealed in protest.

The long plod back to the car in the wind blew away the smell of fish and cats and hatred.

"How did she know about your wife, sir?" asked Clive.

"Not from the bloody spirits, son, that's for sure. It was in all the local papers at the time—'Police Hero's Wife Dies—Funeral Pictures Page 8.' It was probably wrapped round her fish heads." He said nothing for a while, then, "My wife was beautiful when I first met her, you know. I wasn't such a bad catch myself—not the ugly sod I am now," and his hand went to his cheek.

Throughout the drive back he was deep in thought and kept touching his scarred face; then, as they rumbled down the hill to the Market Square, "Tell me something honestly, son. This scar, it doesn't make me look too bad, does it?"

"You can hardly notice it, sir," said Clive, eyes fixed on the road ahead.

Frost looked unconvinced. His finger felt, pushed, and poked. "I can't leave the damn thing alone. The doc says I could have plastic surgery, but between you and me, I'm a bloody coward. I'm terrified of hospitals. I keep having this nightmare—I'm being wheeled into the operating theatre where the surgeon's waiting with blood on his gown and I try to move, but I'm strapped down, and I can see all the knives and hooks and things in a kidney bowl, and I try and yell, and then I wake up in a cold sweat."

Control came through on the radio. "Would Inspector Frost report to the Divisional Commander at once, please?"

Frost sighed. "No wonder I get bloody nightmares. What have I done wrong now?"

WEDNESDAY (4)

Superintendent Mullett's knuckles drummed his desk top in a gesture of impatient irritation. How much longer was he expected to wait? Other officers treated a summons from their Divisional Commander as tantamount to an Imperial Decree, dropping everything in their eagerness to obey it, but Frost . . .

A rap at the door. At last! Even the knock was slovenly.

A pause as the blotter was moved fractionally to dead centre and the silver-buttoned tunic pulled down to pristine smoothness.

"Come in."

And in he slouched, trailing that matted woollen scarf, disintegrating at one end. His shoes made damp marks on the carpet.

Mullett flicked a disdainful hand to a chair. Frost sat on the edge, apprehensively.

"I've just spoken to the head of Forensic," snapped Mullett.

"Oh?" asked Frost innocently, yet knowing what was coming. That slimy sod in Forensic, trust him to waste no time in whining direct to Mullett.

"Do you know how much it costs to send out a full, experienced team like that?"

If I don't, I'm sure you're going to tell me, thought Frost, adopting an attitude of interested concern while slipping his hand into his trouser pocket to play the game of counting his small change by touch alone. It gave him something to occupy his mind while waiting for the Superintendent to finish him moan.

". . . You panicked and you blundered. Even the newest member of the Force would have checked first before calling out a complete Forensic team to look at a dead cat."

Fifty-three pence, thought Frost. Now let's see if I can stack them with heads on one side and tails on the other.

"It wouldn't be so bad if we could keep the shame of your incompetence within the division, but now the press have got hold of the story. I've already had a reporter from the *Echo* asking for details. We'll be a complete laughing stock. It'll be all over County tomorrow, and if the Chief Constable reads it . . ."

. . . bang goes your promotion, thought Frost, but aloud

he said, "Sandy Lane's a pal of mine, Super. If it worries you so much I might be able to get him to drop the story."

Mullett was so delighted he forgot to wince at the "Super." "Excellent. And I can handle the head of Forensic —we belong to the same Lodge." He beamed and stood to indicate that the interview was over. "We all make mistakes, but the secret is the ability to put them right, eh?"

Frost dragged himself up. He was tired and his wet trousers were sticking clammily to the backs of his legs. He wanted to get back to his own office.

"Oh," said Mullett as if it was an afterthought. "There's some more good news . . . er . . . Jack."

Frost waited warily.

"Inspector Allen will definitely be returning to duty tomorrow, so you'll be able to hand all your cases over to him. It . . . er . . . might be a good idea if you slowed down now and concentrated on getting the paperwork up to date. I happened to look in your office earlier and quite frankly . . . the state of your desk . . . I was appalled. You might have to put a spot of overtime in, but it isn't often, and I know Inspector Allen would appreciate receiving things in apple-pie order." His candid smile turned to a perplexed frown as Frost swept out without a word, deliberately slamming the door behind him.

A deep sigh. So uncouth! There must be some way of getting him transferred.

Frost stamped down the corridor and poked his head into Search Control. "Any advance on one sheep?"

Martin smiled. "A couple of other false alarms, Jack, but we seem to be running out of steam. If the weather holds, we'll start on the outlying areas tomorrow, but I can see all Christmas leave being stopped."

"It'll be all over tomorrow," said Frost, cynically. "Tomorrow Inspector Allen will be back, which means the girl will be miraculously found, alive and well, the murderer of Garwood, the dog, and the skeleton will walk into the station and confess, bringing the stolen £20,000 with him, the snow will melt, poverty will vanish, and peace will break out all over the world. But until then, the usual diabolical balls-up from your friendly bemedalled hero."

Back in his office he shrugged off his overcoat and hurled it to miss the hatstand. He kicked it into a corner, then sat on the hot radiator, baking steam from his damp trousers and trying to work up enthusiasm to tackle his desk which had received a fresh delivery of bumf since he was last in. He was getting Inspector Allen's work as well as his own and was neglecting to do either. He groaned. Where the hell was Barnard? Never to hand when Frost felt like bawling someone out. He hopped off the radiator. Nothing for it, he'd been eased off his cases so he might as well steel himself and get down to the reams of nitty-gritty.

He was trying to decipher something he had written on the back of a petty-cash voucher when the door was kicked open and Clive entered, a steaming cup of tea in each hand.

Frost took his gratefully. "Bless you, my son. You're my spirit of Christmas, my star on the tree. Seen anything of the policewoman, Hazel what's-her-name, in your travels?"

"She was in the canteen," said Clive, guardedly. He'd just fixed up another liaison for tonight. "Why?"

Frost stirred vigorously, slopping tea down his jacket. "Just wanted to know how Mrs. Uphill was."

"Oh—sorry, sir—she did mention it. Hazel took her home from the hospital. She's still shaken, but otherwise all right. She wouldn't let Hazel stay with her."

"Not enough business for the two of them, I imagine."

Clive's cup banged angrily in his saucer. "I don't think that's very funny, sir."

Frost looked contrite. "Sorry, son, I'm a bit low this evening. I've been pulled off the case. Inspector Allen returns from the dead tomorrow and I'm to hand everything over to him."

It took an effort, but Clive managed to look as if he thought this terribly unfair. Frost continued. "Our superintendent has kindly suggested I might stay late and slog my guts out on the paperwork. If I thought it would upset anyone, I'd resign, but he's not getting that as a Christmas present." He plucked at the skin round his scar, then realized he was feeling sorry for himself and the dark mood slid instantly away. "Sod it, it's Christmas, why should I feel miserable? If Allen had died I'd have had to subscribe five pence towards his wreath, and in any case, he's not due back until tomorrow so all I've got to do is solve the two cases tonight and present them to him with a two-fingered salute of respect in the morning. Drag up a chair, son, we'll go through the Bennington's Bank file again."

They shared the file between them and smoked and the only sound to emerge through the thick blue haze was the rustle of turned pages, until . . .

"Sir!" Clive jumped up with excitement and pushed some papers across to Frost. It was a wad of photostats taken from the bank's 1951 staff records. On top was a copy of a medical report on the caretaker, Albert Barrow, who went missing shortly after the robbery. The doctor had stated that although Barrow had broken his left arm some nineteen months previously, there was no reason now why it should interfere with the efficient performance of his caretaking duties.

Frost read it through twice, then turned a puzzled face to Clive, who explained. "His *left* arm, sir—the same as the skeleton's. Don't you see, it may not be Fawcus's skeleton—it could be Barrow's!"

Frost let this sink in, then folded his arms on the desk and buried his head in them. After a few seconds he straightened up and smoothed back his fluffed-up hair. "I've given your theory my careful consideration, son, but as Inspector Allen comes back tomorrow, I'm afraid we just haven't got time for it to be anyone else but Fawcus."

"But it's a possibility, sir."

"A possibility we can well do without. If it's not Fawcus's then we might as well pack up and go home and let Mastermind solve it in a couple of seconds tomorrow." He stood up, pushing his chair against the wall. "Let's go for a little car ride."

Clive groaned inwardly. Couldn't the bloody man stick to

one thing for at least five minutes? "We haven't finished looking through the file yet, sir."

Frost retrieved his overcoat from the floor. "It took months to compile that file, son, so we're not going to assimilate it in one night, are we? I want to chat up this retired bank manager—Powell—you've got his address. He should be able to tell us more than a hundred files could." He shuddered as a flurry of snow splattered against the window. "Look at the bloody weather—it knows we're going out." A button came off and he rammed it in his pocket. "I'm sorry we haven't found the girl, though. That upsets me more than anything."

Clive shoved his half of the file to one side and dragged on his coat. "We should have pulled in the vicar, sir, I'm sure he's involved."

Frost grinned. "You've got a down on the poor sod, haven't you? I'll have a word with him about his harmless little hobby."

"Harmless!" exploded Clive. "Taking nude photographs of a schoolgirl?"

"Her birth certificate may say she's a kid, son, but her body says she's nineteen and I know which I prefer to believe," and he clomped off up the corridor, Clive trotting at his heels. "I know the vicar's all right, son, I've got one of my feelings."

"You had one of your feelings about Martha Wendle, sir."

"Which has yet to be proved wrong." He pushed open the swing doors and they braced themselves against the punch of the wind.

The car passed through the Market Square where shops were closing and a few venturesome shoppers scurried for the bus stop.

"I wonder if the snow has much effect on Mrs. Uphill's trade," mused Frost, lighting two cigarettes and popping one in Clive's mouth. "Even the cup of tea she gives you afterwards wouldn't tempt me out in this weather."

Clive's knuckles whitened on the wheel and he spoke as calmly as he could. "I know I'm speaking out of turn, sir, but

I object to your cheap gibes. She may be a tart, but that doesn't mean she's not a good mother. And it's her kid you haven't found, you know." The car plunged on through twisting blobs of white while Clive held his breath, not daring to look at the inspector.

A smoke-ring hit the windscreen and slowly slithered down. "If she was a good mother, son, then she wouldn't be a tart. She'd put the kid first. What sort of a home is that to bring your daughter up in—mirrors on the ceiling, strange men tramping up to the bedroom at all hours of the day and night? If she was any sort of mother she'd have met Tracey from Sunday school even if it meant disappointing a regular thirty-quid-a-time customer." He paused, then shrugged. "But you're right, son, I should be feeling sorry for the poor cow. And I should keep my cheap, personal opinions to myself. Ah, we're here, I think . . ."

Powell's bungalow was pre-war, originally jerry-built as a cut-price weekend retreat for town-dwellers who possibly paid less than £100 for it new, and who didn't get a bargain. Its woodwork was cracked and warped, the paint peeling and flaking, and the entire structure was in a deplorable state of repair. A gloomy, isolated dwelling. A retired bank manager should have been able to afford something much better in which to spend the autumn of his days.

Frost knocked and was answered by a sharp, suspicious voice from within. "Who's that?"

"Police, Mr. Powell. Can we have a few words?"

A warrant card was demanded and Clive's new issue got another airing as a hand poked through the chained door to examine it. Apparently satisfied, Powell freed the door of its fetters and stood revealed, a tall man, bushy eyebrowed and grey moustached with a voice that retained the honed edge of authority. Then they realized he was leaning to one side, supporting his weight on a stick—the sort of stick you would use to smash in the head of a golden retriever, thought Frost grimly.

"Don't just stand there, come in," barked Powell, hobbling his way up a gloomy passage where a low-wattage bulb in an ancient glass shade struggled vainly against the dark and the depressing brown varnished wallpaper.

From the back of the house a woman's voice called thinly, "Who is it, John?"

"Two policemen, dear. About this Fawcus business, I imagine. I'll take them into the lounge. Perhaps we could have some coffee."

He rested on his stick and opened a side door from which an atmosphere of cold clamminess wafted out like mist from a swamp. He ushered them into a miserable room with faded wallpaper, a damp ceiling, and a settee covered in well-worn, brown leathercloth that creaked and exhaled a strange musty odour when they sat on it.

Powell made hard going of bending down and switching on a meagre electric fire. "We don't use this room much, I'm afraid. Strikes a bit cold at first." He stiffly lowered himself into a matching armchair facing them and, clasping his hands firmly over the top of his stick, regarded them with forceful eyes. "Well, gentlemen?"

"You know about Timothy Fawcus then, Mr. Powell?" asked Frost.

The old man nodded. "Read about it in the paper this morning. A dreadful shock. I've been expecting you all day."

"Sorry about that, sir," said Frost, "but we've had the odd shock ourselves. You read he was shot?"

Another nod. "And everyone thought he had absconded with that money. In spite of all the evidence, I never saw him as a thief. A nice lad, a damned good chap." He bowed his head and sniffed deeply. "And for more than thirty years he's lain in an unmarked grave, falsely accused." He fumbled for a handkerchief and trumpeted loudly.

"It's very sad, sir," agreed Frost. "Do you own a gun by any chance?"

Powell stared angrily. "No!" he snapped.

Frost beamed back affably. "How well do you remember the day of the robbery, Mr. Powell?"

Powell shifted his grip on the walking-stick and smiled thinly. "I'll never forget it, Inspector. Some people remember only pleasant days. My recollections seem to be all the awful ones." A cloud passed over his face and he sank into silence.

"It would help if you could tell us about it," said Frost.

Powell brought up his head slowly. "The story really starts the night before."

Clive consulted the notes he had garnered from the various files. "This would be July 25, 1951, sir?"

"That's right, Constable. July 25, 1951. We were living in Peacock Crescent then. Lovely house, backing on to the golf course."

"I know it," chimed in Frost. "Very select."

Powell permitted himself a wry smile. "Yes. Rather different from this place." His nose wrinkled with distaste as he looked round the funereal room. "I got home from the bank about six o'clock. As I entered the house the phone started ringing. It was Stephen Harrington, manager of our Exley branch, in a rare old panic. He wanted to know if we could help him out with a very large cash transfer the following day."

"How large was 'very large'?" Frost asked.

Powell sighed with impatience. "£20,000. We're talking about the money that was stolen, Inspector. Surely you know the basic facts."

"I know them, sir, but my young colleague's a bit vague. I'm asking for his benefit. Why did he want so much cash transferred in such a hurry?"

"Factory wages. Most of the factories in Exley were closing down for their annual holidays that weekend and the workers expected to be able to draw three weeks' wages and holiday pay. Harrington had forgotten to take this into account with his cash stocks. Damned inefficient. Would have served him right if I'd turned him down. That would have put him in serious trouble with the head office."

Frost shifted his position on the settee where a protruding spring was getting sharply rude. "Twenty thousand quid seems a hell of a lot of money just for pay packets, Mr. Powell. I mean, we're talking about 1951."

"Three weeks' money for six hundred employees. Work it

out for yourself," said Powell. Frost stared into space, moving his lips silently as if mentally calculating, then nodded. "Of course, sir," he said in an enlightened voice, hoping Powell wouldn't ask him what answer he'd arrived at.

Powell went on with his story. "It's not unusual for branches to help each other out with these cash transfers, but rarely with anything like this sum of money. But you can imagine the outcry if the factories had to tell their men they wouldn't get paid before their holiday."

"Surely this chap Harrington was cutting it a bit fine," said Frost. "I mean, phoning you after six the evening before he wanted the money. Suppose you only had one and eightpence in the till—what then?"

"He would have had to try other banks farther afield. Any of the big five would have helped, but then our head office would have to be brought into the picture and that was the last thing Harrington wanted."

Frost sniffed scornfully. "He doesn't sound much of a manager to me."

"Well," said Powell with a deprecating smile, "his staff seemed to like him, but there was no discipline, and he just couldn't cope with the paperwork. You know the type."

"Er—yes," answered Frost, avoiding Clive's eyes, "I know the type."

A timid scratch at the door, a rattle of cups, and Mrs. Powell entered carrying, with shaking hands, a wooden tray on which were three cups of coffee and a plate of plain biscuits. The men rose politely, Powell leaving his stick and staggering over to relieve her of the tray.

"My wife, gentlemen."

Mrs. Powell, grey-haired with a careworn face, hovered anxiously as they stirred their coffee. Frost took one sip and nearly choked. It was diabolical, a thinned-down reheat of some earlier brew. He gulped it down like medicine and wished he had something to take the taste away.

"Is it all right?" asked Mrs. Powell.

"What lovely cups," said Frost.

This seemed to be a hit and she smiled with pleasure.

"One of the few things we brought with us from the old house, my beautiful crockery and the car." She plucked at her dress. "Thank goodness we have the car. I'd go mad stuck in this terrible place without it." She caught her husband's eye then looked away, biting her lip. Excusing herself, she left them.

Powell stared at his right leg. He declined the cigarette Frost offered him. "Right, Inspector. We come to the day of the robbery, July 26, 1951."

Frost dribbled out three smoke-rings and watched proudly as they wafted over to Powell in perfect formation. "Before you go any further, sir, why didn't you warn the police you were sending £20,000 by road?"

Powell flicked away the smoke-rings with an irritated gesture. "This was 1951, Inspector. We didn't have security vans, armed guards, or bandits with shotguns. We were civilized. We had the death penalty and life was a lot safer for the law-abiding."

"It didn't turn out very safe for the skeleton, sir," murmured Frost.

Powell's long fingers kneaded his leg muscle. "I've had thirty-two years to reproach myself over that, thank you. At the time I considered the fewer people who knew about the transfer the better. It was all arranged at the last minute, it was a very short car ride and there were several alternative routes that could be used. I wouldn't even fix a time for the operation until about half an hour before. It was hardly giving the criminal element a chance."

"But they didn't do too badly in spite of all your precautions, did they?"

The old man's face hardened. "I hadn't allowed for the thief being a member of my own staff." He hesitated. "At least, that's what we've thought for the past three decades. If it wasn't Fawcus, then I don't know what went wrong."

The coldness in the room was damp and insinuating. Frost pulled his scarf tighter. "Apart from yourself, sir, and the manager at Exley, who knew about the transfer?"

"Until I told Fawcus and Garwood, nobody."

"What about the people at the Exley branch?"

"I don't know. Harrington was emphatic he'd told no-one, but . . ." He compressed his lips and spread his palms significantly. "Help yourself to a biscuit, Inspector."

Frost took one. It was stale and soggy, a perfect complement to the coffee. He hid it in his pocket to avoid giving offence, and brushed imaginary crumbs from his lips. "Scrumptious, sir. But please go on."

"The twenty-sixth of July. A blazing hot day, clear blue sky, just the hint of a breeze. We don't seem to have days like that any more." A pause as Powell's mind travelled its long journey into the past. "I'd briefed Fawcus and Garwood and told them to get the money ready. They brought it into my office a few minutes after eleven. I locked and bolted my door, drew the blinds, doublechecked the money, then watched them pack it into the security case."

"This would be the steel case we found chained to the skeleton's wrist?" asked Frost.

Powell frowned at the interruption. "Of course. I personally double-locked it."

"How many sets of keys were there?"

"Two. I had one set, Harrington at Exley the other. I had decided they wouldn't leave in the pool car until 12:30, but as an added precaution I wouldn't inform Exley until five minutes after they had left. So I snapped the chain on Fawcus's wrist and instructed him and Garwood to wait in my office until the dot of 12:30. Then I left for my appointment."

Frost drowned his cigarette in the coffee cup a fraction of a second before Powell pushed the ashtray over. "What appointment, sir?"

Exasperation rippled across the old man's face. "It's in your files, man. Your chaps checked and doublechecked it at the time. I had to go to a funeral."

"Whose funeral?"

"Old Mrs. Kingsley's. One of our largest private accounts and a dear personal friend. If it wasn't for that I'd have stayed to see the money off, but I had to go. Before I left I tied up all the loose ends. I told our telephonist—now what was her name? A horrible woman."

"Martha Wendle?" suggested Frost.

"Wendle! Of course! A proper troublemaker. She was told to phone Exley five minutes after Fawcus and Garwood left with the money. If she had carried out my instructions it might have made some difference, but afterwards she swore black was white that I hadn't given her the message. I got back from the funeral a little after two o'clock. The first thing I did was to ask if the transfer had gone off all right. I was told by one of my clerks that they had left on the dot of 12:30, but were not yet back."

"Were you immediately worried because they hadn't returned?"

"No. Why should I be? They'd only been gone an hour and a half. They were entitled to an hour for lunch and I assumed they were taking it in Exley before driving back. Nevertheless, I got the Wendle woman to phone and ask what time they had arrived. She was dialling the number when Harrington came through on the other line. He wanted to know what the arrangements were, as it was getting very tight for time. The factory wages clerks were due at three. I realized that, contrary to my instructions, Martha Wendle hadn't phoned when they left, but over-riding that was the chilling fact that they hadn't arrived!" His face relived the horror of that moment. "I can remember going quite cold. A blazing hot day and I was shivering, and Harrington saying 'Hello? . . . Hello?' out of the phone."

He stretched his hands to the dull glow of the electric fire. "I can remember, to my shame, hoping they might have had some minor accident, but that the money was safe. I phoned the police. They put a search in hand right away. They found the car in a lane off Denton Road, young Garwood slumped across the wheel, Fawcus and the money gone. The police asked me to check that I still had the keys to the security case. I opened the safe in my office where I had put them. They were not there."

Clive looked up from his notebook. "Fawcus was able to

open your safe, wasn't he, sir?" He had read the file a little more thoroughly than his inspector who was nodding as if he was just going to ask that himself.

The old man gritted his teeth and moved his right leg with his two hands. "Yes, he had his own safe key."

"What's up with your leg?" asked Frost.

Powell's eyes iced over. "If you must know, I had a stroke three years ago. At one time I couldn't walk at all."

"Oh," said Frost, "I thought it might have been a dog bite. While I think of it, you had a caretaker. What was his name, son?"

"Albert Barrow," supplied Clive.

"That's it, Barrow. My colleague was wondering if it was significant that Barrow went missing shortly after the money vanished."

Powell thought for a moment. "I remember him—bald and shifty. After he left we checked his stores and found that goodness knows how many packets of tea, towels, toilet rolls, etc., were missing. Been helping himself. We'd suspected it for some time. He even had the cheek to go and get himself a job at another of our branches six months later. He cleaned them out as well."

"Exactly what I suggested to my colleague," said Frost, beaming at Clive.

Powell fumbled for an old-fashioned pocketwatch which he consulted pointedly. "If that is all, Inspector."

"Sadly it's not, sir." Frost worried at his scar. "We're now left with rather a tricky question. If Fawcus didn't pinch the money, then who did? Who shot him and chopped his arm off? Who had the opportunity, and the motive?" He cleared his throat. "Now, apart from yourself, very few people knew about the transfer, let alone the exact details." He paused. The old man, his face set, his eyes hard and expressionless, said nothing. Undeterred, Frost plunged into the icy water right up to his neck. "You, for example, sir, had opportunity . . ."

He got no further. With the aid of his stick, Powell heaved himself up and towered over the seated inspector, quivering with rage. He stretched a hand to the door. "Get out! Do you hear me? Get out of my house!"

Frost didn't budge. He lit another cigarette, leaned back, and waited. The effort of standing proved too much. Powell's body sagged and he sank into his chair, fighting to control his breathing.

Frost continued as if nothing had happened. "It's got to be said, sir, whether you chuck us out or not. You had the opportunity, didn't you?"

A weary hand fluttered limply to indicate the miserable room. "Look around you, Inspector. This cold, depressing room. If I had stolen £20,000, do you think I'd be living in a pigsty like this?"

Frost lowered his eyes and found the name on his cigarette of consuming interest. "Now we come to motive, sir. You may not have wanted the money for yourself, but I understand you had a son."

Wind roared down the chimney and rustled the crumpled paper in the fireplace. Powell gnawed at his lower lip, then dragged himself over to an old, dark oak bureau in the corner. A key from his watchchain unlocked it and, from the bundles of papers stuffed in pigeonholes, he pulled a photograph, which he passed over to the inspector. It showed a young man in RAF uniform, a peaked cap at a rakish angle over devil's eyes, and an Errol Flynn pencil moustache under the Powell nose.

"My son, Frank," said Powell stiffly. "The only photograph we have now. I keep it locked away. My wife . . . she gets upset."

Clive took the photograph and studied the medal ribbon. "The DFC, Mr. Powell?"

"Yes." The eyes shone and he drew himself erect as if standing to attention. "We were so proud of him. We went to Buckingham Palace to see the King give it to him. A wonderful day."

"I bet it was," said Frost. "Why does your wife get upset?"

Powell replaced the photograph and locked the bureau, trying the handle carefully to make sure it was secure. "He killed himself." He tottered back to his chair and sat down heavily. "After the war he started a business with his gratuity and with some savings I was able to let him have. He made an awful mess of it, I'm afraid. We helped him out with more money from time to time, but it was like pouring water into a bottomless bucket. In the end everything got on top of him and his mind snapped. He jumped in front of a tube train. Not a hero's death, was it? His mother never got over it. She idolized him. In her eyes, he could do no wrong."

The only sound in the room was the scratching of Clive's pen. The old man stared down at the floor, his eyes glistening.

It was like kicking a puppy, but Frost waded in again. "As I said, Mr. Powell, you had a fair old motive for stealing the money—to pump it into your son's failing business."

Powell turned his head slowly and twitched his lips to a thin smile of contempt. "You don't do your homework, do you, Inspector? The money was stolen in 1951. My son killed himself in 1949—two years before. Would you mind leaving now, please? My wife doesn't like being left alone."

Frost motioned to Clive who put his notebook away. The two detectives rose.

"Sorry if I've upset you, Mr. Powell, but these questions have to be asked." Powell nodded brusquely and followed them out. In the passage Frost hesitated and pounded his palm with his fist. "I've got a memory like a bloody sieve. I meant to ask if you went out at all last night?"

"I didn't," said Powell. "Why?"

"Last night someone shot Rupert Garwood and splattered his eye to bits, but if you haven't got a gun and you didn't go out, I'll have to look around for another suspect. Thank your wife for the coffee, sir, and if I don't see you before, Merry Christmas."

"Well, son?" asked Frost, thawing out in the warmth of the car as it nosed its way back to the station.

"Seems a decent enough old boy, sir. I feel sorry for him.

He poured all his savings into his son's business and now they're left to struggle along on his reduced pension."

Frost considered this. "He tells a good story, I'll grant him that. I haven't felt more like crying since the chip shop burned down in *Coronation Street*."

"You think he's lying, then?" asked Clive.

Frost twitched his shoulder. "It would be hard to prove if he was. He's had thirty-odd years to polish up his story—and it's a real tear-jerker as you say. Son a war hero, decent parents living in penury to save his good name, and to cap it all, he's got a bad leg. But he is lying, son—I've got one of my hunches."

The car sped past white barren blankness which just about summed up Denton to Clive—blank and barren. Except for Hazel, of course, an oasis of warmth in a desert of ice. He squinted down at his watch—nearly eight o'clock and Frost clearly running out of steam. Good. He'd be off duty at a reasonable time for once. Perhaps he could even take Hazel out somewhere first.

At his side, Frost was stirring uneasily. "I keep getting the nagging feeling I've left something undone. It's not my flies, so what is it? Blimey—yes! Turn left here—we've got to go to the Denton *Echo* office. Hornrim Harry wants me to kill the disinterred kitten story. Slam your foot down, son."

Clive increased speed and barren blankness zipped past. As long as Frost didn't think of any more jobs, he could still see Hazel at a reasonable time . . .

Frost's voice cut into his thoughts. "I imagine they'll be putting you with Inspector Allen tomorrow, son. I can't see your Divisional Commander leaving you under my corrupting influence a minute longer than he can help. He's going to do his nut when he finds I still haven't touched that paperwork. But he'll say, 'I realize we've got to make allowances for you, Frost, in view of your recent sad loss.'" He laughed mirthlessly and shook the last cigarette from the packet. "As you'll be leaving me, son, I'll tell you a secret I've told no-one else. My marriage was a flop. Twenty years of stark bloody misery. My wife despised me. She was ambitious; she wanted someone she could be proud of, and the poor cow got me; she hated me for being what I was. I used to dread going home. In the end I decided to leave her—there was another woman I was going to move in with. On the very night I was going home to break the news, her doctor phoned me at the station. He'd sent my wife to a specialist who'd taken X-rays and they now had the result. Inoperable cancer. She had six months to live and they'd be six rotten months. They thought it best the news was kept from her. So I changed my plans and carried on being despised. A couple of days after that this young sod shot the hole in my face and I didn't particularly care if he killed me or not. The wife was thrilled silly when I got my medal, and when they made me up to inspector she nearly burst with pride. The only thing I'd ever done right. She even stopped nagging. She was a hard woman, but it was a rotten way to die—a bloody rotten way for anyone to die." He mangled his cigarette end in the car's ashtray and stared at the roof. "All I'm trying to say, son, is it's not grief and sorrow at my wife's death that makes me sod things up—I'm just a natural sodder-upper and nothing's going to change me."

Clive didn't know how to react to these raw outpourings. He opened his mouth to speak, then decided silence was best. The car slowed outside the Denton *Echo* office building and Frost shot out, asking Clive to wait.

He found Sandy answering two phones at once and making copious notes in beautifully executed shorthand, so he waited for the reporter to bang the phones down. "Sorry, Jack, but it's going mad at the moment. Did you want me?"

"Yes," replied Frost. "First of all I've decided to forgive you for that rotten dinner. I've only been sick three times and the hot flushes are easing off."

"Oh, yes?" said Sandy warily, sensing a favour was about to be asked.

"I'm in trouble with this dead cat story, Sandy. I want you to kill it."

Sandy patted some papers on his desk into a neat pile.

'You're too late, Jack, we're already printing. Sorry—I would f I could, you know that."

Frost leaned forward and dropped his voice. "Supposing I could give you a better story?"

Sandy's nose twitched, but he pretended only a casual interest. "Like what?"

"Fleet Street stuff, Sandy boy. Strictly speaking our press office should send it direct to the agencies, but when you've got obliging friends who think nothing of spending 12p on our dinner . . ."

The reporter studied Frost's face carefully, then, reaching for his house phone, made up his mind. He spoke into the mouthpiece. "George—kill that page one story about the police exhuming the cat, and stand by for something better." He hung up. "It had better be good, Jack."

Frost told him that the gun that killed Fawcus back in 1951 also fired the bullet that put an end to Garwood's life the previous night. Sandy's lower jaw dropped, then a smile travelled from one large ear to the other. "You're an ugly old sod, Jack, but I love you," he said, and snatching up the phone, he dictated a new story direct to a typist. The headline was to be 1951 KILLER STRIKES AGAIN—AMAZING STORY. The various facts and figures he was able to pluck from his fingertips paid tribute to an elephantine memory. Finished at last he spun his chair round to face the inspector. "What chance of an early arrest, Jack?"

"We're following up several leads," trotted out Frost, trying to think of just one.

"Tomorrow, Jack, we'll have a proper lunch. The sky's the limit—up to a tenner a head. Now, off the record, what leads have you got?"

"Damn all," said Frost, "and that's exaggerating. You keep your lunch and give me some information instead. Do you remember a bloke called Powell, manager of Bennington's back in 1951?"

"Stuck-up sod," replied Sandy. "His son killed himself."

Frost stripped the cellophane from a fresh packet and offered a cigarette to the reporter. "Tell me about the son."

Sandy tugged an ear in thought. "A bloody hero during the war but a near crook after it. He started up this dubious investment company, then blew most of his clients' money on horses and women. Criminal charges would have been preferred if the old man hadn't stepped in and made his losses good. Had to sell his house and they now live in a wooden hut in Denton Road."

Ash dropped from Frost's cigarette to his coat. He spread it about with his hand. "And, in spite of the old man's sacrifices, he killed himself?"

"Yes—in front of a tube train. They had to scrape him off the rails. He still owed a couple of thousand then, but the old man dug a little deeper and got it together somehow and all the creditors were satisfied." He looked up. "Hello—that bloke with the wonky hooter—isn't he your assistant?"

And it was Clive, wending his way through the maze of desks, a scowl of urgent agitation on his face. Frost excused himself to Sandy and hurried over to the detective constable.

"What's up, son?" Then he noticed the smouldering anger.

"Not here, sir—outside," and Clive spun on his heels leaving Frost to trot dutifully after him. In the street the young man stopped and, with eyes blazing, almost snarled at his superior officer.

"You and your bloody hunches!"

When the hospital phoned him about his wife, he knew. Before he picked up the phone, he knew . . . and he knew now. He held his breath to still the churning turmoil within.

"What is it, son?"

"Tracey Uphill. They've found her. She's dead!"

The wind groaned and wailed.

He knew where they'd found her, but he had to ask.

"Where, son?"

"Where do you bloody-well think? Stuffed in that trunk at the vicarage, along with the filthy books and the pornographic photographs."

WEDNESDAY (5)

The car screamed round the corner and juddered to a halt outside the front door of the vicarage where other cars were parked, including the Divisional Commander's blue Jaguar with its damaged rear wing.

A uniformed man at the door saluted. "Second floor, Inspector, first door."

They took the stairs two at a time and pushed into the vicar's photographic studio where a silent group of men clustered around the opened cabin trunk. Frost barged through and looked down into the staring, frightened eyes of eight-year-old Tracey Uphill, who was no longer pretty. A swollen tongue protruded obscenely from her twisted mouth. She wore her warm blue coat but would never be warm again. Frost gently touched the marble flesh with probing fingertips. The flesh was soft. He spotted the doctor at the back of the group and looked to him in mute enquiry.

"*Rigor mortis* has gone, Jack, so I reckon she's been dead since Sunday. You'll need a PM to pin it down to the hour, but the pathologist should be here shortly. We've had to drag him from a Christmas dance."

Frost dropped his eyes to the tortured white face. "How was she killed, Doc?"

"Manual strangulation." The doctor moved the head slightly to show the marks on the throat. "No attempt at sexual assault as far as I can see, but I don't want to disturb her too much. You know what a fussy devil that bloody pathologist is."

A uniformed man coughed to attract Frost's attention. "We found these in that corner cupboard, sir," and he pointed to a stack of dirty books and nude photographs. "We imagine they were removed from the trunk to make room for the body."

Frost gave them a fleeting glance and grunted.

"The property of the vicar," said Mullett loudly, deciding it was time to make his presence felt. "We can see the sort of person he is."

"Yes," snapped Frost, still looking at the girl, "exactly the same sort as the rest of us." He waved the books away. The constable was hurt, wanting the inspector to examine them and realize their enormity. "There's nude pictures of young girls, sir—local girls."

"I know," said Frost, impatiently, "I saw them when we searched here the other day." And not a very thorough search, he reflected bitterly, remembering how he'd hustled Clive Barnard along, and the body must have been here all the time. Then he realized Mullett was talking to him.

"Did I understand you to say you saw these books and photographs, Inspector?" The voice was shocked. "There was no mention of them in your report—such as it was."

Frost lit a cigarette and shrugged. "No, sir, I didn't think it relevant at the time." His eyes went back to the body.

Mullett's voice rose to shrill and accusing incredulity. "You saw these pieces of filth, and you didn't think them relevant?"

But Frost, deep in thought, flicked an impatient hand at his Divisional Commander. "Later, sir, later . . ."

Everyone in the room stiffened. Mullett was ready to explode but managed to control himself in time. He took several deep breaths, determined not to create a scene in front of the others, but as soon as he got Frost back to the station . . .

"Who found the body?" asked Frost, completely unaware of the tension in the room.

The area car driver who had answered the 999 call stepped forward. "The vicar's wife, sir. She went to that cupboard to see if she could find any spare hymnbooks for the carol service and found the obscene books and photographs heaped on the floor. She suspected they had come from the trunk. She opened it, and there was the kid."

Mullett reasserted himself. "The vicar's in his study downstairs, Frost. His wife's in the lounge. She's very upset and I thought it better to keep them apart at this stage."

"Has the vicar said anything?" asked Frost.

The area car driver pulled out a notebook. "Another bloody memory man," snorted Frost, but undeterred the constable flicked through until he found the right page. He cleared his throat and read.

"The vicar said he had no idea how the child had got there. He last used the room about a week ago and last saw the child when she left Sunday school last Sunday afternoon. His wife, Mrs. Bell, was hysterical and I couldn't get much sense out of her, but she said—" and he dropped his eyes to the notebook for the exact words, "—'I knew it would come to this one day, I just knew it.' " He shut the book with a snap and replaced it in his breast pocket.

Frost made no move.

"Well, Inspector," said Mullett with forced heartiness, "I expect you'll want to question the vicar right away. We'll hang on here until the pathologist arrives."

Frost ignored him and sank to his knees by the trunk. Heedless of the shocked protests, he turned the body to one side and plucked something from the back of the blue coat, then he jerked his head abruptly at Clive.

"Come here, son. You want bloody facts, do you? Here's a bloody fact." He pointed then looked up at Mullett. "I don't want to speak to the vicar, sir, and I don't need any bloody pathologist to tell me who killed this kid." He gently replaced the tiny corpse in its original position and looked at Clive who nodded grimly. There could be little doubt. All day long they had both been brushing and brushing to get the damned things off their clothes and the back of the girl's coat was smothered in them . . . hairs—black, brown, white, tabby—from the mangy moulting fur of many different cats.

"Come on, son," and Frost moved to the door.

"Where are you going?" asked Mullett, frowning.

"To arrest Martha Wendle for murder," said Frost, and

was clattering down the stairs before Mullett could ask any more stupid questions.

They were going too fast for safety, but fortunately the roads were empty. Frost refused to waste time walking through the woods. "Take the private road, son," he ordered. Then: "Why are you slowing down?"

"We're coming to the gate," explained Clive. "It's locked."

"Drive through it," said Frost.

"It'll damage the car," exclaimed Clive, horrified.

"Sod the car, son. Smash through it. It'll make me feel better."

So Clive gritted his teeth and pressed down hard on the accelerator. The gate grew bigger and bigger until it filled the windscreen, then struck the car with a hammer blow. A splintering sound, something shot up in the air and crashed on the car roof, then there was snow and open road ahead.

"Saves all the sodding about with a key," murmured Frost, looking back at the wreckage with satisfaction. The dark crouch of the cottage leaped up in front of them and Frost was out of the car while Clive was still applying the brakes.

No lights anywhere. He hammered at the front door. Silence. He sped round to the back and rattled the handle. Locked, but a tiny sound of movement from within. He charged it and bounced off, bruising his shoulder painfully. Clive joined him and kicked near the lock as he had been taught and the door crashed open and they fell into the kitchen with its smells of boiled fish and leaking cats.

She was sitting in the dark, waiting for them, green unblinking eyes staring from her lap.

"We've just come from the vicarage," said Frost.

"Yes," she said, not needing to ask any questions.

Clive went into the other room to fetch the oil lamp and the light showed her broken and resigned. "I didn't think anyone went into those rooms," she said.

"You sodded it up," murmured Frost, gently. "The sort of

thing I usually do. You picked the wrong room. It was his photographic studio. Anywhere else and we might never have found her." He cautioned her and asked if she had anything to say.

Martha stood up and the cat leaped from her lap. "They might as well have their fish." A newspaper parcel of fish heads was tipped into a saucepan and the ritual of boiling began.

"Children come here and torment me. They throw stones . . . break windows . . . call me a witch." She screwed up the fishy sheet of newspaper and dropped it into a battered enamel bucket. "Last Sunday that child came—Tracey Uphill. She kept banging on my door. When I opened it, she would run off, calling me filthy names. Where do children learn such language?" The water boiled over and she lowered the gas. "I find it best to ignore them so they get fed up and go away, but this one kept on and on. Then she started throwing stones. My kitten was outside. My lovely white kitten."

"The one we dug up in the garden?" asked Frost.

Martha nodded. "She hit it with a stone. Broke its back. It screamed with pain. I had to put it out of its agony. The child turned to run, but fell. I was so angry, I grabbed her throat. I shook her." She clenched the fingers of her strong hands, then thrust them out of sight under her apron. "I shook her and shook her . . . And then she was dead."

The fish heads rattled in the saucepan. Clive's pen raced across his notebook.

"When I realized what I had done, I was horrified . . . and frightened. I had to hide the body. At first I was going to bury her with the kitten, but it seemed so obvious. Then I thought of Dead Man's Hollow. No-one ever goes there. I took my spade and dug in the dark. It was like some macabre joke. The very spot I had chosen . . . something was already there. Human remains!" She paused and shuddered.

"You'd uncovered the arm of the skeleton?" asked Frost.

"Yes. I think I screamed. Then I pulled myself together, covered it up again, and returned to my cottage."

"So that's how 'the spirits' knew what was buried there?"

"Yes. When you first called, the child's body was still in the cottage. I had to put you off the scent."

"You didn't put me off the scent, Miss Wendle, you confused me—which isn't very difficult, I'm afraid. But Tracey wasn't here when we searched your cottage this afternoon."

"You were too late. I'd already hidden her in the vicarage. I'd just driven back from there."

"Too late! The story of my life," said Frost. "Why did you choose the vicarage?"

"I'd been there many times before with my spiritualist meetings. I knew there were lots of old rooms no-one ever went into. I'd booked the hall for another meeting and had to go there today to make final arrangements. I took the child's body in my car. No-one saw me. I carried her up the stairs into a darkened room. There was an old trunk covered with a sheet. It seemed ideal. There was a padlock, but it just fell off. I opened it. Inside were a lot of old books. I took them out and put the child inside. I didn't think anyone would find her."

She turned the gas off under the saucepan and emptied the contents on to several plates. The floor was alive with cats, purring in anticipation . . . the cats whose fur had betrayed her.

Frost emerged from Mullett's office smoking an enormous red and gold banded cigar which a delighted Divisional Commander had pressed on him from his special VIP box. It forced Frost's lips apart and weighted his head down. Bloody Mullett had been bubbling over with joy as if they had found the girl alive and well . . . but his elation was really due to the fact that the girl had been proved to be dead before the police were called in and no possible blame could be attached to Denton Division for its handling of the search. He was overjoyed that Frost had obtained a signed statement from the Wendle woman, tidying up all loose ends, but even this might have kept his cigars firmly in their box were it not for the telephoned message of praise received from the Chief Constable.

And so, with the token of his commander's esteem reeking in his mouth, Frost tramped the stone corridor back to his office. He felt deflated and tired, what with Mullett babbling away like a bloody girl and the kid cold and dead in the trunk. He'd carried the news himself to the mother, who didn't break down. She'd shed all the tears she could cry. Thanking him in a flat, lifeless voice, she had poured herself a large drink and shrunk down very small into a chair. Frost sat with her for ten minutes, but she acted as if he wasn't there, so he took his leave. And Mullett had given him a cigar.

The door of Search Control was ajar. He peeked in at a room empty and silent for the first time since Monday morning. A poster of Tracey fluttered on the wall—Have You Seen This Girl? Yes, he'd seen her . . . and tomorrow he'd see her again on the autopsy table as the pathologist cut and tore and probed.

Young Barnard was waiting for him in the office.

"You were right about the woman then, sir."

Frost took the soggy-ended cigar from his mouth and mashed it to brown pulp in his ashtray. "Yes, son, for the wrong bloody reason, but I was right. And if you're going to praise me up, for God's sake forget it. I'm up to here with praise from our illustrious commander. To hear him going on you'd think it was the greatest piece of detection since *The Mousetrap*." He found a cigarette packet in his drawer, chucked one to Clive, and lit one for himself. "I did sod all. I suspected the poor cow partly because I hate her mangy cats, but more for the skeleton, and she had nothing to do with shooting Fawcus."

"You spotted the cat hairs on the coat," protested Clive.

"It just happened I was the first to spot them. If I hadn't, then Forensic would have done so, and they'd have analysed them and given us the bleeding things' pedigrees." He patted his scar and yawned widely. "Barely ten o'clock and I'm tired. It must be old age."

Was that the time? Clive checked his watch. "Er . . . will you be wanting me any more tonight, sir?"

"No—you push off early, son. Mr. Mullett says you're to report direct to Inspector Allen tomorrow, so you'll need all the sleep you can get. You don't mind walking home, do you? I'll be hanging on here for a while and I might need the car."

As Clive left him, the earlier mood of depression seemed to have lifted and he was sitting at his desk, dribbling smoke through his nose and moving mounds of paper to new positions. He was singing to himself a parody of a once beautiful Frank Sinatra song.

"Maybe she's waiting,
Just expectorating
Onto her old shabby dress . . ."

WEDNESDAY (6)

The church clock grated and whirled and hurled a salvo of eleven chimes over a sleeping town.

Martha Wendle, awake in her bunk in the women's cells, heard it as a vague sound, barely impinging on her racing jumbled thoughts. The kitten . . . the lovely white kitten, its skull crushed and blood streaming from its nose. And that child. Why didn't she run away when Martha first shouted at her? Why did she stay and throw stones? If Tracey had run away she would still be alive and life would have gone on as usual. But now the child was dead, her cats would die, and children would throw stones at her empty cottage windows. If only she could turn back the clock, relive it again, force the child to run away.

The wife of the Reverend James Bell heard the chimes as she lay rigid in the sagging marriage bed, right on the edge, as far away from him as possible, ready to shudder and recoil at the slightest nauseating contact of bodies. Those books, those disgusting books. And those photographs. And he had taken them himself, actually seen those girls undressed. His eyes dwelling on their naked bodies.

Her husband was huddled in the foetal position and he heard nothing but his own internal mumblings, his pleas to God for forgiveness, his promise that if there could be no scandal—if it could be kept from his Bishop—then he'd stop. No more photographs, no more books. A promise, Lord. A solemn promise.

And in the printing room of the Denton *Echo* nothing could be heard over the chattering and thudding of the presses. They had to completely remake the front page which now carried the familiar schoolgirl photograph and the self-explanatory banner headline TRACEY FOUND—DEAD. It was also necessary to make a slight alteration to the back page where a short paragraph, "Hunt Continues for Missing Girl," was replaced by an equally small paragraph reading "1951 Killer Strikes Again." The public's appetite could only feed on one sensation at a time.

In Vicarage Terrace, Mrs. Uphill was asleep at last, the drained, empty, heavy sleep of exhaustion. Downstairs the phone was ringing.

Clive Barnard heard the chimes and counted. Eleven. The earliest he had been to bed since . . . since Sunday, years and years ago. Hazel's body, cool and hot, hard and soft, was stretched out beside him. He pulled her to him and they kissed and buds of hardness flowered against his chest. His hands slipped down to the swell of her buttocks and . . .

And there was a knock at the bloody door.

"Are you in there, son?"

Stupid, silly, sodding Frost.

She pulled him down, her hands cool, busy, and he was tempted to keep quiet, to let Frost take it out on the door until he gave up and went away.

"Open up, son . . . please!"

There was something about that "please." He pulled

gently from her and swung his feet to the floor. She was angry and covered herself with the bedclothes. "Don't bring him in here," she hissed, then, with heaving shoulders, presented her back.

"Hold on, sir—won't be a minute." He dressed quickly. Out of bed, away from Hazel it was subzero. Grabbing his thickest coat, he opened the door and slid outside.

And there was Frost, in his old overcoat and his tatty scarf, his scarred face troubled and apologetic. He noticed the hump under the bedclothes as the door squeezed shut. "Sorry, son. After tonight you won't be bothered. It's just that I need your help."

Wondering if Hazel would still be there when he got back, Clive tiptoed down the stairs after the inspector. He didn't bother to ask what it was about; whatever it was, he was committed. And, as Frost had said, tomorrow Inspector Allen would be in charge—tidiness, efficiency, regular hours, and undisturbed sex after close of business.

Snow was falling and the car shivered in the street outside. Frost stepped back to let Clive slide into the driving seat.

"Where to, sir?" The engine started first time.

"Didn't I say, son? Mead Cottage."

Clive blinked. Mead Cottage was where old man Powell lived. It would be nearly 11:30 by the time they got there. "Do you think they'll be up, sir?"

"Christ, I hope not," said Frost. "She might offer me some more of her bloody coffee." Then, lighting two cigarettes and poking one in the driver's mouth, "Do you think I'm a nut-case, son?"

Clive shook his head, his nose delicately savouring the heady Hazel perfume that the heat of the car was driving from the pores of his body.

"Well, you will in a minute. I'm going to break into his house."

Clive hammered the horn and a drunken pedestrian leaped back to the safety of the pavement and swore at the car as it swept past.

"Hard luck, son, you missed him," said Frost.

Clive swallowed hard. Then, without looking at the inspector, said quietly, "I'm sorry, sir, but I don't want any part of this."

Frost sighed. "That's all right, son, I quite understand. We'd better turn back."

"Why do you want to break in?" asked Clive and they passed the intersection where he should have turned and Mead Cottage was getting closer and closer.

"After you left tonight, son, I had a word with Sandy Lane. Something had been nagging at me. Do you remember, when we were leaving Sandy's office last night, that young reporter poked his head in and said he'd phoned the bank manager about finding the skeleton but he'd refused to give a statement? I thought, at the time, he meant Hudson, the current bank manager, but he didn't—he meant Powell, the old one. So last night old man Powell was one of the few people in Denton who knew we'd dug up Fawcus. He was also one of the few people in Denton who were actually involved in the 1951 robbery."

"Apart from Garwood, sir."

"Yes, son, but Garwood got himself shot, so I'm chancing my arm and removing him from my limited list of suspects. That leaves Powell. He claimed that the first he knew of Fawcus's being found was when he read about it in this morning's paper. So he lied. And a man who tells lies is the sort of man who wouldn't hesitate to strike down a lovable golden retriever. Which leads me to the inescapable conclusion that Powell killed Garwood."

Clive's cigarette had burned down to the filter tip. He laid it to rest in the ashtray. "With respect, sir, it sounds very thin to me."

"That," said Frost, loosening his scarf, "is because my standards are a bloody sight lower than yours."

Clive declined another cigarette. "But how does breaking into his house help?"

"I didn't like the way he kept that tatty old bureau of his locked. He can't keep valuables in there, the house is hardly burglar-proof."

"He could keep insurance policies or securities, sir."

"He could, son, but I'd guess he'd keep them in a safe-deposit box at the bank. As he's my only suspect, I'm hoping he did the decent thing and killed Garwood and then ransacked his lounge, looking for something, which he found and now has locked up in his bureau. So I'll take a look. If there's nothing there, no harm done."

There must be some way to talk him out of this sheer bloody madness, thought Clive. They'd be at Mead Cottage within minutes. "But, sir," he exclaimed, "if Powell killed Garwood, then he also killed Fawcus—we know the same gun was used. So what has he done with the money, bearing in mind that £20,000 was worth a darn sight more back in 1951?"

"There," said Frost, "you have put your finger on one of the many weak points in my theory. Thirty-two years ago you could go to town, have a woman, a plate of winkles, and a cup of tea, and still get some change from £20,000. But perhaps what's hidden inside his bureau will provide the answer, because I can't. Pull up here, son—the house is round the next bend."

The car slowed and stopped. Clive switched off the engine and they heard the wind. "What exactly is the plan, sir?"

"You stay in the car, son. If there's trouble, you don't know anything. Now, I reckon I can open his lounge windows with a penknife and once inside I've got my spare keys for the bureau. A quick look, anything incriminating, and I lock up again and hoof it back here to pick you up. We then pay an official visit via the front door and demand he opens up the bureau for us. But if I find nothing, I swear fluently and we go home."

"I think it's a crazy idea," said Clive.

"It's bleedin' mad, son, but it's all I've got. Now slap some slush on the number plates, turn the car round, and keep the engine running. If I make my usual balls-up, we may have to attempt a quick getaway." And then the car door opened and closed and Frost was away, up the road and swallowed in a swirl of snow. Clive reversed, switched off the lights, left the engine gently ticking over, and waited.

Frost was making too much noise. The rusty hinges on the front gate gave a jagged scream as he eased it open and the snow on the path seemed to creak and groan with each careful footstep. He kicked a milk bottle which rolled on and on and on. It was pitch dark alongside the house, but he daren't risk his torch. It only wanted some silly sod of a public-minded citizen to dial 999 and Hornrim Harry would have kittens. He moved his hand along the wall until he found the projection of the sill to the lounge window. Pulling his glove off with his teeth he fumbled amongst the lumpy objects in his coat pocket to locate his penknife. What the hell was this? Oh—that soggy biscuit Powell had forced upon him. He found the knife and immediately dropped it and the snow swallowed it like a quicksand. Five wet, numbing minutes were wasted before his hand closed over it again, by which time the cold had sucked all feeling from his fingers and he had to warm them under his armpit before he dared trust them with the knife again.

The window catch refused to co-operate. He pushed the penknife until he was sure the blade was going to snap and his teeth ached with the effort of gritting them tightly. A bead of warm sweat trickled itchily down his nose and suddenly a click, and it was done. Fingers under the window frame and lift. The bloody noise rumbled and rolled round the sleeping house. Someone must hear. He paused, head cocked, ready to run, holding his breath until it hurt, but no-one stirred, no lights clicked on, so knee up on to the wet cold sill, leg over, and he was inside the dank funereal parlour of a lounge. Behind him the curtains flapped in the wind, as he moved cautiously towards the bureau. He pulled the keys from his pocket with a trembling hand that jangled them like a peal of bells, and then . . . *What was that!*

A floorboard creaked overhead. He froze, not daring to breathe, ears straining, hearing the dull, too-fast pounding of his heart. No other sound. Just that one creak. He emptied his lungs slowly and gulped down fresh air. A small voice whispered "Danger . . . danger" over and over again and the open window pleaded with him. Out of the house, back to the car and off to bed. Let Inspector Allen solve the case and get the glory, the handshake, and the fat cigar from Mullett. His heart slowed to its normal pace, the small voice was still hissing insistently, but he ignored it. He'd got this far, he'd broken into someone's house. If they were going to boot him out of the Force, let it be for something spectacular, not for being late with the sodding crime statistics.

He poked a key into the bureau lock. A pistol crack as the catch snapped back, but it was open. Resting his torch on the lowered flap he rummaged through the mess of papers inside, pulling a wad at random from a pigeonhole and finding them to be ancient household accounts, meticulously checked as if every penny counted. He dried his palms on his coat. How the hell was he going to find anything in this lot, especially as he hadn't the faintest idea what he was looking for? There were so many papers, it would take hours to go through them. He pulled out another wad bound with an elastic band. Old bank statements, the microscopic balance at the end of each month just about able to keep its head above water before the next monthly lifebelt from the pension fund. It was no good. Finding a needle in a haystack would be easier than floundering through this lot. Well, at least he'd tried, he'd ram the papers back and go home.

And then the hairs prickled at the back of his neck. Someone was in the room with him.

Suddenly it was no longer dark and he was screwing up his eyes. The light had been switched on and Powell, in a thick, grey dressing gown over red-striped pyjamas, stood in the doorway leaning heavily on his stick. His face was outraged and angry.

"What the hell are you doing in my house?"

Frost shrivelled inside his overcoat. He was caught red-bloody-handed, the window wide open where he had broken in, the bureau flap down, Powell's private papers in his hand. He wouldn't wait for Powell to report him, he'd write his resignation out that very night and hand it in to Mullett first thing in the morning and, in the circumstances, the Divisional Commander wouldn't need to go through the sham of pretending reluctance and regret in accepting it.

But then he saw something that made his heart skip a beat and sent him smack bang on top of the world again.

Powell, in his left hand, was holding a Luger automatic pistol—and both Fawcus and Garwood had been killed by bullets fired at close range from a Luger automatic pistol.

"You've got a gun, sir?"

Powell gave a hollow laugh. "What, this? I thought you were a burglar. It looks real, doesn't it, but it's just an imitation," and he dropped it into the pocket of his dressing gown. He stared hard at the open bureau. "I'm waiting for an explanation, Inspector."

Frost should have got out—made any excuse, but got out. It wasn't safe in here, but he was cold and tired and he wanted to get it over quickly.

He held out a hand. "Can I have a look at it, sir?"

"No!" snapped Powell.

"I think it's the same gun you used to kill the other two men, sir."

The old man looked at him with such incredulity that Frost was convinced he'd made a mistake, but the gun was now back in Powell's hand and was pointing directly at Frost's head, and it was the real thing, not an imitation, and the cold, calculating expression on Powell's face was not an imitation either.

"You're not as stupid as you look, Inspector. It was the case, wasn't it? The fact that it was empty?"

Case? Empty? thought Frost, his mind still busy working out if he could jump the old man before the trigger was pulled. But he had an uneasy idea that the old man was not as slow or as lame as he made out. "You mean the case chained to the skeleton, sir—the money case?"

The hand holding the gun was rock steady, the knuckle of the trigger-finger white under tight skin. "Yes. As long as it was buried, I knew I was safe. But once it was dug up, even after thirty-two years, it would be so obvious."

It's not bloody obvious to me, thought Frost, his face impassive. Aloud, he said, "What did you do with the money, sir?" He looked around. "You clearly didn't waste it on luxuries."

The thin lips tightened. "I didn't take it for myself, Inspector. I took it for my son. I know he was weak. I know he was a crook. But he was a war hero, a decorated war hero. He made us proud. For that I forgave him everything." Powell's shoulders straightened, his chin jutted, but the gun didn't waver a fraction of an inch.

"I've got a medal," said Frost, hopefully. The old man didn't seem to hear him.

"My son thought he was clever, but the rubbish he mixed with were far cleverer. They took him for thousands. I won't go into details, but in order to get him out of trouble he forged some signatures and misappropriated some £15,000 of his clients' money."

Frost dutifully whistled softly, his eye glued to the unwavering gun. "A tidy little sum, sir, especially in those days."

"It was a fortune, Inspector. He came to me. He begged. How could I refuse him, my son, my flesh and blood?"

"You had that sort of money?" asked Frost.

"No. I sold my stocks and shares, drew out my savings, took out a second mortgage on the house. But even so, I could only raise £10,000."

"That must have been disappointing," said Frost. "Can I sit down?"

"Don't move," snapped Powell, and Frost stood stockstill. The old man went on with his story. "The bank was holding the account of an old lady named Mrs. Kingsley. She was in her eighties, bed-ridden, and very rich. Couldn't get to the bank herself, so I handled all her affairs. She trusted me implicitly."

"Senile, was she?" asked Frost.

"No, definitely not. If any bills needed to be paid, I would write out the cheque and she would sign it without question.

There was close to a quarter of a million pounds in her account, so getting the £5,000 for my son wasn't too difficult."

"It wasn't too honest, either, was it, sir?"

"My son would have gone to prison. I couldn't allow that."

"Of course you couldn't. So you fiddled the old dear's account—the one who trusted you implicitly?"

"I borrowed the money. I intended to pay it back, every last penny. My son was positive that, once over this hurdle, he could get his business back on a firm footing, sell out at a profit, and repay me." Powell gave a hollow laugh. "Within a month he was back again for more. A slight miscalculation. Another debt he'd overlooked. To get him out of trouble this time he needed another £3,000 within forty-eight hours."

"And I presume old Mrs. Kingsley was able to oblige him again?"

"Yes. He promised me this would be the last time, the very last time."

"And was it?"

"A month later he was back for more. None of the money had been paid back. He'd blown the lot on some mad scheme that was supposed to make his fortune. This time I refused. He pleaded. But what was the point? It would just have gone on and on. I told him I couldn't help him. He said not to worry—there was a way he could solve everything. He went back to London, wrote me a note, then jumped in front of a tube train. I should have given him the money."

"It wasn't yours to give, sir. He'd already turned you into a thief . . . £8,000 wasn't it?"

"Yes, and I had no idea how I was going to pay it back. As long as Mrs. Kingsley was alive, at least I had breathing space. For two years I scrimped and saved and managed to repay a couple of hundred . . . it would have taken years. And then suddenly in quick succession, I received two body blows."

"Can I shut the window, sir?" asked Frost. "It's freezing cold."

"No," said Powell, "I want it left open. Where was I?"

"Two body blows," said Frost.

"Yes. The first was when Fawcus walked into my office one night after the rest of the staff had left. He didn't have to say anything. The minute I saw his face, I knew he'd found out about the money. He threatened to blackmail me."

Frost raised his eyebrows. "Blackmail? Good Lord, sir, your branch was full of crooks . . . yourself, Fawcus."

Powell moved his position slightly to ease the weight from his bad leg, but the gun in his hand remained steady, pointing unerringly at Frost's head. "His price for silence was £10,000."

"Shouldn't have been any problem, sir. The old lady was still trusting you implicitly, I take it?"

The old man stiffened, and for a moment Frost thought he had gone too far as the trigger-finger seemed ready to pull back. Powell let out his breath slowly, and continued. "The very next day, Fate showed her uncanny knack of hitting a man hardest when he's down. My phone rang. The news I had been dreading."

"The old lady died?"

"Yes. Her solicitors were on top of me for exact details of her bank balance, and the Inland Revenue decided to send someone round shortly to go through her account with the proverbial fine-tooth comb. They wanted to make sure they got the maximum death duties. My forgeries weren't good enough to stand up to that kind of scrutiny. They'd have uncovered the deficit within hours. I was some £8,000 short."

"You hadn't paid Fawcus his hush-money, then?"

"No. I told him there was no chance of that now. He just smiled his false smile and said he'd leave it in abeyance. He was sure I'd find other opportunities of getting the money, providing I wasn't found out in the meantime. So I lived from day to day, praying for a miracle, but dreading every knock at the door, every ring of the phone, for fear it would be the gentlemen from Inland Revenue." Powell shuddered at the memory. "Days passed, the bank's work went on, and Fawcus kept giving me conspiratorial glances. I began thinking my son's way out was the best way. And then, the night before the funeral, Harrington was on about the cash transfer. I'd no sooner informed Fawcus that he'd be required to assist with the movement of the money than he came out with his plan."

"*His* plan, sir?" asked Frost, inching towards the old man.

"He had a quick and cunning brain. He saw this as a chance to get his ten thousand, plus two thousand more. He was kindly going to allow me to keep eight thousand to repay all the money I had borrowed. It was very tempting."

"What was his plan?"

"A fake robbery. Fawcus and Garwood would leave for Exley, the money in a case chained to Fawcus's wrist. They wouldn't arrive. The police would find their car half-way between Denton and Exley, both men unconscious, the case and the money gone."

"How were you going to work that?" asked Frost, inching a fraction nearer.

Powell explained. The plan was almost childishly simple. Young Garwood, the junior clerk who would be driving the car, wasn't in on the plot so had to be convinced that the robbery had actually taken place. At a lonely part of the route the road would be blocked by a couple of wooden boxes. Nothing suspicious, but enough to make Garwood stop the car to remove the obstacles. When the car stopped, Fawcus would suddenly point and yell, "Look out—he's got a gun!" As Garwood's head turned to follow the pointing finger, Fawcus would bring the cosh down. Powell didn't like this part, but Fawcus brushed his objections to one side. "I won't hit him very hard, but when he comes round he'll believe everything I tell him."

When Garwood came round, he would find Fawcus at his side, head bruised and unconscious, the windscreen shattered by a bullet, and the money case gone. And when Fawcus "recovered consciousness," he would tell of the masked man with the gun who had coshed them both.

"But what would actually have happened?" asked Frost. If only the old man would look away for a fraction of a second,

Frost was sure he could grab the gun. The old man gave no sign of intending to look away.

"I'll tell you first what *should* have happened. The way the plan *should* have worked if everything hadn't gone wrong. I'd be attending the church service for Mrs. Kingsley and I'd make certain everyone saw I was there. After the service the cortège was to leave for the crematorium. Some of the mourners, like me, would be following in their own cars. I was to keep to the rear of the procession, gradually falling behind, then I'd put my foot down and speed off to the pre-arranged spot where Fawcus and the unconscious Garwood were waiting. All I had to do was unlock the chain, take the case, fire my Luger into the windscreen, then back to my own car, foot down, and re-join the slow-moving funeral cortège as if I'd never left it. On the way I'd toss the gun and the empty, opened money case into the undergrowth for the police to find later, so even if they were on the scene within seconds there'd be nothing incriminating on me."

"Except for the money," said Frost. "The £20,000."

Powell looked at him incredulously. "But surely you understand, Inspector. That was the essence, the beauty of the whole ingenious plan. The money was in the last place anyone would think of looking for it. It was still in the bank. It had never left. The case was empty the whole time. The police would be searching everywhere for the armed man and the money . . . but how could they possibly find either of them? They were both non-existent. It was so clever, it deserved to succeed."

"But if there were only two sets of keys to the case, the police would have been bound to suspect you, sir. They're not all stupid like me." And again he moved imperceptibly forward.

"How could they suspect me? I had my keys with me all the time—before, during, and after the funeral service. According to Fawcus's version of events, the robbery would have taken place while I was still in full view of everyone in the church. I would be one hundred per cent in the clear, whereas poor old Harrington at Exley was known to have a drinking problem and be slack. That is where the police would direct their enquiries about the keys."

Frost nodded approvingly. Fawcus had thought it out well. Even super-sleuth Detective Inspector Allen would have been fooled. And if he could move just a fraction closer . . . "But something went wrong, sir?"

Powell noticed the slight movement and there was an ominous click as the safety catch was released. Ruefully, Frost returned to his original position.

"Yes," said Powell, "something went wrong."

He'd changed into his dark suit in the office before going on to the funeral service. The church was cool and calm and he hoped the turmoil churning away inside him didn't show as he nodded to acquaintances. He made certain he was seen, but was careful to keep aloof. It would ruin everything if some fool tagged along with him.

When the cortège left for the crematorium, he lagged behind as arranged, then quickly cut through a side street. A fast five-minute drive and there was the pool car. Young Garwood, blood streaming from his head, was slumped across the wheel.

"He's all right," snapped Fawcus. "It would look more realistic if you tied me up. There's some rope in the boot. It'll only take a minute."

But it took too long. The heat, the anxiety, and the thick funeral clothes were making Powell sweat, his fingers fumble. At last it was done, the rope biting into Fawcus who was trussed like a chicken. "Now unlock the case."

And that was when the nightmare started.

"For Christ's sake, hurry!" screamed Fawcus as Powell, the sweat drenching his clothes, went through one pocket and then the next, digging deep, pulling out the lining. But he knew he didn't have the keys. He had put them on top of the filing cabinet as he changed clothes at the office. They were still there. He couldn't unlock the case. And any minute, Exley would raise the alarm because the car hadn't arrived, the police would race along the route to find the car, with

Garwood unconscious, Fawcus tied, and the case double-locked with nothing inside it.

"What the bloody hell's the matter?" hissed Fawcus.

He explained about the keys.

"You fool, you stupid bloody fool. Untie me quickly."

He couldn't untie the knots. He'd need a knife. There wasn't one in the car.

A moan from the driving seat. Garwood was coming round.

Was it panic, or had he suddenly, clearly, seen the answer to all his problems? Fawcus would always be a danger. Like Powell's son he would always be coming back for more. And there was no way he could explain the locked empty case. He had to act quickly. There was no time to examine motives.

He drew the Luger from his pocket, the souvenir his son had brought back from Germany. He pointed it at Fawcus's head and pulled the trigger. Fawcus's scream was lost in the resulting explosion of sound. It was the only way. He couldn't allow the police to find the locked empty case chained to Fawcus's wrist. He had to kill the one to hide the other.

Another groan from Garwood. The butt of the Luger came down with a sickening crack on the boy's head.

God, what had he done? The boy didn't seem to be breathing. Had he killed him? No, a slight movement as the lungs expanded. Garwood was still alive. But there was no doubt that Fawcus was dead, the splattered blood, the eyes wide open in surprised horror. And the sour, bitter irony of it all, as he learned later, was that he would have had plenty of time to drive back and fetch the keys. That stupid Wendle woman had forgotten to pass on the message to Exley that the money had left. Rather than admit her error, she preferred to lie and claim he had never given any such instructions to her.

Even now, insulated by three decades, he could still tremble at the shattering shock he had received when he returned, heart hammering, to the bank from the crematorium, to find calm and normality, and the alarm still not raised. And Fawcus's still-warm body, wrapped in a tarpaulin, jammed in the boot of his car.

"You took a risk leaving him in your car," said Frost, straining his ears. He thought he heard a movement outside, but it was only snow falling from the roof.

"Where else could I put it? But they weren't looking for a body. They were looking for a man on the run. I went into my office. Everything exactly as I had left it, the keys on top of the filing cabinet. I prayed no-one had been in and seen them. On my way home that night, I dropped them down a drain. I should have hung on to them and unlocked the case, but I wasn't thinking straight. I just wanted to get rid of them, to let people think Fawcus had taken them. Later, when it was quite dark, I drove the car to Dead Man's Hollow. That private road hadn't been fenced off then. It took almost until morning, but I buried him."

"His arm was cut off," said Frost, softly.

Powell's face looked ghastly. "I try to forget that. For a week they looked for Fawcus. No-one suspected me. But I kept worrying that someone might find the body. And as soon as they saw the empty locked case . . ." He shuddered. "So, a couple of nights later, I went back. I took a spade and an axe. It made me sick. The flesh was swollen . . . the hot weather. I couldn't get the chain off. I dug another hole and reburied the arm. When I returned home I scrubbed and scrubbed my hands until they bled. I still have nightmares."

Powell looked ready to drop, all of him except the hand holding the gun. "And I needn't have bothered. No-one found him. For thirty-two years, no-one found him. And then it was the arm you dug up. If I'd left the body alone . . ."

"Still, you had the money, sir. You could cover up the deficit in your books."

"I had too much money," said Powell. "£12,000 too much. You can't keep that sort of surplus hidden in a bank for long. I had to destroy it. I burned it. Each night I took some down to the basement and burned it in the furnace. £12,000 up in smoke. Later on, when I realized the full extent of my son's indebtedness to the people he'd cheated, I could have done with that money. But I burned it."

"That's the saddest part of the story, sir. So your son's creditors had to go unpaid?"

"Oh no. I repaid every penny. I borrowed at an exorbitant rate of interest. I'm still not clear of debt, hence this place." His eyes flickered round the cold room.

"Why did you kill Garwood?" asked Frost, realizing he must keep the old man talking, because when the talk finished . . .

"In my anxiety to convince the police that the money had actually left the bank, I told them that the three of us, Fawcus, Garwood, and myself, had each checked the money into the case. I needn't have bothered as it happened. They never suspected otherwise. I saw Garwood in the hospital and asked him to go along with my story. I let him think it was a strict head-office rule that money for transfer was treble-checked, but that I had overlooked this. He agreed to back me up if the police asked, but they never did. I should have kept my mouth shut. I was becoming involved in unnecessary lies. And then when you found what was left of Fawcus, and the empty case, I was certain that you would immediately realize its significance. If you questioned Garwood he would remember how I had asked him to lie for me. I couldn't let that happen. When you've killed once, the second time is so much easier."

"It's a proper balls-up from start to finish, isn't it, sir?" asked Frost. "You turned over all the drawers in Garwood's house. What were you looking for?"

Powell frowned. "I wasn't looking for anything. I was trying to give the impression that robbery was the motive for the killing."

"Oh," said Frost, realizing that there were no secret papers in the bureau, and that he'd rumbled Powell for the wrong reasons. "Like I said, sir, a proper balls-up all round." He gave his friendliest smile. "Now you've got it off your chest, why don't we pop down to the station and get it all sorted out?" He tried to keep his voice calm, but was seriously disturbed by the look in Powell's eyes.

"I'm sorry, Inspector," and the old man shook his head in infinite sadness, "but as I've already said, once you've killed, it becomes sickeningly easy the next time."

Frost stared at Powell and saw death. He made a last-minute attempt to duck. Everything seemed to be happening in slow motion, Powell squeezing the trigger, the gun leaping in his hand, and Frost still trying to move. Then a blood-red shattering explosion inside his skull. Pain. Blackness.

Powell stepped over the body, kicking aside the maroon scarf, which tangled with his foot. He picked up the phone from the top of the bureau and dialled 999. When he spoke, his voice was trembling and barely audible.

"Police? My name is Powell, Mead Cottage, Exley Road. For God's sake, get here quickly. There's an intruder in my house." Then he screamed "No . . . please . . . no . . ." and crashed down his stick, at the same time jerking the phone wire from the wall. For a man of his age he was remarkably strong.

He knocked over some chairs, scattered papers from the bureau about the room, then slumped down on the settee and waited. Through the open window the approaching wail of a police siren.

On the floor, among the scattered papers, Detective Inspector Jack Frost looked untidier than ever.

THURSDAY

THURSDAY

Mrs. Uphill answered her phone. It was Farnham. "Yes," she said. "Sunday, same as usual, but from now on it's £40." She replaced the receiver and lit a cigarette. Life had to go on. Through her lounge window she could see the house across the street with its Christmas-tree lights flashing on and off.

At the vicarage, the Reverend James Bell and his wife avoided each other. Whatever love was once there when he and his girl bride had smiled happily into the wedding photographer's lens had now shrivelled and died. As soon as Christmas was over, she would leave him.

The car taking Martha Wendle to the Magistrate's Court skirted the woods. She pressed her face to the window, but the cottage wasn't visible from the road.

Clive was with Detective Allen. They had scooped up the papers from Frost's desk, which now looked obscenely bare, and were working through them in Allen's office. From time to time Allen would "tut-tut" at work left undone. Clive couldn't keep his mind on the job. Every time the phone rang he would rush to answer it, hoping for news from the hospital. Frost was hanging on to life by a thread and they were operating that morning to remove the bullet.

Powell had been arrested and was waiting for Allen to question him. He had overlooked the significance of the Luger pistol. When the bullet was dug out of Frost's skull, that too would be sent to Forensic for comparison with the bullet in Garwood . . . the bullet in the skeleton.

Mullett was with the Chief Constable and was very happy. The commandership of the new, enlarged Denton Division was definitely to be his, and a replacement for Frost would arrive that morning from County HQ. Shame about Frost, of course, but things couldn't have worked out better.

Frost was having a nightmare—a nightmare he had had many times before. He was in hospital being wheeled to the operating theatre where a gowned and masked figure was waiting. There were instruments—knives, saws—sharp, terrible, and shiny, laid out on a green cloth. At this point he usually woke up, trembling and wet with sweat, but this time the nightmare was going on. They rated his chances at less than fifty-fifty and expected him to die.

But Frost was never any good at figures and never did what was expected of him.

Six days to Christmas. Outside it started to snow again.

ABOUT THE AUTHOR

R. D. WINGFIELD was born in London within screaming distance of the scenes of the Jack the Ripper murders.

Until 1970 he worked in the sales office of an international oil company, writing crime plays for radio in his spare time. The success of his radio work meant the day job had to go, and he became a full-time writer. His plays have been broadcast all over the world and translated into many languages.

R. D. Wingfield is married with one son, and lives in Essex. He is the author of four mysteries: *A Touch of Frost, Night Frost, Frost at Christmas,* and *Hard Frost,* all available from Bantam Books.

R. D. Wingfield's

Jack Frost Mysteries

Jack Frost, Denton Division, is not beloved by his superiors. In fact, he's something of a pain in the brass: unkempt and unruly, with a taste for crude humor and a tendency to cut corners. They'd like nothing better than to bounce him from the department. The only problem is, Frost's the one D.I. who, by hook or by crook, always seems to find a way to get the job done . . . .

HARD FROST	___57170-2 $5.99
A TOUCH OF FROST	___57169-9 $5.99
NIGHT FROST	___57167-2 $5.99
FROST AT CHRISTMAS	___57168-0 $5.99

- -

Ask for these books at your local bookstore or use this page to order.

Please send me the books I have checked above. I am enclosing $____ (add $2.50 to cover postage and handling). Send check or money order, no cash or C.O.D.'s, please.

Name _____

Address _____

City/State/Zip _____

Send order to: Bantam Books, Dept. MC 7, 2451 S. Wolf Rd., Des Plaines, IL 60018
Allow four to six weeks for delivery.
Prices and availability subject to change without notice.   MC 7 12/95